OTHER STAR WARS BOOKS BY TIMOTHY ZAHN

THRAWN

ALLIANCES

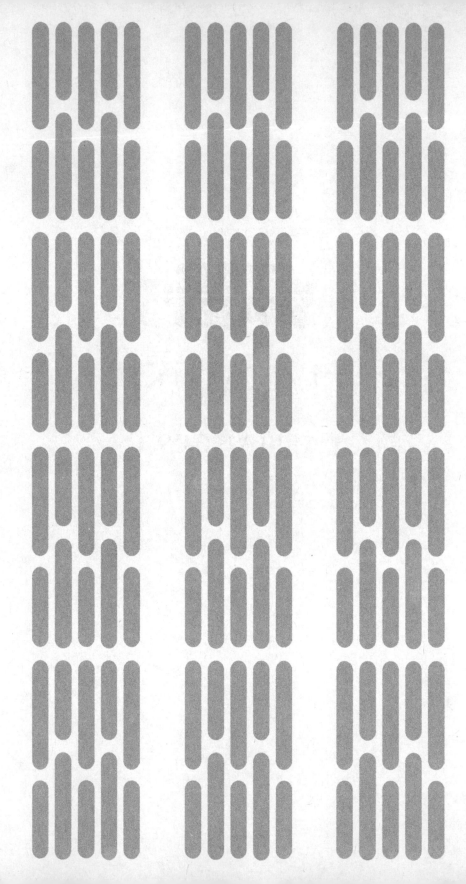

THRAWN
ALLIANCES

TIMOTHY ZAHN

DEL REY | NEW YORK

Copyright © 2018 by Lucasfilm Ltd. & ® or ™ where indicated. All rights reserved.

Published in the United States by Del Rey, an imprint of Random House, a division of Penguin Random House LLC, New York.

Del Rey and the House colophon are registered trademarks of Penguin Random House LLC.

ISBN 978-0-525-48048-8
International edition ISBN 978-1-5247-9892-5
Ebook ISBN 978-0-525-48073-0

Printed in the United States of America on acid-free paper

randomhousebooks.com

2 4 6 8 9 7 5 3 1

First Edition

Book design by Elizabeth A. D. Eno

For all those who've ever wondered if they were
teamed up with the wrong person . . .

THE DEL REY

STAR WARS

TIMELINE

I) THE PHANTOM MENACE

II) ATTACK OF THE CLONES
THE CLONE WARS (TV SERIES)
DARK DISCIPLE

III) REVENGE OF THE SITH
CATALYST: A ROGUE ONE NOVEL
LORDS OF THE SITH
TARKIN

SOLO
THRAWN
A NEW DAWN
THRAWN: ALLIANCES
REBELS (TV SERIES)

ROGUE ONE

IV) A NEW HOPE
BATTLEFRONT II: INFERNO SQUAD
HEIR TO THE JEDI
BATTLEFRONT: TWILIGHT COMPANY

THE DEL REY

STAR WARS™

TIMELINE

A long time ago in a galaxy far, far away. . . .

THRAWN
ALLIANCES

PROLOGUE

NOW

"I have sensed a disturbance in the Force."

Emperor Palpatine paused, stretching out his thoughts to the two men standing before his throne, awaiting their reactions.

No. Not *men*. Of course not *men*. Men were insignificant, pitiable creatures, fit only to be ruled, or intimidated, or sent to die in battle. These were far more than mere men.

A Chiss grand admiral, a strategic and tactical genius. A Sith Lord, ruthless and powerful in the Force.

They were watching him, Palpatine knew, each trying in his own way to glean some understanding as to why they'd been summoned. Grand Admiral Thrawn was observing his Emperor's voice, face, and body stance. Lord Vader, in contrast, was stretching out with the Force toward his Master.

Palpatine could feel all that. But he could also feel the tension between these, his two most useful servants.

The tension wasn't simply because each wished to be the one standing alone at his Master's side at the center of Imperial power, though that was certainly part of it.

There was more. Much more. Thrawn had recently suffered a serious defeat, permitting a small group of rebels he'd successfully trapped on the planet Atollon to slip through his fingers. That failure had earned Vader's contempt.

Thrawn, in his turn, strongly opposed the Death Star project favored by Vader, Grand Moff Tarkin, and Palpatine himself, pushing instead for his own prized TIE Defender project on Lothal. So far Thrawn's opposition had not reached the level of open resistance, but the Emperor knew it was only a matter of time. Vader knew that, as well.

But Palpatine hadn't brought them here to offer an opportunity for reconciliation. Certainly not to mediate personally in their conflict. There were other, far deeper considerations.

Thrawn had given his oath of loyalty to the Empire. But that loyalty had never been fully tested. Vader stood beside Palpatine as the Sith Master's apprentice. But his previous life among the Jedi could not simply be ignored nor casually dismissed.

Here, with this intriguing Force disturbance, was the opportunity to deal with both issues.

Palpatine raised his eyes briefly toward the high window in his throne room. The Star Destroyer *Chimaera* was visible in the distance, a barely discernible arrowhead shape floating high above Coruscant's buildings and skylanes. Normally, military craft that large weren't permitted closer than low orbit. But Palpatine had wished the ship to be present during this meeting, a subtle reminder to both his servants of what had been given to Thrawn, and what could be taken away.

Vader spoke first, as Palpatine had known he would. "Perhaps you sense the rogue Jedi Kanan Jarrus," he said. "Or the creature Admiral Thrawn claimed to have encountered on Atollon."

Palpatine smiled thinly. Of course he wasn't sensing Jarrus. That particular disturbance had long since been noted, codified, and dismissed, a fact Vader knew only too well. The suggestion was nothing more than a reminder to Thrawn—and to Palpatine—of the Chiss's humiliating defeat.

Thrawn gave no visible reaction to Vader's comment. But Palpatine could sense a hardening of his attitude. He'd already promised the Emperor that he would deal with Jarrus and the Phoenix rebels who had so recently escaped him. Much of that failure had been due to factors not under Thrawn's control, which was why Palpatine hadn't taken the Seventh Fleet away from him.

But Vader had no patience for failure of any sort, no matter what the reasons or excuses. For now, he was waiting; but he was more than ready to step in to solve that particular problem if the grand admiral failed.

"This disturbance comes from neither," Palpatine said. "It is something new. Something different." He looked back and forth between his servants. "Something that will require both of you working together to uncover."

Again, neither of them visibly reacted. But Palpatine could sense their surprise. Their surprise, and their reflexive protest.

Working *together*?

This time, it was the Chiss who spoke first. "With all due respect, Your Majesty, I believe my duty and my abilities would be best used elsewhere," he said. "The rebels who escaped Atollon must be tracked down and eliminated before they can regroup and join with other cells."

"I agree," the Emperor said. "But the Seventh Fleet and Commander Woldar can deal with that without you for now. Grand Moff Tarkin will also be joining the commander while his new assignment is being prepared for him."

Palpatine sensed a flicker in Vader's emotions, perhaps a hope that Thrawn would mistakenly believe this was the right time and place to once again raise objections to the Death Star project. Palpatine paused, offering the grand admiral the opportunity to do just that.

But Thrawn remained silent.

"While Woldar and Tarkin find and deal with the rebels," the Emperor continued, "you and Lord Vader will take your flagship to deal with this other matter."

"Understood, Your Majesty," Thrawn said. "May I point out that Governor Tarkin is less familiar than I am with this particular rebel cell. Perhaps a more efficient approach would be for Lord Vader to be offered one of my Star Destroyers and seek out this disturbance on his own."

Palpatine felt a sudden stirring of anger from his apprentice at Thrawn's unthinking choice of phrase. A Lord of the Sith was not *offered* a ship. He took *what* he wanted *when* he wanted it.

But like Thrawn, Vader knew when to remain silent.

"You surprise me, Admiral Thrawn," Palpatine said. "I would have expected a certain eagerness to journey within sight of your home."

Thrawn's glowing red eyes narrowed slightly, and Palpatine felt his sudden caution. "Excuse me, Your Majesty?"

"The disturbance is located at the edge of your Unknown Regions," the Emperor said. "It appears to be centered on a planet named Batuu." Again, he sensed a reaction to the name. This time, the reaction came from both of them. "I believe you have heard of it?"

Thrawn's eyes were hooded, the expression on that blue-skinned face swirling with memories. "Yes," he murmured. "I have indeed heard of it."

As, of course, had Vader. It was the place where he and Thrawn had long ago interfered, albeit unwittingly, with one of Palpatine's own plans.

But again, Vader remained silent.

"Very well, then," Palpatine said. "You, Admiral, will command." He looked at Vader. "You, Lord Vader, will deal with the disturbance."

"Yes, Your Highness," Thrawn said.

"Yes, my Master," Vader said.

Palpatine leaned back into the depths of his throne. "Then go."

The two servants turned and walked toward the door between the double rows of red-cloaked Imperial Guards silently lining their path. Palpatine watched them go: the Chiss in his white grand admiral's uniform, the Sith garbed in black, his long cloak swirling behind him.

The solution to this particular puzzle would indeed require both of them. But more important, it would address Palpatine's lingering questions.

He smiled thinly. Time for Thrawn to face his future.

Time for Vader to face his past.

PROLOGUE

THEN

Anakin Skywalker pursed his lips. "Nope," he said. "Never heard of it."

"No reason why you should have," Padmé Amidala said, shaking her head. She'd left her hair down today, and the tresses flicked with subtle lights as they moved. Anakin had always liked that effect. "It's on the edge of the Outer Rim, right up against the Unknown Regions."

"And it's important *why*?"

"I don't know," Padmé admitted. "All I have is Duja's message that she's stumbled onto something going on somewhere in the Batuu area and thinks we ought to investigate it."

"*Something* going on *somewhere*," Anakin echoed. "Not exactly the most solid intel report I've ever heard."

"That's what everyone else in the High Command thinks, too." Padmé paused, and Anakin sensed the mix of trepidation and stubbornness rising up in her. "Which is why I'm going out there myself to check it out."

Anakin knew his wife well enough to have guessed where this was going. Even so, it was something of a punch in the gut. "Alone?" he asked. Again, not like he needed to ask.

"Of course not," Padmé said. "Duja's already there, remember? Oh, don't look at me like that."

"Like what?"

"Like a—" There was a barely noticeable pause as she reflexively reminded herself where everyone else in the office complex was and confirmed that no one was in a position to eavesdrop. "—husband. Or at least a Jedi protector," she added with an impish smile.

Anakin smiled back. There had been a time when that was all he was to her. Though even then he'd wanted more. "Well, I *am* a Jedi protector, you know," he said. "No reason I shouldn't look or talk like one." He clenched his teeth briefly, forcing back his rising emotion the way his Jedi instructors had taught him. "Unfortunately, I'm also a Jedi general, and there's a battle coming up that I'm supposed to lead. If only . . ."

He broke off. If only Ahsoka hadn't left the Jedi Order. But she had, and she was sorely missed, and not only for her battle skills.

Maybe Padmé was thinking the same thing, and missing Anakin's young Padawan almost as much as he was. At the very least, she understood enough not to ask him if someone else could fill in for him in the upcoming battle. "It'll be okay," she said instead. "You've met some of my former handmaidens. You know how well trained they are in combat and espionage."

"Duja's a decent one?"

"One of the best," Padmé assured him. "Once we're together, it'll be the enemy whose protector needs to be worried."

"Maybe." Anakin cocked an eyebrow. "Not one of your better lines, by the way."

"I know," Padmé said. "I have to save all of those for the Senate." She sighed. "Anakin, do you think this war will ever end?"

"Of course," Anakin said automatically, with an enthusiasm he wasn't really feeling.

Because it was a question they were all asking. *Would* it ever end?

Already it had lingered longer than he'd expected. Longer than maybe any of them had expected. So far Chancellor Palpatine was holding things together, keeping the Republic focused and standing firm. But even he couldn't do so forever. Could he?

So many had died. So very, very many.

But Padmé wouldn't be one of them. Anakin had promised himself that. "When will you be back?" he asked.

"I don't know," Padmé said. "There aren't too many stable hyperlanes in that area, so it'll take some time just to get there."

"You want me to work out a course for you?" Anakin suggested. "The Jedi archives might have something better than the standard charts."

"No, that's okay," Padmé said. "Someone might find a record of your search, and I don't want anyone else to know I'm going out there. You can save that for when you're coming to join us—that's when we'll really need you to crank up the speed."

"Trust me, I will." Anakin shook his head. "I don't know, Padmé. I really don't like you being out of touch that long."

"I don't like it, either," she admitted. "But the HoloNet never worked very well that far out even before the war, and I doubt it's gotten any better. Still, there are five private message services that operate in the region, so even if there's a bit more time lag I should still be able to get information back to you." She reached over and touched his arm. "I'll be all right, Ani. Really."

"I know," Anakin said.

He knew no such thing, of course. Padmé on Coruscant he could protect, at least some of the time. Padmé at the far edge of nowhere he couldn't.

But she'd made up her mind, and he knew that further argument would be futile. Padmé's former handmaidens were fiercely loyal to her, and that loyalty went in both directions. Whether Duja was in trouble, or had simply found trouble, now that she'd asked Padmé for help there was no power in the galaxy that could keep them apart.

"Just promise you'll let me know what's going on as soon as you can," he said, taking her hand in his.

In his *left* hand, of course, the flesh-and-blood one. Padmé never seemed bothered by the difference, but Anakin never forgot.

"I will," she said. "A quick trip, a quick assessment, and straight home. I'll probably be back before you are."

"I'll hold you to that," he warned. "And speaking of holding . . ."

He stepped close to her, and for a moment they stood with their arms wrapped around each other in a lingering hug, a small eye of quiet and peace amid the violent sandstorm that continued to rage throughout the galaxy.

Small, and far too brief. "I have to go," Padmé said into his shoulder as she pulled gently away.

"So do I," he said with a quiet sigh. "I'll miss you."

"I'll miss you, too." Padmé gave him another smile, more tired than impish this time. "At least you'll have Obi-Wan to keep you company."

Anakin made an exaggerated face. "Not exactly the same."

"I know." She stepped back to him for a quick kiss. "We'll spend some time together when we're both back. Some *real* time."

"That's what you always say." But then, that was what *he* always said, too. "Be careful, Padmé, and come home safe."

"You, too, Anakin." She reached up and stroked his cheek. "*You're* the one heading into a war, remember. *I'm* just going to see an old friend."

"Yeah," he murmured. "Right."

The battle played out like so many that had gone before: minuscule gains here, minuscule losses there, both gains and losses all but swallowed up in the accompanying swirl of death and destruction.

Padmé hadn't returned by the time the weary forces returned to Coruscant. Nor had she sent any messages. Anakin checked the service she'd said she would use, then queried all the others that operated in that part of the Outer Rim. Nothing. He searched the mass of recent records that routinely came into Coruscant for consideration and archiving, searching for her by name, by her ship design, by her physical description, even by the jewelry she typically wore. Still nothing. He petitioned the Jedi Council to allow him to go look for her himself, but Count Dooku was on the move again and the request was denied. Another battle, a quick one this time, and he was back on Coruscant.

Still no message. But this time, his document search had found a match. Padmé's ship, or one of the same class and type, had been found abandoned on Batuu. The local hunters who found it said it appeared to be deserted.

Padmé Amidala, senator and former queen of Naboo, had vanished.

CHAPTER 1

There were passengers, Commodore Karyn Faro thought to herself as she stood in the center of the *Chimaera*'s command walkway, and then there were *passengers*.

Darth Vader was definitely one of the latter.

Faro scowled at the starscape outside the bridge. In her opinion, passengers of any sort didn't belong on an Imperial ship of the line. If Vader wanted to fly around the Empire, he should get a ship of his own.

Or maybe that was what the *Chimaera* had now become. Certainly Vader had wasted no time settling in and making changes.

Over the hum of quiet conversation, Faro heard the sound of the aft bridge doors. She turned to see a white-armored stormtrooper step into view. He took an unhurried look around, then continued on toward Faro.

She scowled a little harder. And speaking of unwelcome changes in the *Chimaera*'s routine . . .

She had the scowl safely tucked away by the time the other came to a crisp halt in front of her. "Commodore Faro," he greeted her with the stiff formality she'd come to expect from stormtrooper officers. "I'm—"

"Yes; Commander Kimmund," she interrupted with equal formality.

He didn't twitch, and of course any flicker of surprise would be hidden by his helmet faceplate. But Faro had no doubt the surprise was there. The white-on-white unit and rank designations were nearly impossible to see without stormtrooper optical enhancements, but Faro had long since mastered the technique. "What can I do for you?" she continued.

"I need to talk to you about the positioning and priority placement of our transport," Kimmund said. There wasn't any surprise in his voice, either. Quick on the recovery. "Your chief hangar master is having trouble obeying orders."

Mentally, Faro shook her head. Yes, that sounded like Senior Lieutenant Xoxtin. The woman had her precise, idiosyncratic way of doing things, and it often took a figurative loadlifter to budge her.

Unfortunately, her family was one of the Coruscant elite, and was furthermore close friends with the Emperor's senior adviser on Mid Rim affairs. Xoxtin got away with doing things her own way simply because few naval officers had the nerve to bring the necessary pressure to bear.

Luckily for Kimmund, Faro was one of those few.

"I'll speak to her personally," she promised Kimmund. "Where exactly do you want your transport positioned?"

"Lord Vader's Lambda should of course be in Number One," Kimmund said. "The *Darkhawk* should be in Number Two."

Which would leave Admiral Thrawn's own personal Lambda no higher than the Number Three slot. A clear violation of proper navy protocol, and Kimmund surely knew that.

Still, Thrawn had instructed his officers to cooperate with their guests—that was his word—as much as possible. And it wasn't like a ship in Number Three couldn't get into space as quickly as a ship in

Number One. It was just farther from the prep room and therefore a bit more of a walk. Thrawn would probably be okay with that.

Actually, having the *Darkhawk* in there would go nicely with the other nondescript freighter currently sitting in Number Four, the civilian ship Thrawn had liberated from pirates a couple of years ago and used whenever he felt the need for anonymity. The First Legion's transport was of much the same flavor: an old, Clone Wars–era Separatist freighter that looked decrepit on the outside but had been refitted with all the best weaponry, shielding, and sensor-evasion systems that Imperial technology could provide. For all of Lord Vader's menace and flash, to say nothing of his instantly recognizable appearance, he clearly also understood the uses of subtlety.

Either that or he liked having a captured Separatist ship around to remind everyone which side had won.

"Very well," she said to Kimmund. "I'll make it happen."

"Thank you, Commodore," Kimmund said. Coming briefly to full attention, he turned and strode back down the command walkway.

Faro watched him go, feeling the swirl of calculations that was a frustrating part of an Imperial officer's life. Xoxtin's family was powerful; but Kimmund was the head of the First Legion, the elite unit that Lord Vader had drawn from the equally renowned 501st to serve as his personal stormtrooper force. Theoretically, the Emperor's right-hand man trumped all the rest of the tangled political web.

But only if, when things went to meltdown, Vader deigned to intervene on Faro's behalf. Unfortunately, he was notorious for staying out of political squabbles, and there was no guarantee he would even remember Faro's minor assistance here. Xoxtin, on the other hand, would almost certainly hold a grudge.

There was never a good time for such a balancing act. But this particular time was especially bad. Faro had been promoted to commodore just six weeks ago, with the assurance that Task Force 231 would be hers as soon as its current commander was moved up the ladder to one of the larger fleets.

But that promise, and her task force, had yet to materialize. And with Commander Eli Vanto's unexplained disappearance from the

Seventh Fleet still fueling the rumor mill, Faro was no longer sure where her future lay. Annoying Xoxtin and her family at this juncture could prove fatal.

Still, she'd promised Kimmund. More important, letting a subordinate get away with ignoring orders, even a subordinate as well connected as Xoxtin, set a bad precedent.

She was staring out the viewport, mentally walking through her confrontational options, when the mottled sky of hyperspace abruptly changed to starlines and collapsed into stars.

The *Chimaera* had arrived.

Only it hadn't arrived at its planned destination. It had, instead, arrived in the literal middle of nowhere.

The stars shone through the viewport, their positions matching those on the nav display and confirming Commodore Faro's calculations.

Lord Vader stands just out of sight, motionless, only his labored breathing marking his position. His breathing displays some variance. His body stance likewise holds a muted range of thought and emotion. But there is little there to read. Little to understand. Little to anticipate.

Faro stepped into view. "The hyperdrive has been checked twice, Admiral," she said. *Her facial muscles are tight. Her voice holds a higher degree of anxiety than usual.* "The techs thought it might be the alluvial dampers, but they've been cleared. I've ordered a second check, but so far everything's showing full green." *Her eyes remain correctly on her admiral as she speaks, but her muscles hold a tension that indicates she battles an urge to turn her attention and her speech to Lord Vader. She does not wish his presence on the command walkway, but her expression holds recognition that she has no choice in the matter.*

"Then the fault must lie with the *Chimaera*'s crew," Vader said. *He steps forward. His voice perhaps holds impatience.*

"With all due respect, Lord Vader, I don't believe that to be the case," Faro said. *Her eyes turn to Vader. The stiffness of her stance increases. Her voice holds caution and a degree of fear, but also determi-*

nation. "This hyperlane is sparsely traveled, and its parameters and edges are poorly defined. I believe it more likely we've run into the shadow of some previously unknown mass."

"Indeed," Vader said. *His vocal pitch lowers slightly. His hands rise to his waist, his thumbs hooking into his belt.* "And where is this mysterious mass?"

Faro's throat muscles tighten briefly. "We haven't yet located it, Lord Vader," she said. *Her eyes turn back to her admiral.* "I have our best sensor operators working on the problem, sir."

"Perhaps your *best* are not up to the standards of Imperial service," Vader said.

"The *Chimaera's* officers and crew are more than adequate to their tasks, Lord Vader," Thrawn said. "Commodore, if there is indeed a wayward mass affecting us, perhaps some forward movement will take us clear of its shadow and effect."

"Yes, sir," Faro said. *The tension in her face and voice eases noticeably.* "Helm: Take us ahead at two-thirds power. Scanners: Continue to search for objects."

"And for other ships," Thrawn said.

Faro's expression holds puzzlement. "Other ships, sir?"

"Do you expect us to come under attack?" Vader asked.

"It is possible, though unlikely," Thrawn said. "My concern is that, however it was we were pulled from hyperspace, other ships may be similarly affected. We need to be wary of collisions or other encounters."

"Commodore Faro just explained how poorly traveled this hyperlane is," Vader said. *His words are slightly clipped.* "Do you truly expect a traffic level of two ships a week to present a danger?"

"That is indeed the listing on the navigational charts," Thrawn said. "But the transit profile may have changed since those notations were made. Certainly the ship traffic was even more sparse the last time I was here."

"You were here before, sir?" Faro asked. *Her expression and voice hold surprise.* "I didn't know that."

"Is there a reason you should, Commodore?" Vader asked.

"My apologies, Admiral," Faro said. *She speaks quickly. Her voice holds fresh anxiety.*

"No apologies required, Commodore," Thrawn said. "It was many years ago during the Clone War."

"I see," Faro said. *The anxiety is fading, her voice and expression now holding interest.* "I was unaware you were in the Republic at that time."

"The past is the past," Vader said. "The present and future are all that matter." *He turns, his long cloak swirling, his half-hidden lightsaber glinting in the bridge light. His hands remain hooked in his belt a moment, and then he lowers his arms to his sides. His fingers curl slightly.* "I will be in my quarters. You will inform me when we are again under way."

"Of course, Lord Vader," Thrawn said.

"You will also inform your Noghri that my legion's *Darkhawk* is off limits to him," Vader added. "Commander Kimmund has twice caught him inside. The next time will be the last."

"Understood, my lord," Thrawn said. "Rukh is sometimes overzealous in his attempts to know everything that occurs aboard the *Chimaera*. I will so inform him."

"There was no need for him to be aboard at all," Vader said. *His voice deepens in pitch.* "If his combat and tracking skills are as good as you claim, he should have been left behind to aid Woldar and Tarkin in their hunt for Jarrus and the rebels." *His head tilts slightly.* "Or do you fear for your personal safety after your confrontations on Atollon?"

Faro's facial muscles stiffen. Her body stance holds fresh tension.

"On the contrary, Lord Vader," Thrawn said. "With you and the First Legion aboard, the *Chimaera*'s safety is more than guaranteed. But there may be tasks that require all of us, including Rukh, before this mission is over."

"The mission will be over sooner than you think," Vader said. "We will find the disturbance, I will deal with it, and we will return to Coruscant."

"Understood," Thrawn said.

"Good." *Vader turns a few degrees to face the viewport.* "With all speed, Admiral. I wish to see what exactly has caught the Emperor's attention."

"Of course, my lord," Thrawn said. "As do I."

After the first time Kimmund threw Rukh off the *Darkhawk* he'd ordered Trooper Sampa to rig intrusion sensors on all the hatchways. One of the sensors had successfully been triggered the second time Rukh sneaked aboard, allowing the stormtroopers on duty to catch and evict him much faster.

Kimmund was watching the *Chimaera*'s progress—or more properly, its lack of progress—on the First Legion ready room's repeater displays when the sensor once again warbled its alert.

Two minutes later he was in the hangar, fully armored, blaster carbine in hand, making a quiet bet with himself as to precisely where circumstance and whim would place his first shot. He reached the *Darkhawk* and strode around its bow.

Only to find the diminutive Noghri standing calmly on the deck five meters outside the vehicle under the watchful guard of Sergeant Drav and Trooper Morrtic. Morrtic, Kimmund noted, was holding an extra stormtrooper helmet at her side. "Where did you find him?" Kimmund asked.

"Right here, sir," Drav said darkly. "Standing outside the hatch."

"Pretending he was just out for a stroll," Morrtic added.

Kimmund focused on the Noghri. Short and humanoid, with gray skin and a row of small horns running up from his forehead, he was looking back at the stormtrooper commander with his usual scowl. His arms were hanging casually at his sides, but Kimmund had seen him practice with the fighting staff strapped across his back and knew he could grab it with blinding speed.

With three stormtroopers standing in triangle array around him, Kimmund almost hoped he would try. Especially since there was a certain look on top of Rukh's scowl that he was pretty sure was smugness. "Well?" he demanded.

"Well?" Rukh repeated in a grating voice.

"What are you doing here?"

"This is my master's ship," Rukh said. "I can go wherever I wish."

"The *Chimaera* is Grand Admiral Thrawn's ship," Kimmund corrected acidly. "Lord Vader's *Lambda* and the *Darkhawk* aren't. You've been warned to stay out."

"Your soldiers will tell you I haven't been aboard," Rukh said. "Speak to them. Ask them."

Kimmund shifted his attention to Drav. "Well?"

"We were here ten seconds after the alarm sounded," the sergeant conceded. "If he *was* inside, it couldn't have been more than a ring-and-run."

"Really," Kimmund growled, looking back at Rukh. "Are we reduced to petty schoolchild pranks, then?"

"We are reduced to words," Rukh said. "These are mine: The safety of my master is my task. I will not allow unknowns to threaten it."

"We're hardly unknowns," Kimmund said stiffly. "We're the First Legion, Lord Vader's personal stormtroopers. The entire Empire knows us."

"The entire Empire may," Rukh said. "I don't. But I will learn."

"You do that," Kimmund said. "Just remember that the next time we catch you in one of our transports, we *will* shoot to kill."

"You may try," Rukh said. "I bear you no ill will. But I will do my job." Giving Kimmund a low, obviously sarcastic bow, he turned and strode on his short legs toward the hangar bay exit.

"Should we follow him, sir?" Drav asked.

"No," Kimmund said. "Unfortunately, he's right—Thrawn *has* given him full run of the *Chimaera*. Hopefully, Lord Vader's had a chance to clarify things regarding *our* ships." He gestured to the helmet in Morrtic's hand. "What's that?"

"It's what he used to trigger the alarm," Morrtic said, holding up the helmet for closer inspection. "He apparently stood out here and tossed it through the hatch into the sensor field."

Kimmund frowned, keying his helmet's optical enhancements. Was that—? "Is that *Jid's*?"

"Yes, sir," Morrtic confirmed sourly. "And yes, it was still in the aft electronics shop waiting for its comm upgrade."

"So how did Rukh get in there and get it?"

Morrtic looked at Drav. "No idea, sir," Drav admitted.

"No *idea*?"

"He didn't use that electrostaff of his to short out the sensors," Morrtic put in. "I checked them."

"What about that damn personal cloaking trick?" Kimmund asked. "Did Sampa ever figure out how that thing worked?"

"Yeah, he got a look at the specs," Drav said. "It's a lot like a Sinrich optical dephaser, but it's got a totally different design. Looks like it's limited to three minutes on a charge, doesn't work on humans—needs a Noghri's double-layer skin conductivity or something—and doesn't cover any added stuff once it's been activated."

"That last is the key," Morrtic said. "Sampa's rigged up a gadget that sprays a fine mist of microwave-reflective glitter when the floor weight sensors are triggered. Once Rukh's got that on him, we should be able to track him anywhere he goes."

"Great," Kimmund said. "So that means he never got aboard. Congratulations."

"Yeah," Morrtic growled, wiggling Jid's helmet in her hands. "We'll go over the ship right now and find his diggery hole."

"Yes, you will," Kimmund bit out. He glared at the wayward helmet. "Because the next time he crosses me, someone's going to die. Preferably Rukh; but if it's not him, it'll be whoever let him through. And it won't be *me* who does it. It'll be Lord Vader."

He shifted his eyes across the hangar, fighting to keep from lifting his carbine and blasting the insolent Noghri in the back right there and then. "So pass the word, Sergeant. Pass it to everyone."

The *Chimaera* traveled two hours in realspace before Thrawn ordered Faro to try the hyperdrive again.

Once again, it failed.

"It's almost like there's an Interdictor cruiser somewhere nearby, sir," she told Thrawn as the Star Destroyer continued its realspace journey through the starlit darkness. "But there's no way it could be big enough to have this kind of power without being in scanner range."

"Unless it were cloaked," a deep voice came from behind them.

Faro twitched. Vader had asked to be notified when the *Chimaera* had cleared the mysterious blockage. She'd taken that to mean the Dark Lord would remain elsewhere until that message came.

Apparently, he'd gotten bored.

"My lord," Thrawn greeted Vader calmly. "I believe you'll find it is impossible to run a gravity generator and a cloaking device at the same time. The two fields work against each other."

"Perhaps a new technique has been discovered," Vader countered. "Unknown Regions science may be different from ours."

"Technologies may certainly be different," Thrawn said. "Science itself, less likely. There are certain laws that are universal."

"Perhaps," Vader said. "Regardless, it appears we are at an impasse. What is your proposed solution?"

For another moment, Thrawn remained silent. Faro noted his gaze shifting among the starscape, the regional map, and the close-in diagram of their current hyperlane. "If the existing path cannot be followed, we shall forge one of our own," he said. "Commodore Faro, change course forty degrees to portside."

"Is there another route the Empire is unaware of?" Vader asked.

"None that I know of in this region," Thrawn said. "Our options are to send out a scout ship to map a route for us, or to proceed via those same short jumps ourselves. The latter seems the more efficient choice."

"That will take time," Vader warned, an edge of threat in his tone. "The Emperor's instructions were to proceed with all haste."

"Following the hyperlane has proved less than successful," Thrawn pointed out. "Continuing as we have will likely cost even more time."

"Unless we are already at the end of the blockage."

Thrawn inclined his head. "Helm?" he called. "Make the jump to lightspeed."

"Yes, Admiral."

Faro turned to the viewport, bracing herself. The stars flared into starlines—

And with the sputtering tonal descent from the hyperdrive that indicated a failed jump they collapsed again into stars.

Faro knew better than to swear in front of superior officers. But even so, it was a close thing.

"Interesting," Thrawn murmured. If he was perturbed by the failure, it didn't show in his voice or face. "Commodore: Take the *Chimaera* forty degrees to portside."

"Yes, sir," Faro said. "A suggestion, if I may?"

"Your admiral has given you an order," Vader said.

"Continue, Commodore," Thrawn said calmly.

Faro felt her throat tighten. Vader's comment, underscoring as it did Thrawn's order, was in itself an additional order. Was Thrawn simply going to ignore it? "I've done some calculations, sir," she continued hastily, wondering if Vader was going to interrupt. Or worse. "Traveling to Batuu jump-by-jump will take approximately thirty-nine hours. If we instead travel to Mokivj, we can then take a different hyperlane from there to Batuu, with a savings of fourteen to fifteen hours."

Thrawn inclined his head. "Show me."

Faro keyed the route to the display, bracing herself as she waited for Vader's inevitable question as to what kind of lane could possibly connect two such minor worlds.

And it would be an entirely valid question. The nav charts showed that such a pathway existed, but it was even less well defined—not to mention less well traveled—than the one the *Chimaera* had been following to Batuu. If the same faulty data that had diverted them from the Batuu hyperlane also affected the Mokivj-to-Batuu route, they might find themselves in the same situation they were in right now.

But for once, the Dark Lord seemed to have nothing to say.

"An excellent suggestion, Commodore," Thrawn said. "Set course for Mokivj."

"Yes, sir." Turning to the helm station, Faro caught the eye of the officer seated there and nodded. He nodded back, acknowledging the order, and the massive warship began turning to starboard.

"Eleven," Vader said.

Thrawn turned to him. "Excuse me?"

"Eleven hours' savings at the most," Vader said.

"Agreed," Thrawn said. "Still, it will be worthwhile."

"Perhaps," Vader said. "We shall see."

As Vader had expected, he was right. The jump-by-jump passage to Mokivj took three hours longer than Commodore Faro's estimate, putting their time savings exactly where he'd calculated.

He hadn't wanted to travel to Mokivj. He hadn't wished to see it.

But now that they were here, and within sight of the planet . . .

"Analysis, Commodore?" Thrawn asked quietly as the *Chimaera* circled the planet toward the entry point to their target hyperlane.

"It's a mystery, sir," Faro said, frowning at her datapad. "I don't know any kind of catastrophe other than a comet strike or massive volcanic eruption that could have caused this kind of widespread devastation. But I'm not finding evidence of a comet or any active volcanoes."

Vader gazed out the viewport. Where there had once been lush grasslands and forests there were now lifeless plains and deserts across a great swath of the planet's surface, with only pockets of greenery offering faltering defiance against the surrounding devastation. Clouds covered much of the sky: not white feathery clouds or the gray strata of rain clouds, but brooding masses that promised nothing but the darkness and chill of blocked sunlight.

"Perhaps it was something even more cataclysmic than a comet," Thrawn said. "Commander Hammerly, how many moons are you reading?"

"Moons, sir?" Hammerly asked, sounding bewildered.

Vader turned to face her. Again, one of Thrawn's subordinates questioning the admiral's orders. Perhaps it was time to deliver a reminder of the need for instant and unquestioning obedience. "Yes, sir—moons," Hammerly added quickly.

Vader looked at Thrawn. There was no indication that he was considering punishing the commander, not even with a verbal rebuke, for her questioning of his orders. Indeed, he seemed merely intent on receiving her answer.

Mentally, he shook his head in contempt. Perhaps the admiral's lack of proper discipline of his subordinates was the reason the rebels at Atollon had escaped him.

"There should be ten," Thrawn continued. "Six are relatively small, but four are large enough for their internal gravity to have shaped them into spheres."

"What does this matter?" Vader asked. He hooked his thumbs into his belt, feeling a fresh awareness of the lightsaber hanging there.

"There is little else to occupy our attention while we traverse the system," Thrawn pointed out. "Besides, I am curious as to the completeness of the *Chimaera*'s archives."

It was a reasonable enough answer, delivered in an eminently reasonable tone.

But Vader wasn't fooled. There was a point to everything this Grand Admiral Thrawn did, a hidden plan or motivation or scheme. Once again, he felt the presence of his lightsaber . . .

"Your pardon, Admiral, but that's not what we're reading," Hammerly said, frowning at her board. "I count six moons, only one of which is spherical."

"The other four must be on the other side of the planet," Vader said, feeling a stir of impatience. *That* one was obvious.

"I think not, my lord," Thrawn said. "Note the gravity-interaction overlay Commander Hammerly has placed on the display. It indicates no other significant masses in the planetary system."

Vader looked at the overlay. He couldn't do the calculations himself—that was what droids were for—but the sensor officer's conclusions were laid out at the bottom of the display. "Are you suggesting the missing moons fell to the surface?" he asked.

"Unlikely," Thrawn said, a quiet intensity in his voice. "Four masses that size would have turned Mokivj into a blazing inferno of groundquakes and lava."

Like Mustafar, Vader noted silently. "Then where are they?"

Thrawn shook his head slowly. "That is a mystery we must solve."

"No," Vader said.

A sudden silence descended on the bridge. "Excuse me, my lord?" Thrawn asked, his voice under careful control.

"We are not here to solve random mysteries," Vader said firmly. "We are here to seek out the disturbance the Emperor sensed. That, and nothing else."

"Of course," Thrawn said. "But we may discover that the two are connected."

"*Are* they?"

"I do not know, my lord," Thrawn said.

For a long moment, Vader gazed at him, trying to read that alien mind. But if there was duplicity hidden behind those glowing red eyes, he couldn't sense it. "Then let us be on our way," he said.

"Of course, my lord." Thrawn turned to Faro. "Commodore, as soon as we are cleared to the hyperlane you will make all speed toward Batuu."

"Yes, sir," Faro said.

The Chiss turned back to Vader. "I would point out one other thing, Lord Vader. If the Emperor is aware of a presence in this part of space, that same presence may similarly be aware of *you*."

That thought had already occurred to Vader. Many times. "Perhaps," he said. "But awareness does not necessarily imply preparedness."

"No," Thrawn said quietly. Perhaps the grand admiral, too, was looking back at a distant and unpleasant past. "It does not."

CHAPTER 2

"I'll tell you one thing, Artoo," Anakin said darkly as he detached his Eta-2 *Actis*-class Interceptor fighter from its hyperdrive docking ring. "If something's happened to Padmé, someone on Batuu is going to be *very* unprepared for what's about to happen to them."

R2-D2 warbled his agreement. That was one of the great things about R2-D2, Anakin thought as he maneuvered the Actis away from the ring and headed lower toward the planet below: the little droid's willingness to do whatever was necessary to follow his master on the most difficult and dangerous roads.

Here, the first problem would be to even *find* the proper road.

That wasn't something he usually had to worry about. In space, the Separatist fleets were big and obvious, and on the ground there was always enough smoke and blasterfire to mark the key sites pretty clearly. On the rare occasions when Republic forces got there first, there was usually someone on the ground ready to guide them to where the hostilities were about to begin.

None of those were likely to be the case on Batuu. Still, the planet was sorely underdeveloped, with only a few outposts and small trading communities reading on his scanners. The message Duja had sent Padmé had specified one of the larger settlements, Black Spire Outpost, as their rendezvous spot. If the women weren't there, Anakin would move on to the next outpost until he found them.

R2-D2 had already keyed in the coordinates. Taking a final look at the nav display, Anakin pointed the Actis toward the horizon and poured power to the drive—

Abruptly, R2-D2 trilled a warning. "What is it?" Anakin said, frowning as he checked his rear display.

And felt the back of his neck tingle. There was a ship back there, the size of a medium freighter but of unknown configuration.

Settling into orbit right beside his hyperdrive ring.

There was no question of how Anakin should react. The ring was his only way out of the system. If the intruder stole it—or worse, destroyed it—Anakin would be stuck here until he could get a message back to Coruscant. Swinging his control yoke hard over, he spun the fighter in a tight curve and headed back toward the ring, doing a quick 360 roll to make sure there were no other surprises in the area.

It appeared he and the intruder were alone. He straightened out, checked to make sure R2-D2 had the laser cannons energized and ready, and keyed the comm. "Unknown ship, this is General Anakin Skywalker of the Galactic Republic," he called. "Identify yourself and state your purpose."

Nothing. Maybe they didn't communicate on any of the Republic's standard frequencies.

Or, more likely this far out, didn't speak Galactic Basic.

Anakin pursed his lips, running through his list of trade languages. He knew Huttese and Jawa Trade Language fairly well, but Batuu was a long way from Hutt influence. Meese Caulf? He was a bit far out for that, but it was the best he had. "Unidentified ship, this is General Anakin Skywalker of the Galactic Republic," he said, working hard to wrap his mouth around the Meese Caulf words and hoping he was getting the grammatical structure right. "You are intruding on Republic equipment and interfering with a Republic mission. I order you to pull back and identify yourself."

"I greet you," a calm voice came back in the same language. "Did you give your name as General *Skywalker*?"

"I did," Anakin said, frowning. "Why, have you heard of me?"

"No, not at all," the other said. "I was merely surprised. Let me assure you I mean no harm to you or your equipment. I merely wished a closer look at this interesting device."

"Glad to hear it," Anakin said. "You've had your look. Pull back as ordered."

There was a pause. Then, at a leisurely pace, the ship drifted away from the ring. "May I ask what brings a Republic envoy to this part of space?" the intruder asked.

"May I ask what business it is of yours?" Anakin countered. It wasn't very polite, but he wasn't feeling in a particularly polite mood. Every minute he was stuck out here making sure this prowler behaved himself was a minute he couldn't spend looking for Padmé. "You can be on your way at any time."

"On my way?"

"To continue your travels," Anakin said. "To go wherever you were going before you stopped to look at my hyperdrive ring."

Another silence. The alien ship, to Anakin's annoyance, had halted its sideways drift and was now pacing the hyperdrive ring at a distance of a hundred meters. Still far too close for comfort. "Yes, I could continue on my way," the intruder said. "But it might be more useful for me to assist you in your quest."

R2-D2 gave a puzzled twitter. "I already told you I was on a Republic mission," Anakin said. "It's not a quest."

"Yes, I recall your words," the intruder assured him. "But I find it hard to believe that a Republic at war would send a lone man in a lone fighter craft on a mission. I find it more likely that you travel on a personal quest."

"I'm on a mission," Anakin ground out. This was starting to be *really* irritating. "Directly ordered here by Supreme Chancellor Palpatine himself." Not that Palpatine even knew Anakin was here, of course, let alone sanctioning the mission. But if the stranger had heard of the Clone Wars he'd surely heard of Palpatine, and dropping the chancellor's name might add some weight to his side of the conversation. "And I don't have time for this."

"Agreed," the other said. "Perhaps it would be best if I were to simply show you the location of the ship you seek."

Anakin's hands tightened on the yoke. "Explain," he said quietly.

"I know where the Nubian ship landed," the intruder said. "I know the pilot is missing."

Anakin ground his teeth. "So you intercepted a private transmission?"

"I have my own sources of information," the intruder said, his voice still calm. "Like you, I seek information, on that and other matters. Also like you I'm alone, without the resources to successfully investigate. Perhaps in alliance with a Republic general we may find the answers both of us seek."

"Interesting offer," Anakin said. And now, finally, he was close enough. Taking a deep breath, he stretched out to the Force.

The intruder wasn't human, though of course Anakin had already guessed that. He was near-human, though, like many other species in the Republic.

But the texture of his mind was unlike anything Anakin had ever touched before. It was neat and well ordered, the patterns of thought flowing smoothly and precisely in ways not unlike those of scientists or mathematicians. But the content of that flow, and the muted emotions accompanying it, were completely opaque. It was like a neat and precise array of unfamiliar numbers.

He also wasn't alone. There was a second nonhuman aboard.

"You say it's just the two of us?" Anakin continued, targeting the likely position of the ship's hyperdrive. If the intruder would lie about being alone, he would probably lie about other things, too.

Worse, the most likely reason for him to lie about Padmé's ship was if he was involved somehow in her disappearance. If that was the case, Anakin wanted to keep him here until he got some *real* answers.

"Yes," the intruder said. "Plus my pilot and your droid, of course."

Anakin paused, his finger on the firing controls. "You didn't mention your pilot."

"Neither did you mention your droid," the intruder pointed out. "Since neither will be joining us in our investigation, I didn't think they entered into the discussion."

"Artoo usually comes with me on missions."

"Indeed?" the intruder said. "Interesting. I was unaware that navigational machines had other uses. Do we have an alliance?"

Anakin glowered at the alien ship. If the second being really was just a pilot, maybe that hadn't been a lie so much as a mostly honest omission. Even now, after years of warfare, there were still Republic politicians who refused to accept clones as real human beings. Maybe for some unknown reason this particular culture considered pilots to be second-class citizens, as well. "So what answers are *you* looking for?"

"I wish to more fully understand this conflict in which you're embroiled," the intruder said. "I wish answers of right and wrong, of order and chaos, of strength and weakness, of purpose and reaction." There was a slight pause; and when the voice came back there was a new formality to it. "You asked my identity. I am now prepared to give it. I am Commander Mitth'raw'nuruodo, officer of the Expansionary Defense Fleet, servant of the Chiss Ascendancy. On behalf of my people, I ask your assistance in learning of this war before it sweeps its disaster over our own worlds."

"I see," Anakin said cautiously. There were long-standing rumors of vast civilizations lurking out beyond the borders of Wild Space. Was this Chiss Ascendancy one of them?

And if so, could they be persuaded to join the war effort on the Republic's side? That possibility alone might make it worth coming to an agreement with this Mitth'raw'nuruodo. "Very well," he said. "On behalf of Chancellor Palpatine and the Galactic Republic, I accept your offer."

"Excellent," Mitth'raw'nuruodo said. "Perhaps you will begin by telling me the true story of your quest."

"I thought you already knew," Anakin said, his neck tingling again. "You know about Padmé's ship."

"The Nubian?" There was a brief pause, and Anakin somehow had the impression of Mitth'raw'nuruodo shrugging. "The design and power system were unlike anything else I've seen in this region. Your craft displays similar characteristics. It was logical that one visiting stranger was seeking the other."

"Ah." If there was one thing Mitth'raw'nuruodo had in abundance, Anakin reflected, it was quick and reasonable answers. "You're right, the Nubian is one of ours. It carried a Republic ambassador who came here to collect information from an informant. When she failed to contact us, I was sent to look for her."

"I see," Mitth'raw'nuruodo said. "Was this informant trustworthy?"

"Yes."

"You are certain of that?"

"The ambassador was."

"Then betrayal is unlikely. Has the informant contacted you?"

"No."

"In that case, the most likely scenarios are accident or capture," Mitth'raw'nuruodo said. "We need to travel to the surface to determine which it was."

Finally. "That's where I was heading when you barged in," Anakin growled. "You said you knew where her ship was?"

"I can send you the location," Mitth'raw'nuruodo said. "But it might be more convenient for you to first come aboard. I have a two-passenger shuttle in which we can travel together."

Anakin smiled tightly. He would definitely like a look at the inside of Mitth'raw'nuruodo's ship.

But not yet. Not until he trusted the Chiss a whole lot more. "Thanks, but I'll take my own ship in," he said. "Like I said, we might need Artoo down there."

"Very well." If Mitth'raw'nuruodo was offended that Anakin hadn't taken him up on the offer, it wasn't apparent in his voice. "I'll lead the way."

"Fine," Anakin said. He'd prefer to have the Chiss in front of his laser cannons anyway. "Whenever you're ready."

"I'll make preparations at once," Mitth'raw'nuruodo said. "One additional thought. Chiss names are difficult for many species to properly pronounce. I suggest you address me by my core name: *Thrawn*."

"That's all right, Mitth'raw'nuruodo," Anakin said. Did this being go out of his way to be annoying and condescending? "I think I can handle it."

"Mitth'raw'nuruodo," the alien said.

"That's what I said," Anakin said. "Mitth'raw'nuruodo."

"It's pronounced *Mitth'raw'nuruodo.*"

"Yes. Mitth'raw'nuruodo."

"Mitth'raw'nuruodo."

Anakin clenched his teeth. He could hear a slight difference between his pronunciation and the alien's. But he couldn't figure out how to correct his version. "Fine," he growled. *"Thrawn."*

"Thank you," Mitth'raw'nuruodo—Thrawn—said. "It will make things easier. My shuttle is prepared. Let us depart."

Padmé's ship was parked in a small clearing in a forested area thirty kilometers from Black Spire Outpost. Unlike most clearings Anakin had seen—and the one he'd landed his Actis in a kilometer away— this one was overhung with branches that concealed anything parked there, yet was nevertheless accessible via a narrow corridor through the surrounding trees that allowed for an approach that would leave no traces.

And the ship wasn't alone.

Two rough-looking men and a couple of nonhumans of different species were gathered around the hatch, with another five humans sitting in cargo vehicles parked at the edges of the clearing. The postures and stances of all nine indicated impatience. The group by the ship was working on the hatch with cutting torches.

Anakin glared at them from behind a concealing tree, his light-

saber already gripped in his hand. He and Thrawn had had to land in
different spots, and Anakin had promised to wait outside the clearing
until the Chiss arrived so that they could begin the investigation together.

But that had been before Anakin found the ship under assault.
More important, just because he couldn't sense Padmé didn't mean
she wasn't still aboard, possibly injured or unconscious.

And that changed everything. Waiting for his new ally when nothing was happening was one thing. Waiting for him when Padmé
might be in danger was entirely different.

Behind him, R2-D2 gave a soft, questioning warble. "No, you just
stay here, Artoo," Anakin murmured. "If I need backup, I'll call. And
stay *out* of the line of fire this time, okay?"

R2-D2 made a wounded-sounding gurgle.

"I said no," Anakin said firmly. A month ago, the techs had spent
three days putting the droid back together after he'd taken a bolt
from a B2-RP super battle droid for no better reason than that the
little astromech had wanted to see what was going on.

R2-D2 made one more brief protest, then went silent. Taking a
final, careful look around the area to make sure there weren't any
surprises, Anakin stepped around the tree into view. "Hold it right
there!" he called.

Every eye swung toward him, the torches shutting down as their
operators turned to the unexpected interloper. Anakin started toward
them, watching the group at the hatch, trusting the Force to alert him
to any threat from the vehicle drivers.

He'd taken barely five steps when his peripheral vision spotted the
men in the two vehicles farthest from each other slide blasters from
their holsters. He took one more step, settling his mind and body
into combat awareness . . .

Double vision: the Force showing him the present overlaid with a
glimpse of a moment into the future—two blaster bolts coming from
the drivers of the two vehicles—the first scoring into his upper chest, the
second into his lower side—

With a *snap-hiss* his lightsaber blade blazed into existence—

He swung the blue blade against the first bolt, then the second, and paused.

For perhaps two seconds no one moved. Then, as if on signal, the other seven snatched their blasters from their holsters and opened fire—

Double vision: blaster bolts coming at torso, at side, at head, at side—the Force speeding his perception, slowing down time—moving his hands in a blur—no longer deflecting bolts away, but sending them back to their points of origin—

Anakin had given the first attack what Obi-Wan liked to call a second-thoughts chance, deflecting the bolts into the woods instead of bouncing them directly back into the shooters. Now, with nine-to-one odds, he didn't have that luxury.

Double vision: bolts coming at chest, at chest, at head—controlling with precision, sending back to arm, to leg, to shoulder—

But not to kill. Only to wound, to disable and dissuade. If Padmé wasn't here, they might know where she was.

If Padmé *was* here, and if they'd hurt her, her attackers would need to suffer a little before they died.

Double vision: bolts coming at head, at torso—attack faltering as wounded enemies cease fire—

"*Kunesu!*" a voice called from somewhere.

Abruptly, the attack ceased. Anakin waited a couple of seconds to make sure the barrage wasn't going to start again, then lowered his lightsaber a few centimeters and looked around.

Standing a few meters inside the clearing a quarter of the way around the edge was a tall, slender man. Or rather, not *quite* a man. His eyes were glowing red, his skin blue, his hair blue-black. He was dressed in a black military-style uniform with a burgundy patch on one shoulder and silver bars on his collar. Something was holstered on his right hip—a sidearm of some sort—with a slender, lightsaber-sized tube holstered on his left.

Thrawn.

For a long moment, no one spoke or moved, except for those who were writhing silently in their transports as they clutched their self-inflicted blaster wounds. Thrawn's eyes swept slowly across the men and machines, then he spoke again in a language Anakin didn't recognize.

"Artoo?" Anakin prompted quietly.

The droid made a negative sound. So he couldn't translate the language, either.

Not really surprising. Briefly, Anakin wished there'd been enough room in the Actis to bring C-3PO along.

One of the men at the ship spoke. Thrawn replied. The other spoke again, this time gesturing with the hand holding his blaster. Anakin lifted his lightsaber again in warning, but the man made no attempt to open fire. For a minute the two of them continued to converse in the same language. Then Thrawn said something, the man called out to the rest of the group, and all of them reluctantly holstered their blasters. Thrawn shifted his eyes to Anakin and beckoned to him. Anakin gave the clearing one final scan, then closed down his lightsaber and walked across to the Chiss.

"General Skywalker, I assume," Thrawn said in Meese Caulf as Anakin reached him.

"Yes," Anakin confirmed. "What's going on? Who are they?"

"They claim to be simple merchants," Thrawn said.

"*Armed* merchants?"

"Most travelers in this part of space are armed," Thrawn said. "They claim this landing area is normally reserved for their ship, and that they were dismayed to find it occupied by another. When their attempts to communicate with those aboard failed, they resolved to force an entry to render any aid the crew might require."

"I'm sure they did," Anakin said, watching the men by the hatch. They were clearly unhappy with the situation, but at the moment none of them seemed inclined to continue their attack. "Do you believe them?"

"Partially," Thrawn said. "They're surely smugglers, not simple merchants. I'm furthermore not convinced that they attempted communication before attempting to force their way aboard. But I do believe they expected to find an open landing area and were upset to discover that was not the case."

Anakin eyed the crates stacked on the cargo carriers. There wasn't much reason to haul all of that out here unless they were planning to load it onto another ship.

Or maybe to load it onto *this* ship? "Or else they knew Padmé's ship was here and were planning to steal it," he growled.

"No," Thrawn said. "Note the number of crates on each vehicle, and how low those vehicles lie upon their lift fields. Each crate is far too heavy for the beings here to transfer by hand."

"Unless they have loadlifters."

"There's no room for lifters of sufficient size to be aboard the vehicles."

Anakin nodded sourly. "Which means the lifters are aboard their ship. And since there's no way of knowing if there would be anything like that aboard this one, there's no point in trying to steal it."

"I would put it more strongly," Thrawn said. "The design of this ship is that of a diplomatic or passenger craft. It's highly unlikely that it would have the necessary loading equipment aboard."

"Or enough cargo space for all that," Anakin conceded, the taste of defeat in his mouth. "So if they didn't do anything to Padmé, who did?"

"A question for which we do not yet have an answer," Thrawn said. "Nor do I believe have they. What do you wish done with them?"

Anakin frowned. "What?"

"You are a general," Thrawn reminded him. "I am a commander. You stand higher in military hierarchy."

Anakin looked sharply at him. Was the Chiss mocking him? "You seem to be the expert on things that happen in this region," he said. "You also know their language." He nodded toward the smugglers. "Not to mention that they know you. Or at least, they recognize the uniform."

"They don't know me," Thrawn said. "I also doubt they've ever seen this uniform. But they recognize that it *is* a uniform, and deduce therefore that I'm a person of authority. It's also likely they've heard of the Chiss." He smiled slightly. "Though perhaps only as myths."

Anakin thought about all the places he'd been, all the small backwoods worlds he'd visited while chasing down Separatists. Some of the people there had only distant memories—or none at all—of the Jedi. "Not necessarily a bad thing," he said. "It can be useful for people to underestimate you."

"It can be equally useful for them to overestimate you," Thrawn said. "What do you wish done with them?"

"Tell them to get themselves and their cargo out of here," Anakin said. "We'll move the ship when we're ready to do so. Until then, they stay away."

Thrawn nodded and spoke again.

The smuggler chief replied, his tone clearly indicating a protest. But he nodded and gestured to his crew. The ones still standing beside the ship headed to the vehicles, some of them shoving the injured drivers roughly across the wide seats and taking the controls.

Two minutes later, Anakin and Thrawn were alone.

"I presume you can get us into the ship?" the Chiss asked.

"I think so," Anakin said, looking over at the hatch. He needed to check on Padmé, but the last thing he wanted was to let an untested alien into her ship. "It normally opens to a transponder, but there's also a key code I can punch in. I'll go see if she's inside while you look around out here for clues."

"I might be of more use inside," Thrawn offered. "My eyes see a slightly different spectrum than yours."

"I'd rather you check out here," Anakin said firmly. Even this close to the ship he couldn't sense Padmé's presence, which meant she was either not there, already dead, or critically close to death. He needed to get inside and find out which, and he wasn't in the mood to argue the point. "You can have Artoo to help," he added. Looking back at the tree where the little droid was hiding, he raised his voice. "Artoo?"

There was a twitter of acknowledgment, and R2-D2 rolled into view. Giving a small burst from his jets to fly over a fallen log, he settled back onto his wheels and rolled awkwardly across the uneven ground toward them. "I'm going inside," Anakin told him. "You and Commander Thrawn look for clues out here."

There were all sorts of reasons why Padmé might have changed the key code on her ship. Luckily, she hadn't. A minute later Anakin was inside.

He checked out the most likely places first: galley, sleeping chamber, control cabin. Then, lightsaber in hand, senses alert for trouble, he went methodically through the entire ship.

No Padmé: dead, injured, or alive. No signs of attack, or indications that she might have had to leave the ship in a hurry. The escape pods were still in place, and hadn't been activated or prepped. The comm showed that she'd sent two messages, but with the obligatory encryption overlay he couldn't read them.

His sense of anxiety, which had abated somewhat with the discovery that his beloved wife wasn't lying dead in her ship, was growing again as he finally stepped back outside. Padmé had apparently left the ship under her own volition. But where had she gone?

Thrawn and R2-D2 both turned to him as he joined them at one end of the clearing. "Any news?" Thrawn asked.

Anakin shook his head. "No one inside. No signs of accident or violence. Her computer's nav log shows she came straight here from Coruscant."

"Your ships maintain the data of your travels?" Thrawn asked, frowning.

"Sure, if you don't wipe the nav computer after you arrive," Anakin said. "Why, don't yours do that?"

"We use a different navigational method," Thrawn said. "Yes, of course you would have records."

"Yeah," Anakin said. Odd comment. "There were also two messages in her outgoing file, but they're encrypted and I can't read them."

"Her personal message records are *encrypted*?"

"It's a diplomatic ship," Anakin reminded him. "Nothing an ambassador does or says is truly personal. Transmission records are routinely encrypted in case the ship is intercepted—we don't want the Separatists reading our messages."

"Yes; the Separatists," Thrawn said. "The origins and driving force behind this Clone War are still somewhat opaque to me."

"And we're not going to discuss them now," Anakin said firmly. "Did you find anything?"

"There's no damage to the ship's exterior," Thrawn said. "No indications of fuel loss, sensor failure, or other problems that might have forced a landing. Also no detectable blood or torn clothing." He indicated the ground in front of them. "You spoke of an informant. Was he local, or was he also traveling to Batuu?"

"She," Anakin automatically corrected. "And yes, she was traveling here. Or had traveled here. I'm not sure of the timing."

"Have you details of her ship?"

"Not really," Anakin said. "Artoo, did Padmé ever mention the kind of ship her handmaidens used?"

There was a short pause as R2-D2 searched his datafiles. Then, with a warbled affirmative, he leaned forward and projected a holo of a small ship onto the ground. "That's it," Anakin told Thrawn. "He says it's a Nomad Four, a civilian version of the Seltaya military courier ship."

"What is the scale?" Thrawn asked. "And may I see the underside?"

"Artoo?" Anakin prompted.

The image flipped over, and a scale crosshatch appeared over it. "Yes," Thrawn murmured. "Do you see these marks?"

He pointed to the ground at his feet. If he squinted, Anakin decided, he *might* imagine he could see a wide depression there. "Are you saying that's the mark of a Nomad's landing skid?"

"Yes," Thrawn said. "Furthermore, do you see the grass within the mark?"

"Yes," Anakin said. It looked like all the other grass around them. "And?"

"Note the darker color in the veins on the undersides of the leaves," Thrawn said. "I believe the leaves were crushed in a ship's landing, beginning their return to full life only when it departed."

"Any idea how long the ship was here?"

"No," Thrawn said. "But from the regrowth pattern, I estimate the ship left approximately one week ago."

"You're an expert on Batuu plant life now?" Anakin asked, frowning. That seemed suspiciously convenient.

"I knew the Nubian ship had been in this area," Thrawn said calmly, pulling a small flat box from the back of his belt. "I also know that plant life can offer clues. I therefore loaded all the details that were available on this region's plants into my recorder before leaving my ship."

"I see." Anakin gazed at the ground, clenching his artificial hand tightly. If Thrawn was right, that would put Duja's departure at just about the time Padmé arrived. Could the two women have gone off together?

But why hadn't they contacted him? Or had Padmé tried and the message simply had not made it to Coruscant? Either way, why had Padmé left her ship here in the middle of nowhere instead of in a better-monitored landing field, or even in orbit around the planet? Had Duja found evidence of imminent threat?

"There are no further answers here," Thrawn said. "The nearest native outpost is approximately thirty kilometers away."

"Black Spire?"

"Yes," Thrawn said. "I suggest we travel there and seek information."

"Sounds reasonable." Anakin hesitated. "You said your shuttle had room for two?"

"It does," Thrawn said. "There's a landing area three kilometers west of the outpost. I'll land there and we can take a ground vehicle the rest of the way."

"Okay." Anakin looked at R2-D2. "Head back to the ship," he ordered. "Have it ready to fly if we need backup." He looked back at Thrawn. "Let's go, Commander."

CHAPTER 3

Finally, just over three hours past Faro's original estimate, the *Chimaera* reached Batuu.

Grand Admiral Thrawn, she knew, would recognize the delay as being due to unknown factors and the general uncertainties of travel in inadequately charted territory. Lord Vader, she suspected, would put it down to incompetence, either hers or her crew's.

Both assessments rankled.

"I assume you have a plan, my lord?" Thrawn asked as Vader joined them on the command walkway.

For a moment the Dark Lord gazed out the forward viewport in silence. Possibly thinking; possibly doing one of those Force things that Faro had never quite believed in and certainly never trusted.

Especially not from here. Thrawn had ordered the *Chimaera* to come out of lightspeed at a healthy distance from the planet, and as a result Batuu was a barely visible dot glinting in the light from the even more distant sun.

Mentally, she shook her head. Vader could talk all he wanted about how the Emperor could sense things all the way back at Coruscant, but Faro wasn't buying any of it. In her opinion, it was overblown rhetoric masking private information sources or simple deductions.

"The disturbance we seek is on the surface," Vader said. "Commodore Faro, prepare to take us to orbit."

Thrawn's hand moved at his side, subtly belaying the order. "If I may suggest, my lord," he said, "there may be hostile beings down there. If so, the arrival of a Star Destroyer may be counterproductive."

"It will show them the power of the Empire," Vader rumbled.

"It may also drive them underground," Thrawn pointed out.

"You fear the effort that would be needed to extract them?"

"I note that the effort would be time consuming," Thrawn said. "Our orders were to proceed at all due speed." He gestured toward the planet. "Besides, it is often wise to conceal one's full capabilities from potential enemies."

For a long moment, the two faced each other in silence. Thrawn's expression was calm and respectful; Vader's was as always invisible behind his mask. "What then do you suggest?" the Dark Lord asked at last.

"You and I go alone," Thrawn said. "I have a small freighter that will allow us anonymity. We can land—"

"*Anonymity?*" Vader interrupted scornfully. "Do you truly believe I can travel anywhere in the Empire without being recognized?"

"Anywhere in the Empire, no," Thrawn said, his expression still calm. "But this edge of the Outer Rim is Imperial in name only. There is every chance you can pass unknown among the people down there."

For another, even longer moment, there was silence. Faro held her breath, aware that Commander Kimmund had entered the bridge and was striding toward them, his white armor in gleaming contrast with the darker hues of the naval uniforms around him. Vader had made his disdain for Thrawn abundantly clear throughout the voyage, hinting at the Atollon failure every chance he got.

In fact, among Faro's fellow officers, there was quiet speculation that Vader would at some point simply declare himself the *Chimae-*

ra's master, no matter what navy protocol said. If that ever happened, having Kimmund on the bridge would certainly make the takeover easier to enforce.

Was that why Kimmund was here? Was this the moment that was going to happen?

To Faro's relief, Vader merely inclined his head. "Very well," he said. "Commodore Faro, prepare Admiral Thrawn's freighter."

"At once, my lord," Faro said, pushing back her fears and relief as she pulled out her comlink. Senior Lieutenant Xoxtin had been extra prickly ever since the two of them had had their little talk, and it would save trouble all around if the commodore gave the order directly.

But at least the tension between Thrawn and Vader had subsided. For the moment.

"Commander Kimmund?" Vader called.

"My lord?" Kimmund responded briskly, taking a last step to Vader's side and coming to attention.

"You will go to the hangar deck and supervise the preparation of Admiral Thrawn's transport," Vader ordered.

"Yes, my lord," Kimmund said. "How large a group do you wish to accompany you?"

Again, the black helmet turned to Thrawn, the invisible face behind it seeming to measure him. "None," he told Kimmund. "The admiral and I will go alone."

"Alone?" a gravelly voice came from behind Faro.

Despite her best efforts, Faro started. *Damn* that Rukh, anyway. Thrawn had already given him free run of the ship—why did he insist on using that damn invisibility gadget of his?

"Alone," Thrawn confirmed, not reacting at all to Rukh's sudden appearance. Maybe Chiss eyes could penetrate the disguise better than human ones.

Or maybe Rukh was here because Kimmund was here. Maybe Thrawn had ordered the Noghri to keep an eye on the First Legion's commander.

Kimmund, she'd heard, was openly rooting for the Noghri to burn out his personal cloaking device with overuse. Faro was tending toward agreement on that one.

"Perhaps you do not believe your master and I can travel to a primitive village without your protection?" Vader demanded. He hadn't reacted to Rukh's sudden appearance, either.

Rukh growled something in his native language. "Unknown situations are exactly when the grand admiral needs me the most."

"We go alone," Thrawn said, his tone making it clear the discussion was over. "If you wish, you may accompany Commander Kimmund to the hangar bay and observe the preparations."

Rukh turned his glare on Kimmund. Not that Kimmund probably cared. "It will be done, Grand Admiral," the Noghri said. "I will watch *very* closely."

"Then, with your permission, my lord," Thrawn said, "I will go to my cabin and prepare."

"I will await you in the hangar." Vader gestured toward him. "I trust you will not be wearing your uniform?"

"That is indeed the preparation I spoke of," Thrawn confirmed. "Even if the locals do not recognize the uniform of an Imperial grand admiral, they will nevertheless recognize that it *is* a uniform."

"Very well. Do not be long."

"With all due speed, my lord," Thrawn promised.

He turned to Faro. "While we are gone, you will rig the *Chimaera* for darkness and stealth," he ordered. "Keep a sharp watch, passive sensors only."

"Yes, Admiral," Faro said.

With a final look at Rukh, Thrawn turned and walked back down the command walkway. Kimmund waited until he'd passed, then also turned, following the admiral at two steps' distance. Rukh slipped past Faro, eyed Vader measuringly as he passed, and started to follow the stormtrooper.

"Rukh?" Faro called.

The Noghri paused and looked back. "Commodore?"

"I want you to watch the freighter prep work very closely," Faro said. "And make sure Lieutenant Xoxtin *knows* you're watching."

A malicious smile briefly crossed Rukh's craggy face. "She will know, Commodore," he promised. "Most certainly."

The freighter was of a type Vader hadn't seen before. Still, the controls were in the proper places and the handling was smooth enough.

It was Thrawn's ship, and standard protocol was that the admiral would fly it. Vader hadn't bothered to ask before taking the pilot's seat. Thrawn, for his part, had had the good sense not to argue the point.

Black Spire hadn't changed much since The Jedi had last been there, Vader noted as he brought the freighter in toward the landing field nestled into the forest three kilometers west of the settlement. The trading post with the attached cantina dominated the center of town, pressing up against the edge of the ruins of the ancient civilization that had once stood here. Some of the homes and businesses had been built into those ruins, though most were freestanding buildings. The petrified remains of the giant black trees that had given the outpost its name towered over everything, mysterious and brooding. The house directly behind the trading post, where the owner lived, stood out from the rest with evidence of real money.

"Those are new," Thrawn murmured.

"What?" Vader asked.

"Those houses," Thrawn said, pointing at a wooded area on the eastern side of the outpost, the side opposite the landing field, about three kilometers away from the edge of town. "They were not there the last time."

Vader studied the houses. There were three of them, larger and better built than those in the town, hemmed in by the woods around them. Each house was surrounded by a small ring of garden space, which on some of the galaxy's most prestigious city-worlds would be evidence of the owner's wealth or leisure.

Here in the Outer Rim, though, a garden might simply be a frugal person's attempt to stretch uneven finances by growing some of his own food. "I wonder why they chose to build amid the trees when other, more easily cleared ground surrounds the outpost," the Chiss continued.

"Does it matter?" Vader asked. So far he wasn't sensing the disturbance in the Force that the Emperor had spoken of. Did that mean whatever it was had left Batuu?

He hoped not. Every minute he stayed out here was a minute in which the rebels were free to plot and prepare and attack.

"I suspect it is for purposes of concealment," Thrawn said. "Do you note the additions to that stone tree?"

Vader shifted his attention to the petrified tree remnant Thrawn had tagged on the display. At first glance it looked like all the others, but as a scanner overlay appeared he saw the complex electronics that had been invisibly woven into the stone bark and along the branches. "I believe it is part of a communications triad," Thrawn continued. "It is a system for sending signals over long distances throughout the Unknown Regions."

Vader eyed the display, a whisper of interest tugging at him despite himself. Though unlikely to have a direct bearing on their search, it echoed back to The Jedi's memories of his time here. "The term *triad* suggests there are two other poles."

"Indeed," Thrawn said. "The likely position of the first is in one of the new houses."

Vader looked at the main display. Assuming the triad's poles formed an equilateral triangle . . . "The ship at the far end of the landing area will be the other," he said. "Faded gray paint and a broken landing skid."

"An abandoned derelict, clearly of no use to anyone," Thrawn said. "A perfect hiding place."

Vader eyed the six other light freighters jammed together in the cramped space. "For a planet that is supposed to host few visitors, there are an unusual number of waiting ships."

"I agree," Thrawn said. "Interesting. Unfortunately, it leaves us no room."

Vader pursed his lips. Only two spots were still available: one at the outpost end of the field, the other right beside the derelict ship.

Both would be tight for a vessel their size, but he could do it. "I can land us there," he said.

"There is insufficient space," Thrawn insisted.

"The space is sufficient for a pilot of sufficient skill."

For a moment Thrawn remained silent. Vader could feel the flow of his thoughts and emotions, the orderly mix of what seemed to be calculation and caution. There might have been some annoyance, as well, but the Chiss's mind was still maddeningly closed to Vader's understanding. "You are certain you can land without mishap?"

In answer, Vader swung the freighter's nose toward the landing area. The sooner they searched the outpost and found the source of the Emperor's disturbance, the sooner they would be done with this place.

"What about our goal?" Thrawn asked. "Have you been able to gather any further information?"

Vader glared out the viewport. For someone with no Force sensitivity, Thrawn had a disconcerting knack for reading or anticipating people's thoughts. "Nothing of significance," he said. "The disturbance feels distant, yet somehow also close at hand."

"As if attempting to conceal itself?"

"Perhaps," Vader said, stretching out to the Force again. The disturbance . . . there it was.

But it was flickering, barely there. The thought of the Emperor picking up something this weak all the way from Coruscant bordered on the unbelievable. Yet somehow, he'd done it.

"We shall soon know," Thrawn said. "Perhaps a closer investigation will reveal the truth."

"We think they dropped from lightspeed about fifteen minutes ago," Sensor Officer Hammerly said, pointing at the overlay she'd sent to the *Chimaera*'s tactical display. "It wasn't until they turned toward Batuu that we were able to pick up their drive emissions on passive sensors."

Faro gazed at the display, stroking her lip gently. For a system that wasn't supposed to get much traffic, Batuu certainly seemed popular today. Counting the six ships on the ground that Admiral Thrawn's tight-beam transmission had mentioned, this new set of four made ten. "Maybe they're having a party down there," she said. "What else do you have on the newcomers?"

"Not much," Hammerly admitted. "We can't get configuration or markings at this distance, not on passive sensors. If they're running ID beacons, they're too weak to pick up out of the noise."

Faro looked at the sensor displays, found the line that indicated the background electromagnetic radiation level. It wasn't unusually high for a star of this magnitude and spectrum; the *Chimaera* was just too far out. "Did you do an emission/acceleration profile?"

"Yes, ma'am," Hammerly said. "They read as small freighters. But of course, they could also be small warships running at low power. They're flying in loose formation, so they're definitely together. Near as we can tell from their current vector, they seem to be aiming for the same general area where Admiral Thrawn and Lord Vader landed."

Faro nodded. Before Thrawn and Vader left, the admiral had made it clear that Faro wasn't to signal him except in an extreme emergency, given that a transmission would betray the *Chimaera*'s presence to anyone listening in. And if these ships were just more merchants joining the sales event the admiral had suggested might be happening, it hardly qualified as an emergency.

But if they were warships . . .

"Contact!" the officer at the secondary sensor station snapped. "Straight ahead; distance four hundred thousand kilometers. Two ships."

"On it," Hammerly said coolly, swiveling back to her board. "Two ships—similar sizes; long-range heavy freighters at the least—bearing straight toward Batuu."

"Where did they come from?" Faro asked. It was way too soon to figure the ships' vector, but since everyone seemed to end up at Black Spire, it seemed reasonable to assume the newcomers were going there, too.

"Straight over our shoulder, looks like," Hammerly said. "Down the hyperlane we came in on, I'm guessing."

"Only they're in more of a hurry to reach the planet than we were," Faro said. "Stayed in hyperspace a little longer and came out up there instead of back here."

"Yes, ma'am." Hammerly looked furtively up at her. "Orders, Commodore?"

Translation: Was Faro going to decide this qualified as an emergency and take the risk of contacting the admiral?

Faro looked back at the tactical. The estimated landing for the four small ships was twenty minutes, assuming they were heading for Black Spire. At the larger newcomers' current acceleration profile, again assuming a planetside rendezvous, they would be fifteen minutes behind the original foursome.

Or possibly not. There were now indications that the large freighters might be splitting up, one heading for orbit while the other headed for the surface.

Could that change be because Thrawn's freighter was sitting in their planned landing spot? In which case, could someone down there be annoyed enough to start shooting?

Faro made up her mind. Grand Admiral Thrawn had a passion for information, and right now there was precious little of that commodity that Faro could offer.

Besides, Vader was down there with him. What could possibly happen that the two of them together couldn't handle? "You've got ten minutes to squeeze everything you can out of those sensors," she told Hammerly. "Once we see what you've got, we'll go from there."

The travel corridor between the landing field and Black Spire was rough-hewn, its edges lined with small trees and bushes that marked the forest's continual attempt to reclaim the land.

The lack of precise edgework suggests the earlier care has diminished over the past few months. The air is rich with memory, full of the aromas of exotic plants and the sounds of distant birds.

Three meters ahead and a meter to the right, Vader hunches over the front of his speeder bike, his long cloak rippling rhythmically in the wind of his passage. His body stance perhaps holds tension, perhaps anger.

Black Spire comes into sight. Vader lifts a hand, signaling a halt.

Thrawn slowed his speeder bike and stopped beside Vader's. "Have you a plan of approach?" Vader asked. *His left hand falls back from the speeder bike's control grip to his side near his lightsaber.*

"We will begin with the cantina," Thrawn said. "It may be that the bartender will remember me."

Vader's hand moves a few centimeters closer to his lightsaber. His back stiffens slightly. "We shall see," he said. *He leans forward and again takes the control grips. His wrist twists and the bike moves forward.*

A surprisingly large number of residents were visible on Black Spire's streets as Thrawn and Vader traveled at reduced speed along the twisting paths through the outpost. Perhaps that was due to the hour: The sun was near zenith, and for many residents this would be the time for a midday meal, business meetings, or general conversation. Four species were represented: humans, Darshi, Shistavanens, and Jablogians.

Vader's helmet moves a few degrees back and forth as they approach the cantina. His vision appears to linger on each Darshi that he passes. "You are not familiar with Darshi?" Thrawn asked.

"I am not," Vader said. "Are they from the Unknown Regions?"

"I believe they are a border people," Thrawn said. "I know little about them except their basic appearance. They travel both Wild Space and the Unknown Regions."

"I understood travel into the Unknown Regions was difficult."

"Indeed," Thrawn said. "The hyperlanes are few and not easy to traverse. But system jumps are possible if a traveler has sufficient time and is content with traversing limited distances."

"And if one was *not* content with limited distances?"

"One would need a careful study of the border," Thrawn said. "Millennia ago a set of chained supernova explosions throughout this particular region threw planet- and moon-sized masses at high speeds across the stars. The movements of those masses continually alter the hyperlanes, changing the paths in ways that are difficult to calculate. Other phenomena in other parts of the border created similar barriers. The hyperlanes that remain largely intact are beset with other dangers."

"Are the Darshi one of those dangers?"

"Their culture has not been deeply studied by the Chiss," Thrawn said. "They are not generally believed to exhibit violence to outsiders."

"Yet they are built for violence," Vader said. "Long clawed limbs are ideal for attack. Narrow heads and bodies are likewise excellent for defense."

"I agree," Thrawn said. "I can only state again that the stories do not portray them as violent."

Vader turns his head as he passes another Darshi, keeping him in view until he is lost to sight. "Stories are not always accurate," he said. "I also note that each carries a long knife at his side."

"Indeed," Thrawn said. "From the extensive tooling on the scabbard, I surmise the weapons are largely ceremonial."

"They are still weapons," Vader said. "If not against outsiders, then perhaps against their own kind."

"That is often the case with ceremonial weapons."

There were three other speeder bikes and two landspeeders drawn up in front of the cantina when they arrived. Other Black Spire residents were converging on the building on foot. Thrawn and Vader parked their bikes beside the others and dismounted. "Perhaps our timing was . . . inconvenient," Vader said.

"Perhaps," Thrawn said. "Yet a large group also increases the probability that one or more of those responsible for the Emperor's disturbance will be present. Their reaction to our arrival may prove useful."

"It may," Vader said. "I will watch. You will speak."

The door is tall and wide, designed to accommodate large beings or cargo pods. The texture is subtly different from the rest of the building, and appears newer. Vader pushes one door open with his left hand, leaving his right hand free. He strides in and takes a long step to the side, allowing entry behind him. The interior is dimly lit, the windows mostly closed and covered, with only small gaps allowing in light.

The cantina was well populated, with approximately two-thirds of its tables full. Most of the patrons had turned toward the door as Vader entered, and were now gazing at the newcomers.

With so many faces it would be impossible to fully observe the initial reactions of all of them. Fortunately, only one group was truly important.

Two adjacent tables are attended by five Darshi each. Four of the ten exhibit enlarged eyes. Six exhibit enlarged eyes and suddenly stiffened spines. One grasps at a second's arm. A third leans closer to a fourth, speaking inaudibly. Still, it is impossible to discern whether they are reacting to Vader or the unexpected appearance of a Chiss.

Thrawn strode past Vader toward the bar and the large human working behind it. *The patrons along the route, none of them Darshi, return to their plates and cups, their initial focus fading. The bartender finishes preparing his current drink and looks up at the newcomers. His expression holds puzzlement and a hint of returning memory.*

"Good morning," Thrawn said. "Perhaps you remember me."

The bartender's eyes widen. His expression holds sudden recognition. His lips turn downward, his eyes and expression holding unpleasant memories. "I do," he said. *His eyes change focus as Vader comes forward.* "The other, from before. Is he with you?"

"No," Thrawn said. "I'm told he died some years ago. The fortunes of war."

"Good," the bartender said. *His eyes shift to Vader again. His expression holds hostility.* "Does this one now stand as your bodyguard?"

Visible in the curved metal railing of the bar, Vader's body stance stiffens. "He is a fellow traveler, not a bodyguard," Thrawn said. "What is your name?"

The bartender's expression changes, now holding wariness. "I am Nodlia. Have you come to once again deal with supposed oppression?"

"Do you wish my help?" Thrawn asked.

"Have I a choice?"

"Perhaps," Thrawn said. "You speak of oppression?"

Nodlia hesitates. He lowers his voice and leans a few centimeters closer over the bar. "The newcomers to Batuu," he said. "The Thinfaces."

"The Darshi?"

"If that's their name. They've not spoken much to me. I know only that since their arrival Batuu hasn't been the same."

"When was that?"

"The first group came one hundred seventy-four days ago," Nodlia said. "They said they were on a pilgrimage, that their journey would require them to stay on Batuu for a time. They built houses for themselves to the east, and spent three days in the woods to the north in group meditation. At times they fill our spacefield with their ships, coming and going to distant places on unknown errands."

"That does not sound like oppression," Thrawn said.

"They drove away some of the traders who used to come here," Nodlia said. "Other ships were discouraged by the lack of landing spots at the times when they filled the spacefield. Some of those traders went elsewhere on Batuu. Others abandoned our world entirely. Our people were forbidden from venturing near the Thinfaces' houses, and they took the best food and resources for themselves."

"Did they not pay for it?"

Nodlia hesitates. His expression holds embarrassment. "Yes, they paid. The proper fees and prices. Perhaps even somewhat more. Enough more, truth be told, to calm most of those dissatisfied with their other interference."

He leans yet closer, his eyes shifting to the Darshi at their two tables. "But I wasn't fooled. I remember . . . you know of what I speak. There's the same feel about the Thinfaces.

"And then, eighteen days ago, a new group of them arrived." *He pauses. His expression holds a quiet horror.* "With them came ten coffins."

An armored finger touched Thrawn's arm. "They prepare for combat," Vader said quietly.

Nodlia's expression holds sudden fear. He takes three steps away along the bar. His body stance holds a desire to move far from the up-coming attack.

"How soon?" Thrawn asked.

"They are passing weapons among themselves," Vader said. "Not their knives, but combat sticks. The newly armed are making their way in both directions, no doubt attempting to surround us and launch a coordinated attack."

There was a signal from the comlink on Thrawn's belt. "Perhaps more coordinated than you know." He pulled out the comlink and turned it on. "Speak."

"Large ship, heavy freighter or small warship, heading toward your position." *Faro's voice holds tension and determination.* "Second ship, plus four smaller ships, making orbit. Orders?"

"They cannot be allowed to escape," Vader said. "Order the *Chimaera* to attack."

"It would be unwise to reveal the *Chimaera*'s presence and fire-power at present," Thrawn said. "Let us first see if the survivors of the coming attack can provide us with the information we need."

"Unlikely they will know the incoming ships' space combat capa-bilities," Vader countered.

"The *Chimaera* is even now gathering that information."

"Data from that distance will be insufficient," Vader rumbled. "I have ordered Commander Kimmund to intercept, examine, and en-gage if necessary."

"I am in command, Lord Vader."

"You command the *Chimaera*," Vader said. *His voice and stance are stiff. His hand rests near his lightsaber.* "I command the First Le-gion. You will instruct Faro to release them to the attack."

"Very well," Thrawn said. "Commodore, you will permit Com-mander Kimmund and his men to depart. I place the *Chimaera* under your command. You may act on your own discretion."

"Acknowledged, Admiral."

He returned the comlink to his belt. "The warrior's path lies before us," he said. "Let us follow its guidance."

CHAPTER 4

―――――――――――――――――――――――

"The warrior's path lies before us," Thrawn said, nodding through the windscreen at the cantina looming in front of them. "Let us see where it leads."

Anakin suppressed a sigh. Whether a soldier called it a motto, an aphorism, or a war cry, his personal experience was that most of those who continually spouted them turned out to be not very good at their jobs once the shooting began.

Jedi were the exception to that rule, of course. Most of the ones Anakin had met could trot out an aphorism for nearly any occasion, but despite that most of them did just fine in combat.

Maybe Chiss were like Jedi in that respect. But he doubted it.

The cantina itself looked equally unpromising. It was large but old, bordering on the decrepit, something that had never been all that impressive to begin with and had been going downhill ever since. The windows were shuttered, the door scarred and faded with age.

The people moving back and forth down the streets looked equally scarred and faded, as did the whole outpost. The ruins Black Spire was built beside and into looked ancient, like something lost out of time, with the mixed sense of intrigue, desperation, and ruthlessness that he'd seen in so many similar settlements. In this kind of environment, there was no telling what sort of trouble Duja had stumbled on.

But what level of trouble could have persuaded her to drag Padmé all the way out here with her?

"Do you see them?" Thrawn asked.

Anakin looked around at the people shuffling their way across the dusty streets. "See who?"

"Two beings to our left, three to our right," Thrawn said. "They've begun to slowly converge on us."

"Really," Anakin said, resisting the impulse to look. Ambushes were always easier to turn when the attackers didn't know they'd been spotted. "You think our smugglers are still unhappy with us?"

"These aren't the ones who tried to breach your ambassador's ship," Thrawn said. "Indeed, if they remained in ground vehicles they're most likely still traversing the forest. But they certainly could have signaled ahead."

"Well, if they think getting us out of the way will let them go back and move the ship, they're going to be disappointed," Anakin said grimly. "I bounce-locked the ship's systems before we left. Without the code, they'll never get it to fly."

"Perhaps they've already investigated and know that," Thrawn said as he pulled to a stop by the cantina. "These five may be hoping to extract the release code from you."

Anakin shrugged as he got a hand on the windscreen and hopped over the landspeeder's side. "Like I said. They're going to be disappointed."

The cantina's interior was as depressing as the exterior. There were barely a handful of patrons seated at various tables, a few talking together in low voices but most sitting solitary vigil over their drinks. The bartender was standing behind a wraparound wooden bar, gazing dully at the patrons as he absently polished a small obsidian mug from a line of similar vessels lined up in front of him. Behind him, the wall was covered with a tangle of pipes, filters, bubblers, and other less identifiable devices. Briefly, Anakin wondered if the place was happier, or at least busier, at mealtimes.

He put the thought behind him. They were here for information, not companionship.

The bartender shifted his gaze to the door as the two newcomers walked in, his eyes following them as they made their way through the maze of tables. "Afternoon, visitors," he said in accented Basic as they reached the bar. "What drinks do you choose?"

"We choose the cool quaff of information," Thrawn said in Meese Caulf.

A look flashed across the bartender's face, as if he was mentally shifting gears. "Information, you say," he said in the same language.

"Yes," Thrawn confirmed. "And we're prepared to pay for it," he added, setting a golden coin on the bar beside the row of mugs.

The bartender looked down at the coin, but made no move to pick it up. "Information on Batuu is of two types," he said. "The useless, and the very costly."

"Perhaps we shall find a central ground." Thrawn gestured to Anakin.

"We seek information on these human females," Anakin said, switching on his holoprojector. The ghostly images of Padmé and Duja appeared above the disk. "Have you seen either of them?"

Reluctantly, the bartender lifted his eyes from the coin. Anakin reached out with the Force, caught the flicker of recognition—

"No," the man said, lowering his eyes again. "Neither has been seen here."

"Really," Thrawn said, his voice taking on a smooth coolness that suggested he didn't believe the man, either. "Please take a second look, for this is important. Their father is dying, and would like to see his daughters one last time before the end."

Again with clear reluctance, the bartender lifted his gaze. "I haven't seen them," he said, lowering his eyes back to the mugs and the coin. "They're sisters, then?"

"Yes," Thrawn said. He pulled out a second coin and placed it beside the first. "Their entire family is assembled at his bedside"—he added a third coin—"with these two sisters the only ones unaware of their coming loss"—a fourth coin joined the growing pile—"and who will be heartbroken if their beloved father passes on without their farewells."

The bartender had missed none of the action. "And you were sent to retrieve them?" he asked.

"He carries the burden of that task," Thrawn said, nodding to Anakin. "I was merely hired as guide and translator."

"Yes." The bartender took one last, long look at the pile of coins. Then, taking a deep breath, he stepped resolutely back from the bar. "I'm sorry, gentlebeings. I truly am."

And without warning, the line of mugs on the bar exploded into a cloud of thick white smoke.

Instantly Anakin clamped his nose and mouth shut to keep out the gas. Snatching up his lightsaber, he started to leap back from the cloud—

And staggered sideways off balance as Thrawn grabbed his shoulder and shoved hard against it. Through the smoke he caught an unclear image of the Chiss now standing on top of the bar, turning to face the doorway with drawn blaster. Again, Anakin started to step back from the bar.

But instead found himself swaying further to the side, his balance gone, his knees buckling beneath him. That momentary jolt when Thrawn used his shoulder as an assist for his leap onto the bar had let in enough of the gas to affect him. He managed to get turned toward the door, then found himself toppling to the floor.

As he hit the rough wood, the room erupted with blasterfire.

His vision was starting to fade. But he was a Jedi, and there were ways to fight back against drug attacks. Drawing energy from the Force, concentrating on not losing consciousness, he peered through the smoke.

Four shapes were charging toward them, blasters blazing. From behind Anakin, Thrawn was returning fire, his weapon flashing brighter and making a higher-pitched sound than Republic blasters. One of the four assailants fell, but the other three continued forward.

Even with the gas fogging his mind, Anakin had enough awareness to know he didn't dare ignite his lightsaber—with his muscles uncoordinated the weapon would be as dangerous to him as to the enemy. But there were other ways. Again reaching to the Force, he got a mental grip on the nearest chair and threw it into the attackers' path.

Or rather, tried to. With no accuracy and only limited strength he was barely able to tip the chair over in front of them. But it was enough. For a moment they were distracted, their shots going wild, and in that moment two more of them fell to Thrawn's counterattack. Anakin tried to throw another chair, or even just nudge the blaster out of line.

But the fog was growing thicker, and his mind and hands were turning to lead. He had the vague impression he was tapping his comlink with the emergency code . . .

He woke up with a start to find himself lying on his back on the cantina floor. R2-D2 was standing over him, prodding him with one of his grappler arms, moaning with quiet anxiety. "I'm all right, Artoo," he assured the droid, his voice slurring a little. The air seemed clear; taking a deep breath, he ran a quick mental inventory.

Everything seemed intact. His mind was still fuzzy, but it was rapidly coming back to normal. He flexed his fingers—no problems there. Lifting his head, he looked around.

The cantina, not surprisingly, was deserted, the earlier patrons having fled. Aside from himself and R2-D2, only Thrawn remained, sitting in a chair a few meters away, his back to Anakin. His gun hand was resting on the chair's armrest, his weapon pointed toward the door. A few meters in front of him lay four bodies, and the smell of death was in the air.

"Welcome back," Thrawn said. He didn't turn around, Anakin noted, but kept his face turned toward the door. "Your droid seemed worried."

"Artoo sometimes thinks I need looking after," Anakin said, carefully pushing himself to his feet. There was a moment of dizziness, but it passed quickly. "Any idea what that gas was?"

"Something designed to make us easier to kill," Thrawn said, his voice going grim. "A diversionary attack from in front, with a simultaneous attack from behind. You will note where the first two shots were aimed."

Anakin looked at the bar. Right where he'd been standing were two fresh blaster burns. "I guess I should thank you for pushing me out of the way."

Thrawn half turned, a frown on his face. "That was not my intent," he said. "Such gases are designed to flow downward toward their victims. I therefore used you and the bar to leap upward out of its effect. I assumed you would follow."

"Yeah, I was a little busy being shoved to the side," Anakin growled. A movement on the far side of the bar caught his eye, and he leaned over the wood to look.

The bartender was back there, asleep on the floor. His arms were crossed over his stomach, his hands bound together with thin rope. "Looks like he didn't know it was coming."

"Or else simply didn't move back sufficiently far to avoid the effects." Thrawn paused. "You are a Jedi, then?"

"I'd have thought that was obvious."

"Not at all," Thrawn assured him. "Our myths of the Republic speak of two groups of beings with such powers: the Jedi, and the Sith. But the Sith are reputed to be clever and capable warriors. Tell me, do you recognize any of our attackers?"

Anakin turned back to the bodies on the floor, resisting the awful urge to lift Thrawn out of his chair and dangle him over the bar while he explained the *true* difference between Jedi and Sith.

But for all the Chiss's sarcasm, Anakin had to privately admit the implied accusation wasn't wrong. Focused on dragging the truth about Padmé out of the bartender, he'd gotten unforgivably sloppy. He should have expected a layered attack and been ready for it.

As to the bodies on the floor . . . "I don't think I've seen any of them before," he said, eyeing the three humans and one olive-skinned, amphibious Rybet. "Why, do you think I should?"

"I thought it possible," Thrawn said. "Three points. First: The placement of their initial shots prove they intended your death. That argues against a goal of forcing you to unlock the ambassador's ship. Second: The layered two-prong attack indicates they have knowledge of how to attack a Jedi. Third: The fact that only four of those who were following us attacked while the fifth remained outside suggests these four attackers were considered expendable by their comrade."

"Or else the fifth had been ordered to report to someone else and needed to stay free and clear to do that."

"Indeed," Thrawn agreed. "In which case, he now faces a dilemma."

"Yes, I see," Anakin murmured, looking again at the door. "I assume you locked us in?"

"Yes, and have confirmed that the window coverings were secure," Thrawn said. "No one can see inside."

"So our fifth man knows that at least one of us is still alive," Anakin continued. "Only he doesn't know which one. *And* he knows that all four of his friends are dead, or else they would have come out by now."

"Or possibly are taken alive," Thrawn said. "That may be his greatest fear."

"Yeah." Anakin looked at the bodies again. "Too bad we couldn't have managed that."

"In combat, quick decisions must be made," Thrawn said. "Added to his concerns is the Jedi fighter craft now resting nearby. He has many questions, but no answers."

"And he won't want to leave without them," Anakin said slowly, thinking it through. "So he has to be still waiting out there, either mixing with the rest of the citizens or lurking at the edge with comm in hand ready to call his boss."

"Which we must prevent."

Anakin cocked an eyebrow. "We don't want him talking to his boss?"

"We don't want them speaking via comm," Thrawn corrected.

"Ah," Anakin said, nodding understanding. "We want him to go there in person."

"Exactly," Thrawn said. "I presume your fighter has jamming capability?"

"Yes, and Artoo can switch it on from here." He gestured to the droid. "Go ahead."

R2-D2 warbled acknowledgment. "Jamming is on," Anakin said. "So how do we follow him?"

"Let us first design the story he will return with," Thrawn said. "Since their attack was layered toward Jedi, I suggest we present you as having been injured or killed. I'll carry you to your fighter, place you inside, and allow your droid to fly you away. Once we determine which of the onlookers is our quarry, I can follow him to his residence or vehicle, allow him to deliver his message, then capture him. An interrogation, plus an examination of his equipment, should yield the data we seek."

Anakin pursed his lips. That assumed, of course, that this whole scenario was connected with Padmé's disappearance and wasn't just someone's crazed vendetta against Jedi. So far, they hadn't proven that.

But at the moment this was the only lead he had. He had to follow it, and trust in the Force to guide him to his wife.

"One problem," he said. "Playing dead with you carrying me leaves me in a position where I can't easily react or fight back. What if he decides to take another shot at me, just to make sure?"

"A reasonable concern," Thrawn conceded. "Have you an alternative suggestion?"

Anakin looked around the cantina. None of the bodies was the right size for him or Thrawn to adopt their clothing; nor was there anything else in sight that could be used as a disguise.

On the other hand . . .

"You said he's afraid one of his friends survived," he said. "Let's play on that." Reaching out to the Force, he got a grip on one of the dead humans and lifted him off the floor.

"Interesting," Thrawn said. If he was startled by the body's sudden movement, it didn't show in his voice. "This requires a change in the story, though. The Jedi he sought to kill will now be alive."

"I like this one better," Anakin growled.

"I didn't say it was worse, merely different," Thrawn said mildly. "Can you make him appear to be living?"

"Let's find out."

It turned out to be trickier than Anakin had expected. Life wasn't just limbs moving back and forth, he quickly discovered, but also the more subtle flexing of muscles beneath the skin, plus the interplay of muscle groups with balance and kinesthetics.

An hour's worth of practice, and he would have had it down cold. But a few minutes was all he got before Thrawn called a halt. "That will be sufficient, and we have no more time," the Chiss said. "I suggest you take him out and lay him across the top of your fighter for transport."

Anakin thought about that. Balancing him up there would be tricky, even wedged in between the canopy and R2-D2's dome. "He'd fit better in the landspeeder," he pointed out.

"Would you normally leave your fighter behind while transporting a prisoner?"

Anakin scowled. Under certain circumstances that wouldn't be completely out of the question. Here and now, though, he had no intention of leaving his Actis unattended. "You're right," he said. "Okay, I'll take our puppet and head out. Any particular direction you want me to go?"

"I suggest you fly toward the ambassador's ship," Thrawn said. "If our attackers were alerted by the smugglers, they'll know of that spot and assume you're traveling there. Meantime, I'll endeavor to identify and follow our quarry."

"Right," Anakin said. "I'll go nice and slow to keep the jamming field over the whole area as long as possible."

"Very good." Thrawn eased himself out of his chair and turned around.

Anakin caught his breath. The chest of the Chiss uniform had turned from black to a dirty gray, and was pocked with a dozen ragged-edged blaster burns. "What—?"

"Their blasterfire was impressively accurate," Thrawn said, moving carefully toward the door. "Fortunately, Chiss uniforms are designed to absorb and disperse as much energy as possible." He looked down at his tunic. "It is, unfortunately, not a perfect system."

"Still better than nothing," Anakin said, his respect for the Chiss reluctantly rising a couple of notches. He'd seen hardened clone warriors turn to jelly with fewer wounds than that through their chest plates. "You going to be okay?"

"I've already treated the wounds," Thrawn said. "Until they're fully healed, I'll make do. Are you ready?"

Stretching out to the Force, Anakin started the dead man doing a shuffle-walk toward the door. "Ready," he said. He moved up beside the puppet and put his left arm around the other's waist, supporting him as he might a wounded prisoner. He took a couple of experimental steps forward, moving the body's legs to keep time with his own. "How does it look?"

"Adequate." Walking stiffly to the door, Thrawn unlocked it. "Go. Good fortune."

"Come on, Artoo," Anakin said. The inside of the door, he saw now, was pocked with fresh blaster burns. Apparently, injured Chiss didn't shoot very accurately. Pushing open the door with his free hand, he stepped out into the street.

Black Spire hadn't looked all that big as he and Thrawn rode through in their landspeeder. Not nearly big enough to support four or five hundred people.

But clearly it did . . . and every one of them seemed to have turned out to gawk at the Republic starfighter that had landed in the center of their town.

Perhaps a dozen people turned as Anakin stepped into the sunlight. The rest of the crowd, still fascinated by the shiny fighter, ignored him completely. "Move aside!" Anakin called, pouring on every gram of authority that a lifetime's worth of war command had given him. "Move aside! Republic business."

He wasn't sure that people out here even knew what the Republic was. But if they didn't, the tone of his voice was apparently enough. The crowd began to shuffle aside, opening up a crooked path to the Actis. "Come on," Anakin said under his breath, remembering to move the body's legs as he started down the open path, his senses alert to danger. If their quarry wanted to finish off either him or his injured comrade—or both—this would be the time for him to take that shot.

No attacks had come by the time they reached the Actis. Anakin waited for R2-D2 to jet up and lock himself into his socket, then lifted his burden onto the top of the vehicle, pushing him as he would a wounded man and making it look like the body's arms were searching weakly for handholds.

He got him wedged between the droid and canopy rim. Then, remembering to keep the body's limbs moving in a hopefully realistic manner, he climbed into the cockpit and closed the canopy. Easing in the repulsorlifts, he rose into the sky.

The Actis's jammers were designed to block enemy fighter transmissions hundreds of kilometers away. But that required a focused field, one that was primarily aimed forward toward where those enemies would normally be in battle. Still, the field spread out a short distance in all directions around the fighter, which meant he should be able to block anything from Black Spire up to around a dozen kilometers away. Rotating the Actis in midair, moving at a leisurely pace in order to give Thrawn as much time as he could, Anakin lined up the nose with Padmé's distant ship. He eased in the thrusters—

An instant later there was a dull thud from beneath him and the Actis suddenly rolled sideways, dropping nearly all the way onto its left side.

"Artoo!" Anakin snapped as he jabbed the repulsorlift controls. Even as his brain registered the urgently glowing red lights on the monitor the fighter leapt forward, pressing him back into his seat as the thrusters came on at full power, burning them through the air at maximum acceleration. A second later the compensators kicked in, easing the pressure and letting him get to the controls again.

Only there was nothing he could do. The thud he'd heard, he realized now, had been a small explosion from the Actis's portside repulsorlift. The only thing that had prevented the fighter from dropping onto that side and falling out of the sky was R2-D2's quick thinking in kicking in the thrusters. That had given them enough forward motion to create sufficient lift over the stubby airfoil wings to compensate for the lost repulsorlift.

The only problem was that they were now blazing across Batuu at nearly a thousand kilometers an hour, leaving Black Spire far behind.

Lifting the jamming Thrawn was counting on to force their quarry out into the open.

To make matters worse, somewhere in all of that flurry of activity the body they'd decoyed their quarry with had slipped off the Actis and vanished into the forest far below.

Cursing under his breath, Anakin grabbed the control yoke and sent the fighter into a tight 180-degree turn. Once he was pointed back at Black Spire the communications blanket should come back into play. If their quarry had missed that brief window of opportunity, or if Thrawn had at least tagged him, they might still be able to pull this off.

R2-D2 warbled a question. "I don't know," Anakin told him. "The landing field, I guess. Unless he bought or rented a house here he's probably living out of his ship. How much speed do we need to stay level without the repulsorlift?"

The droid's answer wasn't encouraging. "No chance of going a little slower?" Anakin asked hopefully, cranking the thrusters back to just above R2-D2's estimated danger speed.

The reply this time was more emphatic. "No, landing on our portside wing isn't really an option," Anakin said with a sigh. "What about Thrawn's ship, the one in orbit? Did it have a port we could dock in?"

Another whistled negative. "Yeah, I didn't see one, either," Anakin said. "Nothing to do but head back to Black Spire. Don't worry, I'll think of something."

By the time the outpost was once again in sight on the horizon he had a plan.

It wasn't much of a plan. Anakin himself didn't really like it. R2-D2 absolutely hated it.

But Thrawn was down there alone, injured, and facing a killer who might know where Padmé was. If Anakin was going to be in time to help out, this was his only option.

The landing field was a smaller clearing in the forest to the west of Black Spire. Anakin turned the Actis toward it, dropping to treetop level and keeping his speed as low as he could without losing control. The near end of the clearing flashed beneath him—he caught a glimpse of Thrawn crouched behind his landspeeder exchanging blasterfire with a hooded figure that was moving toward him—

Yanking back on the stick, he turned the Actis straight up, its nose pointed toward the sky, its thrusters blasting at the ground below. The sudden increase in air resistance against the fighter's belly pressed him into his seat and sent its forward momentum plummeting. He watched the airspeed indicator, mentally crossing his fingers . . .

He was halfway across the landing field when he saw that the deceleration wasn't going to be enough. Long before the fighter came to a midair halt it would be over the forest again, with no guarantee that there would be an open area where he could set it down.

Which left him only one option. Punching the canopy control with one hand and his restraint release with the other, he stretched out to the Force and jumped.

His head barely cleared the still-opening canopy. But the gamble worked. With the Actis rapidly slowing, and the Force adding speed and strength to his jump, Anakin found himself dropping almost straight down toward the clearing below. A quick twist of arms and hips to orient himself for a feetfirst landing—

He'd had barely enough time to grab his lightsaber when the hooded figure below raised his blaster and opened fire.

Six bolts blazed through the air at him before he hit the ground amid a crunch and flurry of dead leaves. He bent his knees to absorb the impact, holding that crouching pose as his assailant continued to fire. Through the blaze of red blasterfire against blue lightsaber blade he had a clear view of the face beneath the hood.

Only it wasn't a living face. It was a metal one.

A droid.

His battle-focused brain had only just registered that fact when the droid abruptly twisted and toppled over as its right leg disintegrated beneath it. The blaster fired one final bolt at Anakin's torso—

And the droid spasmed as Anakin sent the shot straight back into one of its photoreceptor eyes. Two more twitches, the death gaspings of a fatally damaged electronic brain, and the droid lay still.

Slowly, Anakin straightened up, his eyes on the droid. He'd seen them fake shutdowns before. But no, this one was finished. He glanced around, noted that Thrawn had emerged from cover and was walking stiffly toward him. Lying next to one of the parked ships was another hooded figure, this one human, his arms locked behind him, making small movements of pain or frustration. One last 360-degree check for threats and Anakin closed down his lightsaber. "Is that him?" he asked, nodding toward the twitching man.

"It is," Thrawn said, coming to a stop beside him. "Interesting flight maneuver."

"There's a lot of improvisation in warfare," Anakin said. He nudged the droid with his foot. "What's *his* story?"

"I succeeded in arriving before our quarry," Thrawn said. "As you anticipated, he was returning to his ship to report. Once it was clear which ship was his goal, I intercepted and neutralized him." He gently touched a fresh burn on his chest. "I didn't expect such an adversary to be waiting inside."

"Consider yourself lucky it was just a general-service droid instead of a full-blown assassin," Anakin said grimly. "They're a lot nastier."

"If we find ourselves facing one of those in the future, I'll permit you to take the lead," Thrawn promised.

Anakin sent him a sideways look. Had that been actual humor? "It's a deal," he agreed. "Let's go see what we've got."

The ship wasn't a style or model Anakin was familiar with. But it had a definite Techno Union feel about it. The hatch was locked, but a few seconds of lightsaber work solved that problem.

And once inside . . .

"It's a Separatist ship, all right," Anakin said, looking around. "The equipment, the markings, even the controls. There's no doubt." He hissed between his teeth. "The question is, what are they doing way out here?

"The layout appears to be that of a freighter," Thrawn pointed out. "Perhaps the cargo will give us a clue to their purpose."

"In a minute," Anakin said, pulling out his comlink. "Artoo? You there?"

There was a disgusted-sounding grunt, followed by a long and unhappy account of his current situation. "I'm sure you did everything you could," Anakin soothed him. "Do you need my help getting down?"

There was another emphatic grunt. "Okay, then," Anakin said. "We need you at the landing field. We're in the gray ship with—look, just go to the downed droid and turn left."

He keyed off. "Is your droid all right?" Thrawn asked.

"He's fine," Anakin assured him. "But my fighter is sitting about five meters off the ground, wedged vertically between three trees. Not sure how I'm going to get it out without setting the forest on fire. Anyway, Artoo's fine and he's on his way. Once he's here, we can check the computer and see if they still have the coordinates of their last stop."

"We shall see," Thrawn said. "While we wait, shall we look at the cargo?"

"Sure," Anakin said, getting a fresh grip on his lightsaber. There might be more droids lurking back there. "Follow me."

CHAPTER 5

"I'm coming into Batuu now," Padmé said into her ship's recorder as the sunlit ground began to rise around her. "I'll signal you once I've found Duja."

She hesitated. Should she add *I love you*?

Probably not. Aside from the chance that someone else might be around when Anakin listened to the message, this was going through an untested public relay service instead of the usual HoloNet. No telling what they might do before sending it on.

Shutting down the recorder, she keyed for transmission. The display indicated that it had been received by the service and—hopefully—sent on its way.

Whether it was or not, there was nothing more she could do about it. Time to find Duja and see what her former handmaiden had learned that was so important.

Hopefully, the information wouldn't already have been preempted by events. The trip here had taken longer than Padmé had expected, with her nav computer's database proving sufficiently out of date to make its proposed courses unsafe. She'd had to plot new segments twice, and at both times she'd wished she'd taken Anakin up on his offer to use Jedi resources to work out her travel arrangements.

But at least he'd be here much faster once she knew what was going on. Keying her comm to Duja's frequency, she leaned toward the cockpit microphone. "Duja, it's Padmé," she called. "I'm here."

No answer. "Duja?" she called again. "Duja, come in please."

Nothing. Not even a carrier or transponder echo.

She frowned, the first stirrings of concern starting to twist their way through her stomach. Duja was one of the best, both at intel and combat. If someone had managed to take her out . . .

She took a deep breath. Okay. Duja wasn't answering, but that didn't necessarily mean something terrible had happened. Odds were she was simply away from her ship, with her comm turned off for a perfectly good reason. The outpost Duja had specified—Black Spire—wasn't all that big. It shouldn't take more than an hour or two for Padmé to have a look around.

The landing field was small, not all that surprising given the size of the outpost itself. But there were only a pair of midsized freighters parked near the middle, leaving plenty of room for her to put down. She did so, picking a spot as far from the other ships as she reasonably could, and shut everything down to standby. Putting on a light-green jacket with a subtle brown brocade running from left shoulder to right waist—the outside sensors said it was a bit nippy out there—and tucking her blaster out of sight beneath it, she cycled the hatch and stepped out.

She had finished getting her BARC speeder bike out of the aft hull storage locker when she heard a voice call to her in an unknown language.

She turned. A lumpy nonhuman of a species she didn't recognize was crouching at the bottom of the nearest freighter's landing ramp. "Excuse me?" she called back.

"He was complimenting you on your magnificent ship," a human called from the top of the ramp. "Excuse us, but your Basic is not my language."

"That's all right," Padmé called back, suppressing a knowing smile. Liar. He was trying hard—a little too hard, actually—to pretend he was struggling with a second language. But the Basic words and syntax were coming just a little too easily and smoothly.

"What are?" the man asked. "I mean, what species?"

"Species?" Padmé asked. "Oh—you mean the model. It's an H-type Nubian yacht. Tell me, do you know someone named Kuseph Jovi?"

"I know nothing of that name," the man said. "Are you here to meet her?"

A quiet warning bell went off in the back of Padmé's mind. Why would he assume that the name she'd rattled off was that of a woman?

Unless there was already an unknown woman in Black Spire who'd caught their attention.

"To meet *him*," she corrected. "I'm here to deliver his new ship."

"Really," the man said, eyeing the ship as he walked down the ramp. There was a lump at his side that probably indicated a hidden blaster. "Nice. What did he pay for it?"

"No idea," Padmé said. "I'm just a courier. Any idea who might know where I can find him? The ship that's picking me up could be here anytime, and I want to finish the transaction so I can go home."

"There's a cantina in the middle of town," the man said, pointing down a ragged-edged corridor that had been cut through the trees and undergrowth toward the outpost itself. "If he's here, someone there will know him."

"Thank you," Padmé said. Climbing onto her speeder bike, she turned toward the corridor and headed in.

She could feel the man's eyes on her as she left the field.

She'd expected Black Spire to be like all the rest of the tiny frontier outposts she'd seen in her travels: carved out of the wilderness, with houses and shops laid out in a more or less orderly fashion along the major streets—though the term *major* was usually granting them more status than they deserved—and other buildings arranged haphazardly wherever their builders had felt like putting them.

But this town had a twist. There were ruins here, ancient ruins of some long-gone civilization, bordering the colonists' town. A few of the buildings were completely or partially within shells of the older structures, while one or two others nestled against them as if for warmth or protection.

Even more intriguing, the black towers she'd seen on her way in, obviously the source of the outpost's name, weren't structures or towers, but the petrified remains of trees, scattered like sentinels throughout the town and the region around it. The whole place struck her as beautiful, mysterious, and a little bit sad.

But the populace, at least, conformed completely to Padmé's expectations. Pedestrians and a few vehicles moved between the buildings, everyone pausing to give Padmé a quick or furtive once-over as she passed. Genuine strangers were apparently rare here.

Either that, or Duja had stirred up more attention than she'd probably wanted.

At the intersection of the two main streets was the cantina the man had mentioned. There was a strange wooden platform off to one side: waist-high, about two meters long, with some kind of yellowish strawlike decoration poking up around all the edges. Probably where the locals gathered for speeches, lectures, or just the general haranguing of their fellow citizens, she decided. There were two other vehicles parked at the other side of the entrance, and she guided her BARC to a spot beside them.

And as she walked toward the cantina door she got her first real look at the platform.

It wasn't a platform at all, but a box about fifty centimeters deep. The strawlike decoration was in fact actual straw, forming a mat at the box's bottom and lining the sides.

Lying on the straw was a body.

It wasn't a political dais like Padmé had thought. It was, instead, an open-topped coffin, possibly being prepared for a funeral pyre.

Duja's funeral pyre.

Padmé had trained long and hard to keep reactions and emotions out of her face and body when she needed to. But even all that practice nearly proved inadequate. She was barely able to maintain an expression of idle curiosity as she stepped over and peered into the coffin.

Duja had been through the crusher, all right. Her face was battered and bruised in several places, and there were small stains on her clothing where blood had seeped through. The amateurishly hand-made brooch she always wore seemed undamaged, and her chrono and data card pack were undisturbed. Not a robbery, then, but a cold-blooded attack.

One thing was sure: If she'd fallen to violence, she hadn't gone down without a fight.

That one quick glance was all she dared for the moment. But she would be back. Turning away, she pushed open the cantina door and went inside.

Given that it wasn't yet local noon she wasn't expecting much of a crowd. She was right. Apart from her and the bartender, there were only three others in the room: two humans and another of the lumpy aliens like the one at the landing field. "You here for a drink?" the bartender called. "Or to pick up your friend?"

"My friend?" Padmé echoed, putting puzzlement into her face and voice.

The bartender pointed through the wall toward the coffin. "The lady out there."

"The—? Oh. No, not at all," Padmé assured him. "I'm looking for a man named Kuseph Jovi. Do you know him?"

It was the bartender's turn to look puzzled. "No one here by that name," he said. "You sure you got the right place?"

"This is the spot where he said to bring his new ship," Padmé said, walking over to the bar. "I suppose he *could* be coming from off-planet, though why he'd pick a spot like this for the transfer I couldn't guess. No offense," she added.

"None taken," the bartender assured her sourly. "Not exactly New Codia, is it?"

"Not really," Padmé agreed, wondering distantly whether New Codia was a system, a planet, or even just a city. There were so many small and forgotten places across the galaxy. "What do you have here?"

"What do you want?" the bartender countered. "We've got Batuu Brew, Black Spire Brew, Blurrgfire, Toniray White, Andoan White, Moogan Tea—with or without alco—" He rattled off another half a dozen drinks, none of which Padmé had ever heard of. Local favorites, probably. She picked the Andoan White and watched as he selected a bottle and poured a few centimeters into a small obsidian mug. "So what's her story?" she asked as the bartender set the mug down on the bar and accepted a five-credit coin in exchange. "The lady in the box, I mean? What happened to her?"

The bartender shrugged. "Don't really know. Some men from one of the trading ships brought her in a few days ago—said they saw her try to take a corner too fast out in the forest and flipped her speeder bike on top of her. She was already dead when they got to her, so they brought her here hoping someone in town knew who she was." He shrugged again. "No one did, so we decided to give it a few days to see if anyone came looking for her. Not good to lose someone and never find out what happened."

"No, it's not," Padmé said, taking a sip of her drink. The story was ridiculous—Duja was one of the best speeder riders she'd ever seen. More likely she'd been poking around a suspicious ship, had been caught and tried to escape, and had either been hunted to ground or else forced into the accident they claimed had killed her.

Which would have left them with a huge problem.

Duja was smart enough not to carry any kind of genuine identification with her. As a result, her killers had no idea who she was, where she'd come from, or whether she had backup waiting for her. And they desperately needed answers to those questions.

So after pawing through her data cards without finding anything useful they'd cleaned her up as best they could, brought her to Black Spire, and talked the residents into setting her outside the cantina in the hope of drawing out her contacts.

The big question for Padmé was whether they'd tracked down Duja's ship and sifted it for its own set of data and secrets. If they had, her investigation was effectively over.

If they hadn't found it—if Duja had hidden it somewhere out of their reach—there was still a chance of taking them down.

And the more Padmé thought about it, the more the latter scenario seemed the most likely. If the killers had already gotten everything they wanted they probably wouldn't have bothered to dangle Duja as bait.

"How's the Andoan?" the bartender asked, the mystery of the dead woman outside apparently already forgotten.

"Good," Padmé told him. It actually wasn't bad, certainly not for a local brand. "Do you think anyone would mind if I wrote a song for her?"

"Wrote a—what?" he asked, frowning.

"If I wrote a farewell song," Padmé said. "It's the custom of my people to sing the departed on their journey with songs of encouragement and hope."

"I thought you said you didn't know her."

"I don't," Padmé said. "But it sounds like no one else here does, either. And truly, it's the lost strangers who lack encouragement and hope the most."

The bartender waved a hand. "I suppose. Fine, go ahead. I can't imagine it bothering anyone."

Padmé took her time with the job, aware that she was running close numbers but also knowing that making it look rushed and anxious might attract the wrong kind of attention. Half an hour and a second Andoan White later, she was ready.

The bartender kept surreptitious watch on her the whole time, either because he'd been instructed to do so or just out of bored curiosity. As she finished her drink and picked up her datapad he came back to her end of the bar. "So what happens now?" he asked. "You want me to gather some folks to come watch?"

"You can come if you want to," Padmé said. Not that she wanted an audience, but it would look suspicious if she refused the offer. "But it's not necessary. I'll be singing privately to her, so there won't be anything for anyone to hear."

The bartender grunted. "Yeah, okay. Gotta get ready for the lunch crowd anyway. Have fun."

There were a few more people in the streets when she emerged from the bar, all of them going about their own business, most of them barely giving her a cursory glance before continuing on. She moved to the head of the casket, held her datapad over Duja's body, and began to sing.

She'd had to write the song as if to a stranger. But beneath the vague words and simple tune she could feel her heart breaking at the loss of her friend and onetime bodyguard. Memories came flooding back of the interweaving of their lives, both the good times and the bad, the hopes and dreams and fears they'd shared that were now gone forever. There was the time when Duja helped her decipher an unintelligible communication from an angry ambassador, a potential diplomatic crisis that had been defused when Duja suddenly realized the ambassador simply hadn't liked the way Padmé pronounced the name of a fellow envoy. There were the late-night conversations, after everyone else had gone to bed, when the two of them talked about the future, and all that they hoped those days would bring.

There was the aftermath of the attempted assassination on Coruscant that had taken Cordé's life, and the private tears Padmé and Duja had shared together.

Now Duja was gone. And Padmé would have to leave her here, and would likely never be able to give her a proper funeral.

Duja would understand, and under the circumstances would certainly not want Padmé to risk her own life and safety merely for respect and decorum. But that didn't make it any easier.

She finished her song and for a moment gazed down at her friend. Then, keeping her expression that of a compassionate stranger merely doing her ethical duty, she pulled out the data card on which she'd written the song and laid it on Duja's chest.

And when she brought her hand up out of the coffin she had Duja's brooch pressed invisibly into her palm. Giving Duja one final look, she turned away and headed back to her BARC.

The man and alien were still loitering by their freighter when she reached her ship. "Any luck?" the man called.

"No," Padmé called back as she stowed the BARC into its hold. "I guess I'll try some of the other outposts. Maybe he just messed up the name and coordinates."

"Yeah, good luck," the man said. "If you can't find him, come on back. I'll take it off your hands for a good price."

"You wish," Padmé said, forcing a casual cheerfulness she didn't feel. With a friendly wave she walked up the ramp, sealed the hatch, and headed back across the sky.

But not very far. Certainly not all the way to the next outpost. This was where Duja had planned to meet, and here—somewhere—was where she'd hidden her ship.

Only now Padmé had the way to find it.

She'd traveled about thirty kilometers when she spotted a promising-looking clearing. She set her ship down at one edge and walked outside, blaster ready while she checked the perimeter for large animals or other threats. Satisfied that nothing was preparing to pounce, she tucked the blaster away and pulled out Duja's brooch.

Duja had taken a fair amount of ribbing over the years by people who couldn't understand why a woman who otherwise knew all the ways of fashion and elegance would wear something that outlandish in public. It was made of moldable plastoid, fashioned with the exuberance and total lack of skill of a five-year-old child.

But then, that was exactly the look Duja had been going for when she made it. A child's loving creation, worn as a tribute by a proud and doting mother.

Padmé smiled sadly at the thought. Duja had talked about one day settling down and having a child who might make such an earnest gift for real. Now that would never happen.

Maybe one day, if the war ever ended, Padmé might find that kind of peaceful life for herself. If so, she would dedicate the first of her firstborn's creations to Duja's memory.

But that was the future. This was the present. Wiping away a sudden tear with the back of her hand, Padmé raised the brooch—the one piece of jewelry no thief would ever bother with—and squeezed it hard in the center.

Whether through luck or simply their long association enabling the two women to anticipate each other's moves, Padmé had landed almost on top of Duja's hiding place. Barely two minutes after triggering the beckon call buried deep within the brooch Duja's ship suddenly appeared overhead, floating down on its repulsorlifts to a sheltered spot at the other edge of the clearing. It settled to a stop and the hatch popped open.

Taking a deep breath, feeling a fresh sense of loss, Padmé stepped inside.

Duja's ship was small and plain, the kind of ship flown by billions of ordinary people across the galaxy. As in so many cases, though, appearances were deceiving. Padmé walked past the twin bunks and the compact galley, squeezed through the cockpit doorway, and slipped into the pilot's seat. "This is Queen Padmé Amidala of Naboo," she announced. She hadn't been queen for years, of course, which made it unlikely that anyone else would think to use that title as an identification phrase. "Duja, talk to me."

There was a short pause. Then, like a ghost from a lost past, Duja's voice came from the speaker. "Hello, my lady," she said. There was none of her usual impish humor, but only a hard-edged focus. "I've been poking around this area, and I believe I've uncovered a Separatist factory on Mokivj."

Padmé blinked. A *factory*? Way out *here*?

"I don't know what they're making, or who's in charge," Duja continued. "But from what I've been able to glean it's a top-notch operation. I've got the location—planetary coordinates are in the attached file—and I'll see what I can learn about its layout and defenses before you get here."

Padmé sighed. That search was probably what had led to her death.

"Of course, I'll wait until you get here before we make our move against it. Depending on what we find, we might even be able to get the chancellor or the Jedi to come out and join us."

"Guaranteed," Padmé murmured the promise to her friend.

Because the minute Anakin heard about Duja's death he would be here in a Coruscant second, whether or not the Council had him slated for some other duty.

"Travel safely, my lady, and I'll see you soon." The recorder clicked off.

For a few minutes Padmé sat silently in the command seat, gazing out at the forest and offering one final farewell to her friend. Then, slowly, she reached to the control board and pulled up the factory's coordinates.

Duja had planned to wait for Padmé before moving against the facility. That hadn't ended well. The smart move for Padmé now would be to send an alert to Anakin and wait until he arrived before taking any further action.

Only the Separatists were onto them now. They'd caught Duja, and the presence of the coffin outside the cantina proved they suspected she had backup on the way. Worse, they'd now seen Padmé and were undoubtedly putting two and two together. If she hung around Batuu too long waiting for Anakin, there was a good chance they'd run her down.

Even if she avoided that fate—if she took her ship into deep space, say, and hid there—what would happen to the factory in the meantime? She'd seen Separatists destroy factories and mining facilities rather than let Republic forces get them. And if this place was as secret as its location implied, it was all the more likely that she and Anakin would arrive to find nothing but smoking debris.

No. Duja had given her life to alert the Republic to this threat. Padmé wasn't going to waste that sacrifice by sitting around doing nothing until Anakin could get free or the Separatists could cover their tracks.

Which wasn't to say she thought she could attack the factory all by herself. Years of terrible risks and narrow escapes had proved that she was anything but indestructible.

On the other hand, the enhanced shields and heavy weaponry lurking beneath the plain exterior of Duja's ship gave Padmé an advantage that the Separatists would never expect. Surely she could at least take a quick look and try to figure out what they were doing there.

Reaching to the control board again, she keyed for a quick preflight diagnostic. She would collect a few supplies from her own ship and send a final message to Anakin, and she'd be ready to go. A quick trip to Mokivj, a brief look around, and she'd be back. Probably before Anakin even arrived.

She smiled to herself as she squeezed back out of the cockpit. It was rare when she was able to surprise Anakin. But it was always so satisfying when she did.

There were two more droids waiting in the rear of the freighter. But Anakin was ready, and it was easy to sucker them into choke points where he had the advantage. Two skirmishes later, he and Thrawn arrived at the cargo bay.

Unfortunately, there wasn't much information to be gleaned once they got there.

"If the labels are correct, these appear to contain various alcoholic beverages," Thrawn commented as they walked slowly between the lines of safety-webbed crates. "Does that seem odd for your Separatists?"

"Not really," Anakin said. "Separatists drink as much as everyone else." He picked a crate of Tevraki whiskey, popped off the webbing, and used the Force to lift it from its shelf and lower it to the deck.

"Twister-sealed," Thrawn murmured, peering at the fasteners. "There should be an opening tool somewhere nearby."

"Never mind," Anakin said. Igniting his lightsaber, he carefully sliced off the top of the crate.

It wasn't a line of bottles that glittered at him in the dim light. Instead, an orderly row of slender metal ingots filled the crate, separated by soft plastoid spacers. "Interesting," Thrawn said. "It appears to be gold."

"You're right," Anakin said, running a finger over one of the ingots.

"Is that metal valuable on your worlds?"

"It is on some of them," Anakin said. "But mostly it's used in manufacturing. Pieces this thin would probably be used in extruding machines for making wire or parts of high-performance circuit modules."

"Machines of that sort will have many uses."

"True," Anakin said. If this was a Techno Union ship, gold ingots implied droid manufacturing. But Thrawn was right: Wires and circuit modules were used in everything from household cookers to major warships. The fact that the Separatists were moving metals didn't tell them anything.

"Still, knowing the ship's destination is a manufacturing facility tells us a great deal," Thrawn said. "It indicates that Batuu is not simply a way point for finished products. Nor is it being used as a transfer point for data or personnel."

"I suppose," Anakin said. Fine; so it told them more than he'd thought. "I guess that's it."

"There may yet be more."

"And you're welcome to poke around as much as you want," Anakin growled. "*I'm* going back to the command deck and see if Artoo's found anything." He turned and headed for the cargo bay hatch.

"A moment," Thrawn said.

Anakin turned back, pushing back a flush of irritation. He'd just *said* there wasn't anything more to learn back here. "What?"

Thrawn was standing in front of one of the other crates. "Do you recognize this one?" he asked, pointing to it.

"Of course I recognize it," Anakin said with strained patience. "I recognize *all* of them. They're the crates in here that we've just seen."

"Indeed," Thrawn said. "The interesting part is that we've seen this one twice."

"What are you talking about?"

"A crate with these same markings was aboard one of the smugglers' land vehicles."

"Similar markings on similar packages isn't that unusual—"

"Not *similar*," Thrawn interrupted. "*Identical.*"

Slowly, frowning at the crate, Anakin walked back to him. "Are you sure?"

"Very sure," Thrawn assured him. "Perhaps we should see what's inside."

"Perhaps we should." Again, Anakin used the Force to lower it to the deck, then sliced off the top with his lightsaber. "Whoa," he said, feeling his eyes widen as he caught sight of the thin plates inside.

"You recognize them?" Thrawn asked.

"I recognize the metal," Anakin said. "It's quadranium. Very hard, very dense, very valuable. It's used for hull plates, heavy armor, and anything else you really want to stand up to blasters and laser cannons."

"Interesting," Thrawn murmured. "I wonder how the smugglers came to own an identical crate."

"Yeah," Anakin said darkly. This one, at least, was obvious. "Let's find out." Igniting his lightsaber again, he sliced off the front of the crate.

Just as he'd suspected. The top two layers were quadranium plates. Below that, the box was filled with scrap metal. "There you go," he said, gesturing to the scrap. "Seems our smugglers are also thieves."

Thrawn gazed at the crate for a long moment. "Indeed," he said. "So we're dealing with two groups of opponents, not one. That explains a great deal."

"Really?" Anakin asked, frowning. "What specifically does it explain?"

"In a moment," Thrawn said. "First, I believe you wished to see if your droid had identified this ship's destination or origin."

"Okay," Anakin said. There was clearly something here the Chiss wasn't saying. But the ship's history—and hopefully Padmé's location—was his first priority. "Sure. Come on."

R2-D2 had indeed found something.

"Huh," Anakin said, frowning at the display. "Cermau. Never heard of it."

"Bear in mind that knowledge of this ship's destination does not necessarily mean your ambassador traveled there," Thrawn reminded him.

"Oh, she's there, all right," Anakin said with a grimace. "She and Duja both, probably."

"That seems foolhardy for an ambassador."

"It's foolhardy for anyone," Anakin said. "But that's Padmé. She never bothers with the odds when there's something that needs to be done."

Thrawn was silent a moment. "She sounds like a remarkable person," he said. "I look forward to meeting her. Still, there's more we need to know before we travel there."

"Fine—you stay here and study the situation," Anakin said. "That's my ambassador out there. I'm going."

"A moment," Thrawn said.

Glowering, Anakin turned back. "What now?"

Thrawn was staring at the display where R2-D2 had put up Cermau's planetary data. "You said this information was stored in the ship's navigational computer."

"Yes, of course."

"Easily accessible to anyone who searched for it."

"Well, not *easily*," Anakin said. "Artoo had to dig."

"Does it seem reasonable that the Separatists would handle such critical data this way?"

"They weren't expecting anyone except themselves to be in here," Anakin reminded him patiently.

"Your ambassador was also not expecting intruders," Thrawn reminded him. "Yet her messages were nevertheless encrypted."

Anakin felt his stomach tighten. That was a good point, actually. "So what are you saying?" he asked slowly. "That this is just a cover for the real data?"

"Perhaps," Thrawn said. "Ask your droid if there were any other navigational files in the computer."

R2-D2 warbled a negative. "He said no," Anakin translated.

"Then the data is accurate," Thrawn concluded. "But the presumed destination may not be."

"What do you—oh," Anakin said, nodding as he understood. "The course points to Cermau, but their actual landing site may be somewhere else."

"Exactly," Thrawn said. "How many inhabitable systems are along that route?"

"Let's find out," Anakin said. "Artoo? Pull up a list of systems. Give me everything we've got on them."

Minutes later, the droid had the results.

They weren't promising.

"Eleven of them," Anakin growled, running his eye over R2-D2's list. "And you've got nothing on *any* of them except Batuu?"

R2-D2 grunted with some mechanical frustration of his own.

"It's not hopeless," Thrawn soothed. "You see that the Separatist have provided datafiles of their own."

"What, *these*?" Anakin demanded, jabbing a finger toward the display. "You've got to be joking. 'Batuu: home to ancient ruins and giant petrified black trees.' 'Umme: galaxy-class hunting.' 'Yakorki: wide selection of edible wild fungi.' 'Mokivj: ten moons, beautiful sunsets.' 'Plood: majestic seascapes.' It's like they pulled these out of travel brochures."

"Then we'll need to narrow down the list," Thrawn said.

"Starting with your captive outside?"

"I doubt he knows anything useful," Thrawn said. "He claims to be merely an engine mechanic."

"And you believe him?"

"The scars and burn marks on his hands tend to support his claim," Thrawn said. "Regardless, I need a larger group for the interrogation I have in mind. Perhaps the drama currently playing out near the cantina will suit our needs."

Anakin frowned. "What drama?"

"Five beings entered the cantina after our departure and carried the bartender away," Thrawn said. "They appear to be awaiting his return to consciousness. From their conversation I deduce they're associated with both the group we encountered in the forest and the four beings who assaulted us in the cantina."

"So they *did* call back to Black Spire to have someone deal with us," Anakin said, nodding.

"It is not quite so simple," Thrawn warned. "You forget they targeted you for death. The five now with the bartender are concerned about the owners of this ship, and fear their thefts have been discovered. They're also unclear whether you and I are associated with the shipowners, your ambassador, or neither."

"You're right, it sounds like we need to have a chat with them," Anakin said.

"Indeed," Thrawn advised. "Again, it's not quite so simple. The human I followed to this vehicle was not alone."

"He had a friend?"

"Four friends," Thrawn corrected. "I believe that even now they're listening unannounced to the smugglers' conversation as they also await the bartender's return to consciousness."

Anakin looked out the viewport. A ship this size . . . a cargo bay this size . . . the one who'd come back, plus the four Thrawn said were waiting for the bartender to wake up . . . yes, that could very well be the entire ship's complement.

And having all the Separatists gathered together in one spot could be very handy. "How do you know all this?"

"After the battle, while you were still unconscious, I took the precaution of putting a listening device on the bartender's clothing," Thrawn said. "I've been following their conversations ever since."

Anakin felt a tight smile tug at his lips. "And since the bartender isn't awake yet, everyone's just sitting around waiting and worrying out loud. And since our jamming's still going, none of them can talk to anyone else—"

He broke off, frowning. "Wait a minute. How are you getting messages from the bartender if we're jamming all communications?"

"My listening device does not utilize normal communication methods," Thrawn said. "It translates speech into powerful sonic signals at frequencies far above those detectable by any known species. The signals are received by another device, which I placed on a wall near the cantina, which further translates the sound into a pattern of invisible flickering lights. The lights are reflected from nearby objects—here, the stone trees—and collected by a device on my vehicle. They're then translated back into high-frequency sound, which is again converted to speech by my earpiece."

Anakin whistled under his breath. "That's quite a system. A lot of work, though, isn't it?"

"It is," Thrawn said. "Yet I have communication, and they do not."

"Can't argue with that," Anakin agreed. "Okay. Artoo, stay here and see what else you can find out. Commander Thrawn and I have a party to go to."

CHAPTER 6

The residents who had gathered earlier to gawk at Anakin's starfighter had long since moved on, some of them gathering around street carts for quick food or drink, others haggling with the owners of the various shops, still others moving furtively on darker errands. A few of the patrons seated at the cantina's handful of outdoor tables were watching Anakin and Thrawn as they approached, but none seemed inclined to comment or question, let alone interfere. "Where are they?" Anakin murmured as they parked their landspeeder across the winding street. The cantina's window shutters, he noted, were still closed. "Inside?"

"A moment." Thrawn reached to the landspeeder's displays and made a small adjustment. "They're indoors, approximately fifty meters away."

"I'm guessing over there," Anakin said, eyeing a doorway that led into one of the many dingy shops. Five hard-looking men were loitering near the door, eating small hand meals that looked like they'd come from a street vendor.

So much for Thrawn's fancy surveillance equipment. Sometimes all it took was someone with eyes and a brain to figure these things out.

"Very possibly," Thrawn said. "I assume the one eating with his dominant hand is the leader."

Anakin frowned. Dominant hand? What was Thrawn talking about?

Then he got it. All five had blasters on their right hips, but only one was holding his meal in his right hand. The others were instead eating with their left hands, leaving their gun hands free. The underlings needing to be ready to fire at a moment's notice, while the boss could be a little more leisurely about it?

It seemed like a leap to Anakin, but possibly Thrawn was seeing something else that he wasn't. Certainly the right-hander didn't seem any less thuglike than the others. With droids making up the main Separatist forces—and with none of the droids he'd seen moving around Black Spire less than thirty years old—whoever was running the secret base had probably had to hire local talent for his muscle. "The boss, and the hired help," he commented.

"Perhaps," Thrawn said. He reached into the speeder's side storage pocket and pulled out a small set of powered optics. He lifted them to his eyes, paused a moment, then nodded. "However, their clothing all follows the same pattern, and not the pattern of those who attacked us in the cantina," he continued. "If they're hired help, they share the same origin as their commander." He held up a finger. "The bartender has regained consciousness. Let us observe the actions of the humans in the street."

The wait wasn't long. Barely ten seconds after Thrawn's announcement the five men were on the move, tossing their food away and settling their hands on their blasters. One of them glanced both ways down the street—

And stiffened as he caught sight of Anakin and Thrawn.

"We've been spotted," Anakin growled, drawing his lightsaber but keeping it below the level of the windscreen where it was out of the thugs' view. All five were now looking surreptitiously at them. "You have a plan?" He nodded his head sideways at Thrawn's damaged tunic. "You're not exactly in top form for a fight."

"Indeed I'm not," Thrawn conceded. "Are you familiar with a beast known as a reek?"

Anakin snorted. The petranaki arena back on Geonosis, and the horned monster that had tried to eviscerate him, Padmé, and Obi-Wan . . . "Quite familiar," he assured the Chiss drily.

"Prepare to emulate one."

Prepare to emulate *one?* Anakin opened his mouth to ask what in the world Thrawn meant by that—

And suddenly the landspeeder leapt forward, accelerating down the winding street directly toward the five thugs.

They'd traveled maybe a third of the distance, and the thugs had all drawn their blasters, when he finally got it. Standing up, he got a grip on the windscreen and jumped over it to land on the vehicle's hood. He slid all the way forward and slipped the fingers of his left hand into an air intake vent to keep from falling off.

And with the landspeeder now indeed looking like a Jedi-horned reek, he ignited his lightsaber.

The thugs had just enough time for their eyes to widen in stunned disbelief and scramble for cover before the landspeeder blew into their midst.

The two closest went flying as the vehicle rammed into them, throwing them five meters backward. The next two had made it just far enough to the sides to avoid getting run down—

Double vision: blaster rising close at hand, preparing to fire—

The first of the two, the one Thrawn had identified as the leader, jerked back as Anakin's close-in lightsaber slash sliced his blaster in half.

Double vision: the thug behind him ducking and shooting from waist-high position—

The second managed one shot. Anakin's blade was already in position to deflect it into the wall beside him.

Double vision: Thrawn braking hard and spinning the rear of the landspeeder around toward the last thug—the thug jumping back out of the way—the thug drawing a thermal detonator from his waistband—

Anakin leapt straight up just as Thrawn began the maneuver, turning in midair as the man dodged to the side and reached for the detonator. His hand began to emerge, his lips curling into a snarl—

Which became a gasp as Anakin hurled his lightsaber, sending the blade spinning through the detonator and half of the man's hand. The thug fell to the ground and lay crumpled against the ancient wall, his face screwed up in pain as he gripped the remains of his hand.

The landspeeder had braked nearly to a halt by the time Anakin landed on the hood again. He used the Force to recall his lightsaber to his hand, then dropped into a crouch to catch his balance and spun back to the thug who had taken that single shot at him.

Double vision: shots coming at torso and head—

He blocked both, sending the second shot into the thug's own chest and dropping him to the street beside his comrade. Even as he collapsed, Thrawn was climbing stiffly out of the landspeeder and hurrying to the two he'd rammed earlier. "Well?" Anakin called, giving each of the other thugs a quick look.

"Both are injured and unconscious," Thrawn said. "Have we one who can still speak?"

"I think so," Anakin said, turning his eyes and his lightsaber toward the leader. The thug was staring back, the grip half of his bisected blaster still clenched in his hand. "Not really sure."

"Indeed," Thrawn said. He crossed to Anakin's thug, drawing his blaster as he walked. "You're not a warrior."

Belatedly, the man's eyes shifted to the Chiss. "I'm . . . no, I'm . . ."

"Your name?" Thrawn prompted.

The man swallowed visibly. "Oenti," he said. "I'm an inspector. Just an inspector. A cargo inspector."

"Haven't done a very good job of it, have you?" Anakin suggested mildly. "Let's take this talk inside, shall we?"

"Yes, let's," Thrawn agreed. "These are your people, General. You'd best lead the way."

"No problem," Anakin said. He got a grip on Oenti's arm and pulled him over to the door his group had been focused on. A double lightsaber slash through the cheap lock and equally cheap hinges, a flick of his hand to send the door flying inward with a crash, and he gave the thug a more insistent shove inside.

The room they were in was a shop of some sort, with shelves and bins loaded with exotic curios, poorly made counterfeits of Core World art objects, and a lot of unidentifiable bits of flotsam and jetsam. A faded damask curtain hung over a doorway beside the counter, and as Anakin pushed his prisoner toward it two long-snouted beings flung it aside and charged out into the front room.

And came to a sudden halt as they spotted the intruders already halfway to them. One of them raised his blaster—

"Don't," Anakin said, lifting his lightsaber a little higher over Oenti's shoulder.

The would-be attacker hesitated, focused briefly on Oenti, then looked back at Anakin. "Who are you?"

"We're not your friends," Thrawn said, moving out from behind Anakin and taking a couple of steps to the side. "But we're not necessarily your enemies. We seek information, and believe you can supply it."

"Or we can kill all of you and get what we want from this one," Anakin offered, tugging on the shoulder of Oenti's shirt with his free hand. "Your choice."

One of the long-snouts swallowed, a long, rippling motion of the throat, and lowered his weapon. "Yes," he said, stepping aside and gesturing toward the curtain. "Come inside. We shall talk."

"Yes, we shall," Anakin said. "You can just leave the weapons here."

The two long-snouts looked at each other. Then, wordlessly, they set their blasters on the counter, pushed back the curtain, and disappeared through the doorway.

Anakin and Oenti were right behind them.

The room looked to be a stockroom of sorts, with crates and shelves and more bins scattered randomly around. The bartender was lying on a dilapidated couch, his head propped up, still looking bleary-eyed from the aftermath of the gas attack. Two humans and another long-snout were seated on stools clustered around him, all three of them now twisted around at the waist as they stared at the newcomers. "Oenti?" one of them demanded cautiously as the first two long-snouts silently walked around behind the rest of the group and took up positions there.

"Hello, Janott," Anakin's prisoner said, a dark note in his voice. "Don't bother to get up. So—Janott the friendly bartender. This explains a lot."

"I don't know what you're talking about," the bartender protested. But his eyes were suddenly awake and alert.

"Oh, I think you do," Oenti said, looking around at the rest of the group. "Your friends are on the duke's list, you know. The whole gang is. You realize I'd have been shot if he figured out what you were doing?"

"I don't know—" Janott began again.

"Enough," Thrawn said. His voice was quiet, but somehow it cut like a lightsaber through the growing argument. "We have no interest in watching you posture. Allow me to save time by telling you what has occurred. You will then tell us what we want to know."

He gestured to Anakin. "And *he* will tell me if you're lying."

Anakin stretched out to the Force, getting a feel for the sense and emotions of each of them, and gave a small nod.

"You are smugglers," Thrawn said, gesturing toward the group seated around Janott's couch. "You are also thieves."

He looked at Oenti. "You are part of the Separatist movement, currently at war with the Republic and Loyalist systems. Your duke has constructed a base and is shipping materials and equipment to it. Because he didn't want anyone to know where the base is, he gathered his supplies from various origination points and sent them to Batuu, where the inhabitants don't pry into others' activities. But he didn't expect interference from thieves."

He pointed his blaster at Janott. "Nor did you know that the man who owned your chosen transfer point, the cantina, was in league with those thieves."

"I'm not in league with them," Janott insisted, starting to rise from his couch. Anakin flicked his lightsaber around Oenti's side, settling the blade warningly over the bartender's chest, and he subsided.

"With your assistance the thieves learned which shipments were the most valuable," Thrawn continued, ignoring the protest. "The shipments no doubt arrived at wide intervals, allowing you sufficient time to steal the best cargoes and leave worthless duplicate containers in their place. You felt confident that the leisurely pace of the shipments would delay detection of the thefts until such time as you were ready to leave Batuu.

"But then another entered the scene, and with her came your downfall."

"Duja," Anakin murmured.

"Indeed," Thrawn said. "She was able to identify one of the shipments and follow it to Batuu. She entered the Separatist ship and learned of the base, then sent a message to alert the Republic."

He gestured to Oenti. "But your comrades detected her intrusion, and concluded that she was a thief."

"Which started them looking for other thieves," Anakin said. "Which suddenly put all of you in their viewfinders."

"You realized you were in danger of being caught, and therefore collected all the gains you could and attempted to escape Batuu," Thrawn said. "But before your ship could arrive, the landing space was occupied and blocked by another ship." He looked at Anakin. "That of your ambassador."

With an effort, Anakin held on to his temper. Flashing his lightsaber around right now wouldn't gain them anything. Better to let Thrawn carry this, at least for the moment. "What happened to her?" he asked quietly, looking at each of the others in turn.

"We don't know," one of the long-snouts said.

"Neither do we," Oenti added hastily. "She landed, went into Black Spire, then left."

"All I know is that she came into the cantina and wrote a poem for the dead woman," Janott said.

"So Duja is dead," Anakin said. That had been the direction the story had been going, but it was still a wrench for him to say it aloud. "Which of you did *that*?"

"It wasn't any of us," Janott said, cringing back a little, his eyes focusing on the lightsaber blade still swinging above him.

"I wasn't there," Oenti said, equally quickly. "I was in the *Larkrer*'s hold, trying to figure out what she'd been trying to steal."

"General?" Thrawn invited.

"They're telling the truth," Anakin growled. It would have been so much easier if he'd been able to sense guilt in one of them. As it was, justice would have to be delayed.

"That's their good fortune," Thrawn said, a dark menace in his voice. "But now the masquerade is over."

"You going to turn us over to the Separatists?" Janott asked anxiously.

"Most of them are currently outside your door," Thrawn said. "Though not, I grant you, currently in a position to deal out punishment. They're now trapped here, as are the rest of you."

Janott flashed a look at Anakin. "What are you talking about?"

"I've seen both the Black Spire landing field and the clearing where your comrades took their cargo," Thrawn said. "I conclude the ship you planned for your escape is too large to land nearby without drawing unwelcome attention. Your only hope is to seize the Separatist freighter."

Oenti stiffened. "You can't let them do that."

"We won't," Thrawn assured him.

"Why not?" Janott asked. "You're Loyalists, right? I heard all Jedi were Loyalists."

"We'll give you a good price for their ship," one of the long-snouts added.

"Shut up!" Oenti snarled. "You couldn't take it anyway—we've got a full squad of combat droids ready to cut you to mulch if you try."

"Hardly," Anakin said. "You have *three* droids, and they're general-service, not combat." He cocked his head. "Rather, you *had* three droids."

"The ship isn't for sale," Thrawn said. "We intend to take it ourselves." He paused. "To the Separatist base on Mokivj."

For a single second they all just stared at him. Anakin had just time to feel the sudden surge of fear and dismay—

Then, as if on a signal, the whole group exploded into action.

Double vision: Oenti spinning and leaping, his hands closing around Anakin's throat—

The Separatist's hands were still thirty centimeters from their goal when Anakin used the Force to send him flying backward across the room. As Oenti sailed past the others, Janott and the three thieves yanked blasters from their tunics, while the two long-snouts snatched weapons from hiding places among the crates.

Double vision: two blaster bolts at torso, chest, one bolt at Thrawn's chest—

Anakin caught the first two shots on his lightsaber, bouncing them into the walls and ceiling. A quick flick of his wrist, and he managed to catch the shot that had been intended for Thrawn, as well.

Double vision: a bolt from the left into his rib cage, sending him toppling to the floor with a burnt lung—

Only now, with his lightsaber stretched out to the side between Janott and Thrawn, there was no chance he could bring the weapon back in time to block the attack.

He tried anyway, spinning as quickly as he could. Over his shoulder he caught a sideways glimpse of Oenti, raised up on his left elbow, lining up a blaster he had grabbed from somewhere. There was a sizzle from behind Anakin, a brilliant bolt scorching the air past his side—

Oenti collapsed to the floor, his dying shot burying itself in Janott's couch.

Double vision: bolts coming at torso from the long-snouts—

This time, there was no problem deflecting the shots. One went into the crates; the other went into the shooter.

And then, it was over.

"Are you injured?" Thrawn asked in the fresh silence.

"No," Anakin said, surveying the battlefield.

Oenti was dead. The five thieves were dead, taken out by Anakin's ricochets or Thrawn's less vigorous but adequately precise return fire. Only Janott the bartender was still alive, breathing in quick, shallow gasps as he stared in horror at the carnage around him.

"I let him live," Thrawn continued, as calmly as if he were talking about the weather. "There may still be information he can give us."

"I don't know," Anakin said doubtfully, eyeing the bartender. "We know the Separatists are bringing in supplies for a base on Mokivj through Janott's cantina. We know this ring of thieves was stealing from those shipments." He raised his eyebrows at Janott. "And we know now that Cargo Inspector Oenti was in on the scheme."

"How do we know that?" Thrawn asked.

"Because otherwise he'd have made a break for the door, either to escape or to call in the others outside, instead of trying to hold me down long enough for the thieves to get to their blasters," Anakin said. "*And* because he wouldn't have known where to find that hidden blaster he came up with unless he'd spent a lot of time here."

"Yes," Thrawn said. "Very good."

"Thanks," Anakin said drily. Normally, he reflected, he would have been irritated by the Chiss's condescending words.

But to his mild surprise, he felt a touch of satisfaction instead. Thrawn was clearly the type who stayed a couple of steps ahead of his opponents. It was nice to know that he, Anakin, could keep pace with him. "So the question is, what can he tell us that would persuade us to leave him alive?"

"She left unharmed," Janott blurted out. "The woman—the second woman. She sang a song to her friend and then left unharmed and unhindered."

"Her ship's still here," Anakin said, lowering his lightsaber blade over the bartender's chest.

"She left Black Spire, but landed somewhere else," Janott said, stumbling over the words in his haste to get them out. "She then left in another ship. A smaller ship."

"How do you know?" Thrawn asked.

"The—" the bartender swallowed visibly. "The police. There aren't many officers here, but there *are* some. They thought she was a smuggler and chased her for a bit. But her ship was fast, and hard to lock onto, and she left them behind."

"Did they fire on her?" Anakin asked.

"I—don't—"

"Did they fire on her?"

"I don't know," Janott said, cringing again. "I think they might have. But they didn't damage her. She escaped. Really."

"Does he speak truth?" Thrawn asked.

"Yes," Anakin said, glaring at the bartender. It was all very well to say that Padmé had escaped; there could easily have been damage from the skirmish that wouldn't show up until later. If her hyperdrive had been damaged, or her hull breached—

Stop it, he ordered himself. She was fine. She had to be.

"So do we kill him?" he asked Thrawn, stretching out to the Force. He had no particular interest in killing the man, but sometimes a threat was enough to shake loose information.

Unfortunately, he couldn't sense anything in Janott that might suggest he was still sitting on any additional bargaining chips.

"No need," Thrawn said. "The fact that the cantina attackers were part of the smuggler group, yet the attack was designed by those who understand Jedi tactics and abilities, suggests that the Separatists themselves either persuaded or hired the smugglers to launch that assault. Possibly knowingly; possibly not."

"Ah," Anakin said. Thrawn had said the cantina attack wasn't simple, but that particular detail hadn't occurred to him. "So the Separatists know all about the ring. And there are still a couple of Separatists alive out there—damaged a little, but alive—to pass the word to the rest of their forces."

"There may be more elsewhere on Batuu, as well," Thrawn said. "As to the thieves, they now know that the Separatists' plan to eliminate us has failed, and that many of their comrades are dead. Given the circumstances, they may suspect the bartender of collusion."

"I'm sure they will," Anakin agreed, closing down his lightsaber. "Which adds up to you not being very popular right now, Janott. If I were you, I'd find someplace nice and quiet where I could stay out of sight for a while."

"Yes," Janott breathed. "Yes. I can do that."

"You *will* do that," Anakin said.

Janott's eyes flicked to the dead smugglers. "I *will* do that," he agreed.

"Then we're done here," Thrawn said. "Let us be on our way."

There was no crowd gathering around the remnants of the street fight as Anakin and Thrawn left the shop. In fact, aside from a few curious looks being directed toward the Separatists slowly coming back to consciousness, the passersby seemed to be ignoring the carnage completely.

But then, death and destruction were probably daily events in Black Spire.

"Do you really think there are more Separatists around?" Anakin asked when they were once again in their landspeeder and heading toward the *Larkrer.* "Or were you just saying that to scare him?"

"There may be others, though no more than two or three," Thrawn said. "You may have your droid examine the oxygen and food usage records during our voyage if you wish accurate numbers."

"We'll see," Anakin said. Right now, exact numbers weren't a high priority. "The question is whether there'll be anyone functional enough to warn the Separatists at Mokivj before we get there."

"There won't be any warnings," Thrawn said confidently. "They've taken great pains to conceal this base. Sending a warning through a private and presumably untested message service would threaten that secrecy."

"Not just untested," Anakin said, shaking his head. "Completely unreliable."

"How do you reach that conclusion?"

"Because if Janott was telling the truth, Padmé was here long enough to send me a message," Anakin said. "Probably more than once. But I never received anything. The question is whether they'll be able to find another ship after we take theirs." He looked sideways at Thrawn. "We *are* taking their ship, right?"

"I have no wish to arrive in mine," Thrawn said. "Do you wish to arrive in yours?"

Anakin felt his lip twist. Showing up at a secret Separatist base in an Actis starfighter. Right. "Point taken."

"As for their finding another ship, that won't be a concern," the Chiss continued. "As long as they're at least a few hours behind us, they won't be a problem."

That assumed, of course, that he and Thrawn could track down Padmé that quickly. Anakin wasn't at all sure about that part. "I don't know," he said. "Maybe we should take an hour and disable everything in the landing area."

"That would only gain a few more hours at the most," Thrawn said. "Really, don't concern yourself with them."

Anakin pursed his lips. But the Chiss was probably right. Unless they could disable every ship on Batuu, they could hardly keep the surviving Separatists from coming after them. "Fine," he growled. "By the way, how did you know that it was Mokivj?"

"The planetary data," Thrawn said. "Only Mokivj's listing included information that would be useful for inbound navigation."

"The ten moons," Anakin murmured. "Nice. But what if you were wrong?"

"The Separatists outside will soon recover," Thrawn said. "If we'd failed to force a reaction with the thieves by naming Mokivj we could have tried a different system on them."

"And you wanted a larger crowd than the Separatist you captured because you wanted to goad them into attacking us?"

"Correct," Thrawn said. "They wouldn't want us to leave with such vital information, but only with what they assumed would be overwhelming odds on their side would they dare to act."

There was a moment of silence. Anakin watched the forest rush past on either side of them, trying not to worry about Padmé. Either she was all right, or she was in danger, and until he got to Mokivj there was nothing he could do about any of it.

"The duke that Oenti mentioned," Thrawn said into his broodings. "Is he the leader of the Separatists?"

"No, that's Count Dooku," Anakin said. "The other real driving force of their military is General Grievous. No idea who this duke might be."

"I've heard of Count Dooku," Thrawn said. "A Jedi like you, is he not?"

"A fallen Jedi," Anakin said, a bit more curtly than he'd intended. "*Not* like me. But don't worry, we'll get him. We've got Chancellor Palpatine on our side, and I'd put him up against Dooku and Grievous any day."

Thrawn was silent for a moment. "Just remember that the goal in war is victory, not revenge."

"Don't worry. We all know that."

"Good," Thrawn said. "Remember that on this mission, as well."

Anakin frowned. "What?"

"This is no longer merely a search for a missing ambassador," Thrawn said. "It's become an important part of your Clone War. Remember that victory is the goal."

"And not revenge?"

"No." He felt Thrawn's eyes on him. "Nor even rescue."

Anakin looked away. Nor even *rescue*?

Unthinkable. Padmé's life was the most important thing in the galaxy. To him, and to many others besides.

"Do you hear me?" Thrawn persisted.

"I hear you," Anakin growled.

And he would *not* give up that life for some vague and probably minor Separatist operation in a forgotten corner of the universe. "We're wasting time. Can this thing go any faster?"

CHAPTER 7

Duja's ship—Padmé had never known its real name, but the current ID beacon listed it as the *Possibility*—was small and cramped and, to the casual observer, completely harmless.

But the casual observer would be wrong. The ship boasted extra shielding, twin laser cannons in the front and one in the rear, and a pair of top-grade proton torpedoes. More a pocket fighter than a simple transport, it had evaded Batuu's pitiful police force with ease.

It should, she thought dully from inside the cockpit escape pod, make for a spectacular crash.

She still didn't know how that vulture droid had gotten her. She'd arrowed straight into Mokivj as soon as she hit the system, then crossed the wide expanses of plain, scrubland, and lake at the lowest altitude she dared. Combined with the *Possibility*'s compact size, that should have let her slip past anything patrolling the area around Duja's coordinates.

Clearly, it hadn't worked. The vulture had nailed her, and she'd never seen it coming. Apparently, the Batuu police pursuit had damaged her ship more than she'd realized. She'd barely had time to kick it high enough to give the escape pod time to deploy before the whole thing began to come apart.

And now, as she burned at a controlled fall toward the hills below, she watched the multiple pieces of the *Possibility* arcing their fiery way toward the distant landscape.

Like Duja herself, the ship had faced its final challenge and lost. Now it was up to Padmé to avenge them both.

Though that was starting to look increasingly unlikely. The fragments of the *Possibility* were still blazing and smoking their way through the air, and already she could see a handful of vulture droids starting to gather over the horizon ahead. So far they didn't seem to have spotted her pod amid the rest of the debris, but the minute her repulsorlifts came on they would probably spot the unnatural shift in trajectory.

Even if they didn't, the terrain below hardly offered much hope for escape. The hillside was covered in jagged rocks, grass, and wide bushes, with no decent cover for several kilometers around her. There was a glint of sunlight from the river meandering its way downslope; she could see the bushes rippling in a breeze coming over the hill—

She caught her breath. *The river.*

It would be risky, but right now it was the only shot she had. Taking a last look at the distant vulture droids, she settled her hands on the controls and got to work.

The pod had the standard range of steering capabilities that would offer the passenger a choice of landing sites. But like the repulsorlifts, using the thrusters ran the risk of drawing the vultures' attention. Fortunately, the river was nearly below her, and it took only a small and brief nudge on the controls to bring her onto the proper vector. She watched the river rushing toward her, trying to judge the exact trade-off point where the risk of droid detection and the chances of breaking her back with the impact were both at their lowest. Fifty meters . . . forty . . . thirty . . . ten . . .

Bracing herself, she hit the repulsorlift control.

The deceleration she'd programmed in was more intense than she'd expected, slamming her hard into her seat with an abrupt multiple g-force. Even so, the pod hit the river with an impressive splash, and she watched the water level run up the viewport as the pod submerged. She shut down the repulsorlifts and huffed out a relieved sigh.

She wasn't prepared for the repulsorlifts to suddenly reactivate themselves.

She grabbed the controls again, forcing a manual shutdown. But it wasn't enough. Even without them the pod had enough buoyancy to start a slow drift back toward the surface. Probably a deliberate safety design, and under most circumstances she would have welcomed it.

Here, though, a bobbing escape pod would pretty well guarantee her capture.

She ran her eyes over the panel, looking for inspiration, trying to find some trick of airfoil or ballast that would let her circumvent the safeties and take her back down again. But the pod's designers clearly hadn't anticipated this particular situation.

Which left only one chance. Clenching her teeth, watching the level of the water on the viewport, she keyed the hatch.

For a moment nothing happened. The water continued to recede down the viewport as the pod made its way upward. Then, with a creak of protest, the servos managed to shove the hatch open against the outside pressure.

And with a hissing rush, the river began to pour into the pod.

Padmé gasped as the icy stream blasted across her side and legs, far colder than she'd expected. The water quickly collected around her feet, rising up her shins, numbing the skin beneath her loose trousers. The pod's slow climb wavered, then stopped; and as the water level approached Padmé's knees the pod began to slowly sink again.

She keyed the hatch, wondering fleetingly what would happen if the water had penetrated the electronics or incapacitated the motors. But the hatch obeyed the command, resealing itself and cutting off the inrush. Peering upward through the viewport, she watched the play of light on the surface of the water as the pod continued to sink, then finally settled at a level of neutral buoyancy.

She checked her instruments. The readings were a little ambiguous, but it looked like the top of the pod was about four meters down. With luck, that would be deep enough to obscure her presence and let her float past the Separatists' search.

In fact, and with even more luck, she might even be able to ride straight to the manufacturing plant itself. Most industrial processes required a plentiful water supply, and her river was heading in the general direction of Duja's coordinates.

At any rate, until she was safely past the search area there was nothing she could do. Shutting down everything she could, propping up her feet on a section of the control board to get them out of the water, she settled in for a long wait.

The trip quickly turned into an exercise in patience and boredom. Still, it wasn't entirely without its interesting moments.

The first of those moments came as she reached the vulture droids' primary search area. Each time one of the flickering shadows interrupted the distant sunlight she felt herself tense, wondering if she'd been spotted or if the droid was merely moving past on another errand. Midway through the activity it occurred to her that, given the angle of the sun, the shadows that passed directly over her were from droids that weren't actually overhead. The realization gave her a short period of relief until the corollary struck her: If one of the droids *was* directly above her, she would never know until it was too late.

But no laserfire sizzled through the water, and no torpedo blasts slammed a deadly shock wave across the pod's surface. Gradually, the overhead shadows became fewer, then disappeared completely.

The next small diversion came an hour later in the form of a sudden swirling and roiling in the river's otherwise leisurely pace. Her first thought was that she'd hit a rocky whitewater section, but then she spotted the large intake pipes that were drawing water out of the river near the left bank. A town, perhaps, since she seemed to still be several kilometers upstream from Duja's coordinates.

Or perhaps not. The river flow had barely returned to its placid pace when she began to notice piles of small rocks along the riverbed's slope. Again, her first thought was that it was something natural, perhaps erosion or runoff from a groundquake. But as the piles continued along the river she realized they were instead tailings from a mine, possibly driven off larger riverside mounds by wind or rain. The tailings continued for nearly a kilometer before dwindling; a hundred meters past them the pod was again buffeted as another set of pipes returned wastewater to the river. The pod's sensors indicated that the temperature of the influx was noticeably higher than that of the surrounding water, again indicating some kind of mining or refining process.

So the Separatists apparently had a mine here associated somehow with their factory. But what in the galaxy could the mine be producing that it made sense to pour time and money into doing it way out here? Even doonium and quadranium weren't *that* valuable.

Unless they'd found an incredibly rich deposit of one of those metals. In that case, the factory would be producing . . . what?

It seemed insane. Surely it would be easier to simply ship the metal to some other, more secure factory that was already geared up to produce hull plates or droid armor. But instead, they'd set up here.

Unless Duja had been wrong. Unless the mine was all there was, and she'd been mistaken about the factory.

Padmé stared out at the murky water swirling around her. No. Duja had never been wrong before. She wasn't wrong now.

So Padmé would cultivate her patience and wait until she reached the coordinates. And then she would see what exactly her friend had sent her to deal with.

The sky overhead had darkened to night by the time the pod reached the factory's coordinates.

Now came the tricky part.

Padmé had already stowed two extra outfits, boots, comm, datapad, glow rod, her favored ELG-3A blaster pistol, and the sturdier S-5 Security-grade blaster/ascension gun in a—hopefully—watertight backpack. Now, taking several deep breaths to flush as much carbon dioxide from her lungs as possible, she again hit the hatch control. This time, though, instead of just a crack she was going for a full opening.

The hatch mechanism had other ideas. It opened to the same crack it had earlier, then stopped as if unable to make more progress against the outside pressure.

Padmé tried again, forcing down the sudden surge of panic. If the hatch stayed jammed she would have bare seconds to dig her blaster out of the bag and try to shoot off the hinges before she drowned.

Fortunately, it didn't come to that. Even as the churning water rose to her waist the pressure on the hatch equalized to the point where it could resume its outward motion. She waited until it was open just enough, then ducked down into the water and maneuvered herself outside. Ignoring the numbing cold, letting out a small trail of bubbles from the corner of her mouth to make sure she was headed the right way, she swam to the surface.

She popped up into a dark night and a welcome warmth of air. For a moment she floated with the current, awkwardly treading water with one hand while she looped the backpack's straps over her shoulders, and looked around.

The river was about thirty meters across at this point, its surface about five meters below the tops of the banks on both sides. On one side, the side where Duja's coordinates put the factory, all was darkness, while the other side showed hints of bright lights somewhere beyond the bank. Above, the stars blazed down, their twinkling occasionally interrupted by wispy clouds.

For a moment she looked back and forth between the banks, trying to decide what to do. The lighted bank was probably a town, where she might find food, warmth, and local clothing. On the other hand, more people also meant a better chance of being noticed, talked about, and captured.

Besides, she wasn't here for her comfort. She was here to make sure Duja hadn't died in vain. Fifty meters downstream she could see a copse of tall trees clustered along the river's edge, trees that might have sent a few roots out through the edge of the bank where they could be climbed. Turning toward them, shivering so hard her teeth were chattering, she began to swim. She'd seen numerous fish moving past the pod's viewport during the day, some of them as long as her arm. Hopefully, any disturbance she made would be attributed to one of them.

Even in the dim reflected light from the town behind her she could see at least a dozen gnarled roots twisting their way in and out of the dirt. Grabbing the lowest, she pulled herself out of the water and started to climb.

It wasn't easy. The roots were wet, and the soil around them crumbled at her touch. But she'd done some rock climbing back in the Gallo Mountains, and this really wasn't all that different. She reached the top and carefully eased her head up to look.

In the distance she could see a long, dark structure, two or three stories high, with castlelike turrets at the corners. Between her and it was rolling grassland and the hint of a deep cut in the ground, possibly a creek or syncline. She could see no sign of the metallic glint that might indicate droids, but in the faint light that didn't necessarily prove they weren't there.

Still, there was nothing to be gained by staying where she was. Pulling herself the rest of the way up onto the bank, she stood up, brushing a strand of hair back out of her eyes. She took a moment to map out her best approach, and started toward the building.

And gasped as a hand shot out from nowhere, grabbed her by one of her backpack's straps, and hauled her sideways into the cover of the trees. "Get back here, you idiot," a gruff voice breathed in her ear. "You want them to see you?"

A second later he abruptly pushed her back to arm's length again, and she found herself gazing at a startled human face, bearded and wide-eyed, resting atop a thick neck and a stocky body. "Wait a second," he said, his voice as surprised as his face. "*You're* not Cimy."

"Will you shut *up*?" a second voice called softly from deeper in the trees. "You want them to hear you?"

"I think they already did," the man said, turning toward the voice. The movement dragged Padmé around with him. "Look—I found a spy."

"I'm not a spy," Padmé protested. "Ow—that hurts."

"What?"

"Your knuckles," Padmé said, wincing. "They're digging into my shoulder."

"Oh." Instantly, the man let go. "Sorry."

"Who are you talking to?" the second voice came. There was a rustle in the bushes around the trees, and a second man appeared, this one taller and less stocky but with a more impressive beard. "Whoa. Who the frost is *this*?"

"I thought it was Cimy," the first man said apologetically. "He—"

"*She*, you idiot."

"What?" The first man peered more closely at Padmé. "Oh. Right. She. Sorry. Anyway, she was standing out in the open and I thought it was Cimy—"

"Who thought who was me?" a third man cut in, stepping into view. He was shorter than the others, beardless but sporting a thin mustache.

Even in the dim starlight Padmé could see that he and the second man had a strong family resemblance. Brothers?

"I thought she was you," the first man said patiently. "So I pulled her back out of sight—" He paused, turning back to Padmé. "You're wet," he said, frowning as he looked her up and down. "Were you in the *river*?"

"I was just out for a swim," she said, trying to keep her teeth from chattering. The air, which had felt warm compared with the river water, was starting to chill her again. The steady breeze now that she was out of the shelter of the banks wasn't helping, either.

"A *swim*?" the second man scoffed. "Yeah, right."

"Okay, fine, I wasn't swimming," Padmé said. Cimy was holding something that looked like a fishing pole . . . "I was out fishing and my boat sank."

"Are you crazy?" Cimy demanded. "Bad enough to be out at night in the first place—but in a *boat*? The scavs would have caught you for sure."

"I suppose," Padmé said. "Must be a lot safer up here in the trees."

"That's why we're here and not someplace else," the first man said. He peered at her again.

Then, to her surprise, he pulled off his jacket and wrapped it around her shoulders. "Here—you look cold. I'm LebJau, by the way. This is Huga and his brother Cimy—"

"LebJau, are you *crazy*?" Huga cut in viciously. "We don't know anything about her."

"She's wet, she's cold, and she was fishing," LebJau said. "What else do we need to know?"

"Let's start with who the frost she is and what the frost she's doing here," Huga shot back. "She wasn't fishing, you frosted idiot."

"Wait a minute," Cimy said, his voice starting to shake. "This morning—remember when the scavs took off and headed upriver?"

"Oh, krink," Huga muttered. "LebJau was right—she *is* a spy. Only not for the metalheads. Who are you? What are you doing here?"

"It's nothing that concerns you," Padmé said, trying to think. Her blasters were still sealed up in her backpack, and with her captors' suspicions aroused there was no way to get to a weapon before they could stop her. Besides, she could hardly justify shooting a group of harmless locals. "If you let me go, I promise you'll never see me again."

"And what if the metalheads find you?" Cimy demanded. "Huh? What if they trace you back to the river, and back to us?"

"Hey, it's not a big deal," LebJau said, sounding puzzled. "We can find somewhere else to fish."

"Will you just shut *up*?" Huga growled.

"It's not the fishing, LebJau," Cimy said patiently. "It's if the metalheads get mad at us for letting her go."

"Well, there's one quick way to fix *that*," Huga said. "Grab her arms. We'll stash our gear here for later and take her in."

"No, wait," Padmé said quickly. "You don't want to do that."

"Why not?" Huga said. "Might even be some reward money in it."

And there it was: the hook she needed. "Is that what you want?" Padmé asked. "Money?"

"Doesn't everyone?" Huga countered. "The duke sure as frost doesn't pay much."

"I don't suppose he does," Padmé agreed, wondering who the duke was. Another local, or one of the Separatists? "Let me show you something." Reaching under her blouse, she pulled out her necklace. "This is a Corusca gem," she said, unfastening the chain and handing it to Huga. "They're used as money some places around the galaxy."

"Not here they're not," Huga said. But his voice had changed as he peered at the gem.

"It's worth a lot of money everywhere," Padmé said. "Way more than the duke would ever give you for handing me over. If he gave you anything at all."

"No problem," Huga said with a shrug. "We can take this *and* turn you in."

"You're not seeing the bigger picture," Padmé chided. "I only have the one gem with me. But the fact that I have one means I'm rich. And my family is rich. So . . . ?"

For a second they looked back and forth at one another. Huga got it first. "Are you saying . . . we hold you for *ransom*?"

"Why not?" Padmé asked. "You want money. I don't want you giving me to the duke or the metalheads. This is a way to keep everyone happy."

"Yeah, but—" Huga floundered. "You're not supposed to *volunteer* to be kidnapped. Are you?"

"I'm hardly volunteering," Padmé said. "You've already got me, right?"

"Yeah, but—"

"If it makes you feel better, you can think of the money as rent," she suggested. "You can put me up until someone from my family can get here with the money, then we go our separate ways. Is it a deal?"

Again, the three looked at one another. "What do you think?" Huga asked.

"I don't know," Cimy said, looking furtively at her. "We can't take her inside—the metalheads know everyone who's supposed to be in there. Anyway, she talks funny."

"We could put her in the riverboat," LebJau suggested. "No one goes there, and we can take food for her out the back door."

"Wait a minute," Huga growled. "*Food?* How long is this going to take, anyway?"

"No more than a week or two at the most," Padmé assured him. "Just long enough to get a message back to my uncle Anakin. He'll bring the money, and you'll be done with me."

"I don't know," Huga said. "A week's an awfully long time. What if they find her?"

"They won't," LebJau promised. "I'll do all the bringing—they don't pay much attention to me. You and Cimy just do your jobs like you're supposed to, and I'll do the bringing."

"You going to give her wood shavings to sleep in, too?" Huga growled. "She's not a pet, you know. If she takes off—or if they catch her—we'll be frosted."

"She won't." LebJau looked at Padmé. "You won't, will you? Run off?"

"Not until my uncle arrives and you get your ransom," Padmé said. "I promise."

"She says she won't run," LebJau said, turning back to the others.

"I don't know," Huga said again. But he was still rubbing the gem gently between his thumb and fingers.

"You've got nothing to lose," Padmé pointed out. "If I run, you'll still have the gem, remember?"

"Okay," Huga said. He still had reservations, she could tell. But for the moment, at least, greed was winning out over fear. "How do we contact this uncle of yours?"

"I have a contract with one of the independent message services in the region," Padmé said. "Interstel Systems. I can—what's the matter?" she interrupted herself as something flashed across all three faces.

"Nothing," LebJau said. "It's just that we heard the other day that Interstel's comm triad is down."

"Someone was grousing about having to hand-ship messages over to Plood or Batuu," Cimy added. "Pain in the neck."

"Really," Padmé said between suddenly stiff lips. "What are they doing about it?"

"Probably just hanging on to the messages until they've got enough to make it worth a trip to Plood to hook 'em into the triad there," Cimy said. "That's what they usually do."

"I see," Padmé murmured. How convenient that the system had just happened to crash right when she needed it.

Could someone have spotted Duja's outgoing messages to Coruscant and wrecked the triad to keep anything else from leaking out? If so, did that mean neither of her messages had made it to Anakin?

Because that would be a disaster. Her ship had copies of all her messages; but assuming he could even find the ship, those records were all wrapped in the Senate's automatic encryption.

She squared her shoulders. So Interstel needed a thick stack of messages before they would do anything? Fine. She was more than happy to oblige. "Any idea what the magic number is that'll get them to send a ship to Plood?" she asked.

Huga shrugged. "Dunno. A couple of hundred, probably. Not that much traffic out here."

"Fine," Padmé said. "We'll send five hundred."

Huga's jaw dropped. "Five *hundred*?"

"Hopefully, that'll get their attention," Padmé said. "*And* Uncle Anakin's. I'll put a message together as soon as you get me settled. Oh, and my name's Padmé. It's nice to meet you."

"Yeah," Huga said, still sounding sandbagged. "Sure. Well . . . come on. Watch out for the roots."

He headed off deeper into the copse of trees, Cimy at his side, Padmé and LebJau walking behind them. They'd gone about ten meters when LebJau wrapped his hand gently around Padmé's upper arm. "Careful," he murmured. "It goes down."

Padmé nodded—she'd already seen Huga's head dip as he and Cimy headed down a steep slope. The defile was nearly five meters deep, she saw as she and LebJau followed, the end running into the river. A dry creekbed, from the look of it, possibly part of a seasonal tributary, and almost certainly the cut in the ground she'd noticed before LebJau grabbed her. Huga turned his back on the river flowing past the end and headed up the gorge.

The defile was deep enough that the Separatist building was mostly out of sight as they made their way along the rocky ground. But there were places where other cuts intersected theirs, and as they passed those spots Padmé was able to catch glimpses of her destination.

Her first impression had been that the place was like a castle. But now she could see that that wasn't quite accurate. What she'd taken to be turrets at the corners were in fact the narrow pyramid shapes of vertical anchors for the vulture droids, sites where they could hook on and refuel, yet could launch into action at a moment's notice without the need to come out of a hangar. The rest of the building was low and wide, no more than fifteen meters tall but a solid half kilometer wide and at least that deep.

"Used to be a multi-factory," LebJau said, nodding toward the building. "Big power generators in the center courtyard, with a bunch of hundred-by-hundred-meter fabricators and manufacturers under the same roof."

"Everyone had windows and sunlight coming in both sides," Cimy added wistfully. "'Course, one side was also kind of noisy, with the generators. But at least there was light."

"Right," LebJau said. "But then the duke and the metalheads came in, threw everybody out, and took over."

"Any idea what they're doing in there?" Padmé asked.

"Stuff that's none of our business," Huga growled back over his shoulder.

"It *used* to be our business," LebJau countered sourly. "We worked in one of the electronics factories. Now they've got us doing maintenance."

"Hey, at least we got jobs," LebJau said. "Not everyone got hired back, you know."

"What kind of maintenance?" Padmé asked, frowning. Maintenance at Separatist facilities was usually a droid job.

"Cleanup, mostly," LebJau said. "Sweeping and carrying out any trash."

"Ah," Padmé said. "I suppose all the tech work is done by other droids?"

"No, that's who else they hired back," Cimy said. "Materials specialists—folks who make new plastoids and ceramics and stuff—and a bunch of engineers to remake some of the assembly lines."

"Took about two months to do it, too," Huga said. "Knocked out a big chunk of the east wing ceiling—the whole thing takes up about half the space of the bottom two floors."

"You've seen the line, but you don't know what they're making?" Padmé asked.

"Never seen any of the finished product," LebJau said. "They shut everything down before the cleanup crews go in and stuff the day's work behind curtains."

"But they *do* have droids, right?" Padmé asked.

"Metalheads? Yeah," LebJau said. "Mostly a bunch of spindly things that walk around waving guns at us. Everything else is our people or the two overseers who work with the duke."

"That's another man and a woman," Cimy put in.

"Right," LebJau said. "I don't think the metalheads can handle the machines and programming work."

Padmé nodded. "I suppose not."

Only she knew that the Separatists *did* have droids that could do that. They were specialized and very expensive, and Dooku and Grievous didn't have very many of them. Still, they were functional and capable, and they didn't need locals to feed them. Something else she needed to look into once she got inside. "So who is this duke? What's he look like?"

"Never seen him," Cimy said. "His overseers or the metalheads give us orders."

"Used to be more men and women, too," LebJau said. "A lot more. They were there for the setup, and for about a month after that. Lot of flights in and out of the courtyard, and a lot of stuff coming in from the mine. Then most of them picked up and left, and it's been pretty quiet since then."

"Probably all the R and D got finished, and they're just doing production," Cimy said.

"Ah," Padmé said. "What do they bring in from the mine? Some sort of heavy, grayish metal?"

"No idea," LebJau said with a shrug. "The mine was never ours—some other group owned it and had their own people working it. Never let us in. Then the duke came along and chased them off, I guess, because they all left a few months ago and haven't come back."

"Got a bunch more people from the town in to work it, though, so that's good," Cimy added. "But the metalheads keep close tabs on them, and they've got their own barracks on the grounds, so we don't hear much from them. The duke's keeping them busy, though."

"I see," Padmé murmured. If they were bringing in doonium or quadranium it would make sense to keep tight security around the mine.

But then why the mass exodus of staff? Even if what they were constructing here could really be so completely automated, shouldn't they have more than just a few people here to oversee things? Maybe it wasn't as big or important a project as Duja had thought.

Or maybe it was such a dead-dark secret that Dooku wanted the absolute minimum of people knowing about it.

Which would also explain why they would use local techs instead of programming droids to watch over the process. Not only would the absence of highly specialized droids from the war effort be conspicuous, but they would have to have their memories wiped and programming reinstalled afterward, which would be both expensive and time consuming. "You said something about a riverboat," she said. "Aren't we going in the wrong direction for that?"

Huga snorted a laugh. "Only if you want a *real* boat."

"The boat's LebJau's baby," Cimy added. "Or maybe *boondoggle*'s a better word."

Padmé looked at LebJau. The big man was staring straight ahead, his lips pressed tightly together. "What does he mean?" she asked.

"He figured he could build a boat here in Kivley's Gulley," Cimy said, waving a hand around. "Up near the factory, where he could get scrap and maybe borrow tools when he needed them. Figured when the spring rains came and the gulley flooded the thing would float down to the river and he'd be sitting pretty." He pointed ahead. "Only then the duke and the metalheads showed up, we got shifted to maintenance, and he can't go outside anymore."

"So now the thing's just sitting there," Huga put in. "Kilometers from town or anything else, and too big to move."

"And nowhere near finished," Cimy said. "So when the rains come, the water will just wash through it and leave it sitting there."

"That's too bad," Padmé said. "How long until the rains?"

"Two months," Cimy said. "Maybe three."

"Ah." So if she and Anakin could bring the Republic down on this place fast enough, LebJau might still be able to finish his boat in time.

She frowned as something he'd said suddenly struck her. "I thought you said you weren't allowed outside."

"We're not," Cimy said casually. "But they don't give us enough food, and most of what we get is packaged stuff that tastes like sawdust. So we sneak out whenever we can to go catch fish."

"We get out the door I always used to get to my boat," LebJau said. "They had a road to it once, back before the metalheads came in, but one of the spring floods washed it away and they didn't bother to replace it. So now it's not used."

"You just need to know how to dodge the scavs when they're out on their patrols," Huga said. "Once we're outside the perimeter they usually don't bother with us. A lot of townspeople come out at night to hunt, and I guess they got tired of stopping everyone to find out who they were."

"Ah," Padmé said. They were close enough to the fortress now that the top edge was in view even from the bottom of the gulley. "How far from the wall does the perimeter extend?"

"You tell me," Huga said. "We're inside it now."

Padmé swallowed hard. And from the way the stars had suddenly gone muted they were also under an umbrella energy shield. Terrific. "How much farther?" she asked, lowering her voice even more.

"Not very," Huga said. "Why, you getting tired?"

"A little," Padmé said. "Also cold."

"We're almost there," LebJau said. He pointed a finger over her shoulder. "There it is, just before that bend. You see it?"

"Yes," Padmé said. At this distance, it looked less like a boat than a pile of junk filling the gulley.

Up close, she soon found out, it looked exactly the same.

"What do you think?" LebJau asked as he helped her over a low railing and led her toward a low-roofed wheelhouse in the middle of a half-finished deck.

"Interesting design," she said in her best diplomat's voice. In fact, the thing was about as rough and amateurish as anything she'd seen in her life. It seemed to have been constructed largely of scrap from one or more of the factories, mostly metal but with some ceramic and plastoid sections thrown in.

There was no way it would take a flooded gulley without sinking. For that matter, it might not even survive an extra-large wave.

"Thanks." LebJau stepped to the wheelhouse and pried open the door. "You can stay down here."

The wheelhouse was bigger than it looked, extending downward below the deck far enough that she could at least stand up without whacking her head. She followed LebJau down the three steps—one of which wobbled under her weight—and over to a plastoid ledge that would probably one day be a bunk. "There's no real bed," he said, apologizing as he brushed some metal shavings off the ledge. "Sorry. I can try to find something tomorrow."

"That's okay," Padmé assured him, handing him back his jacket. "I've been in worse places."

"When are you going to send your messages?" Huga asked. "The five hundred you said you'd send to Uncle Anakin."

"I'll write them out right now," Padmé promised. Sitting down on the ledge, she slipped her backpack off her shoulders and pulled out her datapad. "How are you going to get them to Interstel?"

"We'll have Grubs or someone take them into town," Huga said. "Someone there can transmit them to the Interstel office over in Yovbridge."

"Hopefully, five hundred will be enough to get them to break out their ship," Cimy added.

"Hopefully," Padmé agreed. "Until then, you've got my necklace as a guarantee of my good behavior."

Fifteen minutes later they were gone, Cimy with the message data card and her account number, Huga with the Corusca gem, LebJau with a promise to come back the next evening with food and bedding.

And once again, Padmé was alone.

In the shadow of a Separatist facility.

I've been in worse places, she'd told LebJau. But at least most of those other times *someone* had known where she was.

She took a deep breath and pulled a meal bar from her pack. Worry, she knew, would accomplish nothing. What she needed now was food, sleep, and a plan.

The first two were straightforward enough. The third, hopefully, would come with time.

And once Anakin got here, the two of them would figure out what the Separatists were up to. They'd figure it out, and they would stop it.

CHAPTER 8

"They are encircling us," Vader warned, studying the bar. Reflected in the decorative brasswork were the distorted images of the ten Darshi as they moved quietly around behind him and Thrawn into flanking attack positions.

A simple, yet well-executed maneuver. During the Clone Wars, The Jedi had seen many such attacks from Separatist forces. The attacks from the current epidemic of loudly flailing rebel groups were significantly less professional.

Rebel groups like the one on Atollon that Thrawn had been sent to destroy.

Thrawn had tried encircling them, too, just like the Darshi here in the cantina were trying. The Chiss had failed in his effort, just as the Darshi were going to fail in theirs.

Thrawn didn't reply. Still disapproving of Vader's decision to launch the First Legion at the incoming ships above Batuu?

The grand admiral was hardly in a position to be critical. He'd had the Phoenix group bottled up, in space *and* on the ground, and a few ships had still managed to slip through the blockade.

Here, Vader didn't have those same resources, which meant some of the ships above Batuu would inevitably escape. But the big freighter, the one he'd sent the First Legion to, *would* be dealt with.

He would show Thrawn how it was done.

"Do you hear that?" Thrawn murmured.

"What?" Vader asked, still watching the movements in the brass.

"Their click code," Thrawn said quietly. "Do you hear it?"

Vader frowned. Yes, he could hear the faint tongue clicking now. Odd that he hadn't noticed it before. "Can you interpret it?"

"Not the specifics," Thrawn said. "But most follow similar patterns. The number and frequency of clicks indicate they are nearly ready to launch their attack. Remember that we wish prisoners to interrogate."

Vader glowered at the images in the railing. Simple blasters for hire, most likely. Better to eliminate them and allow Kimmund to deal with the task of finding prisoners. "Do you expect them to be equally courteous?"

"At first, yes, they will," Thrawn said.

That wasn't the answer Vader had expected. "For what reason?"

"Interrogation," Thrawn said. "They will wish to know what I have learned of them." He looked sideways at Vader. "Though they may not offer you the same courtesy."

The Chiss thought highly of himself, that was for certain. "Then they will be surprised."

"They will indeed." There was the soft hiss of Thrawn's combat baton being drawn from its holster. "Once they have lost some of their numbers, they will likely abandon any hope of taking either of us alive."

Vader nodded to himself. And when they reached that point, not even Thrawn would be able to complain about leaving the bodies of their opponents scattered on the cantina floor. "Then their surprise will be short-lived."

"We will first try to disable without killing," Thrawn said, with an emphasis that suggested it was an order.

Not that Vader was in the mood to accept any such instructions, especially not under these circumstances. Fortunately for Thrawn, he'd presented the goal with more subtlety than that.

Subtlety. In an Empire filled with men like Tarkin, perhaps that was what the Emperor found most useful in this Chiss.

Thrawn had refused to send the *Chimaera* against the unknown ships on the grounds that it could be advantageous to keep the full extent of the Imperials' power hidden. Now he wanted to strike nonlethal blows to suggest he lacked the power or the strength of mind to kill?

Very well. Subtlety was a game Vader could also play if he chose.

And in that instant he caught the flicker through the Force as the Darshi charged to the attack.

He turned, snatching his lightsaber from his belt. Three of the aliens were converging on Thrawn, combat sticks of their own ready in their hands, while four more charged at Vader with identical weapons.

Their knives, interestingly enough, remained in their sheaths. Apparently, they *did* have some thought of taking their quarries alive.

Still, they weren't being foolish about it. Standing well back from the battleground, only intermittently visible as the rest of the customers beat a hasty retreat past them through the door, were the other three Darshi, blasters drawn and ready. Either Vader and Thrawn would leave as prisoners, or—their thinking apparently went—they wouldn't leave at all.

The attackers were going to be severely disappointed.

Thrawn had already turned to face his attackers, a bottle of rum he'd snatched from behind the bar in his free hand. But instead of simply throwing it, he spun it around twice in his hand, pointed it at the nearest attacker, and slashed his baton across the bottle's neck, shattering it.

And as the freshly agitated liquid burst from the bottle's confines Thrawn sprayed the stream across all three of his attackers' faces.

Their charge jerked to a confused halt amid gasps and roars as the alcohol hit unprotected eyes. Thrawn threw the now half-empty bottle toward Vader's attackers, then waded into the midst of his own group, slamming his baton with expert precision across arms, legs, and ribs, disabling without killing.

But Vader's group had seen Thrawn's move, and had had time to recover from the surprise attack. As the bottle came toward them the nearest Darshi knocked it away with a flick of his own baton. He turned back toward Vader—

Double vision: the Darshi feinting left, then swinging his stick from the right—

The attacker staggered back, twisting around from the impact as Vader slapped him hard across the side of his head with his lightsaber hilt.

Not the blade. Only the hilt. If Thrawn could take on three opponents with just a stick, so could Vader.

Double vision: stick jabbing at his helmet—

Vader swung his lightsaber, deflecting the attack, then jabbed the end hard into the center of the alien's chest.

Double vision: slapping blows against helmet and right forearm from the remaining two Darshi—

A complete waste of their time, of course, combat sticks against body armor. But Vader allowed the attack, letting the blows land without effect, luring them into moving within range of counterattack. Two more quick jabs with his lightsaber, and they had joined their companions on the floor.

Double vision: bolt coming at right shoulder—

He looked at the three backups, swinging their blasters toward him. He brought up his left hand, catching the bolt on his palm, feeling a brief rise in heat as the energy expended itself against the armored glove.

Double vision: bolts coming at chest, at helmet—

He reached out to the Force, tweaking the attackers' blasters a couple of degrees to the sides, just far enough to throw off their aim. Probably they never even realized what had happened. He strode toward them, feeling his cloak billowing behind him.

Double vision: blaster bolts coming at chest, at head, at chest—

Again, he blocked one and reached to the Force to deflect the other two. He caught up a nearby table and, keeping his hand on it as if using only muscle power, used the Force to hurl it across the cantina into their midst.

One of them was fast enough to dodge out of the way. The other two weren't so quick or so lucky and went down in grunts of pain and the crash of wood table on wood floor.

The one still standing had had enough.

Double vision: blaster bolt at head—

Vader again turned the weapon, sending the bolt to the side as the Darshi made a mad dash for the door. Vader strode after him, trying to decide whether to drop him right there or to let him get outside so that he could find out what kind of vehicle he'd arrived in.

The latter, he decided. The Darshi reached the door and pulled it open—

Sensation surging—rippling and swirling of the Force—something or someone appearing nearby—surprise—confusion—double vision— second vision bringing only darkness—

Vader felt his pace falter. It was the disturbance in the Force the Emperor had sensed from Coruscant. There was nothing else it could be.

But now, in sharp contrast with Vader's earlier attempts to sense the anomaly, it was suddenly right there in front of him, flooding over and through his mind.

Swirlings in the Force—surprise—confusion—darkness—anxiety—

Only what was it? For all the strength of the awareness, the sensation was vague and unfocused. He couldn't tell whether it was a person, a group of people, or something else. Possibly something completely unknown in Jedi or Sith history.

And then, as the Darshi darted out the door and Vader tried to focus on the thoughts and sensations, he heard the distant rumbling of an explosion.

The swirling of anxiety turning to fear—twisting in alien forms and patterns—breaking all ability to concentrate—flashing into unfocused turmoil—

The sudden shift snapped Vader's attempts to isolate it. The distant explosion—had the aliens attacked the source of the disturbance?

The disturbance dissolving into terror—

A second explosion, as muffled and indistinct as the first, rippled across Black Spire, rattling the cantina.

"I believe our freighter has been attacked," Thrawn said coolly. Stepping over one of the three Darshi lying unconscious on the floor in front of him, he hurried toward Vader and the door. "Our opponents are attempting to isolate us."

The terror fading—the swirling collapsing onto itself and silence—

Vader still didn't understand the disturbance. But as the hurricane faded, he made one last focused effort to locate it.

And for a single heartbeat, he was able to do so.

"No," he told Thrawn, pointing in the opposite direction from the door. "Not the freighter. The three houses."

Thrawn's eyes narrowed. "Their communications network?"

"Yes," Vader said. "*And* the Emperor's disturbance."

Vader had never seen Thrawn at a moment of complete surprise. Neither had The Jedi. But now, without warning, the Chiss's face went suddenly rigid, his stride jerking just as Vader's had a moment earlier. The moment passed, and he was once again the imperturbable Chiss grand admiral.

But the moment had been enough.

"We must hurry," Thrawn said, picking up his pace and gesturing Vader to follow. "Come."

And because Vader was still reaching out to the Force, he felt the flicker of warning.

He spun around toward the now empty cantina dining area, the now empty array of tables and chairs, and lifted his lightsaber—

As a cloud of large insects appeared out of nowhere and swarmed toward them.

He ignited his lightsaber, the blade's brilliant glow adding a layer of red light to the relative gloom. Stinging or biting insects were of no threat to Vader himself, protected as he was by his armor. But Thrawn was completely vulnerable to such attacks. Behind Vader and to his side, the Chiss's blaster opened fire, the bolts blazing into the mass of insects.

He might as well have been shooting at a sandstorm. The blaster-fire caught a couple of bugs, but the targets were too small and moving too erratically for even Thrawn's marksmanship to make any real difference. Vader stretched out with the Force, trying to shove the swarm into a more compact space, but again the insects' size and numbers made the effort largely futile. As the swarm reached them, he slashed his lightsaber blade through it, with results that were little better than Thrawn's. The lead group of insects slammed into Vader's shoulder and right arm—

And disintegrated into bursts of gray liquid.

So: no stinging, no biting. Something artificial, bioengineered or possibly even tiny droids.

Acid? Vader peered down at his arm, looking for the telltale smoke as the woven metal, ceramic, and plastoid was eaten away.

But again, no. Instead, the bursts of gray liquid had instantly solidified across his arm and elbow into a sort of smooth gray stone.

His *elbow*?

He tried straightening out the joint as more of the insects slammed into his arm and chest. But it was too late. The elbow was frozen solid.

Thrawn had been right the first time. The attackers were hoping to take them alive.

But where were they? Somewhere among the scattering of tables and chairs, certainly—that was where the insects had come from. But there was no one crouching beneath or beside any of the furniture.

He snarled under his breath. At least, no one he could see.

Thrawn's assassin, Rukh, had a personal cloaking device. Apparently, someone on Batuu did, too.

Out of the corner of his eye, he saw another insect swarm suddenly appear and start buzzing toward them. An instant later a volley of blasterfire raked the area beneath the tables. Clearly, Thrawn had already come to the same conclusion as Vader and was hoping a patterned counterattack would take out their hidden enemy. There was a sudden, choked-off scream, and a Darshi body abruptly appeared, twitched violently, then toppled to the floor and lay still.

"There!" Thrawn snapped.

"There are three more," Vader snapped back. He still couldn't see them, but he could sense them.

Thrawn's response was more blasterfire, this time running a new pattern beneath all the tables.

Only there was no guarantee that was where the other Darshi were hiding. The cantina was dark enough that there were several places where they could be standing or crouching unseen. Especially if they remained still—Vader had noted that Rukh was slightly visible when he moved.

If the Darshi didn't move, and if each of them had a canister of insects, he and Thrawn would be immobilized long before they could smoke out their attackers.

He looked down at his armor. His right shoulder and arm were rapidly being encased in gray stone, as were both legs around the knees and hips. Clearly, the Darshi had some way to aim the insects' attack. But so far his left arm was clear.

With luck, that would be the last mistake the Darshi ever made.

"Visual cover!" he snapped to Thrawn, continuing to swing his lightsaber through the insect cloud as best he could with only his right wrist still free to move. A couple more insects fell, bursting into gray blobs that solidified before they even hit the floor.

An instant later Vader found himself in the middle of a shower of splinters and dust as Thrawn turned his aim upward and began blasting into the ceiling. For a brief moment both Vader and the attacking insect swarm were obscured.

And in that moment of privacy, Vader reached down with the Force and tore a strip of cloth from the bottom edge of his cloak. Bringing it up, he pressed it against his left arm, loosely wrapping the whole area from wrist to chest plate.

The cloth was barely in place when the shower of debris from the ceiling abruptly stopped. Vader looked over to see that the insects had targeted and wrapped Thrawn's gun arm, freezing the elbow and shoulder joints and locking his aim upward. In response, the Chiss had bent over at the waist and was firing more or less blindly in his continuing attempt to take out the remaining attackers. A third insect swarm appeared from near the back of the room, followed immediately by a fourth from the far end of the bar.

Four Darshi. Four swarms. Hopefully, that was all of them. Vader continued to swing his lightsaber as far as he could, his range of movement steadily decreasing as the insects splattered against his wrist, adding layer after layer of stone. His legs were frozen, effectively pinning him to this one spot. His left arm was now under attack, with insects throwing themselves at those joints. Two insects headed for his helmet's eyes; reaching to the Force, he shoved them to the sides. The Darshi might have immobilized him, but he was absolutely not going to let him blind him as well. At his side, Thrawn's blasterfire settled to a single spot as the insects continued to bury him in the quick-setting stone.

And then, as the last of the insects expended itself against the two Imperials, there were three brief shimmers from various parts of the room, and three Darshi abruptly appeared. Each held a weapon the size of a blaster carbine, with large attached cylinders beneath the barrels where the insect swarms had presumably been carried. Walking with what could only be their version of an arrogant swagger, they headed toward their immobilized victims.

Vader waited until they were nearly to him. Then, reaching out to the Force, he stripped away the section of stone-hardened cloak that he'd wrapped around his left arm and sent his lightsaber from his frozen right hand to his left.

The Darshi had barely enough time to jerk to horrified halts before Vader slashed the red blade through all four of them.

He waited until they were lying dead on the floor. "I presume, Admiral," he said into the silence, "that you no longer require us to take prisoners?"

"I believe the situation has moved beyond that point," Thrawn agreed darkly. "Well done, my lord. Can you summon aid from the *Chimaera*? My comlink is out of reach."

Summon *aid*? Lining up the lightsaber blade with his right elbow, Vader carefully sliced through the gray stone wrapped around it. A quick snap of his arm, and the joint was free. Another slice at wrist and shoulder, and the entire arm was once again fully mobile. Shifting the lightsaber back to his right hand, he freed his legs, then turned to Thrawn.

The Chiss was still hunched over, little but his face still visible. He was lucky, Vader thought as he began freeing him, that he hadn't lost his balance and fallen over.

It was one thing to lose a battle, as Thrawn had at Atollon. It was worse to lose both a battle and one's dignity at the same time.

"Thank you," Thrawn said when he was finally able to straighten up again. He sent a quick look around the cantina, then looked down at the freshly dead Darshi. "Can you travel?"

"Can *you*?" Vader countered. Even with his own arms and legs free, he could feel the extra weight of all that stone. Thrawn, without Vader's bioenhancements or the Force, would be hard-pressed to carry the extra load. Not to mention that he looked less like a living being than he did the midway point of some sculptor's artwork.

Though to be fair, Vader didn't look any better. Once back aboard ship, Thrawn could simply change clothing, while Vader would need his armor cleaned in more time-consuming detail. Fortunately, he had another full set in his quarters that he could wear while the *Chimaera*'s techs restored this one.

"Of course," Thrawn said. With an effort, he squatted beside one of the bodies.

"What are you doing?" Vader demanded. "The Emperor's disturbance is elsewhere."

"A moment," Thrawn said. He gazed at the Darshi's knife, gently touched the spot where the scabbard rode the belt, and then drew the weapon. "Do you see?" he asked Vader, holding it up.

"I see that you are here while the Emperor's disturbance is not," Vader said, putting some anger into his voice.

"Yes," Thrawn murmured. He slid the knife back into its scabbard and stood up. "Let us hope we are not too late," he added as he made his slightly staggering way toward the door. "Nodlia? Do not let anyone remove these bodies."

"I'll try," the bartender said, sounding doubtful. "But—"

"You will do as he says," Vader ordered, glowering at Thrawn's back as he followed. Had the Chiss been stalling with the whole knife thing, hoping to delay their travel?

No. Vader remembered the look on the Chiss's face just before the final Darshi attack. Something about the mysterious houses, the explosion, and the Emperor's disturbance had actually startled him.

And anything that could startle Grand Admiral Thrawn was something Vader very much wanted to see.

"I think they've spotted us," Tephan reported from the *Darkhawk*'s helm, her pleasant alto voice glacially calm. "Reading fresh power transfer in their probable hyperdrive section."

"Copy," Kimmund said, cursing silently. The *Darkhawk* had an impressively low sensor cross section, but eventually even the most unobservant scan operator couldn't help but notice it.

The target was already close enough for the *Darkhawk*'s laser cannons to blow it into atoms. But Lord Vader wanted it taken mostly intact, along with at least a handful of surviving prisoners. That meant Kimmund's gunners had to get close enough for controlled, pinpoint fire.

The question was whether they could get there before the target escaped. Lord Vader wouldn't be happy if that happened.

And everyone in the First Legion knew what happened when Lord Vader wasn't happy.

With an effort, Kimmund unclenched his teeth. He was, in fact, the fourth commander this particular unit of the legion had had in the past two years. Two of the others had been demoted and sent back to the 501st. The third had been summarily executed.

But for cause, Kimmund reminded himself firmly. All three had been replaced for cause, either for incompetence or otherwise failing in their missions. None had been executed simply through bad luck or failure of subordinates.

At least, not in this unit. Other units of the First Legion had their own stories.

Some of those stories were painful to even listen to.

"Yeah, they've spotted us, all right," Tephan said. "Breaking orbit and grabbing for deep vacuum."

"Yes, thank you, I got it," Kimmund growled, watching the displays, his mind sifting rapidly through the possibilities. The freighter was too deep in Batuu's gravity well to make the jump to lightspeed, but that particular window was rapidly closing. He checked the displays, hoping Tephan might be able to squeeze a little more acceleration out of the engines. But the *Darkhawk* was already running full-out. Now all he could do was keep going as they were and hope his gunners could rise to the challenge—

"Incoming one eighty!" Tephan snapped.

Incoming one *eighty*? From *behind* them? Kimmund shifted his eyes to the aft display—

Just as a flight of four TIEs roared past the *Darkhawk,* blazing toward the target freighter.

"Whoa!" Kimmund said. "Yeah, that's incoming and a half."

"I guess the admiral decided to give us some backup after all," Tephan said. "They came up through our shadow—never saw them."

Which meant the freighter wouldn't have seen them, either, Kimmund knew. At least Thrawn's people had *some* rudimentary tactical ability.

"Commander Kimmund," a formal voice came over the bridge speaker. "This is Captain Vult Skerris of Defender Squadron One. Hope we're not too late to join in. Anything in particular we can do for you?"

Kimmund mouthed a curse. Not standard TIE fighters, but a quartet of those TIE Defenders he'd heard Thrawn was always going to Coruscant to lobby the High Command for.

Which was a complete waste of everyone's time. With the extra weight of shields and hyperdrives—which standard TIEs didn't have and competent pilots didn't need—not to mention the structural changes necessary to switch the design from two wings to three, the Defenders were bigger, clumsier, slower, and more expensive than any other starfighters in the fleet. Even the navy didn't have infinite funds, and with the High Command's passion for bigger and more powerful ships there was no way even a grand admiral with Thrawn's friends on Coruscant was going to get his way.

Kimmund frowned. On the other hand, given how fast the Defenders were leaving the *Darkhawk* behind, the reports of the craft being waddling ducks might have been a bit exaggerated.

Maybe this was his chance to see if the rest of the rumors were wrong, too.

"Looks like they're heading out of orbit and running up their hyperdrive," he called toward the comm. "Lord Vader wants it more or less intact. You think you can pin it to the sky?"

"Exactly what Commodore Faro suggested," Skerris said. "One pinned freighter, coming up."

"Idiot," one of the stormtroopers behind Kimmund muttered.

"That's fighter pilots for you," someone else reminded him scornfully. "Twice the mouth because half the brain."

A withering salvo of fire erupted from the freighter, coming from a cluster of laser cannons that the *Darkhawk* hadn't spotted. The blasts slammed into the TIE Defenders—

The four fighters broke outward in a perfect open-rose maneuver, taking themselves out of the vulnerable close-in group formation as they poured return fire into the cluster. There was a second salvo as the freighter reacquired its targets, with the same complete lack of effect.

It didn't get a third salvo before the Defenders blew the whole laser cluster into twisted shards.

Someone whistled softly. "Damn things can actually fight."

"Looks like it," Kimmund agreed. So much for the snide rumors.

And now, with the laser cluster silenced, the four Defenders proceeded to dig into the part of the freighter's dorsal area that Kimmund had tagged as being the likely hyperdrive location. A couple of quick salvos into the hull, another pair of slower passes with more accurate fire poured into the gaps created by the first volley—

"That should do you," Skerris's voice came as the Defenders delivered one final series of blasts and then veered away. "Aft quarter looks clear. You want us to open up another hole or two so you can get in?"

Kimmund snorted. Now he was just being insulting. "Thanks, we've got it," he said. "If you want to be useful, see if you can chase down those four smaller ships."

Which were already scattering, he saw, in response to the attack on their friend. At their current distance, there wasn't a chance in the galaxy that the Defenders could get to them in time.

Skerris presumably knew all that, too. But the man was nothing if not ambitious. "Whatever you say," he said. "The commodore said we were to render whatever assistance you thought necessary. Have fun. Call us if you need us." The four Defenders made a hard portside turn and shot off on individual trajectories toward the escaping ships.

"Don't worry, we will," Kimmund muttered under his breath. "Boarding status?" he added, raising his voice.

"Ready," the boarding master called back.

Kimmund nodded, checking the readouts for himself. The grapplers that would lock them onto the freighter's hull were armed and ready to deploy; the hatch the *Darkhawk* would press itself up against had already been scanned, marked, and patterned for the sizzlers that would burn through the rim and blast it open.

"Commander?" Tephan called. "One of the Defenders is coming back."

Kimmund looked at the display. What in the—?

"Sorry, Commander," Skerris's voice came again. "I've now been ordered to open fire on the forward starboard hatch and see if we can convince them you're coming in there instead of the aft starboard. Hang off a second, okay?"

"*Not* okay," Kimmund snapped. "Get your butt out of my combat arena."

"Commodore's orders," Skerris said firmly, making no effort to alter course.

"Podiry, lock onto him," Kimmund ordered the gunner. "Skerris, break off or I swear I'll blow you out of the sky."

"Oh, I wouldn't do that," Skerris warned calmly. "Grand Admiral Thrawn wouldn't like it if you accidentally scratched my hull. I'm guessing Rukh would have something to say about it, too."

Kimmund frowned. Rukh? What did Rukh have to do with this?

"What the *hell*?" someone in the rear of the staging chamber snarled. "Hey, Commander—look what the tooka-cat dragged in."

Kimmund stood up, craning his neck as he looked between the rows of stormtroopers waiting to make their assault. Coming up from the direction of the engine compartment were Viq and Jid—

And the damn Noghri.

"What the *hell*?" Kimmund demanded.

"Yeah, I just said that," Viq bit out. "He was standing outside the engine room door, like he was waiting for someone to notice him."

Kimmund looked back at the target freighter, which was now rotating in a likely—and futile—effort to bring another, undamaged laser cluster to bear. Tephan was looping the *Darkhawk* around to compensate; so was Skerris's Defender.

"Sixty seconds, Commander," Tephan warned.

Kimmund turned back to Rukh. He didn't have time for this. "You two sit on him," he ordered Viq and Jid. "He stays in here—"

"You need my help," Rukh cut in. "The grand admiral would want me with you."

"He stays in here," Kimmund repeated between clenched teeth, "even if you have to shoot him." He leveled a finger at the Noghri. "And *you*," he added darkly. "If you get out I'll have those two men shot. Think about how you'll explain *that* to Lord Vader. Because I guarantee Thrawn won't intervene on that one."

For a few seconds Rukh just stared at him. Then he lowered his gaze to the deck. "It will be done, Commander," he muttered.

"Good," Kimmund said. "They're going to babysit you anyway."

"Thirty seconds," Tephan called.

"Strap him in," Kimmund ordered, sitting back down and strapping himself into his seat. Tephan was famous for not caring how hard she hit during boarding ops. The freighter loomed ahead—out of the corner of his eye Kimmund saw Skerris's Defender raking the forward hull with laser cannon fire—Tephan made a final tweak to the *Darkhawk*'s trajectory—

And with a jolt that rocked Kimmund right to his teeth they were there.

The soldiers at the grappler stations were ready. The *Darkhawk* had barely started to bounce back off the freighter's hull when it jerked again and came to a second, less violent stop against its target. There was a slight vibration as sealant spewed out around the *Dark-hawk*'s oversized hatch, forming an airtight barrier between the two hulls—

"Seal good," one of the grapplers confirmed as the stormtroopers popped their straps and readied their E-11 blaster rifles. "Opening hatch."

The *Darkhawk*'s hatch slid open. Kimmund stepped to the center of the squad as it formed up, confirming that the freighter's hatch was completely enclosed by the *Darkhawk*'s larger opening. That was good; if the hatch was only partly visible the stormtroopers would have to cut through a section of hull metal to get in, a much slower and trickier procedure. The grapplers were already spreading sizzler paste around the hatch's inner rim, while a third stormtrooper attached the detonator to the section of paste already in place.

"Ten seconds," Kimmund warned. The key to successful boarding ops was to hit hard and fast, before the enemy had time to set up a proper defense.

Eight seconds later, the sizzler paste erupted in an acrid blaze of light and a halo of sparks. Kimmund keyed his helmet's optics down a bit, ready to turn them up again once the paste burned down.

A second later the hatch blew, the *Darkhawk*'s deliberately increased air pressure sending it tipping over into the freighter's entryway. The first two stormtroopers charged through the opening, their armor brushing against the remnants of the paste, their E-11s spitting fire at the aliens crouched in the entryway and pressed against the walls of the passageway leading deeper into the ship. Two of the aliens jerked and dropped to the deck as the Imperial fire found its targets, the two stormtroopers breaking to either side of the opening to allow the next in line to join in the fight. Blasterfire stabbed through the air toward the stormtroopers and was answered in kind.

By the time Kimmund's turn came, the initial skirmish was over. The aliens lay motionless on the deck, their weapons scattered around them.

"Engine, hold, cleanup: Go," Kimmund ordered, glancing around.

Given the unknown ship configuration, the first two squads would be running mostly on guesswork as to where exactly the engine room and cargo holds were. The cleanup squad would have an easier time: confirming enemy dead, collecting weapons and equipment for later analysis, and securing the *Darkhawk* and their exit point.

With the cargo hold squad behind him, Kimmund headed out.

After having to burn through eight aliens at the hatch he'd expected resistance to continue at a reasonably stiff level. To his surprise, they encountered only a single pair of aliens guarding one intersection along the way.

To his surprise, and his suspicion. Unless this species had completely missed the concept of a layered defense, they were probably shepherding their resources for something serious. He and his squad rounded a final corridor—

And there they were, eight meters away: eight more aliens, standing or kneeling around a pair of tripod-mounted heavy blasters in front of a large metal hatch. Even as Kimmund and Podiry did a quick backpedaling, the passageway erupted in a barrage of blaster-fire.

"I think we found them," Podiry offered helpfully as he and Kimmund pressed themselves against the wall. Bits of metal and ceramic spattered from the corner as the fire ricocheted from the edge. "Grenades?"

"Waste of good explosives," Kimmund said, crouching down. "High cover."

"Right." Leaning out just enough into the corridor to see where he was shooting, Podiry opened up with a volley of fire into the crowd.

And as the aliens concentrated their attention and firepower on him, Kimmund leaned out and sent a three-shot into each of the heavy blasters' power packs.

He and Podiry barely got back around the corner before the packs exploded.

Kimmund waited until the sound of the blast had faded away before peering around the corner again. The blasters were gone, their death throes having decorated the walls, ceiling, and deck with blackened shards. All eight aliens were down as well, stretched out across the deck. Three were still twitching; the others weren't.

"Come on," Kimmund ordered, keeping an eye on the injured as he rounded the corner and headed for the control panel beside the metal hatch. Oddly enough, it seemed to have been hardly touched by the twin explosions. There were two control buttons on it, plus a small display labeled with squiggly alien writing. Mentally flipping a coin, Kimmund pressed one of the buttons. The hatch slid open—

The first and second stormtroopers in line went down instantly in the firestorm that erupted from the other side of the hatch. The next two Imperials dropped to one knee, opening up the field of fire for those behind them. One of the kneelers took a concentrated burst in his chest plate and toppled over. As the rest of the stormtroopers opened fire Kimmund slapped the other button, sliding the hatch closed again and cutting off the battle.

Apparently, they *did* understand layered defenses.

"Two E-Webs to the hold," he snapped into his transmitter. "Troopers?"

"I saw ten in the firing line," Morrtic said, getting awkwardly to her feet from her knee-down position. She'd taken some shots to the helmet and chest, too, but was still functional. "Two more heavy blasters, plus rifles."

"Hold went back about forty meters," Trooper Dorstren spoke up. "Twin lines of cylinders along the walls: five meters tall, maybe three in diameter. Another eight to ten aliens working on them."

"Not just working," Trooper Elebe added grimly. "I'm pretty sure they were rigging them with explosives."

Kimmund swore under his breath. So they were trying to destroy whatever it was they were carrying. Lord Vader wouldn't like that at all. "Can't wait for the E-Webs," he decided. "Assault formation."

Ten seconds later, they were ready: three loose lines—prone, kneeling, and standing—with the stormtroopers spaced far enough apart to deny the aliens easy group shots. Readying his own E-11, Kimmund slapped the hatch control.

Nothing happened.

He tried again, then tried the other control, then went back to the first. Nothing. Apparently, the aliens had let him open the hatch the first time just so they could launch their attack. Now that the element of surprise was gone, they'd gone for a lockout.

Sergeant Drav was already on it. "Grenades at break points," he ordered. "You, you, and you. *Move* it, troopers."

"Belay that," Kimmund said as the three troopers stepped up to the hatch. During the brief moment the hatch had been open he'd seen the thickness of the metal, the honeycomb cross-section pattern, and the slight inward curvature. "Grenades won't breach it—they'll just open up gunports."

"Which we can shoot through as well as they can," Drav countered.

"Which won't help us save the cargo," Kimmund shot back, trying to visualize the freighter's architecture. If he was right . . .

It was worth a shot. He keyed his helmet's long-range transmitter relay—"Skerris? You still out there?"

"Right here, Commander," the TIE Defender pilot came back promptly. "What do you need?"

"I need you to blow out the ventral cargo hatch," Kimmund said. "Can you do that?"

"Probably," Skerris said hesitantly. "Lord Vader wanted the cargo intact."

"The crew's trying to blow it up," Kimmund said. "I figure a little explosive decompression will discourage that."

"Got it," Skerris said. "Coming around now. Whoa."

"What?"

"That second freighter's coming back up from the surface," Skerris said. "You want me to chase it?"

Kimmund bared his teeth. Last indications from the *Chimaera* had been that that second freighter was heading to the same general area where Thrawn and Lord Vader had landed. "Can you get to it before it makes the jump?" he asked.

"It'll be close," Skerris said. "No one else is in position—they're still off chasing the smaller ships. Tell me what you want me to do."

"Stay here and blow the hatch," Kimmund said, making another quick decision. Whatever that other freighter had been doing, chances were Lord Vader was already on top of it. This one, though, was Kimmund's. "And make it snappy."

The words were barely out of his mouth when a muffled blast rattled the hatch, shaking the deck beneath Kimmund's feet. "Never mind," he growled. "*Damn* it all."

"Yeah, got it," Skerris growled back. "Hull and cargo hatch look damaged but still airtight if you want to go in. I'm guessing there won't be much opposition. I'll go see if I can chase down that other freighter."

"Yeah, do whatever you want," Kimmund said, motioning Drav and his grenades back to the now visibly warped hatch. They'd go in, all right, and they'd see if there was anything left to find.

Lord Vader wasn't going to be pleased. At all.

And maybe the squad was about to get its fifth commander.

CHAPTER 9

There had been three houses in the clearing when Thrawn and Vader approached from orbit. Now a single house stood beside two piles of flattened rubble.

"It is gone," Vader said. *His voice is deeper than usual. Perhaps it holds anger, perhaps accusation.* "The disturbance has disappeared."

"Yes," Thrawn said. *The rubble shows evidence of blasts delivered from above. It shows further evidence of compression, also from above.*

"How do you know that?"

"I believe the source was taken," Thrawn said. "Observe the pressure indications across the area of destruction. The first two houses were destroyed in order to make room for the freighter to land beside the third."

Vader faces the destruction. His fingers rest near the hilt of his lightsaber. "You believe the source was inside the third building?"

"Did the disturbance break off suddenly, as if destroyed in an explosion?"

"No," Vader said. *His voice grows clearer. Perhaps he has followed and accepted the logic. Perhaps he is preparing for more questioning.* "Do you know the source of the disturbance?"

"I have a thought," Thrawn said. "I would prefer not to state it, so as not to influence your own thoughts and analysis."

Vader turned to face him. "I would prefer that you do."

"I do not wish to influence your analysis."

For three seconds Vader remains silent. His hand rests openly on his lightsaber. "Many years ago the Emperor asked what you would do if faced with a choice between the Empire and the Chiss," he said. "Do you remember that question?"

"I do," Thrawn said. "I replied that if I were to serve the Empire, he would command my allegiance."

"And?" Vader asked.

"My word is my guarantee," Thrawn said. "If his servant Anakin Skywalker were here, he would speak to that guarantee."

"Anakin Skywalker is dead."

"So I have heard," Thrawn said. "I also have the Emperor's trust."

"Do you?" Vader countered. "After Atollon do you still have his trust?"

"Yes."

Vader is silent another two seconds. "You must still earn mine." *He pauses, his head inclining slightly.* "Commander Kimmund reports that the freighter that was here has escaped into hyperspace. He further states that the other freighter's crew has successfully destroyed their cargo."

"They will certainly have tried," Thrawn said. "But even the most thorough destruction may leave clues."

"You have a reputation for seeing that which others do not." *Vader removes his hand from his lightsaber and waves toward the remaining building. His voice perhaps holds challenge.* "You will begin here."

The house was of a common design. There were five sleeping rooms holding a total of twenty beds, a large common area, a combined food preparation and eating area, and three bathrooms. Two other rooms contained crates which appeared to hold mostly food and household supplies.

"These four beds have been recently slept in," Vader said as they looked into one of the sleeping rooms. "Their occupants appear to have departed quickly."

"I agree," Thrawn said. The style of the building, the design of the furniture, and the patterns of color and line were consistent with what he'd seen elsewhere in Black Spire. Local design and construction, offering no clues as to the occupants' origin. He pulled several of the garments from the sleeping room lockers and laid them out on the bed for study.

"Admiral!" Vader called. *His voice perhaps holds cautious excitement.* "Come to the rear of the house."

Vader was waiting in a wide archway leading into a long room. "Do you recognize these?" he asked.

There were ten cylinders laid out in the room, lying on their sides on support cradles. Each was six meters long, consisting of a central portion two meters long with a swing-up top and a two-meter-long metal cap on each end. Power cables and liquid delivery tubes were arrayed neatly around and between each cylinder. The tops of all ten were open, revealing contoured body couches inside. "I have not seen such devices before," Thrawn said. "Could they be cloning chambers?"

"They are smaller than any known Imperial design," Vader said. *He steps to one and stoops down, peering first into the open central chamber, then shifting his attention to a control board below the lid.* "Do you know this script?" he asked, stepping aside.

"The script is common in the Unknown Regions," Thrawn said. "But I do not recognize the language. An examination of the internal equipment may reveal its use."

Vader held out a hand toward the cylinder. For a moment the cylinder shook gently, then lifted a few centimeters from its cradle. It tilted a few degrees left, then right, then settled again onto the cradle. "The bulk of the mechanism is there," he said, pointing to the left cap, the one at the foot end of the central couch. "The other end is mainly liquid storage."

"How do you know?"

"The inertial characteristics of solids and liquids are different," Vader said. *His voice perhaps holds confidence, perhaps rebuke.*

"I see," Thrawn said. "We need to bring one to the *Chimaera*. Perhaps the engineers can ascertain its function."

"Agreed," Vader said. "Guard them while I bring the freighter."

"There is no need for a guard," Thrawn said. "I will return to the cantina and examine the bodies."

"We will return together," Vader said. *His voice is again dark.* "We will also question the bartender further. It may be he knows more than he has yet said. *After* the cylinders have been loaded aboard the freighter."

"Very well," Thrawn said. "But be quick. Time is not on our side."

For two seconds Vader stands motionless. "I will return at my own pace," he said. *His voice perhaps holds anger, perhaps grudging agreement.* "And that pace *will* be sufficient."

"Transmission is secure, Admiral," Faro said, double-checking the readings one last time before turning her full attention to the image floating over the aft bridge holopod. At the *Chimaera*'s distance from Batuu a standard transmission cone was wide enough to invite local eavesdropping, and even with encryption running it wasn't a risk anyone wanted to take. "Orders?"

"Information," Thrawn corrected. "What of Commander Kimmund and his assault on the freighter?"

"The First Legion has captured it," Faro confirmed. "The cargo hold was destroyed, though, and there's not much left in there to examine. Kimmund has the vessel under power and is bringing it in."

"I assume you sent assistance?"

Faro felt her lip twitch. "I sent four TIE Defenders, sir," she said. "They were unable to significantly affect the outcome."

"I doubt that, Commodore," Thrawn said calmly. "Even if they merely drove off reinforcements to the freighter they nevertheless contributed to its capture. Did Commander Kimmund take any prisoners?"

"Yes, sir, he reports they have three," Faro said, feeling some of the tension leave her shoulders. Grand Admiral Thrawn always saw the big picture, choosing to concentrate on the successes and learn from the failures. Vader, if his reputation wasn't exaggerated, would probably have left a trail of bodies behind him after such a lackluster report.

It was entirely possible that he still might.

"Excellent," Thrawn said. "Lord Vader and I will be returning with two cylinders of unknown origin and function. Have one of the mechanical assembly rooms cleared and a full squad of engineers assigned to learning their secrets."

"Yes, sir," Faro said, tapping a quick note on her datapad. "Do you wish any cultural downloads sent to you? I have a high-speed transmitter ready."

It was only a small smile; but to Faro it spoke volumes. She had correctly anticipated her admiral's thoughts and orders, and he was pleased. "Thank you, Commodore," he said. "Please transmit everything in the files marked DARSHI and BORDERLANDS."

"Yes, sir," Faro said, making another note. "Anything else, Admiral?"

"Did Commander Kimmund get a look at the cargo before it was destroyed?"

"A brief look, yes," Faro said. "He described it as a group of large cylinders."

"Really," Thrawn said. "Bring him into the conversation."

"Yes, sir." Faro keyed her board, lining up another tight beam on the freighter. "Commodore Faro for Commander Kimmund."

Kimmund's image appeared beside Thrawn's. "Kimmund," the stormtrooper commander said sourly.

"Admiral Thrawn, Commander," Thrawn said as an image of a cylinder appeared between them. "Is this what you saw in the freighter's cargo hold?"

Kimmund leaned forward a bit. "Not really, sir," he said. "Ours were much larger."

"But were they of the same style?"

"We only got a quick glimpse," Kimmund said. "But I don't think so."

"Did Rukh perhaps get a longer or better look?"

Kimmund's expression hardened. "Did you order him aboard the *Darkhawk* without my permission or knowledge, Admiral?"

"I gave no such order, Commander," Thrawn said. "Nor did I order him to remain aboard the *Chimaera*. I presume he believed he could be of assistance to you."

"I'm sure he did, sir," Kimmund said stiffly. "In the future, I'd appreciate it if you'd permit me to choose the parameters *and* personnel for our missions."

"So noted," Thrawn said. Which wasn't, Faro noted, acceptance of Kimmund's request.

"And to answer your question, no, he didn't," Kimmund continued. "I had him kept in the *Darkhawk* during the operation."

Thrawn was silent a moment, and Faro wondered if he would point out that the legion's attack might have ended differently if Rukh had been included. But the admiral passed up the opportunity. "Very well," he said. "Continue to the *Chimaera* and put the freighter in the Number Six slot. It may be that the ship, and even the hold, will yield more secrets than its former owners expect." He paused. "One other thing, Commander. Keep your prisoners away from viewports or visual displays until you are within half a kilometer of the *Chimaera*. Then allow them to see their destination and observe and record their reactions."

"Yes, sir," Kimmund said, frowning. "So we can gauge whether or not they've ever seen a Star Destroyer?"

"Exactly," Thrawn said. "It may be most informative. As you were, Commander. And you, Commodore, may send the datafiles at your convenience."

"On their way, sir," Faro confirmed.

"Which datafiles, may I ask?" Kimmund put in.

"Those of the Darshi and others of this region," Thrawn told him. "It is possible that we have already met our enemy. It is equally possible that that enemy is yet hidden from us." He paused, his face hardening. "It is vital that we learn which is the truth."

———

Nodlia was waiting when Vader and Thrawn returned.

The Darshi bodies weren't.

"Were my orders perhaps unclear?" Thrawn asked. His voice was calm, but Vader could hear the quiet threat beneath it.

So, clearly, could Nodlia. "I'm sorry, my sirs, I'm sorry," he said, his throat working, his hands twitching nervously on the top of the bar. "They had weapons. I had none. I protested, but I couldn't stop them."

"Perhaps you should have protested more vigorously," Vader suggested. He focused on the man's throat, stretching out to give it just the slightest hint of a squeeze.

Nodlia's eyes bulged, his hands grabbing futilely at the untouchable grip on his throat. "Sirs, please—I beg you."

"Calm yourself," Thrawn said. His hand moved a few millimeters in Vader's direction.

A suggestion. Possibly an order.

No matter. Vader had already planned for it to be a small, harmless lesson. The man knew too much to be killed outright. He released the grip, watching as the bartender seemed to collapse a little. "Who were they?" he asked. "More Darshi?"

Nodlia nodded, a jerky motion.

"*Those* Darshi?" Vader added, nodding toward three of the aliens who had come in during the Imperials' absence and were now sitting around a back table, nervously watching the newcomers out of the corners of their eyes.

"No, not them," Nodlia said. "Others."

"Fortunately, the absence of the bodies is of little importance," Thrawn said. "I had already seen what I needed. Lord Vader, would you bring me one of the knives from those Darshi?"

Vader snorted to himself. *One* of the knives? Surely the admiral was joking. Stretching out with the Force, he pulled all three of the weapons from their sheaths and brought them flying to the bar.

Thrawn was ready, reaching up one hand to catch the lead knife as it arrowed toward the wall behind the bar. Vader caught the other two.

One of the Darshi started to rise from his chair in protest, seemed to think better of it, and sat back down.

"Thank you," Thrawn said calmly. "Do you see the blade, Lord Vader, and the pattern etched on the metal?"

"Yes," Vader said, studying the knives in his hands. It wasn't just simple etching, he saw now, but a highly intricate pattern of lines and curves set into the metal.

"There is little in the Imperial files on these beings," Thrawn continued, "but you will immediately see that these knives are not at all like the one I showed you earlier. You will also see that these knives fit the slight curve of their sheaths, while our attacker's knife was too short, too narrow, and with a straight blade. In addition, the grooves worn into our attacker's belt were too deep to have been made by the sheath of a weapon that light. They were created by a knife of this size and heft."

Vader thought back. He'd been distracted at the time, but he saw now that Thrawn was correct. "It was not the knife he normally carried."

"Correct," Thrawn said. "It was a substitute. The question is, why did he not have his normal knife?"

"And why did he not use the one he carried against us?" Vader said. "Even a ceremonial weapon should be used freely when death is the only alternative."

"Indeed," Thrawn said. "I suggest that someone had taken his normal knife, and that the replacement was there merely for show. Perhaps he feared that drawing it would reveal the deception to all around him."

"Interesting," Vader rumbled. "Perhaps the value of the weapons goes deeper than mere ceremony."

"A token of honor and family, perhaps," Thrawn agreed. "Something akin to the Kalikori of the Twi'leks. I note that the etchings on these three blades are of different lengths and complexities, which would support the idea that family heritage is a part of the design."

"Perhaps we should inquire of them," Vader suggested, turning toward the three Darshi.

"Perhaps we should," Thrawn said. "Nodlia, which of them would you suggest would be most forthcoming?"

"Please," Nodlia pleaded, his voice shaking. "I don't want to be in the middle of this. Not again."

"Then tell us what we need to know," Thrawn said. "Tell us what was in the cylinders the strangers took to the houses."

Nodlia looked at him, then at Vader, taking in the broken coating of gray stone on both of them. "I don't know," he said, keeping his voice down as if he was afraid the Darshi would hear. "They didn't say. I didn't ask."

"Did the newcomers look like this?" Thrawn asked. Holding his holoprojector in front of him, he pulled up an image of a wide-shouldered creature with angled brow ridges, a tapered skull, and deep-set eyes.

Nodlia twitched back. "Yes," he breathed. "That's them. They brought in the coffins. The cylinders. They frightened us."

Vader frowned at the image. The creatures weren't pretty, certainly, but he'd faced plenty of bigger and nastier-looking opponents. "You are easily frightened," he rumbled contemptuously.

Nodlia swallowed hard. "The Darshi were afraid of them," he murmured. "Some of the Darshi became their servants." He shook his head. "I've seen a lot of Darshi. Made them drinks, watched them argue. My experience is that they never serve anyone. Not willingly."

Vader gestured to the image. "One of the First Legion's prisoners?"

"Yes," Thrawn confirmed. "Commander Kimmund sent it to me while you were bringing the freighter." He half turned it around to gaze thoughtfully at the alien's face. "So this is a Grysk."

Nodlia inhaled sharply. "That's a *Grysk*?"

"What are Grysk?" Vader asked.

"Grysks are a species living somewhere in the Unknown Regions," Thrawn said. He gazed at the image another moment, then shut off the holoprojector. "Creatures half of myth, whom few have ever seen. It is said that they are nomads, with no fixed home, traveling in spacecraft so numerous they blot out the stars. They are said to be terrifying warriors, overwhelming their opponents by sheer numbers and ferocity."

Vader looked at Nodlia. The bartender seemed to have shrunk a little further with every word. "Myths, you say."

"Yes," Thrawn said. "But many myths are rooted in fact. We must now seek to divide the one from the other." He laid a coin on the bar. "Thank you for your assistance."

"Wait," Nodlia said as the Chiss turned to leave. "That's it? You're just leaving us?"

"Did you expect we would stay?" Thrawn asked.

"What about us?" Nodlia asked. "What about the Grysks? What if they come back?"

Thrawn shook his head. "I do not believe they will."

"And if you're wrong?"

Thrawn's eyes narrowed, his face hardening. It was an expression The Jedi had seen on him once, a long time ago. An expression that spoke of imminent death.

"Because you're leaving a pretty big mess behind," Nodlia persisted. "We're the ones who have to stay and—"

He broke off, his eyes going wide, as Vader once again squeezed his throat to silence. "You have been given your answer," the Dark Lord rumbled.

Nodlia's head bobbed up and down in a hasty nod, his eyes still wide. Vader held him another moment, then released his grip. "We depart?" he asked Thrawn.

"We depart," Thrawn said. Like his expression, his voice also spoke of death. "Come. We have work to do."

The first part of the return trip was spent in silence, Vader piloting the freighter, Thrawn gazing at his datapad. From the shifting reflections of light on Thrawn's face it was clear he was sifting through his artwork collection.

They had left Batuu's atmosphere and Vader had laid in the vector back to the *Chimaera* when Thrawn finally set the datapad aside. "Well?" Vader asked.

"I believe I have gained some insights," the Chiss said. "First, let us discuss the scenario on Batuu. I presume you have reached some conclusions?"

"I have," Vader said, wondering darkly if Thrawn was being patronizing. Surely the Chiss had already learned all that there was to learn. The Jedi, certainly, had usually found himself lagging behind Thrawn in such things. "The Grysks hired the Darshi to set up a base and a communications triad at Black Spire. When all was ready, they brought in the cylinders and moved them from the landing field to the house."

"And the cylinders are . . . ?"

Vader glowered. This time, it was *definitely* a test. "I believe they are hibernation tanks," he said. "Perhaps similar to carbonite freezing. The occupants were brought to Batuu, then put inside the tanks for secret transport across Black Spire to the Darshi houses. It was their sudden fear at the knowledge of what was to happen to them that the Emperor detected as a disturbance in the Force." He paused, stretching out to the Force. "But you already knew they were Force-sensitive, did you not?"

In the brief time Vader had spent with Thrawn, he'd never sensed the Chiss's emotions register as more than small and brief flickers against the orderly array of his mind. The flicker he sensed now was also small and brief. But it was definitely there. "I suspected, but did not know for certain," Thrawn said. "It is not something we speak about."

Vader's fingers twitched, his eyes and his mind focusing on Thrawn's collar. A servant of the Emperor did *not* have secrets. Not from the Sith Master's own apprentice. Perhaps a reminder of the Chiss's true position in the Empire was in order. Some pressure on his throat, as Vader had done with the bartender, would bring such things into their proper perspective.

He resisted the temptation. The Emperor clearly still considered Thrawn a useful tool. More important, the Chiss had knowledge that Vader needed.

So let him play games. Let him even think Vader a simpleton, if that brought them to the Emperor's disturbance and the end of this mission.

Better still, Vader would prove that he wasn't as far behind Thrawn as the Chiss tactician perhaps thought.

"You *will* speak of it in the proper time," Vader warned. "For now, let us continue. The Darshi plan was to move the cylinders and oc-cupants from Batuu aboard one of the two large freighters. But nei-ther freighter could land with ours in the way. So the Grysks ordered their Darshi in Black Spire to distract us while they destroyed the two houses, which provided them landing space. They then evacuated the inhabitants."

"Having been put inside the ship's own hibernation chambers," Thrawn said.

"Yes." And the same reaction, either fear or revulsion at what was about to happen, was no doubt what Vader had sensed in the cantina.

"And the freighter's cargo?" Thrawn asked. "The cylinders the Grysk were desperate to destroy?"

"That will require further study." Vader eyed him. "Or do you al-ready know?"

"I have a thought," Thrawn said. "But as you say, further study will be necessary." He leaned forward and tapped the comm control. "Commodore Faro."

"Faro here, Admiral," the commodore's voice came back promptly.

"Is the captured freighter secure aboard?"

"Yes, sir. The engineers have given it a cursory examination, and are now assembling the tools and equipment necessary for a deeper study."

"The Defenders?"

"Also returned, sir. Captain Skerris is compiling the pilots' reports on their encounters with the enemy."

"Excellent," Thrawn said. "Plot a minimum time course back to the point in the Batuu hyperlane where we left that path and turned to Mokivj."

"Yes, sir." If Faro was surprised by the order, it didn't show in her voice. Probably, Vader thought, odd orders were the norm under the grand admiral's command.

"Execute as soon as we are secured aboard," Thrawn continued. "Inform Commander Kimmund and Captain Skerris that we will confer two hours after the *Chimaera* has made the jump to light-speed."

"Yes, sir."

Thrawn keyed off the comm. "*Two* hours?" Vader asked. "Their reports should be finished in one."

"I am certain they will be," Thrawn said. "But I first wish to examine the remnants of the Grysk cargo."

Vader ran the whole thing over in his mind. So Thrawn wanted to go back to the Batuu hyperlane?

But *not* to the point where the *Chimaera* had first been dropped back into realspace, which should be an easier and quicker point to locate. Did he expect to find something at the exact point where he'd originally given up the effort?

Or was something else going on? Could he be making Faro go to all this effort because he was stalling for time?

And if so, why? What could he possibly be stalling for? "And you expect the Batuu hyperlane will now be open?" he asked.

"Not at all," Thrawn said. "But I believe we now hold the key to its closure."

"The Grysks and their hibernating Force-sensitives?"

"That, and more," Thrawn said, his voice going darker. "We will know soon if I am correct."

"Our first thought was that they were some kind of covert fighter escort," Captain Skerris said, pulling up the images he and the other TIE Defender pilots had recorded from their encounters with the Grysk freighters. "But it turned out they didn't have much in the way of armament, or at least nothing they were willing to show us. They weren't very fast, either." His eyes flicked briefly to Faro. "If we hadn't been ordered to assist the *Darkhawk* I could have taken out one or more of them."

Faro suppressed a grimace. And *that* one was squarely on her. She'd given Skerris and the others the order to put the First Legion's mission at top priority.

And Vader was standing right there.

His helmet turned toward her.

There were rumors about what happened to people who displeased the Dark Lord. None of those stories were pleasant. None of them ended well. Kimmund was still here, so Vader had apparently decided the loss of the other ships wasn't the First Legion's fault. But Faro had no such guarantees for herself.

"The freighter was the more important target," Thrawn said calmly. "Would you not agree, Lord Vader?"

"I would," Vader rumbled. For another moment his blank faceplate remained pointed at Faro. Then, he turned to Skerris. "Flight characteristics?"

"Unimpressive, my lord," Skerris said. "They looked like small, heavy-load transports, and that's exactly the way they seemed to handle." He touched a spot on one of the images. "For what it's worth, all of them had just the single cargo hatch, and it was big enough to handle the cylinders Commander Kimmund saw in the freighter."

He looked at Kimmund, and for a moment Faro thought he was going to add *before the Grysks blew them up*. Fortunately, Skerris, for all his arrogance and propensity for ignoring officers, wasn't the type for cheap shots.

Neither, apparently, was Kimmund. "I concur with Captain Skerris's assessment," the First Legion commander said. "I also agree with his conclusion that none of these ships were particularly well armed. They seemed to be at Batuu for a pickup, nothing more, and weren't expecting trouble."

"Given the bartender's comments about the fear the Darshi and Grysks engendered in Black Spire's residents," Thrawn said, "I am certain they did not anticipate resistance."

"Maybe not," Kimmund said, his voice going a little sour. "But they were sure ready in case it happened. By the time we got to the cockpit the entire computer system had been wiped clean, and every bit of electronics had been fried. In fact, there were places where it looked like they'd taken literal flame to the walls and equipment."

"Yes, I saw," Thrawn said, nodding. "They were no doubt attempting to destroy any evidence of their point of origin."

"Including themselves," Kimmund said. "They were throwing

themselves at us during the incursion, and I don't think it was just to slow us down. I think they all wanted to die fighting so that we wouldn't have anyone to interrogate. The only reason we have any prisoners at all is that we caught three of them still working on the electronics wipe and were able to get into stun range before they could get to their weapons. Which were DL-18s and old DC-18s, by the way," he added. "Probably locally bought."

"So what exactly were they supposed to pick up on Batuu that was worth all that?" Skerris asked. "Do we know?"

"I believe we do," Thrawn said. "To clarify, though, I believe they were at Batuu for both pickup *and* delivery. Consider that several of the small transports were already on the ground near Black Spire. I believe the plan was for the first freighter, the one Commander Kimmund captured, to remain in orbit and transfer one cylinder to each of the four smaller transports that had just arrived."

"They *did* look like they were moving toward the freighter when they spotted us and started running," Skerris said.

"Indeed," Thrawn said. "They would have begun with the four already in space, then continued with those waiting on the ground, which would presumably join the freighter in orbit at their own schedule. The second freighter was to land and gather the"—his eyes flicked to Vader—"Grysks' prisoners, bringing them to orbit and likewise transferring one to each transport."

"All of it taking place off the ground, where the locals wouldn't get a good look," Faro said.

"So who exactly are these Grysks?" Kimmund asked.

"Very little is known for certain," Thrawn said. "But some things can be deduced." He touched a control, and the conference table's holoprojector lit up with a series of images. "These are some of the artistic pieces that have been created in memorial by survivors of Grysk conquests. Compensating for the creators' cultural biases and patterns, I believe that the tales of vast hordes of the enemy are inaccurate. More likely they utilize unfamiliar tactics and weaponry, not simple numbers, to overwhelm their opponents."

Faro nodded. Back when she first came aboard the *Chimaera*, she'd often been frustrated by the fact that she didn't have a clue as to what Thrawn was seeing in all this artwork, let alone understand how he arrived at his conclusions. Now she simply admired the pretty pictures, and trusted him to know what he was talking about.

"Nor do I believe the myth that they are nomadic," Thrawn continued. "Most beings began on planetary worlds, and do not easily give them up. Moreover, the images and designs of their ships in these pieces strongly indicate a preference for sun, sky, and soil to the blackness of space. Commander Kimmund, your report stated that you observed what you took to be surprise on the prisoners' faces when they first saw the *Chimaera*."

"Yes, sir, I believe that was their response," Kimmund said. "We'll hopefully know more when the medical droids finish analyzing the biosensors we connected to their restraints."

Faro forced down a grimace. That had been *her* idea, which Kimmund had supposedly turned down on the grounds that the *Darkhawk* didn't have the necessary equipment and that attaching sensors in the first place might warn the prisoners that something special was in the works. Apparently, somewhere on the return trip he'd found both the equipment and the daring to try it.

And since her suggestion had been oral and on a closed transmission, and his report was written and fully on the record, he would undoubtedly get the credit for it.

In Grand Admiral Thrawn's fleet, such things didn't matter that much. In the rest of the navy, and certainly on Coruscant, they mattered a great deal.

She was pretty sure they mattered to Vader, too.

"That would support your conclusion that they are not nomadic," Vader said. "If they were, a ship the size of a Star Destroyer would not impress them."

"Perhaps," Thrawn said, inclining his head to the other. "But make no mistake," he continued, sending his gaze around the rest of the table. "The Grysks are not to be underestimated. If they fled from combat today, it is because they *chose* to do so."

"Just like we did?" Kimmund asked.

Thrawn's eyes narrowed slightly. "Explain."

"I meant, sir, that we too have the choice of combat or otherwise,"

Kimmund said, his voice steady. "My question was whether you're planning to involve the Empire with these Grysk. A warlike species that doesn't seem to be bothering us."

A dead silence filled the conference room. Thrawn and Kimmund sat unmoving, their gazes locked. Faro found her own eyes shifting between Kimmund and Vader, wondering if the Dark Lord was going to slap down his legion commander for such insubordination.

Only he didn't. Did that mean Vader himself had ordered Kimmund to ask the question?

"When I was first brought before the Emperor," Thrawn said at last, his voice calm, "I warned him there were many dangers waiting to strike from the Unknown Regions. He took me at my word. Ultimately, he granted me the rank of grand admiral. Are you questioning his judgment?"

Kimmund's lip twitched, his eyes shifting once to Vader before returning to Thrawn. "No, sir."

"Good," Thrawn said. "Then be assured, Commander, that when we engage the Grysks—not *if*, but *when*," he added, his gaze again sweeping the table—"it will be because they are indeed a threat to the Empire." His eyes steadied again on Kimmund. "Have you further questions?"

Again, Kimmund glanced at Vader. "No, sir."

Thrawn turned to Faro. "Commodore, how long until we reach the coordinates I set for you?"

"Twenty-three hours and fourteen minutes, sir," Faro reported.

"Good," Thrawn said. "That should allow the engineers sufficient time to finish their initial analysis, and permit the officers and crew to rest."

He straightened to his full height. Even sitting down, the move was impressive. "In precisely twenty-one hours the *Chimaera* will begin a full systems test. Two hours after that, this ship will go to battle stations."

He looked at Vader, and Faro thought she saw a small smile touch the admiral's lips. "And shortly after that," he added, "we will have the answers that we seek."

"One minute," the officer at the helm station called. Lieutenant Agral, if Vader was remembering his name correctly.

"All weapons ready," Senior Lieutenant Pyrondi added from the weapons officer station.

"Orders, Admiral?" Commodore Faro asked.

Vader looked at Thrawn, noting the look of quiet determination there. "Stand ready for navigation mark."

"Ready for navigation mark," Faro called. She glanced at Vader, as if expecting him to make a comment or possibly give an order of his own.

But Vader remained silent. For the moment, at least, this was all Thrawn's show.

A flash and fade of starlines, and the *Chimaera* returned to real-space.

"Navigation mark!" Faro snapped. "Sensors at full range."

"Mark, aye."

"No enemy ships on sensors," Pyrondi called.

"Any other objects in range?" Faro asked.

"None," Pyrondi said.

"Reverse to previous course," Thrawn ordered. "New course as indicated."

Faro looked at the nav display, a frown creasing her forehead. "Sir?" she asked.

"The course is correct, Commodore," Thrawn said. "A microjump to this point, a second microjump to this, and normal hyperdrive to our current position."

"Though from a different angle," Faro said.

"Yes," Thrawn said.

"Understood, sir," Faro said, though it was clear from her voice that she didn't.

But at least she and the rest of Thrawn's officers had apparently learned how to follow orders. "Helm: Execute as ordered."

The *Chimaera* made three more approaches into the blocked hyperlane. The sensors made three more scans. The helm added three more navigation marks.

They were approaching the fourth when Vader finally decided he'd had enough.

He took a step closer to Thrawn. "What do you expect to find?" he asked.

"The source of the disturbance," Thrawn said.

"There is nothing here."

"Perhaps," Thrawn said. "Did you see the engineers' analysis of the freighter debris?"

"I did," Vader said. Changing the subject, he'd observed, was one of the Chiss's favorite tactics. Unfortunately for him, Vader had figured out how to counter that ploy. "The ratio of metals in the fragments was similar to the distribution in an Interdictor cruiser's gravity-well projectors."

"Indeed," Thrawn said. "Then you know what we are hunting."

"You hunt in vain."

Vader looked to both sides, making sure no one else was within earshot. This conversation was for him and Thrawn alone. "You think the destroyed Grysk cylinders were gravity-well projectors."

"It would explain the disruption of the hyperlane and how the *Chimaera* was pulled out of hyperspace."

"Your conclusion is flawed," Vader said flatly. "To remain undetected, the projector would need to be protected by a cloaking device. Yet as you yourself said, and as the engineers have confirmed, a gravity well and a cloaking device cannot be run from the same point at the same time."

"Engineers and their conclusions are sometimes wrong."

"Not this time," Vader said firmly.

"I agree," Thrawn said.

Vader frowned. "You agree that there is nothing to find? Then why are we here?"

"I have said already: to find the source of the hyperlane disruption."

"Explain."

"There are still uncertainties," Thrawn said. "I would therefore prefer not to speak at this time."

Vader's left hand unhooked itself from his belt, shifting over a few centimeters and coming to rest on the hilt of his lightsaber. It was time to have this out. "I am the Emperor's representative," he said, putting all the dark threat of a Sith Lord into his voice. "You *will* speak if I so order."

"The Emperor placed me in command of this vessel and this mission."

"The Emperor does not permit his subordinates to play games."

For perhaps five seconds Thrawn didn't speak. Vader tightened his grip on his lightsaber . . .

"Over my years of service to the Empire, I have sometimes offered explanations without proof," he said quietly. "That has never gone well."

"What do you mean?"

"Most people don't believe me," Thrawn said. "That disbelief then biases them against the proof when it *is* revealed."

"I am not most people," Vader reminded him.

"I know that, my lord." Thrawn said. "But I would still ask you to trust me."

Vader eyed him, stretching out to the Force. The Jedi, too, had been distrusted and his opinions casually dismissed, often by the people he was closest to. He, too, had known how it felt to be powerful, yet somehow still an outsider. "Tell me of the prisoners taken from Batuu."

"I cannot," Thrawn said. "I can say only that it is vital we recover them."

"If I demand an answer?"

"I cannot answer," Thrawn repeated. "I can only ask that you trust me."

Vader clenched his teeth. "One cannot simply ask for trust, Admiral," he warned harshly. "Trust must be earned."

"I agree," Thrawn said. "I ask one more hour."

Vader looked out at the flowing hyperspace sky. "One hour," he agreed. "And then, Admiral, you *will* answer my questions."

CHAPTER 10

"All I'm asking," Anakin said, "is that you trust me."

Thrawn didn't answer. He'd been talkative enough at the beginning of the trip, mostly questioning Anakin about the Republic, the Separatists, and the Clone Wars. Anakin's own questions about the Chiss tended to be answered briefly or not at all.

But once Anakin started talking about his plan for getting into the Mokivj facility, all that had changed. Now it was mostly Anakin talking and the Chiss not answering.

On one level, he really couldn't blame his new partner. The plan was borderline crazy, and with anyone but a Jedi it would be doomed to failure from the outset.

But Anakin *was* a Jedi. More than that, he knew how Separatists thought and acted.

And he was very good against Separatist battle droids.

"I am a commander of the Expansionary Defense Fleet," Thrawn said. "My uniform proclaims my authority."

"Which you won't have any of on Mokivj anyway," Anakin said patiently. "Even if the locals have heard stories of the Chiss, the Separatists in charge of the base aren't going to be impressed." He waved at the blaster damage on Thrawn's uniform. "And frankly, what that outfit mostly proclaims is that you were in a major battle, and that you probably lost."

"I'm still alive," Thrawn pointed out. "Life always tempers defeat."

"I suppose," Anakin said. "But really, we can do this."

Thrawn looked over at R2-D2, sitting quietly in the corner. "You were making modifications to your droid earlier," he said. "Were those modifications part of the plan?"

"Yes."

"Are they detectable by the enemy?"

Anakin considered. Technically, if the enemy was *very* observant . . . but they almost certainly weren't. "Not without taking him apart," he said.

Thrawn pondered another few seconds. "The plan is rash. But the very boldness argues against the enemy being prepared for it. Very well, we'll attempt it. At the very least, it will bring us past their outer defenses."

"Good," Anakin said with a sense of relief. This was theoretically a plan he and R2-D2 could pull off alone, but things like this always looked more believable if there was a team. "There are clothes lockers back in the crew quarters. Hopefully, something in there will fit you."

"Yes." Thrawn gestured to Anakin's clothing. "What about you and your uniform?"

"The Jedi don't have uniforms," Anakin said, looking down at his own outfit. "Neither do the Separatists, really—their soldiers are battle droids, ours are armored clones. Though our navy officers and crewers have uniforms. Anyway, you're right. I should probably change into something that looks more local."

"And less like the garb of a warrior."

Anakin frowned. "What are you talking about?"

"Your sleeves are cut to allow exaggerated movements of your arms," Thrawn said. "Likewise, the long tunic, which appears as if it would impede your movement, also allows freedom of motion. Of equal importance is the fact that in combat its swirling motion will distract an opponent's eyes."

"Interesting," Anakin said, looking at his clothing with new eyes. He'd always known how easy it was to fight in the outfit, but he'd never focused on the individual details before. "I'll see if I can find something that works as well."

"Yet does not appear as a warrior's garb."

"Right," Anakin said drily. "Tricky, though—form and function, and all that." He gestured. "If the coordinates are right, we should hit the base four hours into full night. We'll find some landing clothes, then run through the plan again. They're bound to ask questions, and I want to make sure we've got answers."

"No, I'm *not* Captain Boroklif," Anakin explained for the third time, putting some strained patience into his voice. A glance out the cockpit canopy showed that the two vulture droids that had flown up as escort were still holding their distance. That was something, at least. "Captain Boroklif is, let's say, indisposed."

"I need to speak to him," the voice at the other end insisted. A Serennian accent, if Anakin was hearing it right: someone from Count Dooku's home planet of Serenno. Could the duke be some friend or associate Dooku had set up to run things for him?

"Captain Boroklif isn't here," Anakin growled. "There was trouble at Black Spire. Boroklif and his crew weren't in any condition to fly. Do I have to draw you a picture?"

"Are you saying they're *dead*? *All* of them?"

"I don't know," Anakin said, "because we didn't stick around to see the end. But I can tell you that your boys were definitely losing."

There was a pause. "Why are you here?"

"Because we've got your cargo," Anakin said. "I figured you'd want that. Provided you can pay."

Another pause, longer this time. "You can land in the courtyard," the other said. "Feeding you the coordinates."

"What about the shield?" Anakin asked, eyeing the sensor display. "Or do you want me to just fly in under the edge?"

"Don't be smart," the other growled. "I'll open it when you need it open. Not before. Once you're down, you'll leave the ship—*all* of you—and wait at the foot of the ramp for your escort. Unarmed. If we see any weapons, we'll kill you."

"Yeah, yeah, got it," Anakin said. "See you."

He keyed off the comm. "You get the coordinates?" he asked Thrawn.

"Yes," the Chiss said, gazing thoughtfully at the ground display. "Do Separatist shields in fact end before ground level?"

"Many shields do," Anakin said. "When you run them all the way to the ground the people inside start running out of breathable air. Unless they're just ray shields, of course, in which case that doesn't matter. But ray shields will let in missiles and torpedoes, so they're not nearly as useful."

"Ah," Thrawn said. "I also note that factories don't typically have courtyards."

"That's probably just what they call their landing area," Anakin said. "Having it inside puts the ships under the shield's protection."

"It also requires the shield to be opened for each landing and lift," Thrawn pointed out. "That leaves the base vulnerable. A better design would be for the landing area to be outside the base, so the shield would only need to be contracted to the factory's walls to permit travel."

"So the place was originally built as something else," Anakin concluded. "Not a huge revelation. It's always easier to repurpose someone else's building than put up your own."

"Indeed," Thrawn said. "But once again we come to the question of why *here*?"

"That's what we're here to find out," Anakin said. "Let's do this."

Anakin had been right: The base did indeed look like it had begun life as something else.

What that something was, though, wasn't nearly so obvious.

"That type of square structure is common to fortresses," Thrawn said as Anakin settled them onto their final vector. "The large courtyard can serve as protected storage for air vehicles."

Anakin nodded. The courtyard was currently unoccupied, but it was big enough to hold four freighters the *Larkrer*'s size or a bunch of smaller craft. At the base's corners were vertical vulture droid anchors, also currently empty. Each of the structure's rectangular sides was about five hundred meters long and a hundred meters thick and probably three stories tall. Plenty of room in all of that for a factory, a major research facility, or a sizable droid army. "Could be from a pre-shield era."

"The walls are too low for most ancient fortresses," Thrawn pointed out. "Is that the shield generator in the center?"

"Yes," Anakin said, eyeing the squat lumpy shadow sitting on a permacrete foundation in the center of the courtyard. "Looks like something from the KR series. The Separatists like those."

"Amazingly compact," Thrawn said. "The power supply will be underground?"

"Probably," Anakin said. "But if you're thinking about knocking it out, don't bother. Unless you've got a fleet standing by, that wouldn't gain us anything."

"Sadly, I have no fleet," Thrawn murmured.

"Didn't think so," Anakin said. "Doesn't matter. If Padmé's in there, we're getting her out." He pointed ahead out the viewport. "Looks like that's where they want us to land. See the four droids with lights standing in a rectangle?"

"Yes," Thrawn said. "The defined space looks barely adequate for a ship this size."

"Yeah, I noticed," Anakin said with a tight smile. "I guess they want to see how good a pilot I am. Let's show them."

Years of warfare had taught him how to use the Force to focus on flying, maneuvering, and landing a wide range of spacecraft sizes and styles. Not just Republic and Separatist, but independent designs as well. The *Larkrer* was no exception, and he managed to set it down perfectly in the space that had been allotted him.

He was shutting the engines down when the courtyard abruptly blazed with light.

"I see they have lighting after all," Thrawn said calmly.

"So they do," Anakin said, squinting out the viewport. The illumination was coming from a set of six floodlights spaced out along the top of the eastern courtyard wall, the one the *Larkrer* was currently facing. He leaned forward and looked left and right, confirming that there were no such lights on the north and south walls, while from the shadows it was clear that there weren't any on the west wall behind them, either. Above them, the vulture droids that had escorted them in dipped briefly into the light and then headed back out on patrol. "Probably just for unexpected visitors and other special occasions."

"A dangerously poor design," Thrawn said. "Lighting from a single direction creates shadowed regions that can be exploited."

"Which is exactly what we're going to do," Anakin said. "If we're lucky, the lighting controls will be out here where we can get to them, so keep an eye out for them. Let's get outside before they get nervous."

A minute later he, Thrawn, and R2-D2 gathered together at the foot of the ramp.

Under the dead eyes of two full squads of B1 battle droids, their E-5 blaster rifles trained on the newcomers.

"Interesting design," Thrawn murmured. "Small and only moderately armored, but narrow and therefore difficult to target."

"They're the workhorses of the Separatist army," Anakin murmured back. "But don't get comfortable—they've also got droids that are bigger, better armed, and way better armored. Speaking of which, there are two of them now. *And,* I'm guessing, our host."

A pair of B2 super battle droids were clomping across the courtyard, a tall, slender human striding along between them. With the lights streaming down from behind him the man's features and insignia were impossible to make out.

But streaming behind him was a distinctive cloak, a Serennian symbol of nobility.

The same kind of cloak Count Dooku wore.

"To our left," Thrawn murmured. "Note the vehicle in the corner."

"Later," Anakin murmured back tensely, stretching out to the Force. If that was Dooku, this whole thing was about to fall apart.

In fact, it probably already had. With the light squarely in Anakin's face, there was no way the Serennian hadn't already identified him.

Still, there was no hint of warning from the Force. Nor had the approaching figure so much as broken step. Not Dooku, then?

"Note the vehicle in the corner," Thrawn repeated.

Reluctantly, Anakin sent a sideways glance in that direction. Tucked into the northwest corner of the courtyard, attended by another battle droid squad, was a small speeder truck, dark and grimy, with an open-topped rear section. A local vehicle, most likely. A pair of similarly grimy men were standing outside its loading ramp, talking to a man and a woman wearing the same distinctive Serennian cloaks.

"An atmospheric craft," Thrawn said. "I believe—"

"Yeah, later," Anakin cut in, shifting his attention back to the approaching figure and the two B2s. The human's face was still in shadow, but as he approached he looked less and less like Dooku. He and his escort stopped five meters away—

"Well?" he demanded.

Anakin felt a flicker of relief. It wasn't Dooku's voice. "Well, what?" he countered.

On the other hand, it *was* the voice of the traffic controller he'd talked with earlier. Someone expendable in case the visitors proved to be dangerous? "We got your cargo. You got our money?"

"We're a long way yet from talking money," the Serennian said coolly. "Let's start with who you are." His eyes shifted to R2-D2. "And why you're traveling with a Republic astromech droid."

"Is *that* what that is?" Anakin said, looking down at R2-D2. It was a ridiculous comment, of course—astromech droids were way too ubiquitous for a random unit to be instantly connected to the Republic. The Serennian was obviously seeing if he could spark a reaction. "That means it's worth more, right?"

"You assume we're buying," the Serennian said. "What makes you think we're not simply *taking*?"

"Because we got more than just merchandise," Anakin said. "We also got information." He lowered his voice. "Like how we got this droid in the first place. But we'll only talk to someone who can hand over some real money."

"How about you tell *me* all about it," the Serennian offered, "and I don't have you shot right here and now?"

"Sorry, but this isn't the kind of stuff you give a hired hand," Anakin scoffed. "Don't bother to deny it—I know you're the flunky who vectored us in."

"Ah, but even flunkies here have authority," the Serennian said calmly. He lifted a hand—

Abruptly, the B2 droids snapped their wrist blasters up into firing position.

"You can speak, or you can die," he continued. "Your choice."

Anakin looked at Thrawn. "What do you think?"

"Courage is a virtue," Thrawn said. "Foolishness is not."

"I guess." Anakin turned back to the Serennian. "Fine. Let's start with the woman."

The Serennian seemed to draw back a little. "What woman?"

"You know what woman," Anakin said. "The one your people caught snooping around your ship at Black Spire and killed."

"Ah," the other murmured. "Yes. Her. What about her?"

"Well, for starters, she wasn't alone," Anakin said. "She had a whole team with her." He nodded back at the *Larkrer.* "Which is how we got hold of your ship. Captain Boroklif wasn't going to be using it anymore."

"I see." The Serennian gestured toward R2-D2. "Was that hers?"

"I don't know," Anakin said. "We found it . . . okay, here's how it went down. We got to the ship, found a guy trying to unlock the helm, chased him away. We didn't know he'd left the droid till we hit lightspeed. And then . . ." He hesitated, as if reluctant to say the rest.

"The ship's course was preset," Thrawn put in. "It was locked in. We had no choice but to come here."

"Who did that?" the Serennian asked.

"I assume Boroklif did before they got him," Anakin said. "So we figured, as long as we couldn't go anywhere else, we'd deliver the cargo and maybe you'd unlock it or wipe the whole computer and start over."

"I see," the Serennian said thoughtfully. "An interesting story. I trust you appreciate the fact that you now have nothing left to bargain with?"

"Yeah, well, that's the thing," Anakin said. "See, we told you the course was preset. What we *didn't* tell you was that there was another preset layered underneath it."

"What are you talking about?"

"I'm talking about both sides were playing the same game," Anakin said patiently. "See, Boroklif put this course into the computer, like I said. But he put it on top of *another* course the woman had already laid in. I guess she was setting it to fly to wherever her gang has their base; you know, just in case they had to leave in a hurry. I figure Boroklif found it and couldn't erase it, so he just laid his course on top of it. I don't know—gets kind of confusing."

"Don't worry, I'm following it," the Serennian said drily.

"Good, 'cause it's pretty tangled," Anakin said. "Anyway, the other guy—the guy we caught messing with it—I guess he was part of her group and was trying to change it back when we threw him off."

"And he had this droid with him," the Serennian said, his voice dark. "What makes you think he was one of her robber gang?"

"Well . . ." Anakin looked at Thrawn and shrugged. "Who else could he have been?"

"Lugging an astromech droid behind him?"

"Yeah, that doesn't seem right," Anakin said, screwing up his face as if trying to sort it all out. "Well . . . they *were* trying to steal your cargo. Maybe he stole the droid from someone else."

"Perhaps," the Serennian said. "Was there anything else?"

"Yeah, one more thing." Anakin pointed at the B2s, whose wrist blasters were still pointed at him and Thrawn. "I figured you'd want to know where she was sending the ship. Brix here—this is Brix," he added, nodding to Thrawn, "—Brix thought you might not want to pay us, or might even shoot us. So we . . . well, we kind of locked down the computer."

"Locked it how?"

"Used a two-stage encryption passcode," Anakin said. "I've got one stage, Brix has the other. You need both of us to get in before you can even start scrubbing off the preset to see the course she put underneath."

"I see." For a long moment, the Serennian looked back and forth between them. Anakin stretched out to the Force, mentally urging him to spot the flaw in their scheme. If he didn't, they would have to nudge him.

And then, there it was: a flicker of sudden understanding. If R2-D2 had been present during the encoding, he might have a visual record of the encryption. If the Separatists could pull that out of his memory, the two ship thieves would once again have nothing to bargain with.

"You've certainly thought things through," the Serennian said, clearly trying to sound chagrinned. "I suppose we'd best go inside and discuss what this information is worth." He waved casually at R2-D2. "We'll bring the droid. He may know more about the thieves."

"Long as we get paid, he's all yours," Anakin said. "Lead on."

The Serennian made a dismissive gesture to the B2s, who obediently lowered their arms and blasters. "You, too," he added to the squad of battle droids, still holding their blasters on Anakin and Thrawn. "Go help Palter with the shipment."

"Should we check out the freighter?" the lead droid asked.

"Team Four will do that," the Serennian said. "Wait with Palter until Team Three gets the workers here, then help them make sure they get everything unloaded and stacked right."

"Roger roger," the lead droid said. They turned in unison and headed off across the courtyard toward the dusty vehicle in the corner. The Serennian watched them a moment, then turned and started walking toward a door in the southeast corner of the courtyard, his cloak billowing behind him.

Anakin followed, R2-D2 rolling at his side, Thrawn a couple of paces behind them. The two B2s waited until the newcomers had passed between them, then fell into guard positions on either side.

There was the sound of footsteps behind Anakin as Thrawn closed the gap between them. "Beside the door," the Chiss murmured. "A set of switches. Armored conduits lead upward along the walls to the lights."

Anakin gave a microscopic nod in acknowledgment. So not only had the base been built inside an existing building, but the Separatists' retrofitting had been a quick job, simply fastening the security lights to what was already there instead of installing something more permanent.

Which suggested that the base wasn't intended for long-term use. Whatever they were up to, they were planning to do it and get out.

Another group of B1s was coming across the courtyard toward the *Larkrer,* presumably the Team Four the Serennian had mentioned. Anakin eyed the droids, running a quick calculation of their closest approach to him. It wouldn't be perfect, but it would be good enough. Reaching over, he gently tapped R2-D2's side.

The droid gave a muffled grunt of acknowledgment and slid open the hidden compartment in the top of his dome. Thrawn slipped around Anakin's other side, striding past the two of them and moving to catch up with the Serennian—

"Halt," one of the B2s ordered.

Obediently, Anakin and R2-D2 stopped. But Thrawn kept moving. "I must speak," he called toward the Serennian. The super battle droids snapped their blasters up, hurrying to catch up with him, passing Anakin and R2-D2.

And with everyone's attention elsewhere, Anakin stretched out with the Force and pulled his lightsaber from R2-D2's dome. He dropped it to just above ground level and sent it floating back behind them across the courtyard. It flew out of his shadow, glinted briefly in the light streaming down from the wall, then angled up from the ground and tucked itself alongside the bent gun arm of one of the two rearmost droids. Out of the corner of his eye he saw the Serennian jerk to a halt and spin around. "Stop!" he snapped.

"My apologies," Thrawn said, finally coming to a halt. The B2 droids did likewise, their blasters still trained on him. "I merely wished to ask a question."

"Questions can wait," the Serennian growled, glaring at the Chiss. He looked at the B2s and gestured their blasters back down. "Come."

"The question is important," Thrawn insisted, not moving.

Again, the B2s' blasters came up. "I said otherwise," the Serennian said.

For a moment the human and the Chiss stood facing each other, locking eyes and wills. Anakin stayed where he was, watching the battle droid patrol continue its march, keeping his lightsaber half concealed beside the droid's arm. This was going to take exquisite timing . . .

"This had better be good," the Serennian said at last.

"You've suggested this droid may have come from the Republic," Thrawn said. "The thieves tried to force the freighter to their own destination. In warfare, some believe that if one cannot gain a prize, neither shall anyone else."

For a pair of heartbeats the Serennian just stared at him. Then, abruptly, his head jerked as he turned toward R2-D2. "Droids!" he shouted, backing rapidly away. "That astromech—quick-scan for explosives!"

Anakin looked past him to the row of switches by the wall, stretched out with the Force, and opened all of them, then turned his eyes back to the droid patrol. As the floodlights winked out he caught a glimpse of his lightsaber, falling out of concealment toward the ground, and reestablished his Force grip on it. R2-D2 gave a wailing scream—

And as a chorus of startled human and droid screeches erupted across the courtyard, Anakin ignited the lightsaber and sent it whirling and slashing through the droid patrol.

In the heat of a real battle, such a maneuver would have meant quick death. Not only did he have only limited control over the weapon at this distance, but with his lightsaber that far away he was completely open to enemy fire.

But for making it look like a Jedi had suddenly appeared from concealment, he couldn't have asked for better.

It also wasn't a trick he could play for long. He sent one final slash through the last droid, then closed down the lightsaber and threw it toward the top of the eastern building. He hated to part with it, even for a short time, but someone could turn the lights back on at any second and the last thing he wanted was for the Serennian to see a Jedi weapon sailing toward his outstretched hand.

It was just as well he hadn't dawdled. An instant later the flood-lights came back on, one of the beams catching the lightsaber hilt for a fraction of a second before the weapon arced out of its reach into the darkness.

And in the newly restored light, he saw that the courtyard had dis-solved into chaos.

Droids were everywhere: the two remaining groups of B1s trotting across the open space, their long, cylindrical heads turning rapidly back and forth as they searched for a target; four more B2s appearing from somewhere and lurching along, their arms stretched out with wrist blasters pointed stolidly in front of them. The two Serennians over in the corner were racing toward the pile of scrap metal that Anakin had just created from the droid patrol, their cloaks flapping behind them, comms held urgently to their lips as they barked out orders. A door at the courtyard's northeast corner opened and an-other group of B1s streamed out.

"What was *that*?" Anakin gasped.

"You fool," Thrawn bit out. "The droid was no bomb. It was a dis-traction. *He stowed away aboard our ship!*"

"Oh, *esehigi!*" Anakin snarled, spitting out a local curse Thrawn had taught him. "Come on—we need to get out of here."

He took off, slapping Thrawn on the shoulder for emphasis as he passed, sprinting past the still-backpedaling Serennian toward the door.

"Wait!" the Serennian shouted.

Anakin kept going, reaching to the Force for warning. If the other was suspicious, or if the B2s were programmed to act on their own—

But no double-vision warning came of blaster bolts blazing toward his back. The Serennian had seen the lightsaber; and if he hadn't ac-tually seen anyone wielding it, Anakin knew that human minds and memories were very good at adding in unseen but logically obvious details.

Anakin had covered half the distance to the door when he heard footsteps coming up behind him. He half turned, assuming it was

Thrawn, just as a heavy hand came down on his shoulder. "I said *wait*," the Serennian snapped, forcing Anakin to slow to a fast jog. "You can't be in there alone."

"You don't get it," Anakin insisted. Out of the corner of his eye he saw Thrawn trailing behind him, running along slightly behind the lumbering B2s, with R2-D2 gamely trying to keep up. "We threw him off the ship. Now he's coming after us."

"Don't be stupid," the Serennian said scornfully. "Didn't you hear your friend? He *let* you throw him off so that he could stow away."

"What?" Anakin asked, giving the Serennian a bewildered look that gained them another five steps toward the door. If he could keep up the charade long enough for him and Thrawn to get out of view of everyone out here, they should be able to ditch the Serennian and lose themselves in whatever maze of rooms and corridors they found inside.

They were ten steps from the door, and he was starting to think this whole thing would go off without a hitch, when the door swung violently open and two more B2s strode out, stopping just inside the courtyard and completely blocking the opening.

"But you're right—we *don't* want him getting to you," the Serennian continued, again getting a grip on Anakin's shoulder. "Don't worry. I've got a nice, safe spot for you."

"You've got to be joking," Anakin protested as he stood in the doorway of his new home. The door, a swing-up panel that was stretched out like a canopy above him, was a slab of transparisteel attached to the upper cell wall by a pair of hinges the size of his forearm. Aside from two horizontal thirty-centimeter-long slits, the door was completely solid. The cell itself, four meters square and three meters high, was made of plain white permacrete slabs.

To Anakin's right, Thrawn had already been ushered into his own cell, and out of the corner of his eye Anakin watched as one of the B1s the Serennian had picked up along the way swung the door down into place across the opening and slid a pair of tapered dowel pins through the fasteners at either side of the bottom edge. Across the corridor, R2-D2 was standing nervously beside the Serennian, with the two B2s flanking them. One of the B2s held the prisoners' comms and weapons, including the small hold-out blaster in Thrawn's boot that the Chiss had somehow forgotten to mention. "What if he comes after us?" Anakin asked again. "You're only guessing he wanted us to throw him off."

"I don't *guess,* thief," the Serennian said, finally putting away his comm. He'd been on it since they all fled from the courtyard, jabbering orders to someone to drag the techs out of bed and put them to work. What the techs were supposed to do, Anakin hadn't been able to figure out from the one-sided conversation. "He wanted to get here, and this was the simplest way to do it." The man lifted his blaster. "For that alone I should shoot you."

"Your boss wouldn't be too happy if you did that," Anakin warned. "You still need us to get your freighter back."

"The *Larkrer*?" The Serennian wrinkled his nose. "It would almost be worth it not to have to listen to your voice anymore." He drew himself up to his full height. "And for your information, I *am* the boss. I am Duke Solha of the Free System of Serenno."

Anakin snorted. "Am I supposed to be impressed?"

"You will be," Solha promised darkly. "Trust me. Now: inside."

Glowering, Anakin backed into the cell. The B1 reached up and took hold of one of the side hasps, pulling the door closed, then lowered the two dowel pins into their eyelets. Solha turned and strode away, pulling out his comm again. The two B2s lumbered along in front and behind, followed by a clearly reluctant R2-D2, with the two B1s at the rear.

And as R2-D2 passed, and only because Anakin was watching for it, he spotted the small drops of lubricating oil begin to slowly drip from the droid's underside. A trail that would hopefully remain unnoticed by the Separatists and allow Anakin to track down the droid wherever Solha ultimately took him.

Assuming, of course, Anakin and Thrawn could get out of here.

The footsteps continued down the short passageway and through the outer door that led into the cell block. The door closed with a thud.

And he and Thrawn were alone.

"You okay?" Anakin called softly, looking around. Like the cell door, each of the walls also had a pair of slits. His first thought was that they were for observing or feeding prisoners, but he realized now that they were more likely ventilation openings.

"I'm unharmed," Thrawn said. "As I assume you are as well. Let us review. We're inside the base, as desired, though perhaps not in the most preferred situation."

"That's okay—this was always one of the possibilities," Anakin assured him. "I know Separatists, and their first answer to any problem is to throw it behind a locked door."

Though he'd hoped that the locked door would be that of an office, someplace with a dataport where he and R2-D2 could sift out the base's secrets and figure out where Padmé was.

Still, the sudden revelation that there was a Jedi on Mokivj *had* gotten them inside the facility and into a spot where they weren't being watched. Good enough.

"I'm glad to hear that," Thrawn said, perhaps a bit too drily. "Do you know this Duke Solha?"

"Not really," Anakin said. "Padmé mentioned him once, though. He's from the same planet as Count Dooku. He's got some family— a brother, I think, and maybe a sister."

"The other two humans in the courtyard?"

"Could be," Anakin said. "Padmé said the whole family's as ambitious as they come."

"Is the duke currently involved with Separatist politics or military?"

"Well, he's *here*," Anakin said. "Aside from that, like I said, I don't know anything. Other than Padmé's one comment, I'm not sure I've ever even heard his name mentioned."

"My point precisely," Thrawn said. "Count Dooku would need someone who wouldn't be missed to run this facility."

"And who was ambitious enough to work for promises of future glory," Anakin said sourly. "I wonder what Dooku offered him."

"With the highly ambitious, there are many options," Thrawn said. "What do you propose as our next move?"

"We run a test," Anakin said. "Hold on a second." Settling himself cross-legged on the thin mattress of the cell's bunk, he closed his eyes and stretched out to the Force.

And caught his breath. There she was.

Padmé was here.

Not here in the cells, but definitely somewhere close at hand. On this part of the planet at least, maybe even near the factory.

"She's here," he told Thrawn, stretching out to try to pick up every nuance of her mood and emotions. She didn't seem to be a prisoner, but there was a dark grimness to her sense. "Somewhere nearby. Possibly in some trouble—I can't tell whether she's worried or just in the middle of something."

"Can you communicate with her?"

He shook his head and opened his eyes. "Sorry. It doesn't work that way."

"A pity. I wonder what she's planning."

"Whatever it is, it'll be good," Anakin assured him. "She's a lot more clever than most people give her credit for."

"A remarkable person," Thrawn said. "An equally remarkable association you have with her."

Anakin felt his eyes narrow. He'd taken great pains to conceal his true relationship to Padmé. "What do you mean?"

"It's clear from the way you speak that she's not merely an ambassador of your Republic. There's a personal bond between you."

"Of course there is," Anakin said. "I've known Padmé since I was nine years old. We've been through battles and prisons—" He felt a flicker of pain as the death of Qui-Gon suddenly flashed to mind. "—and seen a lot of friends and colleagues die. Too many. Not to mention we've lived through a long war. Yes, we're close companions. But that's all."

For a long moment, Thrawn was silent. Anakin stretched out to the Force, trying to read the other's sense, wishing they'd been put together in the same cell so that he could at least see his expression. "I understand," the Chiss said at last. "The first step in locating her is to escape ourselves. Have you a plan for that?"

"Yes," Anakin said. "We start by waiting."

There was another pause. "For what?"

"To see if Padmé heard about the ruckus we just pulled off," Anakin said. "If she's free and on her own, she'll know I'm here and figure out how to get to us."

"She'll recognize your weapon?"

"She'll recognize my style," Anakin said. "And this is the first place she'll come looking for me."

"Is falling into enemy hands part of your style?"

"*No*," Anakin growled. Thrawn had a real talent for digging under people's skin when he wanted to. "It's just that she'll start with the most urgent scenario. If I've been captured, I'd need help right away. If I'm still free, the situation is a lot less critical."

"And if she doesn't come?"

"We'll give her two hours," Anakin told him. "If she hasn't broken in by then, or at least set up a ruckus of her own as a diversion, it'll mean she isn't in a position to act. In that case we'll get out by ourselves and figure out some other way to find her."

"I see," Thrawn said. "You clearly know each other very well. As I said, a remarkable relationship."

Anakin took a deep breath, preparing to again fend off the Chiss's inferences—

"The local ground vehicle in the courtyard," Thrawn said. "Did you recognize it?"

"Not really," Anakin said. "Should I?"

"It appeared to be an ore carrier of some sort," Thrawn said. "Its surface was marked by dirt and stone damage."

"So the place is definitely a factory or manufacturing facility and not a staging ground," Anakin said with a flicker of relief. He hadn't been looking forward to tackling a whole droid army by himself. The guard complement for a factory, on the other hand, should be much more manageable.

"The layout we've seen would support that," Thrawn said. "But the ore carrier's cargo didn't appear to be native rock."

"Could have been already refined."

"Perhaps," Thrawn said. "Yet it looked more like fibrous material, such as raw grain or plants. Could this factory be for the refinement of foodstuffs?"

"Not likely," Anakin said. "Not with most of the Separatist army being droids. Though if there's some exotic food they can sell for quick money, that might be worth all this trouble. The war's bleeding the Separatists as dry as it is the Republic."

"Perhaps," Thrawn said, sounding doubtful. "Regardless, I believe that cargo is the key."

"Right," Anakin said. "Any other insights you'd like to share?"

"I believe this eastern section of the factory is the main center of interest," Thrawn said. "There's also activity in the northern section, though to a lesser degree. The southern section holds human workers, most likely locals, possibly slaves, while the western section appears to be unused."

Belatedly, Anakin realized he was staring at the dividing wall between them. "Okay, you're going to have to explain that one," he said.

"My eyes see slightly more into the infrared than yours," the Chiss said. "The major heat sources are in the eastern and southern sections, with some lesser amounts in the northern."

"So machinery and personnel in those areas," Anakin said, nodding.

"Correct," Thrawn said. "The droids all came from the doors in the northern and southern ends of the eastern section, which again supports this area as the most prominent. I also note that the windows in the northern and eastern sections have been permanently sealed with thick slabs of ceramic, indicating the areas they most wish to defend from attack or surveillance. The windows on the western and southern sections are still open."

"Where they don't care as much about being seen," Anakin said. "How do you figure they're using slave labor?"

"Isn't that a reasonable assumption from Separatist patterns?" Thrawn asked. "But I also note that the edges of the corridors we traveled along were less clean than the center. Either the laborers are slaves, who do only the minimum work required, or else they are locals, whom Duke Solha wishes to rush quickly through their jobs lest they see something he wishes to keep hidden."

"And the fact that these cells are also in the eastern wing implies that this is where they can keep the best eye on us," Anakin said.

"Indeed," Thrawn said. "Though the design of these spaces suggests they were originally storage compartments and not cells. That may make escape easier."

"It may," Anakin said. "So now we at least know where to begin our investigation once we're out of here. *And* after we find Padmé."

"Yes." Thrawn paused. "Remember what I said about victory being the most important goal."

"Yes," Anakin said. Yes, he remembered. He remembered very well.

But that didn't mean he'd ever agreed.

CHAPTER 11.

The first day, as Padmé had expected, was the hardest.

She spent the whole day in the unfinished boat's cabin, moving around as little as possible, listening to the occasional sound of vulture droids flying in the distance, listening for the rhythmic clanking that would indicate battle droids on patrol along the dry riverbank or swishing through the bushes and grasses surrounding it.

Fortunately, the vultures never came close. She heard no sign of battle droids at all.

The boat itself proved to be more of a problem. The metal of the deck slowly heated up in the sunlight, and by midafternoon the temperature had become oppressive. Still, the additional heat carried its own hidden benefit, making it less likely that any of the vulture droids would pick up her infrared signature.

Though it was hard to think that positively when her clothing was plastered to her body with sweat.

LebJau had promised to come back that evening with food and bedding. But she knew better than to rely on promises from strangers, and so rationed herself to one meal bar and a liter of water for the day.

She was feeling hungry and more than a little dehydrated when, to her relief and mild surprise, LebJau slipped back aboard the boat two hours after sunset with a thin bedroll, some dried meat, bread, and vegetable paste, and four liters of water.

He also brought the news, equally welcome, that the metalheads didn't seem to have noticed her presence.

Still, he was skittish enough about that possibility that he didn't stay long. But before he left he promised that he would return the next night with more food and water, and assured her that Grubs would be heading into town the next day to send out her messages.

Padmé spent the second day sitting beside one or the other of the cabin's rough-edged portholes, waiting for droid patrols to make an appearance so that she could start mapping out their routine. But none came within her sight. During the afternoon she switched to looking up, watching for vulture droids. She spotted a few, but not enough for her to work out any pattern.

At first that bothered her. Separatists were usually better than this at local security. Maybe the operation was smaller than Duja had thought.

And that thought *really* bothered her. For Duja to give her life for an important discovery was one thing. To give it for something minor that would hardly affect the overall war effort was something else.

Still, LebJau had said there used to be more people here, and Cimy had suggested that the bulk of the earlier work had been research and development for whatever they were doing. The fact that this *had* been a major facility, coupled with the fact that they hadn't simply shut it down and left, suggested that Cimy had been right.

Whatever it was, though, Padmé would see that it was demolished. She owed Duja that much.

Though she was still having problems with the reason the factory was here in the first place. Whatever they were doing, why couldn't they do it somewhere else? There were thousands of places closer to home where the Separatists could set up a factory without anyone knowing about it.

Was it something to do with the mine? But that didn't make sense, either. Granted, high-value cargoes like doonium or quadranium attracted pirates and thieves, and might easily come to the Republic's attention. But losing a cargo or two en route would hardly be a disaster, even if it opened the possibility that this secret base wouldn't remain secret.

Unless it was supposed to be secret from *everybody*. Could this be some faction of Separatists trying to build up funds or resources without the rest of the Confederacy knowing about it?

If so, that might be the crack in Separatist unity that Coruscant had been desperately hoping for. If the member systems or corporate backers fell into squabbling among themselves, the whole thing could collapse in a matter of weeks.

That might explain the puzzling lack of security, as well as the absence of high-end programming droids. The fewer the personnel, and the fewer the droids, the easier it would be to keep anyone from noticing that valuable resources were inexplicably missing.

It was an intriguing thought. It also led to another, even more intriguing one.

If the Separatist droid patrols were really cranked back down to barely visible levels, maybe Padmé could sneak upriver and see what exactly they were digging out of the ground.

Anakin would disapprove of such a plan. Probably vehemently. But Anakin wasn't here, and until he arrived there was precious little else that Padmé could do. If she could at least find out whether it was doonium, quadranium, or something else, they might have a head start on figuring out what the Separatists were making.

She spent the next couple of days studying the maps of Mokivj that Duja had included in her report, looking for a path that might get her to the mine undetected. The fastest way would be to cross the river and make her way through the town on the far side, where most of the region's roads connected. But interacting with locals required local clothing and money, ideally accompanied by local speech and mannerisms.

The speech and mannerisms she couldn't do much about. But the money and clothing were another matter.

The obvious source for such things was LebJau. But cultivating the big man proved surprisingly hard. LebJau's second visit was just as brief as his first. For all his willingness to take a few risks to help her out, he was clearly still afraid that the metalheads might catch them together. Padmé tried to get him to sit down and talk, but he brushed off her efforts and disappeared back into the night and the factory.

Still, for all his obvious fear, it was also obvious that he found her intriguing, and not just because of her family's supposed wealth. On the third night she finally managed to exchange a few sentences with him, focusing her questions on his day and his plans for the boat once the Separatists left. The fourth night saw the conversation stretch out a bit more.

Finally, on the fifth night, she broached the subject of new clothing, suggesting that her outfit was starting to chafe from lack of proper cleaning and repeated exposure to her own sweat in the daily heat. But even her best smile and the full range of her diplomatic skills couldn't make any headway against his fear that a set of missing clothing might be noticed even faster than missing food, bringing the Separatists down on him.

She spent the next day sweating, studying maps, and trying to find an alternative route to the mine area. When LebJau appeared again, at his usual two hours past sundown, she could sense that something was different.

Starting with the food itself.

"This is really good," she told him as she bit off a piece of the dried fish that had come instead of the usual slice of meat. "Is this one of the fish you caught the night I arrived?"

"Yes," he said. "Not too dry, is it?"

"No, it's fine," she assured him. "The spice mixture complements it perfectly, too. Thank you."

"No problem." He sat in silence while she ate a few more bites. "I've been thinking about you wanting new clothes."

"It really *would* help," she said, hunching her shoulders as if the material was sticking to her skin. As it actually had been earlier in the day.

"I told you I couldn't get anything that wouldn't be missed," he said. "Not a lot of women here, and nobody has more than a couple of changes of clothes. But maybe there's something else I can do."

"Any help you can give me would be wonderful," she assured him.

"Yeah." He took a deep breath. "Okay, here's the thing. You can't come into any of the work or living areas without one of these." He pulled back his sleeve to reveal a bright yellow wristband. "It lets you get through the doors. Not the big main doors," he added, "but all the little ones where they don't mind us going."

"So there's some kind of transponder inside?" Padmé asked.

"I guess," LebJau said. "The metalheads also make spot checks sometimes in the south wing, where most of us live. You get caught without one, and they'll take you to the Bins."

Padmé frowned. "Mokivj factories come with their own prisons?"

"No, the Bins were storage compartments for extra-valuable stuff," LebJau said. "The duke changed them into holding cells for people who break the rules or go where they're not supposed to. Anyway, what I was going to say is that we're not using the west wing at all. If you're quiet and don't go near the windows during the day you could probably hide there until Uncle Anakin gets here with the money."

"Really," Padmé said, feeling a surge of hope. Wristband or no wristband, if she could get into the factory proper she could at least get started on some rudimentary surveillance. "What's it like in there?"

He shrugged. "Quiet. Empty. Everything movable was taken out when the duke showed up and kicked everyone out. But our back door into the wing isn't easy to use. Once you're in there, you're not getting out without my help."

"That's okay," Padmé assured him. "Not much different than here, really, except more comfortable. When can we go?"

"I want to make sure you understand," he persisted. "You can't go into the south wing where we are, not without a wristband. The only way into the west wing is through the service level underneath everything."

Padmé pricked up her ears. There was a service area that offered access to the whole place? "They haven't blocked it off?"

"They've blocked off everything that matters," LebJau said.

"Like the refinery areas?"

"There's no refining here," LebJau said, sounding puzzled. "Why would there be? The stuff they're bringing in just needs sifting and sorting, and that's all done in the western part of the north wing. After that they take the stuff to the east wing and the eastern part of the north wing."

"Ah," Padmé said. So it wasn't doonium after all? "You said you used to work in one of the electronics factories. Where was it?"

"West wing, third floor," he said. "But like I say, once you're in you're not coming out. And there's still no guarantee the metalheads won't catch you."

"You said all the important work is in the north and east wings," Padmé reminded him. "So that's where the metalheads will be watching. Shouldn't be too many left to bother with the west wing."

LebJau sighed. "Okay, if you're sure," he said. "I just want to make sure you know what you're doing."

"I do," Padmé said. "Just get me inside the west wing. I'll handle everything else."

His eyes narrowed. "What do you mean, everything else?"

"Just that I won't get caught," Padmé said, wincing. She'd spent so much time soothing frightened people and assuring them the Republic was on their side that the words had automatically slipped out.

"Uh-huh," he said, glowering. "I was right, wasn't I? Back when we first saw you. You're a spy."

"I'm here to help you," Padmé said. "All of you. This place, with all its secrecy—do you really think the Separatists will just leave you all alive when they close it down?"

"They'd have a job of it," he rumbled. "Just because we're not in the big fancy center of the galaxy doesn't mean we don't know how to fight."

"You haven't seen what vulture droids can do to a town," Padmé said grimly. "And trust me, you don't want to. I'm your only hope of keeping that from happening."

LebJau stared down at the empty food wrapper on her lap. "I don't believe you," he muttered. "But I suppose it doesn't really matter. When do you want to go?"

"Right now," Padmé said, setting the wrapper aside and picking up her backpack. "The sooner we find out what they're up to, the sooner we can stop it and chase them off your world."

"Yeah," he said. "Victory or death, huh? Yeah. Probably death. Fine. Come on, and stay close."

Earlier, during one of the long, tense nights Padmé had been stuck on the boat, she'd considered trying to find LebJau's secret door into the factory on her own.

Now, as he led her through the darkness, she was very glad she hadn't.

For starters, the dry riverbed itself was trickier than she'd realized. Not only was it littered with debris that had probably been part of the washed-out road, but the gaps beneath some of the larger pieces had become home to various creatures or even whole families of them. Padmé didn't know which of them were dangerous, and it wasn't something she wanted to find out the hard way. Luckily, LebJau knew where to walk to avoid unpleasant encounters.

The entrance itself, once they got there, also proved a surprise. The door LebJau had talked about was still there, an imposing panel set into the wall about five meters above the rocky floor with a small section of the old road still attached to a support mesh at its base. But LebJau didn't even glance at it, instead leading Padmé to another pile of debris and a hidden gap tucked away behind a large slab of broken permacrete. Twenty meters and three switchback turns later, they were finally inside.

"Careful," LebJau said, flicking on a glow rod. "The footing is tricky."

"Right," Padmé said, looking around. The area they were in was all permacrete, low-ceilinged and with fat floor-to-ceiling pillars every ten meters or so. The floor was littered with bits of wire, discarded cable ties, and occasional whole coils of cable. A second look at the ceiling showed spots where more cables rested in permanent loops. "Is this the service level?"

"Yes," LebJau said, turning to the left and picking his way carefully through the debris.

"And you said it runs under the whole complex?" Padmé asked, digging out her own glow rod and turning it to narrow beam. Sure enough, there were no walls or other barriers as far as the light reached.

"I know what you're thinking," LebJau said. "But forget it. The permacrete is two meters thick—has to be, to support all the weight—and there are only eight ways up into the rest of the building. And the metalheads have sealed all the ones leading into the north and east wings."

"Yes, that could be a problem," Padmé agreed.

Only Anakin would be here soon . . . and even two-meter-thick permacrete was no match for a lightsaber.

If LebJau had sent those messages. "What about my messages?" she asked.

"Grubs says he sent them two days ago," LebJau said. "How long before someone comes with our money?"

"Once Uncle Anakin gets the messages, a few days at the most."

LebJau gave a grunt. "Fine. Okay. This way."

The next ten minutes were spent picking their way through the rubble to a rusty ladder leading up into a conical indentation in the ceiling. At the top was a hinged trapdoor, which seemed to take all of LebJau's strength to push open. "The wristbands don't open these service hatches," he said as he offered her a hand up the ladder. "We can turn on the ones in the south wing, but only for a minute or two at a time."

"Power here is shut down, I assume?" Padmé asked as she climbed.

"Yeah," LebJau said. "And I'm going to have to close this behind me when I go. Leaving it open would create air currents the metalheads might notice. You won't be able to use your glow rod in here, either."

"I know," Padmé said, looking around. The room they'd entered was much larger and less confined than the service level, with high ceilings and windows at both sides. With their glow rods off the place was pretty dark, but there was some starlight coming in. All the windows looked like they were mesh-barred, blocking any movement either in or out.

"I'm saying again that you won't be able to get out," he said. "You got that, right? With the power off, these lids are heavy. Too heavy for someone your size."

"I understand," Padmé said, looking around. The level was virtually empty, with only a row of support pillars down the center of the building breaking up the monotony.

Maybe she could find something useful on one of the higher levels? "How many floors are there?"

"Three." LebJau pointed across the floor. "There's a stairway over there in the middle, and two more at the corners. Come on—my old workplace was on the third floor. That'll probably be safest."

Minutes later they emerged from the stairwell into another deserted factory. This one was laid out differently from the one on the lower level, with the space sectioned off into smaller cubicles hemmed in by thin, meter-tall partitions. "My station was over here," he said, leading her through the maze.

Padmé followed, looking around. Even up here, the windows were mesh-barred. As for the factory itself, aside from the cubicle barriers, there was nothing. The desks and chairs had all been removed, along with tools, electronics parts, and basic office supplies. The shelves along the walls were hard to see in the faint light, but they also looked like they'd been cleaned out.

"This was mine," LebJau said, stopping at one of the cubicles in the middle. "We used to have a few fold-up cots, but I guess the boss took them when the metalheads made them leave."

"That's okay," Padmé said. "I'll manage. Are you still going to bring me food and water?"

"There's a water dispenser by the lavatory over there," he said, pointing to the side of the room. "Should still be running. Food . . . I'll try. But they've been shifting our cleanup times lately, and I might not be able to get here every day."

"Don't worry about it," Padmé said. "I've still got food bars—it was the water I was worried about. How are they shifting your work times? Earlier, later, more often?"

"More often," he said. "They cover everything and rush us in, we clean up the mess, then they rush us out again."

"And then they go back to their work?"

LebJau shrugged. "I guess. Look, I gotta get back. Huga's already twitchy about someone noticing I've been leaving every night. If someone tells the metalheads, we'll be in the Bins in nothing flat."

"We certainly wouldn't want that," Padmé said. So getting captured by the droids would get someone taken into the east wing. She tucked the idea away for possible future use. "How secure are they, anyway?"

"Very," LebJau said, giving her a suspicious look. "The Bins are in a block, all thick permacrete, inside another enclosure that has just one access door."

"Locked?"

"Double-key system, yeah."

"Are there any similar Bins in this wing?" If she could see what she was up against, maybe she could figure out an escape trick. If she could, it might make sense to let the droids take her.

"No, just in the east wing," LebJau said. "They always promised to put some in here, but that never happened. I wish they had—people were always stealing other people's stuff. Didn't happen in the east wing, not after the Bins were set up. Why do you want to know all this?"

"I'm just concerned that you might get tossed into one," Padmé said. "If that happens, I'll want to know how to get you out."

He snorted. "Yeah, good luck with that. Look, I better go."

"Sure," Padmé said. "Get some sleep, and I'll see you whenever you can get back. And thank you again."

"You're welcome," he said. "Good night."

A minute later he was gone. Two minutes after that, Padmé felt a faint, brief draft as he opened and then closed the service-level trapdoor again.

Her first task was to check out the windows. She started with the outer set, approaching at an angle and as low to the floor as she could manage. In theory, an unused and sealed wing shouldn't be under close surveillance, but all it would take would be a chance glance by a droid or one of their overseers to ruin everything.

Unfortunately, the mesh barring the windows was as solid as it looked. Whoever had built this place had been serious about keeping out intruders.

Which just served to underline what LebJau had said about the secure storerooms. Maybe getting herself captured and stuck in there wouldn't be a good move after all.

A check of the inward side windows yielded the same negative results. If she was going to get out of this part of the factory, it wouldn't be through the windows. Not without some tools and a *lot* of time.

A search of the entire room came next. Again, her original cursory assessment proved accurate: no tools, no equipment, no scraps or bits of electronics, nothing.

But at least she was out of the boat and into the facility itself. Progress, however slight.

Tomorrow, she decided, she would set herself up by one of the inner windows where she hopefully wouldn't be seen and give the other wings of the factory a few hours' worth of surveillance. She would look for traffic patterns in the courtyard, see which windows had the most activity behind them, and try to get a count of droids and the people overseeing them.

Though she'd have to use her monocular without its enhancements, lest someone pick up the electronic signature and track it back to her. Still, straight optical magnification would be better than nothing—

And right in the middle of that thought the inner, factory-side windows exploded with a blaze of light.

She was flat on the floor in an instant, her heart pounding, her squinting eyes fighting to recover from the blast and adjust to the glare. Her backpack was on the floor a meter away; snagging it with her foot, she pulled it up to her side and slid out her S-5 Security blaster. The cubicle partitions wouldn't be much use as defensive barriers, but they would at least let her play catch-the-mouse for a while before they ran her to ground. She eased her head and blaster around the edge of LebJau's cubicle, lining up the weapon on the stairwell—

A shadow suddenly cut across the blaze of light. She jerked around again, to see a pair of vulture droids in escort formation hover briefly in the light and then rise again out of her view.

Her gun hand sagged to the floor as her whole body went limp with relief. So that was it. No intruder alert, no sudden recognition that a spy had penetrated their defenses. Just turning on the landing lights for an incoming ship and its escort.

She gave it a couple of minutes anyway, just to be on the safe side. Then, tucking her blaster into her belt, she crawled on elbows and knees toward the inner windows. If she was lucky, maybe it would be a passenger ship and she'd see someone she knew. If so, that might give her an idea of which Separatist faction was involved. She got to the wall, slid carefully up alongside one of the windows, and eased one eye around the edge.

The freighter wasn't a style she was familiar with, though it had a Techno Union feel to it. Two passengers and an astromech droid had emerged and were standing midway across the courtyard, their backs to her, talking with a human who was himself flanked by a pair of B2 super battle droids. Off to one side of the conversation a group of six B1 droids stood with their blasters trained on the newcomers.

So: not anyone in authority, or at least not someone who'd been expected. Too bad. She shifted her focus to the other man, whose cloak was rippling with his movements as he spoke and gestured.

She caught her breath. That wasn't just a cloak. The style, the throat clasps, the color and ribbing—all of it identified it as a royal

Serennian cloak. The man was a fellow nobleman, possibly even an associate, of Count Dooku.

And if Dooku was even peripherally connected with this place, its significance suddenly jumped a whole lot higher.

She felt her eyes narrow. Had that been a flicker of reflection from somewhere near the conversation? But if it was, it was gone. The Serennian was heading toward the far side of the courtyard, aiming for a door in the south corner of the east wing. The newcomers were following, the B2s lumbering guard alongside them. The B1s had apparently been dismissed and were heading toward a ground vehicle parked in the courtyard's northwest corner. Another group of battle droids was already there, along with a couple more human figures. The lights shut down, plunging the courtyard back into darkness.

And in that same instant a new light flared out right in the middle of the first group of B1s. A blue light: tight, compact, brilliant.

A lightsaber.

Even as Padmé gasped in surprise the blade was in motion, slashing with dizzying speed through the patrol, turning the droids into scrap. It finished the last one, and closed down—

And then the floodlights blazed back on, revealing a scene of sudden chaos erupting among the droids and people as the whole group converged on the site of the brief battle.

Only the attacker—and the lightsaber—had vanished.

Quickly, Padmé ducked back away from the window. With the Jedi intruder nowhere to be seen, the hunt would immediately turn every direction at once, and she didn't dare risk someone spotting her.

But even as she pressed herself against the wall, a sudden thrill of excitement rippled through her. There was only one Jedi she knew who had both the skill and the sheer audacity to pull off a stunt like that.

Anakin was here.

She really should stay hidden, she knew. But the temptation was too great. Once again, she eased an eye around the edge of the window. Was he hiding somewhere, or was he one of the two newcomers?

He was. Despite still only seeing his back, and despite the fact he was in strange clothing, she could see now that that was indeed her husband.

Who was now walking toward a second pair of B2s flanking that southeast door, their wrist blasters leveled at him, the first two super battle droids pressing close behind him.

Anakin's hands, and those of his companion, were pinioned behind their backs with heavy-duty binders.

Again, Padmé ducked back from the window, her mouth gone suddenly dry. Anakin had been captured. His lightsaber was surely gone by now, either taken by the Separatists or deliberately hidden after his long-distance attack on the battle droids. He was probably on his way right now to the Bins.

And here Padmé stood. Trapped in a cell every bit as escape-proof as his.

Powerless to help him.

CHAPTER 12

Seven times the *Chimaera* had made forays into the same region of space. Each time they came in from a different angle. Each time they found nothing. Each time they accomplished nothing.

Grand Admiral Thrawn had failed seven times. Now he was trying it an eighth.

Vader watched the Chiss, listening as he gave orders or studied the displays or gazed out at the hyperspace sky. Madness, an old saying went, was doing the same thing over and over and expecting different results. By that definition, Thrawn was clearly mad.

But he wasn't. Vader knew he wasn't. More important, the Emperor knew he wasn't.

And the grand admiral's hour was nearly gone.

What Vader couldn't decide was what all this was supposed to accomplish. Thrawn had already agreed that there were no cloaked gravity-well generators out here, and any generator large enough to project its effect beyond the *Chimaera*'s inner sensor range would be running such a huge power generator that it would practically light up the sky.

What was Thrawn doing? Was he really thinking he would find something after seven failed attempts?

Or was he simply stalling for time?

The Grysk had escaped with the source of the Force disturbance. Thrawn had tacitly admitted that, as well. But what was it? Force-sensitive beings of some sort? Force-sensitive animals, if such a thing existed?

Rogue Jedi?

True, the thoughts and emotions Vader had sensed from the disturbance hadn't been like anything he'd ever experienced. But that could have been distortion caused by the hibernation process.

Were the Grysk hiding some Jedi from Imperial justice?

Was Thrawn helping them?

Unthinkable. Thrawn had sworn loyalty to the Emperor and the Empire. Such a betrayal would be treason.

And yet . . .

Thrawn had claimed that his failure to capture or kill Kanan Jarrus at Atollon had been due to the strange creature that had unexpectedly intervened in the battle. The reports from the death trooper guard had appeared to corroborate that.

But what if they were wrong? What if Thrawn had deliberately allowed Jarrus to escape?

Ahead, the hyperspace sky became starlines and collapsed back into stars. "Navigation mark!" Faro snapped. "Sensors at full range."

"Mark, aye."

"No objects in range," the sensor officer reported.

"Very good," Thrawn said. "Again."

"Yes, sir," Faro said. "Helm: new course on board. Execute."

"Yes, Commodore." The *Chimaera* began wheeling around in preparation for its return to hyperspace.

Abruptly, Vader came to a decision. Eight failures now on record, and the hour Thrawn had begged for was nearly over. "Admiral," he said.

Thrawn turned to face him. What he saw in Vader's stance, or what he'd heard in Vader's voice, apparently warned him this was serious. "Yes, my lord?"

"We will speak," Vader said.

Again, the grand admiral knew better than to argue. He nodded and gestured Vader toward the forward viewport, where they would be out of earshot of Faro and the men and women in the crew pits.

Vader strode past him, sensing Faro's sudden uneasiness as his cloak brushed her shoulder. Thrawn turned again as Vader passed, and the two of them continued on, walking shoulder-to-shoulder.

Vader stopped an arm's length from the viewport. Thrawn, again with proper deference, waited until then to also stop. For a moment they stood in silence, still shoulder-to-shoulder, gazing out at the mottled hyperspace sky. "You asked me to trust you," Vader said quietly.

"I did," Thrawn agreed. "I continue to ask that."

"Then you will tell me what we are doing," Vader said. "And I do not wish to hear again of your search for weapons that are clearly not here."

"Then I will not speak of them," Thrawn said. "But your opposition to this experiment is not solely because of that."

So Thrawn was daring him to come out with it? Fine. "No, it is not," Vader said. "Your actions on Batuu and your continued refusal to speak of the Grysk prisoners strongly suggest that you are walking the edge of betrayal and treason."

"In what way?"

"You swore an oath of allegiance to the Empire," Vader said. "Yet you seem intent on putting the needs of your own people above the wishes and desires of the Emperor."

Thrawn turned to face him, an odd expression on his face. "Is that what you fear?" he asked.

"I do not *fear* it," Vader growled. "I accuse you of it."

"I see." Thrawn turned back to the viewport.

But not before Vader caught a hint of a smile. "Do you find this amusing?" he demanded.

"No, not at all, my lord," Thrawn said. "I was simply . . . perhaps *gratified* is the wrong word."

Vader frowned. "Gratified? By what?"

For a long moment, Thrawn continued to gaze out the viewport, an orderly flow of thoughts and emotions running through him. "I have experienced a great deal of opposition during my time in the Empire," he said at last. "Some of the hostility was because I am not human. Much of it stemmed from the fact that I was not part of the Empire's social and political elite, nor did I have family or friendship ties to that elite."

He turned back to Vader, the faint smile now taking on a note of sadness. "Not until now have I faced opposition that stemmed solely from loyalty. Your loyalty, specifically, to the Emperor. I am pleased, and gratified, at the reason for your reservations, my lord. For I, too, prize and cherish loyalty."

"Breakout in ten seconds, Admiral," Faro called from behind them.

"Very good, Commodore," Thrawn called back. He paused, the smile fading. "This will be the end of it," he said quietly. "May I have your trust one more time?"

Vader stared at the hyperspace sky. He should say no, of course. Order the *Chimaera* onto a new course, and follow up with a lesson Thrawn wouldn't soon forget. The Chiss was already pushing the limits—*had* already pushed the limits—and any lesser person would have been dealt with long ago, both for the impudence of it and for wasting the Dark Lord's time.

But he could sense that orderly mind working hard. He could feel the confidence and the anticipation. Whether Thrawn's expectations turned out to be correct, the Chiss clearly *believed* they would turn out that way.

And for all Vader's impatience, he had to admit that he was curious.

"One more time," he said.

A moment later the stars again shone around them. "Navigation mark!" Faro called in the now familiar litany.

"Mark, aye."

"No objects in range."

"Very good," Thrawn said, lifting his datapad and transferring the mark to the group he'd already compiled. "Hold here."

For a minute he gazed at the datapad in silence. Then he held up a finger, paused another moment, and tapped a new spot on the map. "Here," he said, keying the point back to the others. "Lieutenant Pyrondi, that is your target zone. Full spread; ion cannons only."

"Full spread with ion cannons," she repeated briskly. "Ready."

"Fire."

The glowing red-tinged bursts of green ion clusters shot away from the *Chimaera,* blasting through the area Thrawn had marked. Vader watched, wondering if this was yet more stalling. For all Thrawn's talk about loyalty, he noticed that the Chiss hadn't actually answered his question.

Abruptly, one of the ion bursts seemed to explode into a small cloud. Vader frowned, keying in his helmet's electrobinocular setting. A second ion cluster struck that same area, coming apart into the same sort of splash—

And then, suddenly, there it was: a large cylinder floating in the blackness of space.

"*There,* Admiral," the sensor officer snapped. "Bearing—"

"I see it, Commander," Thrawn said calmly. "Commodore Faro, move to intercept and retrieve."

"Yes, sir," Faro said briskly. "Helm, take us into tractor range."

"As you see, my lord," Thrawn said quietly. "Your trust was not unwarranted."

Vader gazed at the object. It was indeed the size and shape of the objects Commander Kimmund had seen in the freighter's wrecked cargo bay.

"As you said, it is impossible for a gravity projector and a cloaking device to operate at the same time," Thrawn continued. "But the designers of this device knew that was not necessary. At the moment when a gravity projector brings a passing ship out of hyperspace there is a brief power surge. The designers simply used that power surge to shut down the projector and activate the cloaking device. By the time the ship is fully into realspace, the projector is completely hidden. When the ship leaves sensor range, the cloaking device shuts down and the projector is reset."

"Yes," Vader rumbled. Like everything else Thrawn saw or deduced, it was very simple once it was explained. "Then we could have returned to hyperspace immediately?"

"Indeed," Thrawn said. "Rather, we could have returned until we reached the next projector in line. In fact, that was exactly what happened during our first trip through this region. Several projectors were laid out along the hyperlane to disrupt all traffic."

He pointed at the distant object. "The challenge in finding it was that the gravity well was not spherical, but was projected asymmetrically to cover as much of the hyperlane as possible. I needed to find the edge of the field from several different directions in order to calculate the asymmetry and define its precise position."

The projector's slow drift abruptly became a rapid approach as the *Chimaera*'s tractor beam locked on and began reeling it in. Vader thought back to their earlier attempt to pass through the hyperlane, to the hours of travel and the repeated and failed attempts to return to hyperspace. "Why?" he asked.

Thrawn half turned to him. "Explain."

"Why did the Grysk do this?" Vader asked. "What did they hope to gain by blocking the route to Batuu?"

"I do not yet know if Batuu itself is of any significance to them," Thrawn said. "Sealing the Batuu corridor could be a test project, the first step in closing this part of the Unknown Regions to Imperial incursion."

"So they wish to avoid the might of the Empire."

"They wish to block Imperial incursion," Thrawn said. "That is not necessarily the same thing."

"How is it not?"

"The hyperlanes are not the only way to move in and out of the Unknown Regions," Thrawn said. "A jump-by-jump method is also able to breach the boundary. But that method is far slower. More significantly, it does not lend itself to the passage of an armada."

Now, finally, there it was. "No, it does not," he agreed. "So you fear that when these Grysk attack your people, you will be unable to bring Imperial forces to their defense?"

"That is one consideration," Thrawn conceded. "There are others."

"But none so close to your thoughts."

Thrawn was silent a moment. "We spoke earlier about loyalty," he said. "The Emperor, too, once asked where my thoughts and heart would lie if the choice came to defend the Chiss Ascendancy or the Empire."

"Your answer?"

"My answer to him then was the same as my answer to you now," Thrawn said. "I am a warrior. A warrior may retreat. He does not flee. He may lie in ambush. He does not hide. He may experience victory or defeat. He does not cease to serve."

"But to serve whom?" Vader countered. "That is the question you have yet to answer."

"I do not believe I must make a choice," Thrawn said. "I believe in this instance we can serve both."

"*We* do not serve both," Vader ground out, waving an arm to encompass the *Chimaera* and its entire crew. "*We* serve only the Empire. And while you stand aboard this ship, that is your duty as well."

"The Grysk are a threat to us both, my lord," Thrawn persisted. "I believe I can demonstrate why our service to the Empire requires their defeat."

Vader shook his head. "Not good enough, Admiral."

Again, Thrawn remained silent. Vader stretched out to the Force, trying to read the sense of the figure standing beside him. But the Chiss's thoughts were as closed to him as always. "Many years ago, I served briefly alongside General Anakin Skywalker," Thrawn said at last.

Vader felt an unpleasant sensation creep across his back. Was the Chiss really going to invoke The Jedi's name *now*?

"There came a moment when I had completed the task the Chiss Ascendancy had set for me," Thrawn continued. "At that point I was free to abandon him to his own task." He turned to face Vader. "You have that same freedom of choice. I am asking that you remain at my side."

Vader stared into those glowing red eyes. No—it was impossible.

The relationship between him and The Jedi was one of the darkest and most impenetrable secrets in the galaxy. It was unthinkable that the Chiss could have found his way through the barriers.

Unless the Emperor had told him.

At Vader's belt, his lightsaber twitched, reacting through the Force to the surge of emotion that suddenly boiled up within him. No— that was even more impossible. The bond between Master and apprentice was unbreakable. No matter how deeply the Emperor might have taken Thrawn into his confidences—no matter how close the two of them might have become over the years—that was a boundary Vader's Master would never cross.

He scowled, forcing back the emotion. That couldn't have been what the Chiss meant by that comment. Vader had simply misread it, that was all. "Anakin Skywalker is dead," he said.

"So I was informed," Thrawn said. He bowed his head slightly— acknowledgment or sorrow; Vader couldn't tell which. "But for his sake, and for the sake of the Republic he served and the Empire that the Republic became, I ask you to return the debt of my service to its proper balance."

Vader clenched his teeth. Balance to the debt. *Balance to the Force.* Without knowing it, Thrawn was hitting all the trigger words, and in the process pulling up far too many of The Jedi's unwanted memories. "There is no debt," he said. "You had a choice. You made it. The Empire does not owe you."

"No, it does not," Thrawn said.

For a long moment, they gazed at each other in silence. "We will continue," Vader said. "For now. What is your plan?"

Thrawn inclined his head. This time, the intent was unambiguous: a gesture of respect and gratitude. "The crew of the Grysk freighter took great pains to destroy all evidence of their home and base," he said. "We shall need another source of that information."

"And you know such a source?"

Thrawn smiled. "I believe so," he said. "Do you recall your suggestion that the Grysks were surprised by the *Chimaera* because they had never seen a warship of this size before?"

"Yes," Vader said, frowning. "Are you suggesting I was wrong?"

"We shall soon find out," Thrawn said. "Come. Let us examine our new prize, and then gather the others."

Seated in the freighter's copilot seat, Kimmund gazed out at the hyperspace sky. Somewhere along in here, if Grand Admiral Thrawn was right, they would find their target.

Mentally, he shook his head. This was crazy.

Beside him, Tephan muttered something under her breath. "What was that?" Kimmund asked.

"I said this crimped freighter handles like a dropped rock," the pilot growled. "I thought it was supposed to be this wonderful six-tricked surprise package."

"I assumed all the cool add-ons were out of sight," Kimmund said. "Extra armor and shielding and all." He pointed to a section of Tephan's board. "Not to mention a pair of fire-linked blaster cannons."

"Which we can't use."

"Well, not yet anyway," Kimmund conceded. "Doesn't mean—"

And even though he was expecting it, the sudden switch from sky to starlines to stars caught him by surprise.

Evidently, it did Tephan, too. "Whoof!" she puffed. "I guess Thrawn was right."

"I guess he was," Kimmund said, keying for a sensor sweep as he punched the intercom. "We're here," he announced. "Incoming . . . two ships. Elliptical shape, about the size of *Corona*-class frigates—"

The freighter shuddered as a pair of laser blasts burned into a section of hull. "And heavily armed," Kimmund added drily. "Damage?"

"Shot directly over the hyperdrive," Tephan reported. "Damage . . . outer hull, nothing else. Well, damn—I guess this thing *is* tricked out."

"So it seems," Kimmund said. "Looks like one's standing off, and the other one's coming in for boarding." He slapped Tephan on her shoulder as he popped his restraints. "I'm heading back to suit up," he said, levering himself out of the cramped seat. "Don't forget to look scared in case they peek in through the window."

"Right—sitting here looking like a vagabond," Tephan groused.

"Don't be snobbish," Kimmund reproved her, looking at her grubby merchanter's jumpsuit. "Most people in the galaxy *always* have to dress like that. Stay sharp."

Thirty seconds later, he was in the ready room. Two minutes after that, he was suited up in full stormtrooper armor. One minute after that, he was standing with his fellow First Legionnaires at the freighter's cargo hatch.

Ten seconds after taking his place, he heard the metallic screeching as the attacking frigate grappled onto the freighter's side, followed by another pair of thuds as the boarding tunnel locked an air seal around both hatches. Kimmund waited . . .

With a sudden multiple crisscross shower of sparks around the edges and across the face of the hatch the attackers began burning through. "Get ready," Kimmund murmured into his comm. "Remember, we're just clearing the hatch." The sizzling reached a crescendo, and with a scream of stressed metal the hatch disintegrated. A dozen armored Grysks charged in through the opening, dropping to one knee just inside as they began exchanging fire with the waiting stormtroopers. A set of spotlights at the rear of the hold blazed to life, lighting up the attackers and shining squarely in their eyes.

And through that glare, probably visible only as an indistinct shadow, strode Lord Vader.

It was doubtful that the Grysks, fully engaged with the stormtroopers, even saw him coming. But as the attackers began falling from the Defenders' concentrated fire Vader reached the firing line, the red blade of his lightsaber cutting through the enemy like a scythe through ripened grain as he walked through their midst. A couple of Grysks near the edge of the battle spotted him and swung their weapons around; the Dark Lord countered by waving a hand at one, sending him smashing against the edge of the hatchway, then blocking the shots of the other with his lightsaber and spinning him through the air to land on the deck at Kimmund's feet.

The Grysk had just enough time to reflexively bring up his weapon, his eyes wide with disbelief and confusion, when Kimmund's stun blast ended his part of the fight.

"Secure him," Kimmund snapped to Viq, looking up again. With the initial wave dealt with, Vader was striding into the enemy ship, lightsaber blazing, heading for the bridge. "Troopers: flanking!" Kimmund ordered, gesturing them forward as he set off at a quick run after the Dark Lord.

"Commander, the second frigate is moving in, weapons hot," Tephan reported. "Orders?"

"We've got this one," Kimmund said. "As per Admiral Thrawn's orders, go ahead and dust it."

"Yes, *sir*."

And as Kimmund and the rest of the squad ducked into the enemy ship, following the blazing lightsaber ahead of them, he felt a tight smile pinching at his cheeks. Let the Grysks try to destroy all the data and evidence this time. Let them just try.

They did indeed try. They didn't succeed.

The curves on the left half of the helmet denote a people of grace, likely with a close affinity to the air and sea creatures of their world. The right side of the helmet has been distorted and defaced by metal tools, the colored sections coming under special attention. More than half of the helmet is so defaced, but the marks are not recent, indicating that the desired level of degradation was achieved.

"Well?" Vader asked. "Will this be sufficient?"

"Indeed it will," Thrawn said. "You and your legion have succeeded brilliantly."

"As the Emperor ordered, we serve at the grand admiral's command." *The tone perhaps holds deference, perhaps holds pride.* "How did you know there would be an attack?"

"I did not know for certain, but suspected it would occur," Thrawn said. "While the primary purpose of the gravity projectors is to block traffic through the hyperlane, it is seldom that a marauding people ignore a chance at plunder. When the *Chimaera* first encountered the trap, its size discouraged those watching against launching an attack. I reasoned that a smaller vessel, approaching from the opposite end of the lane, would present a more inviting prize and draw out the enemy."

"And that with a proper military response, we could capture their records intact," Vader said. *His voice perhaps holds satisfaction, perhaps understanding.* "The other reason the freighter's prisoners were surprised at seeing the *Chimaera.* Not because of the size, but because they had seen it in the hyperlane and were not expecting to see it again at Batuu."

"Indeed," Thrawn said. "Perhaps that was also the reason all the Grysk ships arrived together. Their leaders feared someone had noticed their presence and had ordered them to quickly withdraw from the Black Spire region."

"Yes." Vader pointed at the row of helmets and weapons on the wardroom wall. "What do you read here?"

"Perhaps the key that the Chiss have long sought," Thrawn said. "I believe this is the trophy collection of this group of Grysk marauders. Assuming it is representative of overall Grysk military history, I may be able to use it to learn the location of their home."

"Explain."

"You see how each helmet or weapon has been ritualistically disfigured on the right side," Thrawn said. "I speculate that the degree of destruction is related to the depth of animosity the Grysk have for that particular species, or perhaps indicates the length and bitterness of that particular conflict."

"They appear to be in chronological order, as well," Vader said. "The damages to the leftmost show more signs of age."

"Agreed," Thrawn said. "There are tales of some of the Grysks' wars, a history which I will attempt to connect to these artifacts."

"Tales and histories often lack accuracy."

"That is true," Thrawn said. "But two of these helmets may alleviate some of that difficulty. You are aware, I presume, that I have some skill in anticipating enemies' tactics from a study of their artwork."

"I am."

"That skill can also work in the opposite direction," Thrawn said. "If I am familiar with a warrior's tactics, I can in some measure identify that warrior's artwork."

"Interesting. You have fought some of these species before?"

"The Chiss have records of many battles. Some we participated in, others we merely observed. I believe I know the species involved with these two helmets. If I am correct, I can match this part of the Grysk timeline with known historical events."

"Will that gain you their location?"

"It will narrow it down," Thrawn said.

"And then?" *Vader's voice perhaps holds interest, perhaps suspicion.*

"We will not attack, if that is your concern," Thrawn said. "Not with a single Star Destroyer. At any rate, our first responsibility is to seek out their local base and free the prisoners they took from Batuu."

"Those who created the disturbance in the Force."

"Yes."

"You said you would tell me who they are."

"If we take them alive, I will tell you," Thrawn said. "If not, there is no reason for you to ever know."

"I disagree," Vader said. "The matter is of interest to the Emperor. It is therefore of interest to me."

"I will reveal the secret if we free them," Thrawn said. "That is all I can do."

"*All* you can do?" *Vader's voice holds perhaps warning, perhaps outright threat.* "You have sworn loyalty to the Emperor, Admiral. Is your loyalty to him, or to your own interests?"

"The two are not incompatible, my lord."

"So you say," Vader countered. *His voice holds impatience and growing anger. His hand reaches to hook into his belt near his lightsaber.* "But you have offered no proof."

"The Emperor has great interest in the Unknown Regions, my lord," Thrawn said. "This secret is strongly connected to that interest, and to his ultimate goals in this part of space."

Vader tightens his grip on his belt. "Is that to always be your excuse,

Admiral?" Vader demanded "The Emperor and his goals? The Emperor is my master, as he is yours. Do you suggest I would betray him?"

"Not at all, my lord," Thrawn assured him.

"Then you will tell me," Vader said. "All of it."

Vader's body stance holds menace. But his hand does not move closer to his lightsaber. His voice holds threat, but it also holds self-control. "I offer a compromise, my lord," Thrawn said. "I will tell you some of the truth now, and the rest when the prisoners are recovered."

Vader remains silent for four seconds. His hand does not move in that time. "You ask a great deal of trust, Admiral," he said. *His voice holds perhaps slightly less threat.* "I will not be mocked or toyed with."

"I do not mock, my lord," Thrawn said. "When you hear the truth, you will understand my reasons and my concerns, as well as those of the Emperor."

Again, Vader is silent. But this time only for two seconds. "Very well. The Emperor has confidence in you. I will honor that confidence. For now."

"Thank you, my lord." Thrawn keyed his comlink. "Commodore Faro."

"Faro, Admiral." *Her voice holds anticipation.*

"Bring the *Chimaera* to our location," Thrawn said. "We have seventeen more Grysk prisoners, whom you will secure in the starboard ready block."

"Not the brig, sir?"

"No," Thrawn said. "I do not wish them communicating with the other Grysks."

"Yes, sir."

"You will also prepare to bring the Grysk frigate aboard for further examination," Thrawn said. "I have no doubt that its secrets will soon be ours."

"Yes, sir."

Thrawn keyed off. "And now, my lord," he said to Vader, "I will tell you all that I can."

CHAPTER 13

The TIE pilots from the starboard ready block were not happy at being ousted from their ready room and quarters so that Commodore Faro could put a bunch of Grysk prisoners there. Luckily for the pilots, they got to share their frustration with the First Legion by ousting *them* from their own hangar-side quarters.

Hangar Master Xoxtin was upset on both counts, though mainly because her routine and private little fiefdom had been disrupted. Rumor had it that she hadn't been shy about expressing that annoyance to Commodore Faro, either.

"This is ridiculous," Sergeant Aksind fumed to Kimmund as he slapped his bedroll down on the *Darkhawk*'s common room deck. "What does Thrawn think he's doing, putting them in personnel quarters instead of the *Chimaera*'s brig?"

"He said he doesn't want them taken through the ship to the brig," Kimmund said. He wasn't exactly happy with this, either. But part of

his job as the First Legion's commander was to smooth over superi-
ors' orders with his stormtroopers as best he could.

Under Vader's leadership, that often meant a *lot* of smoothing. It
hadn't always made him popular, but it *had* kept him alive.

Still, that was pretty much the way things were in the modern Imperial fleet. So many commanders were busy playing politics, or were
trying to one-up each other, or were simply petty tyrants in their own
right. Everyone else aboard those ships had little choice but to keep
their heads down and try to make it through without becoming
someone's pawn or fall guy.

Except, apparently, aboard the *Chimaera*.

There was only so much a visitor to a ship the size of a Star Destroyer could learn in the limited time Kimmund and his stormtroopers had been aboard. But even from the beginning, the attitude
of the officers and crew had struck him as unique. The ship had its
share of midlevel tyrants, certainly—Xoxtin was an obvious exam-
ple. But at the same time, none of the senior officers had the self-
centeredness of men and women looking out solely for themselves,
or the deadly inertia of people simply going through the motions.
Everyone from Faro on down seemed intent on working together to
do their jobs and complete their assigned tasks to the best of their
ability.

The reason, of course, was obvious: Thrawn.

The grand admiral was smart and subtle, but never used his bril-
liance to show up or humiliate anyone. He demanded results, but
never perfection, and had amazing stores of patience for those who
were truly working to their fullest ability. He cared about his people,
to the point of standing up for them even against the disapproval of
powerful men like Lord Vader.

Which wasn't to say he tolerated those who were lazy, or who
wasted his time, or who were simply uninterested in giving their very
best for the Empire. Kimmund had heard stories from the *Chimaera*'s
crew about how such deadweights were sent packing in short order,
usually to commanders who also weren't interested in giving their
best. On some occasions, they ended up back on Coruscant to stand

for court-martials, much to the relief of those who'd had to put up with them.

The result was telling: a degree of loyalty Kimmund had seldom seen except within the ranks of his own First Legion.

It was a pity Thrawn's style of leadership hadn't spread through the rest of the navy. Still, he was certainly having an influence on the younger officers. If he lasted long enough, maybe those lessons would someday become the military standard.

If that happened, he suspected, the Empire would stand forever.

"And the brig is, what, three whole decks farther away?" Aksind scoffed.

"The prisoners from the freighter are in there," Kimmund reminded him. "Maybe he doesn't want the two groups talking to each other."

"He should try just locking them in different sections," Aksind grumbled.

"You're welcome to rack with the others in the pilots' mess," Kimmund offered. "Has to be more comfortable than here."

"Which begs the obvious question," Aksind said, raising his eyebrows.

"Because I don't like leaving the *Darkhawk* unwatched with alien prisoners just down the corridor," Kimmund said sourly. "Like I said, you don't have to stay."

"No, that's okay," Aksind said. "Following my commanding officer into hell, death, and sore backs. Inspiration for the troops, and all that."

"I'm honored," Kimmund said. "So why in here instead of aft in your rack?"

"Because I never get enough air in there," Aksind said. "Out here, more space. Plus, if I can't sleep the game table's right there."

"Which Tephan will probably have already taken over."

"That's okay," Aksind said. "Heckling Tephan's games is almost as fun as playing myself. Speaking of whom . . ." He cupped his hands. "Tephan?" he called.

"What?" the pilot's voice came drifting from farther aft.

"You got any food going back there?"

"At *this* hour?" Tephan demanded. "Where do you think you are, Coruscant? You want a night bite, come fix it yourself."

Aksind sniffed the air. "Yeah, she's cooking something," he said. "You want a third of whatever it is?"

"I'll take a spoonful," Kimmund said drily. "Tephan's cooking isn't exactly—" He broke off, frowning, as another sound came faintly from the other direction. "You hear that?"

"A kind of soft thud?" Aksind asked, frowning back. He leaned the side of his head against the common room bulkhead. "Don't hear . . . wait a second. Sounds like someone's moving out there."

Kimmund pulled out his comlink and keyed for Tephan. "Tephan, drop what you're doing and get up here," he murmured. "Bring a couple of E-11s."

"Someone probably just forgot something," Aksind said quietly. But he was already moving forward, angling toward the side of the hatchway where he'd have some cover. Another thud came, a shade louder this time . . .

Kimmund caught his breath as a faint breeze washed past him.

Someone had opened one of the *Darkhawk*'s hatches.

There was another breath of air, and he turned to see Tephan coming up behind them, three E-11 blaster carbines cradled in her arms. "What is it?" she murmured as she handed one each to Kimmund and Aksind.

"Company," Kimmund murmured back, settling the carbine into combat position and flicking off the safety. "Don't know who yet. I'll take point, Tephan at rear."

They headed forward, moving as silently as they could. They crossed the rest of the common room and stepped through the hatchway into the midship storage compartment, a narrow passageway lined on both sides with lockers and cabinets. A bad place to be caught if there was trouble, and Kimmund hurried them forward through the hatchway at the other end and into the staging area.

The staging area, converted from the *Darkhawk*'s old cargo bay, was wider than the storage compartment, but in some ways was more cluttered. There were restraint harnesses hanging from the ceiling for troopers about to charge to the attack, a pair of long back-to-back bench seats down the center facing to the sides, and narrow equipment lockers beneath the seats. More important at the moment were the large hatches on both sides of the ship that the stormtroopers utilized for rapid deployment. If whoever their visitors were had come through there . . .

They hadn't. Both hatches were still sealed, with no sign of having been opened. "Farther forward?" Aksind murmured.

Kimmund nodded, giving the hatches one last look. There were slit viewports on both of them, and for a moment he wondered if they should pause and take a look. But the viewports' angle wouldn't let them see to the *Darkhawk*'s bow, which was where the intrusion was clearly taking place.

Of course, popping one of the hatches would let them out into the hangar, offering the option of coming up behind whoever had moved into the forward part of the ship. But with only the three of them available, flanking maneuvers were pretty much out of the question.

Leading the way around the starboard bench seat, he continued forward. Just beyond that final hatch was the short corridor that led past the forward air lock into the cockpit.

He was halfway there when the hatch slid open, and a Grysk holding an E-11 stepped through.

Kimmund had already guessed the intruders were the enemy warriors. The Grysk, on the other hand, seemed completely surprised to find himself facing an opponent.

That split second of hesitation cost him his life as Kimmund sent a pair of blaster bolts into his torso.

The small victory was short-lived. Even as the alien collapsed to the deck Kimmund could see more of them milling around behind him.

And with the flash and soprano scream of the blaster shots, the whole crowd had been alerted.

"Back!" Kimmund snapped, firing into the shadowy mass now surging toward the hatchway. He'd taken only a couple of steps backward when the shadows disappeared as the Grysks dived for cover on both sides. The stormtroopers had gotten maybe three steps more when a barrage of blasterfire erupted from both sides of the hatchway.

"Back!" Kimmund shouted again, backing up as fast as he could while still firing, forcing himself not to flinch as Aksind's and Tephan's own return fire burned past a shade too close. So far the Grysks' shots weren't all that accurate, but he had little doubt they would pick up the necessary technique with the stolen Imperial weaponry quickly enough.

Fortunately, the three stormtroopers made it back into the storage compartment by the time the Grysks' aim started to solidify. Kimmund continued to retreat, throwing open some of the cabinet doors as he passed, using them as a partial blockage against the enemy's attack and giving him and the others a few extra seconds of breathing space.

But it was a temporary ploy at best. The storage compartment was a ten-meter-long choke point, and he and the others needed to get back to the common room where they'd at least have the partial protection of the hatchway sides.

For the last few seconds it was touch and go as the Grysks found the range. But the three stormtroopers reached the common room without picking up more than a few minor burns. A second after that they were crouched by the open hatch, Kimmund and Aksind standing on opposite sides, Tephan crouching beneath Aksind. "Tephan?" Kimmund prompted as the Grysks crossed the staging area and gathered at the sides of the storage compartment's forward hatchway.

"Already tried," Tephan bit out. "They've jammed our comms."

Kimmund hissed out a curse. And now that they'd gotten through whatever security Thrawn had set up outside their makeshift cells, the only one watching over the hangar bay itself would be the duty officer. If he hadn't called in an alert by now, it meant he hadn't noticed the aliens slipping across the deck through his territory.

Which meant Kimmund and his troopers were on their own. "Okay," he said. "There should be a couple of suits in the maintenance bay. Go armor up—Aksind and I will hold them here."

"Right." Scrambling back to her feet, Tephan sprinted aft across the common room and disappeared through the hatchway.

"Whole bunch more E-11s up there," Aksind warned. "If they find them we're in trouble, armor or no armor."

"Yeah, thanks, got it," Kimmund said, trying to think. As Aksind had pointed out, the bulk of their weapons and armor were in the storage compartment and staging area, sectors either disputed or already under enemy control. All Tephan would find in the maintenance bay was a couple of suits of armor in for refurbishing, some extra power packs that were being recharged, and—if they were *extremely* lucky—maybe an E-Web heavy blaster that Elebe or Dorstren had sent back to be sighted in.

But in the *Darkhawk*'s close confines, numbers were likely to be more of a deciding factor than heavy weaponry. Even if the Grysks were willing to let things sit at a stalemate—

With a teeth-jarring sound of metal on metal two of the underseat equipment boxes from the staging area were shoved into view across the hatchway.

Kimmund's first thought was that the Grysks were trying to block the stormtroopers in, to keep them neutralized at the back of the ship. But a second later the boxes began to move as the two Grysks behind them started pushing them down the corridor.

Kimmund grimaced. Not a barrier. A moving shield.

So much for the Grysks settling for a stalemate.

Still, the boxes didn't quite fill the corridor, and there were other Grysks behind the vanguard. Kimmund shifted from barrage to sniper fire, shooting carefully and deliberately between and above the boxes, trying to hit anything back there that was unwary enough to present a target. The Grysks countered with return fire of their own around the boxes' edges. Aksind continued his own volley fire, focusing his attack on the rightmost box in an attempt to shatter it or otherwise end its usefulness as a shield.

Which would, Kimmund knew, only delay the final confrontation. Opening up one side of the corridor might allow them to nail an additional Grysk or two before the others could retreat, but there were another six under-seat boxes the enemy could move in as replacement shields.

And then, midway between the stormtroopers and the Grysks, one of the storage cabinet doors opened a crack, then closed.

Kimmund's first thought was that he'd imagined it. His second thought was that the blasterfire had somehow popped the catch.

But that wouldn't explain how the door had closed again.

Then, even as he tried to get his mind back on focus, it happened again: The door swung open just enough for him to see the crack, then closed again.

He caught his breath. That cabinet, if he was visualizing the *Darkhawk* correctly, was back-to-back with one of the ship's outside weapons lockers. One of the *large* weapons lockers . . .

The Grysks were still on the move, pushing their way slowly down the corridor behind their shields. A little *too* slowly, Kimmund decided.

Well, he could fix that. "Fall back," he ordered Aksind. "Regroup at the galley hatch."

"What?" Aksind asked, sounding confused.

"You heard me," Kimmund said. "Go—I'll cover you."

"Right." Pushing away from the bulkhead, Aksind backed his way across the common room, continuing to fire. Kimmund gave him a five-count, then fell back as well, also still firing.

The Grysks weren't fooled. Despite the continuing blasterfire, they could see that the stormtroopers were retreating. Their suppression fire around the box edges intensified, and the metal-on-metal screeching grew louder as they picked up their pace, pushing rapidly forward in the hope of catching the stormtroopers in the open before they could reach the next defensive point.

There was a good chance they would make it, too. The moving shield had passed the self-opening cabinet now, with maybe three meters to go before the Grysks behind it reached the end of the corridor. Behind him, Kimmund heard Aksind gasp and swear as one of the Grysk shots got him—

Abruptly, the Grysk advance stopped. There were two more wild shots, and then their blasters fell silent. Kimmund stopped firing. There was a single muffled scream, followed by a pair of thuds.

And then, nothing.

"Damn it," a filtered voice came from behind him. He looked back at Tephan, now fully armored, as she crouched down beside Aksind's body.

"Dead?" Kimmund asked.

"Yeah," Tephan said, straightening up. "You get the rest of them?"

"*I* didn't, no," Kimmund said. "You remember that secret back door to the ship, the one we were never able to find?"

"What?" Tephan said, sounding a little bewildered.

"Well, I think we just did," Kimmund said.

And right on cue, one of the Grysks' shields toppled forward onto the deck.

Standing behind it, a fighting stick swinging casually in each hand as he stood among the dead or unconscious Grysks, was Rukh.

"What the hell?" Tephan growled. "I thought you kicked him off the ship."

"Special occasion," Kimmund said. Lowering his E-11, he hurried toward the Noghri. "Welcome aboard. How did you know?"

"I saw blasterfire through the hatch viewports," Rukh said. His eyes flicked to Aksind's body, and Kimmund thought the Noghri's expression hardened a little. "I thought you might need help."

"Certainly aren't going to turn it down," Kimmund agreed, peering over Rukh's shoulder. There were six Grysks laid out along the storage compartment deck, a combination of Rukh's sneak attack on their rear plus the stormtroopers' earlier fire between the shields. The ends of the Noghri's fighting sticks had a bit of a glow to them— probably they were the halves of his usual electrostaff weapon—but even without that boost Kimmund had no doubt Thrawn's body-guard would have handled his opponents just fine.

So: six here, add in the three or four he and the other stormtroopers had taken out in that first exchange . . . "I figure there are seven or eight left up front," he said. "Maybe as many as eleven if they brought the freighter prisoners with them."

"I didn't count numbers," Rukh said. "But I saw some in the cockpit, standing over the control boards."

"Trying to figure out how to fly it," Kimmund said grimly.

"Oh, no they don't," Tephan growled. "They are *not* taking my ship."

"No, they're not," Kimmund said, coming to a quick decision. Until the Grysks up front realized their force back here had been taken out, the Imperials had the element of surprise. Played right, that was worth half a squad of fully armored stormtroopers any day. "We hit them hard—right now, full-bore, all-out."

"While they're waiting for their friends to come back and report our deaths," Tephan said. "Okay. Let's do it."

"What do you want me to do?" Rukh asked.

Kimmund frowned at him. "So *now* you're taking orders from me?"

"I always took your orders." Rukh waved a stick around to encompass the *Darkhawk*. "First Legion ship. First Legion orders. Otherwise I would have come out for the freighter attack whether you said no or not."

"That would have been nice to know sooner," Tephan muttered.

"Well, we know it now," Kimmund said. "You have your personal cloaking device with you?"

"No," Rukh said. "But I won't need it."

"Probably not," Kimmund said. "Okay. We'll go in hot, keeping our fire high. You go in low wherever you get an opening and make as much of a mess as you can."

Rukh gave an evil grin, spinning one of his fighting sticks deftly across his fingers. "I can make a great deal of mess," he promised.

"We'll make it together," Kimmund said. "And remember we want to come out of this with the ship still flyable. Lord Vader might want us to use it again someday."

From the time the seventeen Grysks escaped from their makeshift cell to the time they boarded the *Darkhawk* was approximately four minutes. From then until Commander Kimmund and his forces re-captured the ship was approximately eight minutes. Returning the surviving prisoners—four of them—took another ten minutes. All told, the entire incident covered less than half an hour.

And there was every indication, Faro thought bleakly, that the death and destruction had only just begun.

Grand Admiral Thrawn normally dominated every room he was in. Not this time. He normally carried an air of calmness that extended out to all those around him. Not this time. He always seemed to be in complete control of everything.

Not this time. Standing here in the cramped space of the *Dark-hawk*'s cockpit, facing Lord Vader from barely thirty centimeters away, he seemed small and helpless, a man who was facing death itself.

And yet, there he stood.

"Commander Kimmund cannot be blamed for his actions," Thrawn said, gazing calmly up at the faceless black helmet. "On the contrary, his actions and those of his stormtroopers were exemplary."

"Which does not change the fact that they ruined the entire plan," Vader ground out.

"I warned you that keeping the secret of the prisoners' marginal imprisonment and the homing beacons could have unwanted consequences," Thrawn said.

"It was necessary for the *Chimaera*'s crew to behave as normal," Vader countered. Astonishing as it was to Faro that Thrawn was chiding the Dark Lord, it was even more astonishing that Vader was actually standing still for it. "The prisoners needed to believe their escape was genuine."

"I don't disagree," Thrawn said. "I merely suggest that a middle ground might have been taken. Commander Kimmund, at least, should have been brought into our confidence, as well as any troopers or stormtroopers who stood between the prisoners' cells and their frigate."

Vader didn't respond. But then, really, there wasn't much he could say.

Faro had been at the private meeting where Vader had proposed this plan. Thrawn had agreed, and in fact had added a few small suggestions. Neither of them could have known that Kimmund and his stormtroopers would unknowingly get in the way.

They certainly couldn't have known that Hangar Master Xoxtin would choose to send three off-duty crewmembers across that precise section right when the Grysks made their break.

Xoxtin was furious. For once, Faro didn't blame her.

Four dead . . . and with nothing to show for it.

The *Chimaera*'s techs had made a thorough search of the *Darkhawk*'s computer. It showed only the route from the Grysks' hunting ground back to Batuu, where they'd apparently been based, without referencing any other systems. Thrawn's analysis of everything artistic aboard their ship had yielded some interesting points, but gained them nothing about the Grysks' local base.

"Still, even a partial success can bring long-reaching results," Thrawn said into the awkward silence. "As it is, we have now learned a great deal about our new enemies."

"Such as the fact they have no teeth?" Vader said with an edge of bitterness.

"That, as well," Thrawn agreed. "Removing a warrior's teeth and replacing them with upper and lower moldings that contain break-apart weapons, communicators, and lock-breakers is quite ingenious. The ultrasonic signals they sent to their colleagues through the metal bulkheads is also a technology that could be of future use to the Empire."

"None of which has brought us closer to our goal."

"Actually, my lord, I believe it has." Thrawn turned to Faro. "Commodore, you have the record of the communications between the two groups of prisoners. How much information do you estimate could have been passed during that time?"

Faro started. She'd been hoping against hope that Thrawn had brought her into the cockpit solely to serve as a witness to the conversation. As she'd watched Vader's menace continue to darken she'd further hoped her presence would be mostly forgotten.

Instead, Thrawn had just dropped a conversational grenade in her lap.

How in the world was she supposed to answer such a question? "They were in communication, back and forth, a total of two minutes and eight seconds," she said. "We can't tell right now which signal originated from which group of prisoners. Also, without knowing the encryption method they were using—or even their language, for that matter—it's impossible to know how much they could have said."

"Understood," Thrawn said. "So let us assume clear language, with whatever coding they used for the speech but without any encryption to burden or lengthen the message. Under those parameters, what information could *you* transfer in that time?"

Faro felt her throat tighten. Normally, she didn't mind Thrawn's mind games. They helped her stretch her thinking, and anything that made her a better officer was worth seeking out.

But to do it here and now? Especially with Vader on the verge of wrecking the whole place?

The whole place.

She looked around the cockpit with new eyes. Having this conversation aboard the *Darkhawk* had been Thrawn's idea, not Vader's. And Thrawn never did anything without a reason.

She turned back to Thrawn. The admiral had a small smile on his face, the indication that he was once again comfortably ahead of her. "I could tell the Grysk warriors about this ship," she said. "A brief description, plus where it was located in the hangar bay."

"And instructions on how to fly it?" Thrawn prompted.

"No, sir," Faro said firmly. "Not in two minutes. Not a chance."

"Thank you, Commodore," Thrawn said, inclining his head to her and then turning back to Vader. "Your personal shuttle was closer to their prison. Their own frigate was farther, but with the advantage that they knew how to fly it. Yet they chose the *Darkhawk*."

He gestured to the control board. "More than that, we see that they had already activated the engines and begun the preflight sequence when they were stopped."

He paused, apparently waiting for Vader to speak. But the Dark Lord stood silently, gazing at the board.

"The *Darkhawk* is equipped with modern weapons and equipment," Thrawn said. "The prisoners from the Grysk freighter had seen it in combat and knew it would be a prize worth capturing. But at the same time, it is at heart a relic of the Clone War. And there is only one place in this region where they could have studied this type of freighter and learned how to operate it."

Vader rumbled something under his breath. "Mokivj."

"Indeed, my lord," Thrawn said. "More specifically, the Separatist factory on Mokivj that we once assaulted."

Vader straightened to his full height. "That *you* once assaulted," he corrected. "No one else aboard the *Chimaera* was ever there."

"Of course," Thrawn said, inclining his head. "I misspoke."

For a long moment, they gazed at each other in silence. Faro found herself holding her breath, feeling a fresh edge of tension crackling through the room. There was something going on here, something deep beneath the surface.

Only she had no idea what it was.

"You are the commander," Vader said at last. "If you believe this factory is the key, that is where we shall begin."

"Thank you, my lord." Thrawn again turned to Faro. "Commodore, prepare a course for Mokivj. We leave in two hours."

"Yes, sir," Faro said.

"That will give you time, my lord," Thrawn added, looking at Vader, "to speak with the remaining prisoners. If you so choose."

"Indeed, Admiral," Vader rumbled in a voice that sent a fresh chill up Faro's back. "You have uncovered some of their secrets. *I* will uncover the rest."

CHAPTER 14

Padmé wasted another twenty minutes searching through every inch of the factory's west wing, all three floors, in search of something useful the previous occupants might have left behind. But the entire place had been cleaned, down to the bone.

The low barriers that marked out the space in LebJau's old work area, however, were held in place by metal uprights: sturdy metal rods, hollow, with square cross sections five centimeters across. On one of the uprights the fasteners were loose enough that she was able to carefully work them the rest of the way out with her fingernails. Once she had one bar free, she was able to use its end to unscrew others.

Even with that to help her many of the fasteners were still too tight to work free. But in the end she was able to gather twenty-three of the rods.

It cost all twenty-three of them, broken or bent, to lever the trapdoor lid far enough for her to squeeze back through it.

She didn't know exactly where the corresponding trapdoor into the south wing was located, but if the access points had been laid out symmetrically she should be able to find it. After that, the next task would be getting it open. Hopefully, LebJau's comment about how heavy the lids were without power meant that the south wing's lids *did* have power, and that the controls were someplace where Padmé could get to them. If not, she was going to have to get creative.

From the confident manner in which LebJau had walked through the service level she gathered the droids didn't come down here very often, if at all. But it wasn't an assumption she was willing to bet her life on. She used her glow rod sparingly as she worked her way across the permacrete floor, keeping it on its lowest setting and only flicking it on for a half second or so every dozen steps, just to make sure she wasn't heading straight toward a pillar or a pile of debris. Better to err on the side of caution.

It was just as well she did. She was halfway back to the spot where she and LebJau had entered when she spotted a faint glow in the distance.

She froze, pressing against the pillar beside her, straining her eyes and ears. The glow was still there, moving slightly with the rhythm of someone walking. She couldn't hear anything, but the light was far enough away that even soft voices would probably be inaudible.

Soft voices, or the muffled clank of droid feet on permacrete.

So: either LebJau or his friends heading back to the south wing, or a battle droid patrol that would ultimately return to the east wing. Either way, it was a direction she needed to go. Taking a deep breath, she headed off toward it, using her own light even more sparingly.

She had nearly caught up when the light suddenly stopped and swiveled upward. Padmé slowed her pace, and a few seconds later she felt the familiar puff of air that marked a trapdoor lid opening.

And now, finally, she was close enough to hear a pair of muffled human voices as the figures climbed the ladder. The lid closed, and darkness and silence returned.

Padmé hurried forward, using her light openly now. Ahead, she could see the cone and the ladder with the lid above. She rounded the last pillar—

And nearly dropped her light as a pair of arms snaked around her shoulders and yanked her back against a hard, muscled torso. The arms twisted up and to her right, trying to throw her to the ground, while a knee jabbed hard into the back of her right knee, further threatening her balance. "Whoever you are—" a voice muttered in her ear.

And broke off as Padmé snatched her blaster from her hip holster, twisted it around and over her left shoulder, and pressed the muzzle against his throat. "You should let go now," she murmured back.

His whole body twitched, his arms loosening but not completely letting go. "*Padmé?*"

"Yes, Huga," she confirmed, recognizing his voice now. "I mean it. Let go."

This time, finally, his arms fell away. Padmé stepped forward and turned around, leveling both her blaster and her glow rod at him. "How was the fishing tonight?" she asked.

His eyes had gone wide, his mouth hanging open. "How did you get in here?" he demanded.

Above her, the trapdoor lid swung open. "Did you get him?" Cimy's voice came from above.

"Sort of," Padmé called back.

"*Padmé?*" Cimy gasped. "But you're outside."

"Not anymore," Huga growled. "LebJau did this, didn't he? He let you in. *Frost* that idiot—he's going to wreck everything." He jabbed a finger in the direction of their secret exit. "Get out. Now."

"Not yet," Padmé said. "I need your help."

"I don't care," Huga bit out. "You need to get out before the metal-heads catch you."

Padmé felt her stomach tighten. So the droids *did* come down here? "Not yet," she repeated. She had a sudden inspiration—"Uncle Anakin's here," she said. "But he's in the droid section—"

"He's *here*?" Cimy cut her off. "Already? That's great!"

"Has he got our money?" Huga added.

"Of course," Padmé said. Anakin was bound to have at least a *little* money with him. "I just need a couple of things to get in there and get him out."

"Yeah, but you can't do that," Cimy said, his enthusiasm fading. "Get in, I mean."

"He's right," Huga said, eyeing her blaster. "Unless you're planning on shooting your way in."

"I think we can come up with something a little more promising," Padmé assured him. "Where's LebJau? We can use his help on this."

"He's up in the barracks," Huga said, his voice going suddenly casual. "But we can do this without him."

In other words, a two-way split of the reward was better than a three-way split? "Fine," she said. "I'll need to borrow some clothes from one of the women—these aren't exactly local," she added, waving toward her outfit. "Then I'll need to get hold of one of those wristbands."

"We don't have any spares," Cimy said. "And once they're off, they don't go back on."

"Really," Padmé said. "How do you know?"

There was a moment of awkward silence. "One of the workers died a few weeks ago," Cimy said at last. "We thought we could bring someone else in and give them his job. But we couldn't get the ends to match up right."

"You couldn't just glue it?"

"We tried," Huga said grimly. "The first metalhead who checked it could tell it was stolen. Or maybe that it was on the wrong person— I don't know which. Beppi tried to run, and it shot him."

Padmé felt her throat tighten. "I'm sorry."

"We've still got it," Cimy offered. "They gave us back the body to bury, and we took the wristband. But it's useless."

"You think we can take this conversation upstairs?" Huga asked, glancing nervously around. "We're not supposed to be down here."

"Certainly," Padmé said. "You can start by finding me some new clothes. After that, I want to see this useless wristband."

Anakin had told Thrawn they would wait two hours before breaking out of their cells. In fact, though, practically from the moment Solha and his entourage left he'd been working out how exactly he was going to do that.

Now, with the two hours gone, he was no closer to finding a way than he'd been at the start.

The door was solid. The dowel pins were wedged in, and just outside his view through the door. Without being able to see them he couldn't get a solid enough grip through the Force to pry them loose. The cell walls seemed old, and for a while he'd hoped he could start at one of the ventilation slits and tear away bits and pieces until he had a hole big enough to squeeze through. But the material had been glazed around the openings, and again he couldn't get enough of a grip on the edges. The cot was too flimsy to use as a prybar, and too light to make an effective missile.

"Interesting structures," Thrawn's voice came from the next cell, echoing oddly off the hard surfaces. "I wonder what they used to store in here."

"Hadn't really thought about it," Anakin said shortly, stretching out a hand toward the door for focus. If he used the Force to pull, and then immediately to push . . .

No good. A trick like that required a certain amount of slack in the fit, with a chance to build up momentum in one direction before abruptly sending the door in the other. But the fit here was well-nigh perfect, with no more than a millimeter's worth of give. Not nearly enough.

"The two hours are over."

"Yes, I know," Anakin growled back, looking around the cell yet again. Still nothing.

"Have you found an exit?"

"No," Anakin admitted between clenched teeth. "But don't worry—I'll figure out something."

"Perhaps this will help."

Frowning, Anakin looked over toward the other cell.

And watched in amazement as a thick, two-meter-long cord slithered through the air vent and landed in a heap on the floor.

"Where'd you get this?" he asked as he stepped over and picked it up. It was made of thin strips of cloth, braided together, with a slip-knot at one end.

"I made it from the fibers of my clothing," Thrawn said.

"Nice," Anakin said. He'd heard the muffled sound of tearing early on in their imprisonment, but the outfits they'd taken from the *Larkrer* were a little tight and he'd assumed Thrawn was just making himself more comfortable.

"Since the dowel pins are tapered, I thought you could perhaps loop it over the tops and remove them."

"Worth a shot. Hang on."

Anakin took the cord to the door and carefully fed it through the vent opening. It was long enough for him to hold on to one end as he lowered the other to the left-hand dowel. It didn't need to be that long, of course; either Thrawn had forgotten he could manipulate a shorter cord with the Force or else the Chiss was just being thorough. He worked the slipknot over the dowel, pulled the cord gently to tighten the loop, and gave a careful pull.

Nothing. He pulled a little harder, easing a bit more muscle into the task, painfully aware that a makeshift cord like this could only take so much strain before it broke. But the dowel pin was too tightly wedged.

"Perhaps if you try to oscillate the door you can loosen it," Thrawn suggested.

Anakin smiled. No; not oscillate.

Lubricate.

"You have another strip of cloth handy?" he asked. "Doesn't have to be big."

"Will this do?" A ragged square of cloth, maybe five centimeters on a side, popped through the vent and fluttered toward the floor.

"Perfect," Anakin said, catching it in midair with the Force and sending it through the vent in his door. Holding out a hand to focus his mind, he eased it to the floor outside his prison.

Into the first drop of oil R2-D2 had left behind.

He let the cloth soak up the whole drop, then moved it to the next, and the next, as far down the corridor as he could see. Then, bringing the now wet rag back, he eased it against the dowel pin below the slipknot. He wiggled the door once, then again pulled gently on the cord.

And with that final tug, the pin came free.

"Got it," he told Thrawn as the pin swung on the cord into his view. He pulled the slipknot off the pin and shifted the cord and the oil cloth to the dowel on the other side of the door. Thirty seconds later, he was free.

"Excellent," Thrawn said.

"Couldn't have done it without you," Anakin said, carefully pushing the door open and looking down the passageway.

The fact that no one had interrupted him during his door work suggested that Solha hadn't left any droids on guard duty inside the room. He was right—the passageway was empty, the single door at the end closed.

Still, he doubted their captor had been careless enough to leave them completely unguarded. That meant droids outside the door, and he had no way of knowing what types or how many of them there were.

Time to remedy that.

"Get ready," he told Thrawn, setting his palms against the door. "It's about to get a little noisy in here."

The first woman they found who was the right size was already fast asleep. Huga didn't bother to wake her, but simply helped himself to her spare robe, sash, and boots and handed them to Padmé. Their next stop was more dark-edged: the unused corner where the former possessions of workers who had died were stored.

"Do people often die here?" she asked as she dressed. The worker's robe was rough and smelled of sweat. But of course, so did she.

"One time each," Huga said shortly as Cimy sifted through the mass of castoffs. "Come on, come on."

"It was worse at the beginning," Cimy said as Padmé knotted the sash around her waist. "Their leader, Duke Solha, pushed everyone—"

"Duke *Solha*?" Padmé interrupted, feeling her eyes go wide. "Solha is here?"

"You know him?" Huga asked, his voice suddenly heavy with suspicion.

"I met him once," Padmé said, thinking back to one of those pre-war diplomatic excursions that had sometimes seemed to be the bulk of her job as a senator. "A long time ago."

"Long enough that he won't recognize you?" Huga pressed. "Because if he's going to know you, we're bailing right now."

"I'll be fine," Padmé assured him. "Let's just get in there, okay?"

"Hey, *I'm* not the one holding things up," Huga growled. "Cimy, you've got ten seconds to find that thing, or I swear—"

"It's here, it's here," Cimy growled back. "Give me a second. Anyway, Duke Solha pushed everyone too hard. Mostly lifting and carrying, and sometimes just too much weight."

"I'm sorry," Padmé murmured.

"It's better now," Huga said. "Ah—finally."

"This is it," Cimy said, getting back to his feet and offering Padmé the discarded wristband. "But like Huga said earlier, we couldn't glue it."

"I'm not surprised," Padmé said, peering at the wristband in the light of her glow rod. It was simple, thin plastoid, bright yellow, with a couple of barely visible wires running through the edges. "There's an induction loop embedded in the material. If the ends aren't lined up right, or if there's glue or something blocking the circuit, it won't give the right echo when it's sparked."

"Could we overlap and use tape or something?" Cimy asked.

"Ordinary tape won't stick to this well enough," Padmé said. "And you'd have to make sure the circuit ends were solidly together."

"So what are you doing to do?" Huga asked.

Padmé pursed her lips. It was risky, but at the moment it was all she could come up with. "There are some metalheads patrolling this wing, right?"

"A few," Huga said. "Mostly at the edges, to keep us from wandering off."

"Do they patrol singly or in pairs?"

"Singly, most of them," Huga said.

"The ones guarding the doors into the east wing are in pairs," Cimy added.

"She didn't ask about the door guards, dummy," Huga admonished him.

"No, I need to know about those, too," Padmé said. "You said you were in a work crew. Does it have a name or numerical designation?"

"A numeri—what?" Cimy asked.

"She means a number for all of us," Huga said. "Yeah, we're Maintenance Crew Herf Two. So what are you going to do?"

"Kill two birds with one rock," Padmé said, wrapping the band loosely around her left wrist. She slipped her S-5 blaster into one of the robe's side pockets and tucked the more compact ELG-3A into the sash at the small of her back, where it would be mostly out of sight but easily accessible. "Let's go find one of the singles."

Anakin pushed the door open about a meter, then released it and jumped back into his cell, letting the door crash shut.

The thud was quieter than he'd expected it to be. But it should be loud enough. If it wasn't, he'd just have to try again.

"If you expect the guards to come in, bear in mind there's little I can do while still locked in," Thrawn warned.

"That's okay," Anakin said. "All you need to do is sit back and enjoy the show."

Padmé's plan had assumed that, with a Jedi supposedly running loose, Duke Solha would have patrols all over the factory.

But he didn't. As she and her two companions headed toward the east wing they saw no one. For all appearances, Solha might have barricaded himself into his stronghold in the hope that the Jedi would eventually give up and go away.

Still, that didn't mean he'd left the approaches to that stronghold unguarded. They rounded one final corner to find two B1 battle droids flanking a solid-looking door, their E-5 blasters leveled.

"Halt!" one of them called as the three humans appeared. "Where are you going?"

"What do we do?" Cimy whispered from beside Padmé. "You said we needed just *one* metalhead."

"Don't worry, we'll make it work," she whispered back. Squaring her shoulders, she started toward the droids. "Maintenance Crew Herf Two," she called. "Got an order to come clean something on the first floor."

The droids looked at each other. "We were not alerted," the first droid said. "Who gave you this order?"

"One of the others," Padmé said, continuing to walk forward. "I don't know which one—you all look alike."

"Where is your wristband?" the second droid said.

"Right here," Padmé said. She stopped in front of him and pushed back the sleeve of her robe, revealing the band balanced across her wrist.

"It is not correct," the droid said. It lifted its blaster to point at her chest. "You will come with me for examination."

"What about them?" Padmé asked, beckoning toward Huga and Cimy with her right hand. "We have a job to do, remember?"

"They will wait here," the first droid ordered, waving its blaster back and forth between them for emphasis. "I will call for a supervisor."

"Okay, but we were told to rush it," Padmé said. She started walking again, watching both droids out of the corners of her eyes. The first continued to hold his E-5 on the two men as it popped the lock on the door. The second swiveled toward Padmé as she passed, its blaster tracking her movement, clearly intending to let her go by and then fall in behind her. She stepped directly between the droids—

Abruptly, she stopped. For an instant the second droid's blaster tracked past her, out of alignment with her body—

And sweeping the blaster with her left forearm to keep it pointed away, she snatched the ELG from her sash, jammed the barrel up under the droid's long chin to the intersection of head and neck, and fired.

The droid went limp, its processor vaporized. Padmé didn't wait to see it fall, but spun around to face the other droid. It was trying to bring its own blaster to bear, but the weapon was too far out of line. Before it could swing the blaster even halfway around, she delivered her second kill shot.

In the silence, the double clatter as the B1s collapsed to the floor seemed to boom. The noise half covered Huga's startled curse. "Are they dead?" Cimy asked, sounding awed. "I didn't know you could do that."

"You need a blaster with enough punch," Padmé told him, crouching down beside the second droid. Her shot had burned straight through the top of its head, leaving a smoking, red-edged hole. "Come here and give me a hand."

"What do you need?" Cimy asked, gingerly dropping to one knee beside her.

"Hold the other end," she said, taking one end of her wristband and pointing a finger at the other end. "Get a grip a couple of centimeters back. Now hold it steady."

Carefully, Padmé touched her end to his, making sure the thin wires of the induction loop were lined up. Then, holding the ends together, she laid the plastoid against the glowing edge of the blaster hole.

"I'll be krinked," Huga muttered as he watched over her shoulder. "Is that going to work?"

"We're about to find out," Padmé said, sniffing the air. There was the faint smell of scorched plastoid. "Let's ease it back . . . go ahead and let go, Cimy."

He did so, and Padmé lifted her wrist for a closer look. "Seems okay. We'll find out inside if I got it right."

"Whoa," Huga said. "What do you mean, *we'll* find out? Cimy and I aren't going in there."

"I thought you were going to help me get Anakin out," Padmé said as she stood up.

"We were helping you get in," Huga said. "We're not going in there without orders." He nudged one of the droids with his toe. "Not after this."

Padmé looked at Cimy. "Cimy?"

"Sorry," he said. "I'm with Huga on this one."

"I understand," Padmé said, feeling a twinge of guilt. These were just normal people, trying to live their lives and survive under the Separatists' thumb. Now, because of her, they were having to put their lives and the lives of their friends at serious risk. "Where exactly are these Bins?"

"The cells?" Cimy pointed at the door. "Inside, turn left, and the outer entrance door is in a plain permacrete wall about fifty meters in and on your right."

"Thanks," Padmé said. "One other favor. Would you find LebJau and tell him where I've gone?"

Huga snorted. "Why, because he still believes there's a reward?"

"What do you mean?" Padmé asked. "I promised."

"That was when you needed to let your uncle know where to find you," Huga said. "But he's here *now*, before he ever got your messages, so I guess he found you all right on his own. So tell me he can see the future and knew to bring money with him. Go ahead—tell me."

Padmé sighed. Putting their lives on the line *and* now convinced there would be nothing to show for it. "Just tell LebJau," she said. "And don't worry—I *will* get you your money."

The door the B1s had been guarding had relocked itself sometime during the past couple of minutes. But as LebJau had suggested, her newly restored wristband clicked off the lock as she approached, allowing her to push it open and slip through. Tucking the ELG back behind her sash and pulling out the more powerful S-5, she opened the door and slipped inside.

There was a distant thud, a subtle puff of air through the ventilation slits on Anakin's door, and the soft clatter of rushing droid feet.

The guards had arrived.

"Hurry!" Anakin said, loudly enough for the droids to hear, softly enough for them to think he was talking to Thrawn or someone else. "They're coming!"

He braced himself . . . and then, there they were: two B1s, their

E-5s raised, rushing forward to see what had made the noise they'd heard from outside. They reached the cell doors—

And stopped, their heads turning back and forth in confusion.

And as they stood there, Anakin stretched out to the Force and shoved the first droid backward across the narrow passageway, slamming it hard into the permacrete wall behind it. The second droid managed to get its blaster up and aimed before Anakin smashed it into another tangled heap beside the first.

"Impressive," Thrawn said.

"Thanks," Anakin said, pushing open the door and stepping into the passageway. One of the E-5s had been damaged when the droid holding it had hit the wall; picking up the other one, he leveled it at the distant cell block door. If the commotion had been heard, they could be getting company any moment.

But the passageway was empty, the door at the far end having apparently closed by itself behind the droids. That wouldn't last, he knew, but at least they should have a little breathing space. "Looks clear," he said, keeping an eye on the door as he stepped to Thrawn's cell and pulled out the dowel pins.

"Thank you," Thrawn said. "The stories we tell of Jedi don't do you full justice."

"We'll try to send you back with some fresh material," Anakin said as the Chiss pushed up the door and slipped out of his cell. "Okay. First job is to get my lightsaber back. After that we'll take a look around and figure out what Solha and his friends are doing."

"Have you a plan to retrieve your weapon?" Thrawn asked as they headed toward the door.

"Not really," Anakin said. "It'll probably depend on how easy it is to get up on the roof. I set it right next to one of the floodlights, so it shouldn't have been noticed by any of the vulture droids."

"We'll hope there are no rooftop foot patrols."

"I didn't see anyone up there on our way in."

"There was no Jedi on the loose then."

"Point," Anakin conceded. "We'll figure it out." He pulled open the door.

The first thing he saw was the blaster leveled at him from barely a meter away. The second thing he saw, above the blaster—

"Ani!" Padmé said, her eyes going wide, her lips parting in a relieved smile. "Are you all right?"

"I'm fine," Anakin assured her, turning his blaster away from her. Focused on the problem of his lightsaber, he'd completely missed her approach. "Are *you* all right?"

"I'm fine," she said. She started forward, her arms opening for a hug—

"This is Thrawn," Anakin said, twitching a hand in warning. "He's here to help me find you. Oh, and he speaks Meese Caulf."

"Ah," Padmé said, her arms dropping quickly as she peered past Anakin's shoulder. "Thank you," she added in Meese Caulf.

"My pleasure," Thrawn said gravely. "You, obviously, are Ambassador Padmé. Is that a grappling hook on your weapon?"

Padmé looked down at her blaster, a flicker of surprise crossing her face. But then, she was new to Thrawn's observational skills. "Yes," she said. "It's a combination blaster and ascension gun."

"Then the plan is obvious," Thrawn said. "You and I will travel to the rooftop to retrieve General Skywalker's lightsaber. He'll remain here and draw enemy attention away from us."

"Wait a minute," Anakin said, frowning. "*You* and Padmé? Wouldn't it make more sense for *me* to go up and get it?"

"We cannot create nearly as wide-ranging a diversion as you can," Thrawn pointed out.

Abruptly, somewhere in the distance, an alarm began to sound. "Well, *that's* going to wake them up," Anakin said. He *really* didn't like the idea of letting Padmé go off alone with the Chiss.

But he was right. With the Force allowing Anakin to throw objects and even fire blasters from a distance, he could make the Separatists think they were facing a whole army. Even Padmé and Thrawn together couldn't do that.

And it wasn't like Padmé couldn't take care of herself. "Fine," he growled. "If Padmé's okay with it."

"No problem," Padmé said, eyeing Thrawn thoughtfully. "I've

been told there's a massive assembly line taking up the first and second floor just down the hall. Stairway's right behind me."

"I'll check it out," Anakin said, taking her arm and turning her back out of the doorway. "We'll go up together, and then you can head to the roof."

"We'll do better to go out the hole in the south wing service level," Padmé said. "There are a couple of trapdoors leading down from that wing that the locals use to sneak in and out. I don't think the droids know about the hole, and we can go up the outside of the building and get to your lightsaber. It's on top of the east wing, right?"

"Yes, next to one of the floodlights," Anakin said. It was all he could do to keep from taking her in his arms . . . but Thrawn was here, and the Chiss already was suspicious of their relationship.

Though why Anakin should even care about that he didn't know. It wasn't like Thrawn would ever go to Coruscant and tell anyone.

"We'll bring it to you," Padmé promised. "Second floor of the assembly line?"

Anakin nodded. Trust Padmé to quickly grasp all the details and their tactical significance. The second floor of a two-floor operation would give him the best overall view, and launching an attack at the assembly line itself was his best guarantee of keeping Duke Solha from looking anywhere else in his little kingdom. "I'll be doing a one-man Marg Sabl."

"Sounds good," Padmé said. "Be careful." Her hand twitched, as if she, too, was fighting the urge for a quick hug. Then she turned and hurried away.

Anakin caught Thrawn's arm as he started to follow. "Protect her," he said quietly, handing him the droid's E-5.

"I will," the Chiss promised.

And then they were gone.

Over the still-warbling alarm Anakin could hear the sounds of voices and hurrying footsteps. Taking a deep breath, forcing himself to hand Padmé's life and safety to the Force, he prepared for combat.

CHAPTER 15

Padmé and Thrawn had passed the two downed droids and were halfway to the trapdoor she was aiming for when LebJau suddenly appeared around a corner in front of them.

"Look out!" the big man called, leaping toward her.

"It's all right," Padmé said quickly, holding her left hand palm-outward toward him and lifting her blaster, muzzle-up, in front of Thrawn. The last thing she wanted was a battle between two allies, especially with her in the middle. "He's a friend."

"Doesn't look like a friend to me," LebJau rumbled. "*Or an uncle.*"

"He's a friend of Uncle Anakin's," Padmé said. "Listen, I've got a job for you. This place is about to get very unhealthy. I need you to wake up everyone and get them out of here."

"What?" LebJau asked. "What are you talking about?" His eyes narrowed. "What are you planning?"

"I'm sorry, but I'm afraid we need to take this factory down," Padmé said. "I need you to get everyone to the river—"

"No," LebJau bit out, bunching his hands into fists. "This is *our* factory. *Our* jobs. *Our* world. You can't just come in here and—frost it, Padmé, this isn't fair. It isn't *right*."

"Let me explain your choices," Thrawn put in. "Your factory is going to be destroyed. That is not negotiable."

"Who do you think you—?"

"Your only options," Thrawn continued, "are to watch that destruction from a distance, or to watch it from the inside."

A shiver ran up Padmé's back. Thrawn's voice had been measured, without emotion or emphasis. But there was a strength behind it, and an absolute conviction, that she'd seldom heard even in the most passionate Senate speeches.

LebJau heard that conviction, too. He swallowed, looked furtively at Padmé, then gave a reluctant nod. "All right," he said, his voice shaking a little. "I just—how long do I have."

"We'll give you all we can," Thrawn said. "But understand that we're not fully in command of that timing."

"Just go," Padmé added. "Please."

LebJau's lips compressed briefly. Then he nodded again and hurried away.

"Where's this trapdoor you spoke of?" Thrawn asked. His tone, Padmé noticed with another shiver, hadn't changed.

"This way," she said, continuing on. "Are you really planning to destroy the whole factory?"

"That's a decision for you and General Skywalker," Thrawn said. "This is your war. These are your enemies. But the workers need to be prepared for the worst."

"I suppose," Padmé said. Put in that light, it didn't sound nearly as heartless.

But the voice and the tone still nagged at her.

"Here," she said, stopping beside the trapdoor.

"Is this where you came up?" Thrawn asked, crouching down for a closer look at the lid.

"No, I came up through the one at the other end of this wing," Padmé said. "But this one's closer. *If* we can get it open."

"Let's find out."

Laying down his E-5, he got a grip on the lid and pulled upward. To Padmé's relief, it opened without trouble or even a noticeable squeak. "This one's been used recently," he said, retrieving the blaster and peering down the opening. "Have you a light?"

"Right here," Padmé said, pulling out her glow rod and offering it to him.

He made no move to take it. "You know the route," he pointed out. "You lead."

"Fine," Padmé said, making a face as she got a grip on the ladder and started down. Again, not unreasonable. But having an armed unknown at her back didn't exactly help with her already high sense of vulnerability.

Still, Anakin vouched for him. That counted for a lot.

Once again, the service level seemed deserted. With Thrawn behind her, Padmé led the way toward LebJau's secret exit, feeling a little strange about the lack of opposition. Earlier, she'd speculated that Duke Solha might have barricaded himself in with his main assembly line. If that was true, she may have just sent Anakin into the dead center of a droid army. Alone, and without even his lightsaber.

"What's a Marg Sabl?"

Padmé blinked away her sudden fears. "What?"

"General Skywalker said he'd be a one-man Marg Sabl," Thrawn reminded her. "What did he mean?"

"Oh," Padmé said, trying to remember the details. It had been a long time since Anakin had told her about Ahsoka's inspired maneuver. "It's a battle tactic invented by his former Padawan apprentice. A warship turns its hangar bay away from its attacker and launches its fighters unseen. They stay in the ship's visual shadow while they form up and accelerate to attack speed. Then they come around their ship from all sides, attacking the enemy from every direction at once."

"Interesting," Thrawn murmured. "I can see how that could be useful against certain species. Those in particular who have difficulty focusing in more than one direction."

"It worked pretty well against the droid fighters Ahsoka was up against at the time, too," Padmé said. "Anakin told me that a *marg sabl* is a type of Togrutan flower that opens its petals in a sunburst shape every morning."

"I see," Thrawn said. "So the one-man Marg Sabl he referred to will involve appearing to strike from all directions?"

"Probably," Padmé said, feeling a fresh twinge of worry. A one-man anything sounded risky at this point. "Did you happen to notice what the rooftop was like when you flew in? I'm wondering if there's a parapet that'll take a grappling hook."

"No, there isn't," Thrawn said. "The surface is slightly concave, toward a drainage line in the center. There's a small ridge at the edge, but not large enough to properly engage a hook. We'll need an alternative plan."

"Don't worry," Padmé said. "I've got one."

Anakin had hoped that Duke Solha would keep him, Thrawn, and R2-D2 together for the hurried interrogation that he assumed would follow the courtyard lightsaber show. But splitting R2-D2 away from the others had always been a possibility, which was why Anakin had set up the oil drip in the first place.

He followed the trail out the door and down a wider corridor heading north along the east wing's western side.

Right up to where it disappeared beyond a locked and armored door set in a solid permacrete wall.

Anakin scowled as he studied the door. All the other ones he and Thrawn had been rushed through since leaving the courtyard had been simple latch-and-hinge swinging doors, probably the factory's original equipment, with no special security added in. Apparently, Solha didn't care whether the locals Padmé mentioned could get into and out of those areas.

The main assembly chamber, though, was a different matter. For a moment Anakin considered going back to the stairway Padmé had pointed out and seeing if the security there might be easier to bypass. But unless Solha was incredibly stupid, that door would be just as well protected.

Still, they probably needed to bring workers in there on occasion, and of course the guard droids needed to get in and out as well. In a remote location like this, working among primitives who might never even have heard of the Separatists, security might reasonably be traded for convenience.

Battle droids, Anakin had long since learned, were heavier than most people realized. Occasionally that had proven useful, such as when he or his clone troopers needed to hold a prisoner for later pickup and didn't have any binders with them. A couple of downed B1s settled across the captive's arms and legs usually did the trick.

None of that weight mattered to a Jedi, of course. Using the Force, Anakin floated one of the droids he'd crumpled in the cell block up the stairs to the second floor. Mentally crossing his fingers, he maneuvered the droid's torso up to the door.

It was still a meter away when he heard the faint *snick* of a disengaging lock.

He smiled tightly as he pushed open the door and floated the droid through. Convenience over security; and he wasn't going to make Solha's mistake himself. Closing the door behind him, he balanced the droid against it on his side. Its transponder should be close enough to keep the door unlocked for when Padmé and Thrawn returned, but opening the door and pushing the droid aside should make enough noise to alert him.

The door opened onto a short foyer that ended in a section of scaffolding. Staying low, his hand automatically reaching for the lightsaber that wasn't there, he moved to the edge of the scaffolding and looked down.

He and the 501st had attacked plenty of droid assembly facilities over the years, and most of them followed one of only a few standard patterns. Not this one. The line was creating a version of B2 super battle droids—that much was clear from the molds and the size of the conveyers, not to mention the eight finished B2s standing rigidly against the far wall. But unlike other droid factories, the armored sections weren't coming out of red-hot injection forges; they were instead laid out along a pair of separate belts with only low-temperature plastoid molds in sight. Between the belts were bins of metals, plastoid pellets, and something that looked vaguely fibrous. Possibly the material he and Thrawn had seen in the courtyard, though he still had no idea what it could be. The assembly process was also far outside the norm, with what looked like an adhesive or catalytic process for putting the pieces together instead of the usual welding torches. A set of support pillars ran down the center of the room, maybe ten meters apart, and he wondered briefly if there might be unpleasant surprises lurking behind any of them.

The only occupants were three men and two women, working feverishly at a large control table near the center of the room. A B2 droid stood motionlessly beside them, a thick cable leading from the console to the programming access port under the droid's left arm. Three more B2s stood guard nearby, though whether they were protecting the techs or preventing them from leaving wasn't clear.

R2-D2 was on the opposite side of the table, and for a moment Anakin wondered if the techs were doing something with him, too. But a closer look showed that the little astromech wasn't connected to the rest of the system by any cables. Apparently, the techs were trying to upload the proper programming into the B2's brain, and R2-D2 had simply been parked there out of everyone's way.

Anakin frowned. Programming was normally part of the whole droid assembly process, with the new droids coming off the assembly line fully functional and ready to fight. This batch had apparently been created as blanks, with programming to be added later.

That was probably a decision Solha was regretting. Every B1 Anakin had seen in the courtyard—minus the ones he'd shredded—seemed to be here, along with seven hulking B2s besides the three at the control table. Solha was hunkering down, and the fact that he had his techs activating his new blanks was evidence that he wasn't feeling particularly safe.

On the other hand, if the duke was running scared, why wasn't he in here where droids could protect him? For that matter, the more Anakin studied the B2s, the more it looked like the ones that weren't at the table had been deployed mostly to defend the bins of fibrous material beside the armor plate molds.

Thrawn had pointed out the mining truck in the courtyard, with the suggestion that it and its cargo were important. But at the time Anakin had been too preoccupied with choreographing his disappearing-Jedi trick to pay much attention.

Far across the room, the armored door at the far end swung open—

Anakin felt his jaw drop . Marching into the factory as if he owned the place, a blaster gripped in his hand and a pair of B2s trailing behind him, was a clone trooper.

Anakin's first, wild, thought was that he was imagining things. His second was that it was a crazy coincidence, that somehow this far-flung world had managed to come up with armor that mimicked that of Republic troopers.

Neither was correct. The person striding along down there was indeed wearing genuine clone trooper armor. Not only that, but it looked from the markings like he was from the 212th, Obi-Wan Kenobi's unit.

So that made him . . . what? A loyal clone who'd somehow gotten innocently mixed up in this? A non-loyal clone, who was deliberately working for Solha and the Separatists? Or was he a decoy, here to create the precise confusion and uncertainty that Anakin was currently feeling?

The trooper stepped over to the programming table. He dropped his blaster back into its holster and pulled off his helmet.

It wasn't a clone, of any alignment. It was, instead, Duke Solha.

Anakin puffed out a silent breath. At least that cleared up the question of why Solha hadn't been here. Apparently, he'd been off scrounging up some extra protection.

Where he might have come up with clone armor was an entirely different set of questions. But Anakin didn't have time right now to wonder why the duke had such resources at hand. Even as Solha set his helmet down on the edge of the desk, the door opened again and two more clone-armored figures came in. This pair was leading a group of B1s that were lugging bins of more fibrous material, with another pair of B2s running rear-guard behind them.

The two troopers popped their helmets as the door closed behind them, revealing the other man and woman who'd been in the courtyard. The B1s, for their part, headed to the armor conveyer and the other bins, the B2s following to reinforce the droid guard already there. Solha left the table and crossed to the other Serennians, meeting them halfway, and the three of them paused for a quiet but clearly intense conversation.

Anakin pursed his lips. This whole thing was starting to look way more complicated than he'd expected.

Still, sorting it out could wait until he had Padmé safely back at his side. And the best way to ensure her safety was to keep Solha and his droids busy right here.

Reaching out to the Force, he focused on one of the B1s near the door. A little nudge to its blaster's aim; a small twitching of the trigger . . .

The blast echoed off the high ceiling as the bolt slammed into one of the B2s standing stoic guard beside the bins.

It was a glancing blow, and the B2 barely even twitched from the impact. But even as the B1 yelped in confusion the super battle droid's programmed reflexes kicked in, spinning it around and raising its right arm, its dual wrist blasters tracking toward the source of the attack.

Luckily for the B1, Solha was faster. "Hold!" he shouted, cutting short his conversation and yanking out his own blaster. Anakin briefly considered snatching it away from him, then decided it would be better to keep the true situation muddled as long as he could.

Unfortunately, Solha was quick on that one, too. "It's the Jedi!" he shouted, swinging around in a slow circle, his eyes darting back and forth. "He's in here somewhere, making you shoot at each other. Spread out and find him."

And here, Anakin knew, was where it got fun.

First on the list was to create a little confusion. Stretching out to the switches by the far door, he turned off the lights.

———

Four of Mokivj's ten moons were high in the night sky as Padmé led the way through the hidden exit. They were small moons, smaller than any of Naboo's three, but even through the attenuation of the energy shield their reflected light was enough for her to get a clear view of the south wing's outer wall as it towered above them. "What's your plan?" Thrawn asked, coming up beside her.

"The windows on the west wing were covered with a protective metal mesh," she told him, slinging her backpack over one shoulder and pulling out her monocular. "So are these," she confirmed, peering through the device. "The mesh is open enough for the grapple to catch, and should be strong enough to hold our combined weight. We fire the grapple, engage it, then the motor in the grip pulls us up."

"How many grapples do you have?"

"Three, but we won't need more than one," Padmé said, putting the monocular away. "The telescopic sight cylinder rotates ninety degrees and locks, and is reinforced to work as a second handhold. You hang on to that one, I hang on to the main grip, and we go up together."

"Once we've reached the top of the line, how do you propose to gain the rooftop?"

Padmé peered up at the wall again. That was a good question, actually. The top of the upper window was a solid meter below the level of the roof, and she couldn't see anyplace where they could brace their feet. "I guess one of us will have to stand on the other's shoulders in order to reach the top."

"A difficult maneuver," Thrawn warned. "I doubt you can take my weight, and my own chest and shoulder muscles have been somewhat compromised."

"By . . . ?"

"Enemy weapons fire," Thrawn said. "I suggest instead that you set a grapple at each of two adjacent windows. If your ascension gun is sturdy enough, the cables would form a V-shape that one of us could use as a foothold while stretching to the roof."

Padmé measured the distances with her eyes. "Yes, that should work," she agreed. Her backpack was still hanging by one strap. She started to shift it back into proper position on her back—

"I'll take this," Thrawn said, deftly pulling it off her shoulder.

"That stays with me," Padmé said, trying to snatch it back. But he kept it moving out of her reach as he slipped it on. *"Thrawn—"*

"I need these," he interrupted, sliding the E-5 blaster Anakin had given him through the straps. He winced a little, she noticed, as the weapon slid across his chest. "Your weapons are smaller and can be secured without using your hands. Mine cannot."

She glowered at him. But again, his argument made sense. "Fine," she said. "But I get it back once we're up top."

"Agreed." He gestured toward the wall. "At your convenience, Ambassador."

Padmé had never tried using two separate lines and grapples from the ascension gun at the same time. But she remembered the manual saying it could be done, and the operation came off without a hitch. The next part, climbing that last meter up to the roof, was a bit trickier. But Thrawn had apparently done something like this before. With Padmé hanging from the gun, he used the lines to climb to their intersection point, balanced on the S-5's muzzle, then continued holding on to one line while he walked his hand up the wall to a grip on the narrow rim at the top. Once he was up, he set the E-5 and backpack aside and lay down at the roof's edge, pulling up on one of the lines until the gun was within reach. After that, it was a matter of gripping Padmé's wrist, giving her a steady pull upward until she could get her other hand on top, then retrieving the S-5 and the grapples. A moment later, with Thrawn in the lead with his E-5, and Padmé following with her backpack and the S-5 once again in blaster mode, they headed off across the moonlit roof.

Padmé had assumed this would be the most dangerous part of the trip. Even if Duke Solha hadn't sent any of his B1s up here, the vulture droids were surely keeping a close watch on the factory. But she and Thrawn reached the eastern edge of the south wing and continued onto the east wing roof without so much as seeing a vulture, let alone being challenged by one.

Thrawn seemed to think it odd, as well. Six paces ahead of her, he was muttering something under his breath in an unknown language, as if trying to work out the puzzle aloud.

They reached the line of floodlights. Padmé looked up, making a quick visual sweep of the sky. Sooner or later, at least *one* of the vultures ought to show up.

"Wait a minute," Padmé said, frowning as something caught her eye. In the distance to the east, a small, shimmering-white sphere was falling slowly from the sky. "Thrawn—over there," she said, pointing. She glanced around again—

And tensed, her eyes sweeping the horizon. All around them, several kilometers away, more of the faintly glowing spheres were drifting downward. Three—five—ten—*twenty*—"Thrawn!" she called again.

And then, even as she watched, two of the spheres directly in her line of sight abruptly blazed with spears of green light. They flared briefly and were gone.

But not before their dying light illuminated the dark shapes shooting past them.

The vulture droids had finally come out to play.

"Don't worry," Thrawn called as the distant vultures came around and fired at another of the spheres.

Padmé looked back. He was crouching beside one of the floodlights, Anakin's lightsaber in his hand. "Come," he called, beckoning to her.

Two more spheres had been destroyed by the time she reached him. "What are they?" she asked.

"Decoys," he said. "Give me the ascension gun."

"Decoys for what?" she asked, wincing as three more spheres were caught by the vultures' fire. Still, there were at least fifteen more drifting across the sky.

"My ship," he said, taking the ascension gun from her. "Do you see it?"

Padmé scanned the horizon, paying particular attention to the dark sections where none of the spheres were falling. Conventional military doctrine was to put decoys where you wanted the enemy to look.

But she could see nothing. "Where?" she asked.

"Not there," he said, hooking one of the grappling hooks into the lighting support struts and getting a grip on the ascension gun. "Above."

Padme looked up. There it was: a shadowy shape, visible only as it blotted out the muted starlight, dropping straight out of the sky toward them. "What in—?"

But Thrawn was already gone, falling backward off the roof and rappelling along the wall toward the courtyard.

And he'd taken the lightsaber with him.

In a two-person, single-line rappelling exercise, the Naboo military manual recommended the first person to the ground return the ascension gun to lift mode and let it reel itself up to the person still on top. Padmé had no intention of waiting that long. Shrugging off her backpack, she wrapped the straps around the line for padding, got a good grip, and rolled off the edge of the roof.

Thrawn was apparently in even more of a hurry. By the time Padmé reached the ground he was already in the center of the courtyard. "Hold it!" she snapped, scooping up the S-5 where he'd left it and cutting off the line. "Where do you think you're going?"

A second later, she got her answer. He came to a halt beside the shield generator, peered for a moment at the lightsaber—

And the brilliant blue blade flashed into existence.

Padmé stopped short, raising her blaster, her first horrified thought being that Thrawn was about to turn the lightsaber on her. But even as she wondered where he'd learned to use such a weapon the blade slashed downward, digging into the ground beside the generator. He stepped to the next side and slashed downward again.

Padmé wrinkled her nose. Of course. Thrawn's ship was coming for him, and the factory's shield was blocking its way. And so here he was, using Anakin's lightsaber to cut through the power cables. Above her, the starlight suddenly brightened as the shield collapsed.

And then, to her surprise, Thrawn crouched down and shifted to a horizontal cut, slicing through the permacrete foundation beneath the generator. "It's already down," she called to him.

"I know," he called back. He finished the cut, looked up at the sky above him, then shut down the lightsaber and walked over to her.

"General Skywalker's weapon," he said, holding it out to her in his right hand. "And your communicator," he added, holding out the comm in his left.

Padmé stared at the weapon and comm. So he hadn't been talking to himself on the trip across the rooftop. She'd wondered how his ship had known to come for him at that precise moment. "What are you doing?" she asked quietly, making no move to take either device.

"I was given a mission, Ambassador Padmé," he said. "We'd observed this factory from afar, and seen the generator of the shield protecting it. We have nothing that holds this much power in such a compact form. I was ordered to obtain it and bring it home."

"Anakin said you came to help him find me."

"We'd observed the arrival of your companion on Batuu," Thrawn said. "But we were unable to discern her fate. As I was observing the planet General Skywalker arrived. It seemed to me that we could help each other with our respective missions."

"Did he know *this* was your true mission?" Padmé asked, her stomach twisting with the all-too-familiar ache of betrayal.

"No," Thrawn said. He lifted the lightsaber a few centimeters. "He'll need this. And he'll need you."

"So you're just going to leave?" Padmé demanded. "Duke Solha's up to something here, something terrible. You're not going to help us find out what it is?"

"I was given a mission."

"We need you," Padmé said, a part of her wondering why she was fighting so hard on this. A reluctant ally was often worse than no ally at all. But something within her couldn't just let it go. "Is this how your people do things? Just go along until you've gotten what you want, then abandon everyone else?"

"Is that how your Republic does things?" Thrawn countered.

"This isn't about politics," Padmé shot back. "It's about individuals. People. Honor."

"Politics is built from individuals," Thrawn said. "The Separatists wished to leave the Republic. Why didn't you simply allow them to go?"

"Because they attacked us. *They* started the war." Padmé slashed a hand of dismissal through the air between them. "That's not the issue here."

"Perhaps it is," Thrawn said. "We need to understand you. We need to know what drives you."

"Right now, what drives me is that my—friend—Anakin is going to die in there if we don't help him," Padmé said. "We can't do this alone, Thrawn. We need your help."

"My mission comes first," Thrawn said. "My people come first."

For a long moment, Padmé gazed into those glowing red eyes. But there was no emotion there; no regret, no shame, no triumph. He was just a soldier, obeying his orders, with neither satisfaction or regret.

He might as well have been a battle droid.

"I'll say goodbye for you," she bit out. Snatching her comm and Anakin's lightsaber from his hands, she spun around.

"The door at the south end is closest to where he'll be," Thrawn called as she jogged toward the east wing.

Padmé didn't answer.

Maybe she was right. Maybe she and Anakin couldn't do this alone.

But they would have to try.

CHAPTER 16

"There," Faro said, pointing out the *Chimaera*'s main viewport. "That moon right there."

"I see it," Thrawn said calmly.

Calmly, but Faro could sense the grimness beneath the words.

From behind them came a set of heavy footsteps. "We have arrived?" Lord Vader asked.

"Yes, my lord," Thrawn said. "Have we arrived in time?"

Vader stopped beside Thrawn, his long cloak settling around his shoulders, and for a moment he stared out the viewport in silence.

Or at least, Faro assumed he was staring out the viewport. For all she could tell from his helmet faceplate, he could be taking a quick nap in there.

Mentally, she slapped herself across the cheek. *Stop that.* It was rumored the Dark Lord could read people's thoughts, and that was *not* a thought she wanted him to know about.

Vader stirred. "Yes," he said. "They are there."

"Excellent," Thrawn murmured. "I had hoped the Grysks would believe themselves safely hidden here. Can you tell where precisely they are?"

"Not from this distance," Vader said. "We shall need to move closer."

"Commodore?" Thrawn asked.

"Velocity unchanged, sir," Faro reported. "Do you want the drive activated?"

Thrawn eyed the distant planet. "Not yet," he said. "Let us close the distance a bit more before we announce our presence."

"Those ships," Vader said, raising a gloved hand to point out the viewport. "What are they doing?"

"What they have done at least four times before," Thrawn said. "They are taking one of the moons."

For another moment Vader was silent. "That makes no sense."

"On the contrary, my lord, it makes perfect sense," Thrawn said, his voice dark. "We have already seen their goal of closing off this region to easy and rapid hyperspace travel. The gravity projectors are effective, but they are costly and have only limited range and lifetime. Far more efficient in the long run to move lunar- or planetary-sized masses into hyperlanes, where they will continue to disrupt travel for decades or centuries to come."

"How is this achieved?" Vader asked. For once, even the Dark Lord sounded awed. Faro guessed that didn't happen very often. "What is their technology?"

"I do not know," Thrawn said.

Vader rumbled in his throat. "Whatever it is, I have no doubt it will fall to turbolaser fire."

"I agree," Thrawn agreed. "But not yet."

Faro smiled to herself. Of course not yet. There was nothing Thrawn valued more than information and knowledge. He would absolutely not attack until he figured out a way to infiltrate a team into the network of ships surrounding the moon and collect the Grysks' secrets.

"Commander Hammerly?" Thrawn called.

"Not yet, sir," the sensor officer replied from her crew pit position.

"What are you waiting for?" Vader demanded.

Faro mentally shook her head. They were waiting for Thrawn to come up with his infiltration plan, of course.

"The moon they are moving still endangers the planet," Thrawn said. "We must wait until they have given it escape velocity."

Faro frowned. Endangering Mokivj . . . but surely that wouldn't matter if Thrawn was simply sneaking into the enemy fleet. Was he actually thinking—?

"Clear, sir," Hammerly confirmed. "Escape velocity achieved. The moon can no longer impact the surface."

"Stand by to attack," Thrawn said. "Commodore, is my ship ready?"

"It is, sir," Faro said, feeling the universe tilting a little around her. When he'd ordered her to prepare the *Chimaera* for combat, she'd assumed it was merely a contingency plan in case his real plan was somehow disrupted.

Did this mean that simply wading in and destroying the Grysk forces *was* his real plan?

"Activate all systems," Thrawn ordered.

"Activating all systems, sir," Faro repeated, looking over at the status board. Lights were rapidly turning from orange to green as the systems that had been on standby while the *Chimaera* drifted unseen toward the planet came back to life. "Combat readiness in twenty seconds."

Thrawn nodded acknowledgment. "Lord Vader, I will need to know as soon as possible in which ships the prisoners are located."

The twenty seconds had passed, and the *Chimaera* had lit its thrusters and was driving toward the distant Grysk ships before Vader answered. "A small number are located aboard the ships. Two, perhaps three. The remainder are on the planet."

"Understood," Thrawn said. "Commodore Faro, you will initiate an attack on the Grysk forces. Lord Vader, I request a favor: that you assign the *Darkhawk* and a squad of First Legion stormtroopers to accompany me to the surface."

"What of your duties to the *Chimaera*?" Vader countered.

"Commodore Faro is more than capable of handling the assault," Thrawn said. "Commodore, the enemy response to your attack will most likely be to launch multiple counterattacks from—"

"Precise orders to the commodore are unnecessary, Admiral," Vader interrupted. "You will remain aboard the *Chimaera* and lead the attack."

"My lord—"

"*I* will take the First Legion to Mokivj," Vader continued. "You will deal with the ships, Admiral Thrawn. *I* will deal with the planet."

For a moment Thrawn was silent. Then he inclined his head. "Very well, my lord," he said. "Prepare your stormtroopers. The battle now begins."

There was, Vader had noticed, a strange sort of symmetry in the Force, a balance that often manifested in patterns and resonances and strange reunions. People long separated would unexpectedly meet again; events of significance would see echoes of themselves within new events; places once visited would somehow draw a person back to create new memories, whether for good or for ill.

Mokivj.

The dry riverbed Padmé had described to The Jedi was still there, matching the fresh data Vader had extracted from the Grysk prisoners. He strode along it, ignoring the airspeeders that swooped past overhead as they traded fire with his stormtroopers. The airspeeders clearly hadn't been expecting this kind of attack and usually came out the losers in the exchange, often bursting into flames right there and crash-landing somewhere out of sight.

Vader hardly noticed. His full focus was on the sensations coming steadily nearer; the swirl of thoughts and emotions, the mixture of hopes and fears, all of it rippling across space through the prisoners' Force sensitivity.

And through it all wove The Jedi's memories . . . and the simmering anger that Vader should have long ago recognized what the Emperor's disturbance truly was.

Vader hadn't seen this before. But The Jedi had. A long time ago; but he *had* already seen it.

The secret entrance into the factory was narrow and cramped. Vader didn't even slow down, but slashed out a larger opening with his lightsaber as he strode through it. Two of his stormtroopers—Commander Kimmund and Sergeant Viq—slipped around in front of him as the stormtroopers filed into the service level, the two of them moving into vanguard positions ahead of Vader and the rest of the squad.

There were no defenses or other hindrances down here. Not that Vader was expecting any. The Separatists whom The Jedi had faced had sealed the east wing against intrusion from this direction, and the Grysks had undoubtedly confirmed the security of that protection when they moved in.

That the enemy *were* in the east wing was not in question. Vader could sense the Chiss minds, now lying directly ahead of him.

The same sense that The Jedi had felt aboard Thrawn's ship at that first meeting over Batuu.

A pilot, Thrawn had identified her back then. But it was clear now that there was far more involved. These Chiss were Force-sensitive, and most likely Force-users as well.

Was that what Thrawn and the Emperor were being so secretive about in their private talks together? Were there Chiss Jedi in the Unknown Regions? Were they perhaps one of the threats Thrawn had warned the Emperor about at their first meeting, a threat that they were discussing together? Was the war against the Jedi, so long and so very, very painfully won, about to begin all over again?

Or could it be that the Chiss Force-sensitives were Sith?

That could be even more disastrous. The Rule of Two was all that had saved the Republic's Sith from the level of internal warfare that could have brought about total self-destruction. Was there an echo of that same warfare going on even now on the Chiss worlds?

Vader frowned, a sudden realization breaking his train of thought. Earlier, when the *Darkhawk* landed near the river, he had sensed eight Chiss minds in the old factory. Now, somehow, the swirl of thoughts had diminished.

And the minds that were left had changed to the overpowering terror he'd felt back on Batuu.

The Grysks were putting them back into hibernation chambers. Or worse.

"Ahead," he ordered the stormtroopers, picking up his pace. Whoever these Chiss were—*whatever* they were—he'd promised Thrawn he would bring them back. And no group of Grysk soldiers was going to stop him.

The dry riverbed had been exactly as Lord Vader described it to Kimmund and the other stormtroopers. So was the entrance to the sublevel, and the sublevel itself.

Clearly, the Grysk interrogation had gone well.

Of course, if Vader was right about all this, he was probably right about their east wing target area being loaded with machinery and other large objects the enemy could hide behind. Kimmund had been in enough urban combat missions to know those were among the most dangerous a stormtrooper could face.

His troops would see it through, of course, and they would succeed. How many of them Kimmund lost along the way would largely depend on how well Vader had anticipated their opponents, and whether the secret weapon Podiry and Tephan were lugging behind them functioned as well as Vader had said it would.

Hopefully, none of the aircars that had buzzed them earlier had had the necessary sensors for peeking into the coffin-sized box. Secret weapons never worked as well when the enemy knew they were coming.

The trapdoor that was their goal was just ahead, its ladder still sticking out of a plug of permacrete that had been sealed around it. At an order from Vader, Kimmund and Viq stepped to either side to let him pass, then watched as he ignited his lightsaber and stabbed upward into the material, digging a circle into and through it. He finished his cut, holding the plug in place long enough to move out of its way before releasing it to crash to the ground.

The ladder still hung precariously at the edge of the hole. But Vader clearly wasn't in the mood to do this the slow way. Kimmund felt something invisible wrap around him, and a second later found himself flying upward through the hole. He got a glimpse of dark, half-ruined equipment and storage boxes scattered around a large, high-ceilinged room—

He jerked sideways as a last-second twitch by Vader sent him past the opening and dropped him onto solid floor. He keyed in his scanners, noting at least a dozen hot spots of hidden enemies as Viq flew up and landed on the other side of the hole.

And as Dorstren flew up behind them, his heavy DLT-19 cradled in his arms, and landed beside Viq, the entire room erupted into a blaze of blue-edged lightning bolts.

Kimmund ducked to the side, feeling a sudden tingling in his skin as one of the bolts barely missed him. A second later he staggered off balance as something small and hard slammed into his armor. No idea where the projectile shot had come from; the lightning weapon, in contrast, marked a clear path back to the gunner. Kimmund sent a volley of blasterfire to that point as another lightning bolt lashed out, this one targeting Viq. Kimmund shifted his aim toward that shot's origin and again returned fire.

That latter shot went wide as another pair of impacts jolted against his chest and shoulder. Some kind of pellet weapons, apparently, which the First Legion's armor was fortunately strong enough to block.

He snarled under his breath. Whoever was running the defense here knew what he was doing. The lightning weapons were hard to aim, but had the capacity to do serious damage if they hit. The pellet guns didn't do much damage, but they came out of nowhere and could keep the stormtroopers off balance, impeding their ability to stay clear of the more dangerous weapons. In addition, the lightning flashes briefly overloaded the stormtroopers' targeting sensors, making the pellet gunners that much harder to spot and eliminate. Out of the corner of his eye Kimmund saw Morrtic fly up into view, her BlasTech E-11 blindly spattering cover fire everywhere she could reach. She hit the floor, shifting her blasterfire to another of the lightning-gun nests—

And then, with a dramatic flourish that never failed to send a shiver up Kimmund's back, he was there.

Instantly the weapons shifted aim. But to no avail. The black armor shrugged off the lightning flashes with ease, and Kimmund could barely see the small twitches caused by the pellet impacts. The figure strode forward like something out of dark myth, heading toward the nearest pile of rusted machinery, a spot Kimmund's sensors had tagged as the hiding place of at least four of the attackers. With the Grysk focus distracted, the other stormtroopers were emerging from the opening, adding their firepower to the battle. A final burst of lightning lashed out—

From dark shadows far to the rear of the main battle floor, half a dozen clouds of insects burst into view.

The figure stopped, lightsaber raised, as if daring the insects to attack. For a couple of seconds they buzzed almost aimlessly; and then, as if at a silent order, they swarmed forward.

Kimmund smiled tightly behind his faceplate. Once again, Lord Vader had called it. The Grysks were going with the same attack plan they'd used on Batuu: swarms of insects, directed by invisible controllers, carrying loads of immobilizing liquid stone. Layered with the pellet guns and the lightning weapons, it was a strategy the aliens probably assumed was unbeatable.

Only they'd forgotten something. They'd forgotten that this time there was a squad of stormtroopers along. Stormtroopers who were good at evasion and counterattack. Stormtroopers who also had enhanced sensors in their helmets.

Stormtroopers who had known this exact moment would be coming.

"Viq?" Kimmund called into his comm.

"Got 'em," Viq said with dark amusement. "Feeding coordinates now."

The first wave of insects reached their target, and the glistening black armor erupted in multiple splotches of gray as the insects delivered their payloads and died. On Kimmund's heads-up display six hazy red marks appeared, the locations where the swarms had appeared—seemingly from nowhere. "Targets marked," he said. "Take them."

The entire chamber lit up as the stormtroopers opened fire, concentrating everything on the cloaked Grysks.

The insects didn't care, of course. They continued their mindless attack even as their masters abruptly became visible, choked or screamed or snarled, and died. The pellet guns belatedly opened fire again, but the lightning blasts remained silent, their owners no doubt reluctant to shoot through the swarms and possibly undermine the insects' attack.

Not that there was much need to worry on that score. By now almost the entire suit of armor was covered in gray, with each successive wave adding new layers, to the point where it was barely even human-shaped. Only the lightsaber remained untouched, the blade frozen in place as it blazed uselessly toward the ceiling.

The final wave of insects splattered themselves and died. Kimmund looked carefully around, feeling the impacts of the pellets, knowing that the lightning guns would soon open fire again. With the stormtroopers pinned down, and the greatest threat fully encased in stone, the Grysks no doubt felt confident of victory.

They'd forgotten that Vader had already seen their attack. They'd perhaps not realized that the Dark Lord was himself a master tactician.

And they'd probably never known that Vader had *two* full sets of armor.

The lightning guns were beginning to open fire once more when the Dark Lord of the Sith appeared from below, for real this time. He stepped forward, calling his lightsaber to him from the now loosened grip of the hollow suit of armor that he'd walked so convincingly across the chamber and into the Grysks' trap.

Someone hidden among the machinery gave a startled-sounding shout. But it was too late. Even as the lightning weapons shifted their full fury to Vader, he strode toward them, deflecting the bolts into the ceiling as he used the Force to twist their weapons off target, hurling his lightsaber to bring down sections of machinery onto the enemy, grabbing anyone who came into view and throwing them into the rapidly diminishing number of lightning bolts.

"Find the prisoners," Vader's voice came through Kimmund's headset.

"Yes, Lord Vader," Kimmund said, rising from his crouch and looking around. Off to his right, tucked away behind another wall of rusting machinery, were a handful of hot spots. Keeping one eye on the battle, making sure the rest of his squad was doing their job of laying down cover fire, he headed toward the hot spot, beckoning to Viq and Elebe to join him as he passed them. He motioned them to head to the far side of the hiding place, waited until they were in position, then stepped around his side.

And felt his eyes widen. Crouched down on their haunches in defensive positions, their lightning guns pointed in opposite directions to cover both approaches, were a pair of Grysks. Sitting hunched together between them, their faces rigid with fear and horror, were the prisoners.

Five young Chiss girls.

Chiss? *Children?*

A tiny corner of Kimmund's mind noted that it would have been nice for Vader to have at least given them a bit of warning. But First Legion stormtroopers didn't let something as simple as the unexpected deflect them from their battle plan. "Don't shoot!" he called, stopping and raising his E-11 to point at the ceiling. *"Don't shoot!"*

The Grysk facing him swung his lightning gun onto the target. The enemy facing the other way glanced reflexively over his shoulder in response to the sudden shout.

Neither had time to do anything else before Viq and Elebe appeared around the opposite corner and coolly put a single shot each into each Grysk's skull.

"It's all right," Kimmund said, keeping his E-11 pointed away from the children as he hurried toward them. They were gazing up at him, their blue-skinned faces pinched with fear, their glowing red eyes narrowed, their bodies flinching back against the machinery behind them. One of them, perhaps braver than the others, lifted a tentative finger to point at something across from them.

Kimmund looked that direction, feeling his stomach tighten. Nestled beneath an overhang of old machinery were more familiar devices: eight hibernation tubes like the ones Vader and Thrawn had retrieved from Batuu. Three seemed to be active, which probably explained why there were five children still sitting here instead of the eight prisoners Vader had said might be present.

"Do you have them?" Vader's voice came through his helmet speaker.

"Yes, my lord," Kimmund confirmed. "Five Chiss children. There may be three more in hibernation chambers."

"Good," Vader said. There was no hint of surprise in his voice, Kimmund noted. At least *he'd* known what they'd come here for. "Prepare them for travel," Vader ordered. "Are the courtyard defenses you detected on our approach still active?"

"I believe so, my lord," Kimmund said, shaking away the questions and getting his mind back to the tactical situation. "But now that we're inside, we should be able to take them out from behind."

"Do so, Commander," Vader said. "When you have secured the courtyard, summon the *Darkhawk* to meet us there. I do not wish to bring Admiral Thrawn's prizes out through the underground passages."

"Understood, my lord," Kimmund said. "Drav?"

"On it, Commander," Sergeant Drav said briskly. "We'll have you clear to fly in ten minutes, my lord."

Kimmund motioned to Viq and Elebe. "Go and assist," he said. He watched them go, then stepped closer to the children and dropped down onto one knee. "Don't be afraid," he said.

No response. Probably didn't understand a word of Basic.

Still, Thrawn would be able to talk to them. Once they were aboard the *Chimaera* the children could be told they were no longer Grysk prisoners.

In the meantime, he'd been ordered to make them ready for travel.

"Come on," he said, standing up and motioning back over his shoulder. He looked around, hunting for a safe place to put them in case the battle for the courtyard spilled back in here.

And felt his lips compress. Off to the side, well away from where the Grysks had set up for battle, was a large conveyer belt flanked by various pieces of assembly equipment. On the belt, in varying stages of construction, were five more of the gravity projectors the Grysks had used to close off the Batuu hyperlane.

It was a project the Grysks had clearly put a lot of time and effort into, equipment they would presumably be hesitant to damage. Ergo, a good place to put someone you didn't want them to shoot at.

"Come on," he said, beckoning to the girls and heading toward the conveyer belt. It was, he decided, going to take a lot more cargo capacity than the *Darkhawk* to get all this back to the *Chimaera*.

But that was all right. Once Vader and the rest of the stormtroopers cleared out the courtyard's defenses, they would have all the time in the world.

"Two ships breaking to the sides," Weapons Officer Pyrondi called. "Attempting to flank."

"Order Squadrons Three and Five to intercept," Thrawn said. *The flanking ships do not go through the web, but maneuver around it for their attack. Possible conclusions: The web cannot be easily breached, or cannot be shut down in individual sections, or is being kept in place for additional purposes. The Grysks are likely keeping their options open while testing Imperial resolve, hoping to yet escape with their prize.*

"Squadrons Three and Five moving to intercept," Commodore Faro confirmed. "Looks like they're launching fighters."

The smaller craft emerge from their host ship in single file. The host ship's hatch is not armored. The smaller vessels' acceleration is low as they move to the sides to permit those behind to exit. Their drive nozzles are wide-spaced for high maneuverability, and are overly large. "They are not fighters, Commodore, but more likely tugs," Thrawn said. "Possibly for positioning the nodes of the web."

"Not coming to fight, but to distract us and keep the TIEs busy so they can't get after the real targets," Faro said. *Her voice holds understanding.* "So we bypass them?"

"Correct," Thrawn said. "Target them with the *Chimaera*'s turbolasers, but do not fire without command. The TIEs will continue on toward the web and the larger ships."

"Yes, sir," Faro said. *Her voice and body stance hold wariness and growing suspicion.* "I find myself concerned, Admiral, that they haven't already abandoned the moon and tried to run. Surely they realize they can't outfight us."

"The launching of tugs in an attempt to slow our approach would seem to indicate that," Thrawn said. "Why might they remain?"

"I'm thinking they may be expecting reinforcements."

"That is one possibility. Another?"

"They could think they can still escape with the moon in tow," Faro said. "They should be clear of Mokivj's gravity well now. However it is that a hyperdrive works with something that massive, a few more minutes might be enough."

"Indeed," Thrawn said. "There is a third possibility."

"A third," Faro murmured. *Her voice holds concentration. The TIEs swarm past the group of tugs and continue toward the moon and the Grysk web.*

"Perhaps an unfair question," Thrawn said. "You do not possess all the facts."

Faro's back and shoulders straighten. Her body stance holds fresh understanding. "The Chiss prisoners," she said. *Her voice holds satisfaction at having solved the puzzle.* "They want the moon, but they want the prisoners more. The ship holding them wants to escape, but its hyperdrive isn't ready yet. *And* it's still in the moon's own gravity well. Until they're ready they don't dare run, because that would show us which ship has them."

"Very good, Commodore," Thrawn said. "And the reason all the ships do not leave now, which would maintain the prisoners' concealment within numbers?"

"Because they can't," Faro said. *Her voice holds dark amusement.* "The two ships that came out to play were at the edges of the web. The others are deeper inside, and they can't simply disengage. The ship we want is either at the edge—" *She breaks off, her body stance holding a fresh level of understanding.* "Or it's hugging the web but not actually inside it." *She raises her voice loud enough to be heard in the crew pits.* "Hammerly?"

"Yes, Commodore," the sensor chief called back. "Scanning as per the admiral's orders. The web's emissions are still interfering with readings, but it's clearing as we get closer."

"How soon?" Thrawn asked.

"Two minutes," Hammerly said. "Maybe less."

"Signal Lieutenant Skerris," Thrawn ordered. "Defender Squadron launch now."

"Defender Squadron: Launch."

The TIEs sweep past the tugs. The tugs in turn rotate a few degrees and turn full power to their drives. The emissions blast across the fighters, but have no effect on them. The momentary drive surge increases the tugs' forward velocity. The tugs continue on their current vectors.

"Destroy all the enemy tugs," Thrawn said. "Now."

The Chimaera's *turbolasers open fire against the tugs.* "Sir?" Faro asked. *Her tone holds puzzlement.*

"If their task was to intercept or slow the TIEs, they would have turned and attacked the squadrons from the rear," Thrawn said. "They did not. Therefore, their purported attack against the TIEs was a ruse."

"They're armed," Faro said. *Her voice holds understanding.* "Or carrying bombs."

"I suspect the latter," Thrawn said. "Their commander will know by now that I pursue information, and that I prefer capture to simple destruction. He seeks to use this against me."

The tugs begin to disintegrate before the turbolaser barrage. The explosions are larger than expected from the detonation of reactors or thrusters. Conclusion: They are indeed carrying bombs.

"Yes, I see," Faro said. "And now that that's failed, and with the Defenders heading for them—"

"Admiral, one of the ships is breaking away," Hammerly called.

"Outside the net—we couldn't tell that until just now. Accelerating and heading into the moon's shadow."

"Defenders: Intercept and disable," Thrawn said. "Do not destroy. Repeat, do *not* destroy."

The Defenders sweep around the surface of the moon in pursuit. The Grysk ship is not visible behind the moon, but the navigator has projected its course and vector on the tactical display. The Defenders are closing the gap. They will intercept before the Grysk ship escapes the moon's gravity well.

Two areas on the moon's rim shatter, sending dense clouds of dust and rock into the paths of the approaching Defenders.

"Turbolasers: Aim above and below the moon," Thrawn said, "Low power; continuous fire."

"They've changed vector?" Faro asked.

"I assume so," Thrawn said. "The debris from those explosions could not possibly damage the Defenders at their range. I conclude therefore the object was to create a visual obstruction while the Grysk ship veered off its projected path."

"Signal from Skerris, Admiral," Lieutenant Lomar called from the comm station. *His voice holds tension and frustration.* "The Grysk ship has jumped to lightspeed. The Defenders were unable to intercept."

"Understood," Thrawn said. *The web around the moon is disintegrating. The Grysk ships are moving outward, intent on escaping the gravity well.* "Fighter squadrons, turbolasers: full attack. Destroy them all."

The turbolasers open fire. Across the starscape, the TIEs engage the enemy.

"Should we try to take some prisoners, sir?" Faro asked. *Her voice holds cautious concern.*

"The Grysks have tried once to lure us into a deadly trap," Thrawn said. "We cannot risk them doing so again."

"Yes, sir." *Faro is silent a moment. Her body stance continues to hold concern.* "Sir . . . the Chiss prisoners. If we don't take one of the Grysk ships, how will we find them?"

"We may not," Thrawn said. "But we may. Lieutenant Lomar, is there word from Lord Vader?"

"Commander Kimmund just reported in, sir," Lomar said. "They have the prisoners and have cleared the enemy from the courtyard. They're bringing the *Darkhawk* in now for a pickup, and expect to be back at the *Chimaera* within the hour. They also request a transport for additional equipment."

"Request denied," Thrawn said. "Inform Commander Kimmund that we will be satisfied with just the prisoners. Order quarters to be prepared for them, and inform Lord Vader that I wish to speak with him immediately upon his return."

CHAPTER 17

The Grysk ships had been destroyed and the errant moon was drifting along its path toward eternity by the time Vader and the *Darkhawk* returned to the *Chimaera* with the freed children. Quarters had been prepared for them near Thrawn's own suite, and the grand admiral had taken a few minutes to speak with them.

Vader couldn't understand what they were saying, and their minds had the same opaqueness as Thrawn's. But he could sense the slow calming of the children's emotions as they finally grasped that their nightmare was over. One of the girls spoke a little Sy Bisti; Commodore Faro located an assistant maintenance tech who also knew some of that obscure trade language and left the children in his care.

And it was time for Thrawn to stand to judgment.

"You lied to me," Vader said when they were once again alone in the admiral's office.

"I did not lie, my lord," Thrawn said, inclining his head.

"You withheld some of the truth," Vader countered, keeping a firm grip on his anger as he stretched out with the Force. The sand bridge Thrawn had been continually walking since they first arrived at Batuu had been steadily blown away by the admiral's words and actions. Now it had eroded to something perilously thin. One more misstep, one more evasion or lie, and Vader would forget that the Emperor still had use of this person. "That is the same as a lie."

"I told you what I could," Thrawn said. "What I deemed the Emperor would permit me to reveal."

"The Emperor knows the whole truth, then?"

Thrawn hesitated, the orderly array of his mind bending a bit under the strain of Vader's glare and presence. "I have not told him," the admiral conceded. "But I have no doubt that he does indeed know."

Vader felt his thumbs tighten in his belt. In that, the Chiss was probably right. "You will tell me all of it," he said. "Now."

"As I promised," Thrawn said, again inclining his head. The deference was real, Vader could sense, as was the caution behind it. The admiral knew exactly where he stood, and recognized that his life was hanging by a thread.

Good.

"You will first appreciate that this is among the most closely guarded secrets of the Chiss Ascendancy," he said. "As I noted when we first reached this region of space, there are few stable hyperlanes into and through the Unknown Regions. Because of this, most species stay close to their own systems, preferring to travel along shorter lanes and unwilling to take the time necessary for the much slower jump-by-jump travel."

"But the Chiss do not wish to be so limited?"

"Indeed not," Thrawn said, a hint of contempt creeping into his voice. "For all their pronouncements of non-interference in others' activities, the Aristocras have a deep desire to know what those activities consist of. Our scouts range far and wide, entering even into the parts of space once claimed by the Republic and now claimed by the Empire." He gestured. "As you well know."

"I have been so informed by the Emperor," Vader said stiffly. Again,

Thrawn was poking uncomfortably close to the edge. "Tell me about the children."

"We do not have nav computers able to plot safe paths through the chaos of the Unknown Regions hyperspace," Thrawn said. "Nor do the Chiss produce appreciable numbers of Force-sensitives, though we call their gift Third Sight. But when such rare individuals *are* born, they come to us with but one ability, that of precognition."

And suddenly Vader understood. The same ability that allowed him to peer into the future far enough to know when and where an attack was coming was being used by the Chiss to sense dangers looming ahead of a ship in time to avoid them. "They navigate and pilot your ships," he said. "Finding and mapping temporary hyperlanes even as they steer new paths along them."

"Exactly." Thrawn waved a hand in the direction of the girls' quarters. "You can now appreciate the reason for our secrecy. An enemy wishing to duplicate our success cannot simply steal a computer or computer program. He must take rare and precious living beings from us." His eyes narrowed. "That cannot be allowed."

"And now your secret is known, and your fears are realized."

"Indeed," Thrawn said heavily. "The Grysks must be dealt with, and taught not to test the will of the Chiss Ascendancy."

As the rebels within the Empire needed to be taught that same lesson. "Why children?" Vader asked. "And are they all female?"

"The ability unfortunately fades with time," Thrawn said. "No level of training or practice can change that. Young adults retain perhaps half of their childhood strength; older adults only a small fraction. Only children have enough precognitive power to safely guide our ships at the speeds the Aristocras demand. As to their gender—" He hunched his shoulders slightly. "Those with the gift are nearly always female. There are exceptions, but that is the general rule. No one knows why."

"I see," Vader murmured. The Jedi's memories drifted across his vision: training with Obi-Wan, observing the younglings at the Temple in instruction and practice, the gradual achievement of each step on the long road toward strength and proficiency.

Apparently, that wasn't what it was like for the Chiss. Their Force-sensitives worked and trained for years, only to see their strength fail and their accomplishments fade. "And then they are set aside," he said. Not even the Jedi were that cruel to their chosen slaves.

"Yes," Thrawn said. "The sacrifice . . . most make it willingly, for the sake of the Ascendancy. But all with the ability must make it." For a moment his eyes seemed to unfocus, as if facing unpleasant thoughts and memories. Then his mind came back. "But that is not our concern now. We must find the Grysk base and retrieve the children before the alarm is given and they are able to mount a response to our attack." He stood up. "Come, my lord."

"A moment," Vader said, making no move to follow. "What exactly are you proposing?"

"Did you not hear me?" Thrawn asked, frowning. "We must find the Grysk base."

"Which is deep within the Unknown Regions?"

"Presumably not too deep," Thrawn assured him. "Their home-world and main center of power is thought to be a considerable distance away. But they will hardly use that location to run an operation at the edge of Imperial space." He started toward the door. "Come."

"No," Vader said.

Thrawn stopped. "My lord?"

"You propose to risk an Imperial warship and Imperial personnel on a matter that concerns only your own people," Vader said. "I cannot and will not allow that."

"The Emperor placed *me* in command of this mission."

"As he also accepted your word that your first loyalty was to the Empire," Vader countered. "That appears to no longer be the case. If, indeed, it ever was."

For a long moment, Thrawn stood motionless. Then he retraced his steps to his chair and again sat down. "If we do not move quickly, all may be lost," he said, his voice low and earnest. "The Grysks will be alerted. They will abandon that base and relocate elsewhere. The children will disappear into their domain and never be returned to their homes and families."

Their families. A swirl of The Jedi's memories swept across Vader's eyes. The Jedi's mother . . . The Jedi's lost wife and child . . .

He shook the thoughts away. Those were The Jedi's memories, not his. "That is the concern of your people," he said. "It is not yours. Unless you intend to break your oath of loyalty to the Emperor?"

"The Grysks have already made an intrusion into Imperial space," Thrawn pointed out. "Their closure of the Batuu hyperlane is clearly an aggressive move."

"Batuu is hardly a major Imperial system."

"And their current attempt to move Mokivj's moons to more permanently block Imperial movement?"

"There is no proof their intention is anything more than to seal themselves away from potential threats."

"Yet that potential threat is part of the Emperor's design," Thrawn said. "He is very interested in extending his rule into the Unknown Regions."

Vader frowned. Had Thrawn just said . . . ? "Which you of course know a great deal about."

Thrawn seemed to draw back, as if he belatedly realized he'd said too much. "As I said, the Chiss Ascendancy seeks to know all that happens around it."

Vader nodded to himself. So that was it. All those private meetings, all those secret conversations. The Emperor was taking advantage of Thrawn's knowledge to prepare for the next great Imperial expansion. "A point that is irrelevant," he said. "I asked for proof this mission concerns the Empire. So far, that proof has not been forthcoming."

"I have a long record of service to the Empire and the Emperor," Thrawn said. "Have I ever failed you?"

"What about Atollon?" Vader countered. "You were unable to stop the rebels there. Now it will fall to me to find and destroy them."

"My war with the rebels is not yet over," Thrawn said softly. "I *will* defeat them."

"Good," Vader said. "Let us return to Coruscant, that your campaign may begin."

Thrawn was silent another moment. "You spoke of proof," he said. "If I could prove the Grysks are a threat to the Empire as well as the Chiss, would you assist me in retrieving the children and destroying their local center of operations?"

"What is this proof?"

"It lies aboard the *Chimaera*," Thrawn said. "In time I hope the evidence will be sufficiently complete to establish conclusive proof. But if we wait until then I fear the children will be lost. I must ask you once again to trust me."

Trust. It was something Thrawn continued to ask for. It was something The Jedi had valued greatly.

It was a quality Vader himself had little experience with.

"I was right about the gravity generators," Thrawn continued. "I ask you to trust a little longer."

Vader gazed at him. *Trust.* So little experience . . .

Still, the Emperor trusted Thrawn. Trusted him enough to promote him to Grand Admiral and give him the Seventh Fleet. If Vader's master was willing to offer the Chiss that much authority, shouldn't Vader be, as well?

Trust.

"Very well," he said. "You may locate and attack this base, and attempt to rescue the children. But if the battle goes against you, you *will* pull back."

"Agreed," Thrawn said, inclining his head. "Thank you, my lord." He hesitated. "But I will need more from you than merely your permission. I will need your direct assistance, as well."

Vader frowned. "In what way?"

"Come to the bridge," Thrawn said, standing up again. "I will show you."

Vader looked down at the console from the command walkway. He listened to Thrawn's explanation of what he wanted.

And he wondered if the grand admiral had gone insane.

"There is no other way," Thrawn said. If he sensed Vader's displeasure, he gave no sign of it. "The Grysks have a long lead on us. But they must rely on the Chiss children to navigate them back to their base."

"Children who have done this many times before," Vader reminded him. "We have such children aboard. Why can they not serve us as they served the Grysks?"

"Because those aboard the *Chimaera* are no stronger in the Force than the children currently in Grysk hands," Thrawn said. "We must arrive at the base before the Grysks, and our Chiss navigators cannot achieve that."

"Yet you believe *I* can?"

"The children are not as strong in the Force as you are," Thrawn said. "You have their same precognition ability, but you have more strength and stamina." He gestured at the crew pit. "You should be able to sufficiently outstrip the enemy's speed."

The bridge crew had gone very quiet. The helm was studiously not looking up at Vader and his admiral. Commodore Faro was carefully not joining into the conversation. The rest of the crew was looking like they would very much prefer to be elsewhere. "And if you are wrong?"

"Then we arrive behind the Grysks," Thrawn said. "We will still engage them to the fullest, but we will have lost the element of surprise."

"Or we shall arrive so late that they will have escaped?"

Thrawn's glowing red eyes shifted to the viewport and the starfield glittering across the darkness. "Yes," he said quietly.

"Yet you still ask me to do this instead of using navigators of proven ability."

"Yes."

Vader stretched out to the Force. He had never attempted anything like this. In fact, the idea of navigating without a nav computer or an astromech droid had never even occurred to him.

Thrawn was asking him to try it, with the *Chimaera* and every Imperial asset aboard at risk.

The bridge was still silent. Did they think he would defy their admiral's order and refuse? Did they think he wouldn't do it?

Did they think he *couldn't* do it?

He squared his shoulders beneath his armor. "How will I know our destination?"

"You have touched the minds of the children who have been there," Thrawn said. There was no gloating in his voice, no hint of satisfaction at having won out over Vader's resistance. All Vader could sense was relief, perhaps even gratitude. "That knowledge, plus the guidance of the Force, should show you where the other children are being taken. For the rest, your skill and power in the Force will guide you along the quickest and safest path."

"Very well," Vader said. Sweeping his cloak behind him, he walked back along the walkway to the stairs leading down into the crew pit.

The crewers pressed themselves closer to their consoles as he passed by. The helmsman was already out of his chair, backing away to give the Dark Lord plenty of room. Vader reached the helm console and lowered himself into the chair.

The chair that had already been adjusted for his height. Either the helmsman had reset it while Vader was on his way, or Thrawn had already had it preset for the taller soon-to-be occupant.

Vader scowled. Yet more of the Chiss's abundant self-confidence.

Or maybe it was his confidence in Vader.

He reached for the ship's controls. It didn't matter. What mattered was that Thrawn needed something, and Vader could supply it, and the Empire would benefit from his actions.

At least, the Empire had *better* benefit by it.

"Stand by to go to lightspeed," Thrawn called from the command walkway. "Systems clear."

Vader listened to the familiar cadence as the various stations confirmed their readiness. It wasn't much different from the countdowns The Jedi had heard aboard Republic attack cruisers during the Clone Wars. Capital warships were capital warships, no matter who commanded them.

There was a flicker in Thrawn's sense. Vader looked up, to see a small smile on his face. "Do you find this amusing, Admiral?" he challenged.

"No, not at all, my lord," Thrawn hastened to assure him. "I was simply recalling a memory. I told you the Chiss call this talent Third Sight. What I hadn't yet spoken of is the title these navigators are given once they take their posts."

"Which is?"

"The Cheunh word is *ozyly-esehembo*," Thrawn said. "In Basic, it translates to 'sky-walker.'" Another small smile. "You can imagine my momentary confusion when I first encountered General Anakin Skywalker."

Vader nodded. He'd forgotten that The Jedi, too, had wondered about Thrawn's reaction at that meeting. A small mystery, now put to rest.

The recitation ended. "Lord Vader, the *Chimaera* awaits your guidance," Thrawn said.

That one, at least, was new. Stretching out to the Force, Vader keyed the hyperdrive.

Double vision: a cometary object approaching the starboard bow—

Not seriously dangerous, but a tweak of the course heading avoided any potential trouble. Ahead, he sensed the boundary of the Mokivj system as the *Chimaera* once more entered interstellar space.

Double vision: a large, star-sized object above the ship—

Again, a small touch on the drive avoided the risk of collision. Two more stars flashed past, without triggering any warning.

Double vision: the ship angling to portside—

The correct direction to take them to the Grysk base? Vader let his mind sink deeper into the Force, seeking confirmation.

Double vision: the ship angling to portside—

He touched the controls again, realigning the *Chimaera* onto the vector in his vision.

He'd never done this before. But it seemed he could indeed do it.

Trust me, Thrawn had again pleaded with him. *Have I ever failed you?*

Double vision: a white dwarf star directly ahead—

Once again, he adjusted course, and settled in for the long journey ahead.

CHAPTER 18

B1 battle droids weren't very smart, but they were reasonably quick to react to falling objects, thrown objects, and sudden changes in illumination or visibility. The bigger B2s were even dumber and slower, though they carried better firepower.

Both types were equally persistent. And it didn't help that Duke Solha and his two cohorts were there to shout them on to greater efforts.

It had been only a few minutes, but the numerical superiority was already starting to tell. Without his lightsaber, Anakin's options were dangerously limited. The only thing that had kept him alive this long was his mobility and the fact that the Serennians seemed extremely reluctant to damage their assembly-line setup.

At least their little Jedi hunt should be keeping them too busy to bother with Padmé and Thrawn. That was the important part.

Still, even given the logistics involved in getting to the rooftop, it seemed to Anakin that they should be back by now. Hopefully, they were just being cautious.

The droids were closing in, and Anakin was looking for yet another good spot to move to, when he felt the distant thud.

The Serennians and droids heard it, too. For a moment the blasterfire faltered a bit as everyone paused to listen. There was a second thud, and a third . . .

Anakin caught his breath. Something—multiple somethings, now—were slamming into the courtyard side of the factory wing.

Was the factory under attack? There was a fourth thud—

Abruptly, the blasterfire ceased as Solha shouted some frantic-sounding orders. On the floor below, the droids turned and headed at top speed toward the room's two exit doors. Another order, and the four B1s that had come up to the second floor to try to chase Anakin down turned and also waddled away.

Anakin crouched lower behind his current bit of cover, staying alert. This could easily be a setup, with Solha planning to reverse the orders as soon as Anakin showed himself, turning the supposed exodus into a trap.

The trap didn't happen. A moment later the only ones left were the five techs still working on the B2's programming, and the three B2s looming guard over them.

Anakin eyed the droids. Three against one. Certainly better odds than he'd had so far today. But without his lightsaber—

He froze, stretching out to the Force as a sudden breeze touched the side of his face. The door the droids had left through had just opened again. He turned in that direction, looking for something handy to throw—

"Anakin?" Padmé's soft voice came.

"Here," he stage-whispered back. Checking the B2s on the floor one last time, he made a low jump back to the area by the door where he'd first started this game. Padmé was at the edge of the platform, crouched in the partial cover of a rusty bin, her S-5 blaster in one hand and his lightsaber in the other. She looked over as his movement caught her eye, some of the tension lines smoothing from her face as she saw him. She started to stand up; he motioned her to stay where she was and hurried over.

"You all right?" he asked as he crouched down beside her.

"I'm fine," she said, passing him the lightsaber.

"Where's Thrawn?" he asked, hefting the weapon. The weight felt good in his hand.

"He's gone," she said shortly. "What's going on here?"

"Solha and most of the droids went charging off to deal with the other attack," Anakin said, frowning. There was an edge of weary bitterness he'd seldom sensed in her before. "If you'd been half a minute sooner you'd probably have gotten run over."

"Yes, I had to hide from a group of B1s heading for the courtyard," Padmé said, frowning. "What other attack?"

"Didn't you hear the thuds? I think someone's shooting at the outer wall. What do you mean, he's gone?"

"He brought his ship in, stole the shield generator, and took off," Padmé said. "I guess that's all he came for."

Anakin felt his stomach tighten. He should have known the Chiss hadn't teamed up with him out of the goodness of his heart. "Well, at least he was helpful enough to pop off a few shots as a diversion on his way out," he said. "I'm heading down. Wait here until I clear out those droids and then you can help me figure out what this is all about."

"Right," Padmé said, squeezing his hand briefly. "Be careful."

"Always." Stretching out to the Force for strength, Anakin stood up and jumped off the platform, aiming for an empty spot on the control table that would put him in easy reach of all three B2s. A crouched landing, three quick slashes with his lightsaber, and it would be over.

The techs, absorbed in their work, never saw him coming. All five of them jerked violently backward as he suddenly slammed down onto the table in front of them. The B2s, probably just as surprised, didn't even twitch. As Anakin ignited his lightsaber they raised their arms, bringing up their wrist blasters. He slashed across the nearest droid's upper torso—

And the brilliant blue blade vanished.

For half a second Anakin just stared at the empty space in confusion. There were a few weapons like electrostaffs that could block a lightsaber, but he'd never before had the weapon simply shut down.

The droids were still bringing up their wrist blasters. Igniting the lightsaber again, Anakin slashed a second time. Again, the blade disappeared before it could do more than leave a scratch on the droid's metallic skin.

There was no time to figure out what was going on. The wrist blasters were almost on target; stretching out to the Force, Anakin leapt up and over the top of one of the droids, landing five meters away and again igniting his lightsaber.

They turned to face him, their arms swinging around. The first to get his blasters lined up fired.

Double vision: bolts coming at torso, at torso—

Anakin swung the blade around, catching the two shots and bouncing them into the walls. At least *that* still worked. He dodged to the side as the second droid came on target and added its blaster-fire to the first's.

Double vision: bolts coming at torso, at head, at torso, at torso—

Letting the precognition and the Force guide his hands, Anakin deflected the salvo as he tried to think. All right. Somehow, something about the B2s' armor was able to shut down his lightsaber.

But maybe whatever it was wasn't so good at blocking blaster bolts. Time to find out.

Double vision: multiple bolts coming at torso, torso, head, torso, torso, torso, head—

Again, Anakin blocked the salvo. Only this time, instead of sending the shots across the room, he turned them straight back at his attackers.

No good. The impacts looked strange, the bolts hitting with a sort of shimmering splash instead of just digging into the surface. But there was no damage he could see. Certainly the droids weren't slowing down.

The blaster bolts were coming faster now as all three B2s came on target. Anakin dodged to the right, still blocking the shots. A pair of shots angled down from above as Padmé opened up with her S-5, her attacks leaving the same odd splash and the same lack of damage.

Anakin continued to dodge, deflecting the bolts, trying to think. Blaster bolts didn't affect Solha's new brand of B2s. That was bad enough; but the fact that they could somehow shut down lightsabers was far worse.

But the droids had to have *some* vulnerability. If they couldn't be stopped, then the Separatists had won. Anakin wouldn't accept that. He dodged again, leaping left this time, watching the droids' slitted eyes as they again tracked their blasters toward him . . .

Their blasters.

It was a slim chance, he knew, not to mention a nearly impossible shot to make. But right now, it was all he had.

Unfortunately, it would also require him to get a lot closer to at least one of his attackers. He dodged left again, still blocking their shots, then leapt up and over the droids, spinning in midair and landing again on the control table.

Directly behind the motionless B2 still wired into the console.

The five techs, he noted, had wisely fled the combat area. Anakin's three attackers turned again toward him.

But now, with Anakin partly shielded behind the blank B2, only one of them could bring its blasters to bear. It swung into range.

Double vision: a blaster bolt at his torso—

Anakin crouched down, putting his eyes on a level with the droid's wrist.

And as the bolt screamed across the gap at him he slashed his lightsaber across it, sending it directly back into the blaster's muzzle.

The *pop* of the impact was surprisingly quiet. But the result was all he could have hoped for. The entire wrist blaster shattered, sending a shower of small pieces cascading onto the floor. The droid itself didn't seem to notice, but continued striding forward, its arm extended as if its blaster was still spitting death toward his target.

Double vision: bolts coming from the other two droids at torso, at head—

Anakin deflected and dodged, again doing his best to keep the stationary B2 between him and the still-functional attackers.

Only now, it suddenly occurred to him, he had *two* shields available. Bouncing the latest salvo back toward the attackers' blasters— missing with all of them—he leapt in front of the droid still trying to attack with its shattered weapon. The B2 loomed over him, its wrist blaster nearly bumping up against his chest—

And on sudden impulse Anakin stabbed the tip of his lightsaber blade directly into the droid's right photoreceptor eye.

There were clone troopers in his 501st who claimed to have taken down B2s by shooting them in the eye. Anakin had never quite known whether those stories fell into the category of fact, boast, or wishful thinking. Now, for the first time, he knew that the stories *could,* at least, be true.

Because he'd just done it.

The B2 staggered back like a brawler punched in the jaw. Anakin twisted his wrists, hoping to slice further through the head and destroy more of the droid's processor; once again, as the blade hit the edges of the eye socket the lightsaber shut down. Anakin took a long step backward as the droid's knees buckled and it pitched forward to crash onto the floor.

Double vision: bolts coming at torso, at head, at torso—

Anakin swung around, igniting his lightsaber again as the other B2s came around the obstacles and back into range. One down; two to go. He moved to his right, getting into position to once again leap into the shadow of the blank B2, where he could hopefully take the remaining droids one at a time.

He was three steps away from making his move when a lightning bolt ripped down from Padmé's level directly into one of the droids.

The effect was startling and vaguely comedic. Instead of merely falling over, the B2's arms and legs snapped straight out to both sides, turning the droid into a bizarre caricature of a child making a sand angel. It held that pose for a second before, overbalanced, it toppled to the floor.

It was still falling when a second lightning bolt blasted through the air, turning the last B2 into its own sand angel and dropping it to the floor.

For a moment Anakin just stared at the droids, the acrid smell of burnt plastoid curling his nostrils. Then he looked up.

Padmé was standing at the edge of the second-level platform, her S-5 held loosely in two-handed sharpshooter stance, her mouth hanging slightly open in astonishment at the sight laid out below her. Two steps behind her and to the side stood Thrawn, holding a long, shoulder-slung rifle in the crook of his arm. As Anakin watched, the Chiss stepped forward, slinging the rifle behind his back, and casually plucked the S-5 from Padmé's hands. He hooked the grapple around a nearby bracing strut, stepped off the platform, and dropped smoothly to the floor below. Resetting the ascension mode, he sent the blaster back up.

"Well done," he said, walking toward Anakin, his glowing red eyes looking back and forth. "Interesting variant on the Separatists' usual combat machines."

"Glad you enjoyed the show," Anakin said, eyeing the unfamiliar weapon as the other stopped in front of him. "Thanks for the assist. Next time, feel free to join the fight sooner."

"If I had, you wouldn't have learned how to defeat them," Thrawn pointed out. "Besides, this particular weapon carries only three shots."

Anakin felt his lip twitch. So the Chiss *could* have taken out all three B2s. Instead, he'd held back while Anakin ran around like crazy trying not to get his head blown off.

Still, he had to admit that Thrawn had a point. If this whole factory was geared to making more of these invulnerable droids, the Republic needed to know how to fight them. "Well, thanks anyway." He nodded at the droid he'd taken down. "You have any idea how they're doing this?"

"I have a thought," Thrawn said. "Let us examine the bins."

Padmé caught up with them on the way. "I thought you were leaving," she said to Thrawn, her eyes hostile, her voice not sure whether to be angry, relieved, or some combination of the two.

"I never said I was leaving," Thrawn told her calmly. "I merely said that I'd been sent for the shield generator, and that my first duty was to my people. Once that duty was fulfilled, I was free to return to General Skywalker's aid."

"Hey!" a voice called from the side.

Reflexively, Anakin spun around, igniting his lightsaber, peripherally aware that Thrawn had swung his own weapon back up to firing position.

A big man was coming toward them from the direction of the first-level door, a battle droid's E-5 blaster rifle gripped in his hands. He jerked to a halt, his eyes widening as he saw the lightsaber blade. "Whoa!" he said, stooping down hastily and dropping the E-5 to the floor.

"It's okay," Padmé said quickly. "That's LebJau—he's been helping me."

"What do you want?" Anakin asked, glaring at the intruder over the pulsing blade. Generally, he trusted Padmé's judgment. But the man had charged in on them without warning while carrying a Separatist weapon.

"I got everyone moving, like she said," LebJau said, his eyes seemingly locked on the lightsaber. "I just thought she might need me, that's all."

"I promised him and his friends some reward money if they didn't hand me over to Duke Solha," Padmé added.

"Is the payment of ransom for ambassadors a common practice in the Republic?" Thrawn asked.

LebJau's eyes widened a little more. "*Ambassador?* You didn't say you were an ambassador."

"Don't worry about it," Anakin said. "Those." He pointed at the group of techs still cowering beside the row of B2 blanks. "They're still here. Get rid of them."

"Sure." LebJau beckoned to the techs. "You heard the man, Vipke. Let's go. I said let's *go.*"

Silently, the techs unglued themselves from the wall and headed across the room. Their expressions, Anakin noted, ran from nervous to frightened to angry. "Frost you," one of them muttered, glaring balefully as he passed Anakin. "You've ruined everything."

"Move it," LebJau growled. Still watching Anakin, he stooped and gingerly picked up the blaster again. The last tech passed him, and he fell in behind them, holding the blaster at the ready. Thrawn set off again toward the bins, Anakin and Padmé behind him.

"You know, we could have asked *them* about the droids," Padmé said quietly.

"Yeah, we could have," Anakin agreed. "Didn't really want them around. Okay, Thrawn—let's hear it."

"An experiment." Thrawn pointed to the bin with the fibrous material. "Touch your lightsaber blade to this."

Anakin did so. Once again, the blade instantly vanished.

"The material is called cortosis," the Chiss said. "It's very rare— I've heard stories about it, but never seen any. It's rumored to have unusually high energy absorption and transmission coefficients, to the point where many energy weapon blasts will be dissipated along the fibers without damaging the fibers themselves."

"That's why the blaster shots didn't hurt it," Padmé murmured.

"Yes," Thrawn said. "It's also soft and frangible, useless for building into armor or other protective materials."

"Solha seems to have solved that problem," Anakin said.

"Indeed," Thrawn said. "It appears they've found a method for weaving the cortosis into a network within a protective matrix. An energy impact is therefore dissipated across the entire network and throughout the entire droid armor shell."

"They've covered the walls with it, too," Padmé said. "The blaster bolts you deflected did the same sunburst thing as the ones you sent into the B2s."

"I imagine it took considerable experimentation to learn how to use a minimal amount of cortosis while still weaving it into a pattern where each fiber touches at least one of the others," Thrawn said. "It would appear they used their failures to add extra protection to their factory."

"So blasters won't work unless you give a really massive jolt?"

Anakin said, looking over at the two sand-angel droids Thrawn had taken out with his lightning gun.

"Or perhaps a very specific jolt," Thrawn said. "A blaster shot is a single energy pulse, which can be dissipated throughout the matrix. The arc-cannon delivers a prolonged energy profile that overloads even the cortosis's ability to dissipate."

"Not to mention putting a massive charge on the skin so that the limbs repel each other," Padmé pointed out. "That's a nice touch."

"Completely unexpected, I assure you," Thrawn said. "The side effects of combat can be unpredictable."

"So what's the deal with my lightsaber?" Anakin asked. "It delivers a prolonged energy profile, too."

"There I can only speculate, as the stories of cortosis include no such weapons," Thrawn said. "But I suspect it's analogous to the functioning of a superconductor. Most such materials can be overloaded by a sufficiently large surge. The far sharper energy gradient at the edge of the lightsaber blade may momentarily block the cortosis effect, sending the energy bouncing back into the blade. There must be something in the return profile that causes the mechanism to shut down."

"That doesn't make any sense," Anakin insisted. "I can bounce against another lightsaber blade without anything like that happening."

Thrawn shook his head. "As I say, I can only speculate. But certainly the ability to block lightsabers would be of paramount importance to the Separatists."

"That it would," Anakin agreed heavily, igniting the blade again. It looked, felt, and sounded exactly as it usually did. "So what we need to do is destroy all this"—he waved at the cortosis bin—"so they can't make more of these super battle droids."

"You could do that," Thrawn agreed. "But there may be more of the material available that we have no access to."

"There's also a mine," Padmé said. "That's where they're getting it."

"Then we have to shut that down, too," Anakin said impatiently. "So let's get started."

"A moment," Thrawn said, his glowing eyes narrowed in thought. "Instead of attempting to shut down the factory, a better solution might be to let them waste their time and resources on a lethally flawed project."

Anakin glanced at Padmé. She looked as puzzled as he felt. "And how do you propose we do that?"

"We have the assembly-line control system available to us," Thrawn said, pointing to the control table. "We have your astromech droid. Why not reprogram the war droids for failure?"

"You mean leave some spots open so blaster bolts can get in?" Padmé asked. "Won't they notice that?"

"I suggest something more subtle," Thrawn said. "The mesh encompasses nearly all of the droid's surface. We can merely extend it slightly by adding a few threads across the discharge capacitor within the blaster emission cylinders."

Anakin frowned. And then he got it. "So that every time it fires, it'll send a burst of energy of its own into the system?"

"Exactly," Thrawn said. "If we also reroute some of the inner mesh threads to lie closer to the control processor . . . ?"

"Then the more it fires, the faster it fries its own brain," Padmé said, a cautious excitement creeping into her voice. "Only it'll do it slowly enough that they won't notice. It'll look fine and pass all the tests."

"And then five minutes into combat it'll start falling apart," Anakin said. "Sounds like a plan. Let's plug Artoo in and see what he can do."

Standard Republic protocol called for astromech droids to be memory-wiped after every mission, lest a Separatist capture offer the enemy a treasure trove of classified information. Anakin had routinely ignored that order, despite the trouble it had occasionally gotten him into with both the military leadership and the Jedi Council.

But as a result, R2-D2 still had all the stray bits and pieces of data and procedure that he'd picked up over the years. One of those bits of procedure involved factory architecture and graphic rewriting.

"Okay, he's on it," Anakin said as the droid warbled his confirmation. "Any other suggestions?"

"Only that he hurry," Thrawn said, cocking his head. "My pilot's diversionary attack has ended. They may return at any minute."

"I thought you said you weren't bringing your ship," Anakin said, focusing on the sounds around them. Sure enough, the rhythmic thudding from earlier had stopped.

"I said I didn't wish to arrive with it," Thrawn reminded him. "We may need to create a diversion to permit Ambassador Padmé and the droid to complete their task."

"LebJau said they did the cortosis sifting and sorting in the western end of the north wing," Padmé said. "Then they took it to the eastern north wing, and here to the east wing."

"They're making unstoppable B2s here," Anakin said. "Any idea what they're making in the north wing?"

"He didn't say. He probably doesn't know."

Anakin cocked an eyebrow at Thrawn. "You feel like finding out?"

"It would be as good a place as any for a diversion," Thrawn said.

Anakin suppressed a grimace as he headed across the floor toward the wing's northern door. With his *real* mission now completed, had the Chiss lost interest in what else the Separatists might be doing here?

It didn't matter. Anakin still cared. More to the point, if Thrawn had really sent his ship away, their borrowed freighter was still the Chiss's only way off Mokivj.

And he didn't just need the freighter; he needed Anakin. The only reason for Thrawn to have a pilot was if he couldn't fly a ship himself. Interested or not, he would still have to tag along.

"Fine," Anakin said. "I'll take point. Try to keep up."

As Padmé had pointed out, the walls were at least partially immune to lightsabers. Fortunately, the door leading to the north wing wasn't. As she watched from the control desk, Anakin carefully sliced through the lock and hinges. A wave of his hand, and the heavy panel floated back out of the doorway. Anakin and Thrawn stepped through, Anakin with his lightsaber ready, Thrawn with his lightning gun still slung over his back.

Padmé watched as they disappeared from view, her mind churning with mixed feelings. She was glad that Thrawn had come back, especially given that Anakin might well be dead if he hadn't. But the fact that he'd apparently been perfectly willing to abandon them once he had what he needed still rankled.

Maybe that wasn't unreasonable. Maybe in his place she would do the same.

Maybe what *really* troubled her was his suggestion that the Republic and Separatists all played by those same rules.

Because she'd seen that happen all too many times. Diplomats, senators, governors, entire planetary systems—the minute they got what they wanted they were gone, without a single thought for anyone else.

Was that how it always was?

A movement caught her eye: The door Anakin had just gotten rid of was being set up back in the opening. Just before it blocked Padmé's view she had a glimpse of Anakin on the other side, an annoyed set to his mouth.

Which probably meant that putting the door back up had been Thrawn's idea, not his.

Padmé smiled. Anakin had never been one to take orders graciously. Some days even good suggestions were pushing it.

R2-D2 beeped. "You're in?" Padmé asked, looking down at him. "How long?"

The droid warbled an estimate: ten to fifteen more minutes. "Good," Padmé said. That should give Anakin and Thrawn enough time to figure out what Solha was doing in that wing. Hopefully, they could find a fix as clever as Thrawn's plan for the B2s. She reached up and gently touched the super battle droid's arm. It felt a little warmer than the usual metal armoring, but aside from that not much difference.

At least now she knew why the Separatists had set up their droid factory here instead of just shipping the cortosis somewhere else in their territory. A captured ship carrying an unknown material would spark suspicion and investigation. A captured ship carrying super battle droids wouldn't even raise any eyebrows, but would merely be sent somewhere to have its cargo crushed or dismantled. Odds were the workers or droids handling that task would never even notice anything unusual about them.

Without warning, the B2 twitched.

Padmé jerked her hand back. "Artoo?" she breathed. "You *did* shut down the data transfer, right?"

She wasn't sure she completely understood the little astromech's response. But it sounded like the transfer had already been completed, and the B2 was simply waiting on its internal processor to sort the data and set up the internal programming. "How long?" she asked.

The answer was almost inevitable: ten to fifteen minutes.

"Great," she muttered, looking up at the big droid. "Work fast, Artoo."

He gave a slightly snooty beep—of *course* he was working at top speed.

"Right," Padmé said, smiling. No matter what danger might be threatening, despite being in the middle of chaos, R2-D2 just kept on doing what he had to. It was a lesson a lot of people she knew could benefit from.

She looked over at the row of B2s still standing along the walls. Thrawn's bit of sleight of hand—almost literally, it belatedly occurred to her—would hopefully work for any future battle droids. But those eight finished ones could give the Republic forces serious trouble if they got out.

Maybe there was a way she could sabotage them, or at least mark them so that the clones and Jedi could see them coming. Leaving R2-D2 at his task, she crossed to the B2s. She studied their torsos, wondering if she dared put scratch marks on them—

"Hello, Jedi," a calm voice came from across the room.

Padmé stiffened, resisting the urge to go for one of her blasters.

From the direction of the voice, he'd probably come in through the south door. From the sound of his footsteps, he was walking casually toward her. If he had his own weapon ready—and he undoubtedly did—she would never get into position to take a shot before he nailed her.

She frowned. *One* set of footsteps. More important, one set of footsteps not accompanied by any of the distinctive muffled clanking of battle droids. Had he actually come alone?

"Good evening," she called back, thinking fast. Anakin had said Duke Solha was in charge of this operation, and that was definitely a Serennian accent. But facing down a Jedi alone seemed beyond even the famous cultural arrogance of Serennian nobility.

On top of that, there was something wrong with his voice. Padmé frowned . . .

"I see you're admiring my handiwork," the voice continued, the footsteps still continuing in her direction. "Be good and I'll tell you—"

Abruptly, the footsteps faltered. "What the—?"

Padmé smiled tightly. "I gather you've noticed *my* handiwork?" she countered. She turned around.

And caught her breath. The puzzle of his odd voice, at least, was now answered. Instead of the nobleman she'd seen from her hidden perch in the west wing, a man dressed in elegant Serennian tunic and cloak, she found herself facing a fully armored clone trooper. He was holding a blaster rifle on her—not the Republic's standard-issue DC-15, oddly enough, but a battle droid's E-5—but his helmet was turned to the side, toward the three B2s Anakin and Thrawn had destroyed. "Impossible," he said, as if talking to himself. "They assured me . . . ah," he said, the confusion suddenly gone from his voice. "Very clever. Where did you find an arc-cannon to use against them?"

"I'm very resourceful," Padmé said. So he knew Thrawn's lightning gun could take out the droids? Interesting. "Invulnerable battle droids. Very impressive."

His head jerked back toward her and he leaned forward as if peering at her face. "Senator *Amidala*?"

"Yes," Padmé said. "Duke Solha?"

For a moment the figure hesitated. Then, keeping his grip on his E-5, he lifted both hands and awkwardly pulled off his helmet.

It was the duke, all right. But not quite as she remembered him. Whereas the old Solha had had the look of someone whose ambitions and desires had been thwarted at every pass, this new Solha's eyes and face were on fire, brimming with hope and purpose and anticipation. "So you remember me," Solha said. "I'm impressed. So many in the Republic and Senate thought of me as a joke, or didn't notice me at all."

"That's not true," Padmé said carefully. Solha was clearly working with Dooku . . . but in any such alliance there was always a chance of persuading someone to change sides. She needed to stall him another few moments anyway; she might as well use that time to try to sow a few seeds of doubt. "You were seen as one of the quieter but more solid supporters of justice and order."

"When they remembered my name, you mean?" Solha scoffed. "Well, that will change. After the final Confederacy victory, *everyone* will know my name."

"I'm sure they will," Padmé assured him. "I should warn you, though, that Dooku has promised victory any number of times, and somehow the Republic still manages to survive."

"I hope you'll remember that boast while you await trial for crimes against the Confederacy," Solha said. "Once Dooku has an army of these droids"—he smiled slyly—"plus a couple of other surprises, your precious Grand Army will be doomed. If you're lucky, maybe the count will allow the Republic to continue to exist. If not—" He shrugged again. "Either way, I imagine the most bothersome members of the government will be eliminated."

"So I would assume," Padmé agreed, throwing a surreptitious look at the south door. Still no sign of any droids. What was Solha waiting for? "Though as a professional politician, I have to tell you that raising the level of your threats at this point really isn't productive."

Apparently, the glance hadn't been surreptitious enough. "If you're waiting for my siblings and my droids to make their appearance, you're looking in the wrong direction," Solha said. "Some are still in the courtyard, making sure the stolen freighter your friends arrived on won't be flying again, at least not anytime soon. The others"—he gave her an evil smile—"are even now making their way through the north wing. Once they've dealt with your friends, they'll be coming through the other door over there—"

He broke off, sudden understanding on his face. "Of course," he said. "*Skywalker.* I *thought* that freighter thief seemed familiar. But I couldn't place the face. Oh, that's unfortunate."

"Why, because you've lost?" Padmé suggested. "Because I can offer you good terms if you surrender right now."

"No, no," Solha said. "It's unfortunate because it means a great hero of the Republic will die here, unnoticed, with no one ever knowing what happened to him." His face hardened. "As, of course, will you."

CHAPTER 19

The factory area in the north wing wasn't so much an assembly line as it was an artisan's studio—smaller, more crowded with tables, and filling only a single floor. But the work being done there was very familiar.

"So that's why Solha was wearing clone trooper armor," Anakin said as he and Thrawn stood beside a section of the assembly table. "They've got the same system going here as with the B2s."

"Yes," Thrawn murmured. "This is a puzzle, General."

"How so?"

"You've stated that the battle droids being created in the east wing fight for the Separatists," Thrawn said. "Yet this armor is worn by the clone troopers who fight for the Republic. Why would the Separatists want lightsaber-resistant armor for their enemies?"

"That's obvious enough," Anakin told him grimly. "Dooku must be planning a massive infiltration of the Republic forces." He nodded at the rows of completed armor lined up on hooks along the center of the room. "In fact, right now he's got almost enough to run rough-shod over the whole Senate District."

"The Separatists also have human soldiers?"

"They have enough to fill this many suits," Anakin said. "In fact, that's probably why Dooku has Solha running the factory in the first place. A Serennian-run operation, with Serennian troops in the armor, and Dooku will have first crack at the best Coruscant has to offer once he's taken down the Senate."

"And eliminated the Jedi, as well?" Thrawn suggested. "They're the only ones in the Republic who use lightsabers, are they not?"

"They are," Anakin confirmed, his throat tightening. "You're right, armor like this would be perfect for attacking the Jedi Temple. If Dooku could destroy the Jedi and the Senate and maybe capture Chancellor Palpatine—"

He broke off as a sudden emotional flood rolled over him. "Pad-mé's in trouble," he said, turning and starting toward the door.

He stopped in midstride as Thrawn grabbed his arm. "No."

"Let go," Anakin said, snapping his arm free of the Chiss's grip. Thrawn countered by half turning and getting a fresh grip on Ana-kin's collar with the other hand. "I said let *go*."

"You cannot," Thrawn said firmly. "*This* is the danger to your Re-public. *This* is where you must focus your efforts."

"We'll reprogram this factory like Artoo's doing to the other one," Anakin said, snapping up his arm, aiming his forearm at Thrawn's wrist to try to break the other's grasp. Thrawn countered by letting go just as Anakin's arm swung harmlessly past, then reacquiring his grip. "*Stop* it, damn you—she's going to *die*."

"We can't reprogram here," Thrawn said. "Clone troopers don't have the droids' built-in weaponry."

"I can't abandon her."

"We won't," Thrawn promised. "But your mission—your *true* mission—must come first."

My true mission is *Padmé,* Anakin wanted to snarl.

But again, he couldn't. Thrawn didn't know the truth, and Anakin didn't dare tell him.

And down deep, he knew the Chiss was right. There was little point in rescuing his wife here only to see her executed in a Separatist purge after Coruscant's fall. "You have a plan?"

"Yes," Thrawn said. "Let's see if our opponents will allow us sufficient time."

"I'm sure you'll try your best," Padmé said, forcing her voice to stay calm. If the rest of Solha's B2s were as invulnerable as the three Anakin and Thrawn had already tangled with, her husband was in deadly danger.

Behind him, R2-D2's dome swiveled to face her.

And suddenly she realized something that hadn't occurred to her. The way the control table was positioned, Solha wouldn't have seen R2-D2's data arm on his walk across the room.

More important, he wouldn't have been able to see that the arm was plugged into the data socket.

But he *would* see it now if he simply turned around. At all costs Padmé had to keep him from doing that. "Why don't you tell me about Dooku's grand scheme?" she asked. "I seem to remember Serennian custom permitting a condemned prisoner a last request."

"Such dramatics, Senator," Solha chided. "Really, I'd tell you if I could. But I believe the count is still working out the details."

"Ah," Padmé said drily. Right. The Count Dooku she knew would have the whole thing planned down to the centimeter and millisecond by now. Odds were that he did, and that Solha simply wasn't important enough for such information.

"But really, the plan should be obvious," Solha continued. "Invulnerable battle droids to destroy your clone armies—"

With a clank, the B2 beside R2-D2 abruptly came to full life. Solha half turned toward it—

Snatching out her S-5, Padmé aimed at the left side of Solha's lower ribs, a shot that should get his attention without seriously injuring him, and fired. The bolt blazed into the edge of his chest plate.

And disappeared.

Solha jerked back around to face her, a startled look on his face. "You *shot* me?"

Padmé fired again, more toward the center of his chest this time. Again, there was no effect.

But this time she spotted the distinctive sunburst effect.

Like the B2s, Solha's armor was wreathed in cortosis fibers.

"So much for a civilized conversation," Solha snarled, his casual arrogance gone. Slipping his helmet back over his head, he spread his arms wide to both sides. "Go ahead—take your best shot. Then maybe you'll accept the fact that the Republic is doomed."

Padmé glanced past his shoulder, to see R2-D2 withdraw his data arm from the console. The reprogramming was finished.

Time to get out of here.

"If you insist," she said, focusing on Solha again. She sent a final blaster bolt at him, this one sunbursting off his helmet, again with no damage.

Thumbing the S-5's selector switch, she braced herself and fired her last grapple squarely between his eyes.

The impact snapped his head back, staggering him backward as he fought for balance. Padmé rushed forward, reeling in the grapple as she ran. Solha recovered his stance and started to swing his E-5 back toward her.

And fell flat on his back as she again slammed the grapple into his helmet. Reeling it in again, she reached him and kicked the blaster out of his hand.

He grabbed at her ankle, started to pull himself to his feet. She slammed the grapple off his faceplate one final time, bouncing the back of his helmet against the floor. This time he collapsed and lay still.

"Come on," she said, beckoning to R2-D2 as she turned and ran toward the north door. Solha's brother and sister were out there somewhere, and Anakin and Thrawn didn't know their clone armor was as invulnerable as the B2s'.

They were halfway to the door when Padmé heard the woken super battle droid stir behind them. It made a strange sound deep within itself.

And began lumbering its way toward them.

"Fill it completely," Thrawn said.

Anakin blinked, looking at the clone trooper helmet in his hands. It was indeed only half full. "Right," he said, dipping it into the cortosis bin again, his full focus on the sensations coming to him from the east wing. Padmé was still alive, still unhurt, and her anxiety level was back under control. But that was all he could see. He desperately wanted to hand the rest of the prep work over to Thrawn and rush to her aid.

But he couldn't. Thrawn was right: They had to beat this thing right here, and right now, or the Republic would be in deadly danger.

And already he could hear the sounds of approaching droids from the western end of the north wing. He and the Chiss were running out of time. "You sure this will work?" he asked as he set the helmet on the floor with the others.

"I'm certain of nothing," Thrawn admitted. "Stories and legends are useful for gauging a culture, but aren't always reliable sources of tactical data. Yet from what I've seen I believe this has a good chance of success."

"Well, if it doesn't I'll never let you hear the end of it," Anakin said. The sounds of droid feet were getting closer—

There was a sudden thud from behind them. He spun around, drawing and igniting his lightsaber in a single motion.

To his relief, it was Padmé, with R2-D2 jetting his way through the air right behind her. "Padmé!" he called.

She turned toward his voice, her stride faltering for a split second at the sight of him and Thrawn encased in their new clone trooper armor, then hurried toward him. "The other B2," she called tensely. "It's right behind me."

Anakin hissed between his teeth. An invulnerable B2 behind, an unknown number of battle droids in front. Great. "I'll take care of him," he said, starting toward her.

"Wait," Thrawn called after him. "You must disable the droid in such a way that you block the door."

"Don't worry, none of the other blanks have been activated," Padmé said.

"The blockage is for us," Thrawn said. "They must not wonder afterward why we didn't return to that chamber and destroy it."

"Yeah, yeah, got it," Anakin said impatiently. Unfortunately, even a hulking super battle droid wouldn't fully fill the whole doorway. "Suggestions?"

"Try to spread-eagle it, as I did the two with my arc-cannon," Thrawn said.

"Why don't *you* do it?" Padmé asked. "You still have one shot, right?"

"We need that here," Anakin said, thinking fast. "Okay, I'll get it. Padmé, stay here and give him a hand—we're filling as many helmets with cortosis as we can. Artoo, you're with me."

"And don't let the B2 see your lightsaber," Padmé called after him.

"Okay," Anakin said. Prying back the top of his chest plate, he dropped the weapon between his chest and the armor, and sprinted toward the doorway, feeling decidedly awkward and more than a little claustrophobic. He normally fought with only minimal armor, as Thrawn had already noted, and with his arms and legs free to move. Going into battle fully encased this way was a new experience, and not a particularly pleasant one.

A screwdriver lying on the floor a few meters away caught his eye, and he used the Force to draw it to his hand. A couple of quick instructions to R2-D2—

The little droid warbled a warning.

"Right," Anakin said, slipping on the helmet.

And now he felt awkward, claustrophobic, *and* blind. Great.

B2s weren't terrifically fast, fortunately, and the battle droid was still a few paces away when Anakin and R2-D2 reached the doorway. The B2 caught sight of Anakin and stopped, raising its wrist blaster. "Identify," it demanded in a flat voice.

Anakin smiled inside his helmet. So that was what Padmé had meant. The three Serennians were also in clone armor, and they probably hadn't had time to work out a proper ID code system with their droids. As long as the B2 didn't see his lightsaber, it couldn't tell he wasn't one of its masters. "Duke Solha," he said, just to see what it would do.

The B2 paused, thinking or else confused. "Artoo?" Anakin murmured, nodding toward the droid.

R2-D2 twittered and rolled forward, gunning his little wheels for all they were worth. He reached top speed and kept going.

And rammed straight into the B2's legs.

Given the difference in size and weight, Anakin hadn't expected the astromech to topple the battle droid. Sure enough, the B2 staggered with the impact but stayed on its feet. It looked down, as if amazed by R2-D2's sheer impudence, and Anakin took advantage of the distraction to reach up and drive the end of the screwdriver into the wall just above the door lintel, using Force strength to shove it through the ceramic nearly handle-deep.

The B2 swept its left arm down, shoving R2-D2 off to the side, and started toward the doorway again. Anakin backed up a couple of steps, then reversed direction, running forward toward the droid. He reached the doorway and jumped up, catching hold of the screwdriver and using the pivot point to swing himself forward. He shoved off the screwdriver, arced briefly through the air, and slammed feet-first into the B2's torso.

The battle droid nearly fell over that time, barely managing to maintain its balance. Anakin landed on his back on the floor and scrambled to his feet.

Double vision: shot coming at torso—

Just as the B2 fired its wrist blaster at full power into his chest.

Anakin jerked back, feeling a warm glow spread rapidly from his chest to envelop his whole body. The droid fired again as Anakin backed through the doorway; this time the glow was almost painfully warm. Even cortosis, apparently, had its limits.

The B2, its balance now restored, started forward again, its blaster tracking Anakin's chest. Behind the droid, apparently unnoticed, R2-D2 was coming up, preparing for another run at its legs. Anakin watched the B2, judging his timing—

"Now, Artoo!" he snapped and again charged forward.

In general, B2s weren't very bright. But this one was perhaps smarter than most. More important, it had already had a taste of its opponents' preferred mode of attack. Even as Anakin sprinted forward it reached the doorway and stretched its arms out to both sides, bracing itself against the jambs for the coming impact. Behind it, R2-D2 trilled a sort of battle cry and increased his speed; the B2 responded by splaying its legs to both sides, bracing its feet against the doorway as well in preparation for the little astromech's attack.

Thereby putting itself in exactly the position Thrawn had requested.

Jumping up to the screwdriver, Anakin grabbed it with his left hand and slammed his feet against the B2's torso. With its arms and legs braced, the droid didn't even quiver. Still holding on to the screwdriver, his feet braced against the B2's torso, Anakin yanked off his chest plate with his right hand, grabbing his lightsaber before it could fall.

He jammed the end up against the droid's right eye and ignited the blade.

A shudder ran through the B2's frame. The reaction passed, and the droid seemed to sag in place. For a second Anakin thought it would fall, but it had braced itself too well and remained upright in the doorway. Sealing it from any approach, just as Thrawn had wanted.

Sealing it, unfortunately, with R2-D2 trapped on the other side.

Anakin's satisfied smile vanished. "Artoo?" he called tentatively.

The droid gave an exasperated grunt. "Yeah, sorry," Anakin said, dropping back to the floor. "Hang on, I'll get you out of there."

"Anakin!" Padmé called urgently. "They're coming."

"Correction: They've arrived," Thrawn added coolly.

Anakin looked back. A door leading into the western half of the north wing had opened, and a line of B1 battle droids was filing in, their blasters held high, their heads moving back and forth as they searched for a target. Behind them, visible above the crowd, were seven B2s.

He winced. And if all seven were the indestructible type . . .

"There!" one of the B1s called, leveling its blaster at Anakin. "You! Stop for questioning!"

"Don't shoot," Anakin called, starting toward them with his hands behind his head, his lightsaber concealed from their view. The lead

B1s had passed the row of nine cortosis-filled helmets, possibly oblivious to their presence, certainly unaware of their significance. All he had to do now was stall them long enough for all the B2s to clear the doorway.

He grimaced. Nine helmets. Seven B2s. This could get tricky.

The droids were still moving forward, half the B1s focused on Anakin, the other half continuing their visual sweep to both sides. The B2s were still behind them, their arms raised, their wrist blasters also sweeping the room. All of the super battle droids were inside now, with another squad of B1s bringing up the rear.

Without warning a blaster bolt sizzled across the room to slam into one of the B2s.

Instantly the droids turned, swiveling their weapons toward the shooter. But before they could fire a second bolt came at them from the other side of the room, this one splashing off a different B2.

Splashing.

Anakin smiled tightly. Of course. Padmé and Thrawn were targeting the B2s in order, watching for the telltale sign of cortosis armor.

The droids were returning fire now. But the attacking blaster bolts were still coming in, their sources shifting each time as Padmé and Thrawn fired and then quickly changed positions to avoid the droids' counterattack. One . . . two . . . three . . .

The seventh and final shot split the air.

And Anakin had the numbers. Three of the seven B2s were of the normal type. The other four, clustered together in the center of the droid formation, were the invulnerable ones.

"Ready!" he shouted, bringing his hands and lightsaber back into view and igniting the weapon. One of the B1s gave a squeak at the sight of the blue blade, and the entire front rank opened fire.

Anakin deflected the shots, edging toward one of the support pillars, trying to draw as much of their attention toward him as he could. They would only have one shot at this. He reached the pillar and ducked behind it.

And instantly ducked around the other side as blasterfire blasted chips of ceramic off the edge where he'd just disappeared. For a fatal half second the B1s had lost their target.

That half second was all he needed. Stretching out with the Force, he lifted the nine helmets and hurled them at and above the four invulnerable B2s. Another twitch, and the helmets turned over, dumping their cortosis fibers into a drifting, swirling cloud around the droids' heads. From across the room, the final shot of Thrawn's lightning gun shattered through the air.

An instant later the four B2s were wreathed with a blazing, twisting, pulsating cloud of energy as the falling fibers connected to one another, disconnected, then reconnected, sending the energy through one another and into the threads embedded in the droids' armor.

Thrawn had hoped that the sudden flood of energy would destroy the droids. Anakin hadn't been convinced that would happen. But he also hadn't cared. All he cared about was dazzling the B2s long enough for him to get in before they recovered. Ducking around the pillar, he charged into the droid formation, slicing and shattering every B1 in his path. He reached the four invulnerable B2s and leapt into the air, fatally stabbing two of them as he arced past. He hit the floor, spun around as those first two toppled over, and jumped on the third's shoulders. Two more stabs, and all four were down. He dropped to the floor again—to find that the rest of the droids, not as affected by the lightning storm as the cortosis version, swung to the attack.

Double vision: bolts coming at chest, at head, at legs, at head, at legs, at chest—

There were probably twenty of them in all, B1s and B2s. It didn't matter. Anakin was deep in the Force, turning and blocking and slashing and destroying. Dimly through his combat haze he could sense other blasterfire cutting through the melee: Padmé and Thrawn picking off the more vulnerable B1s where they could.

The threat to Padmé—the danger to the Republic—the murder of Duja—

Double vision: bolts at chest, at head—

He continued his attack, a memory swirling up through the mist: the slaughter of the Sand People who'd tortured and murdered his mother. Then it had been justice. Now it was war.

Double vision: one bolt at chest—

He deflected the solitary bolt, raised his lightsaber. Before he could attack, the last remaining B1 fell, its torso burned through by the shot from Padmé's S-5.

He looked around. They were down. Destroyed. All of them.

"Are you all right?" Padmé asked as she hurried over to him.

"Sure," Anakin said, breathing a little harder than he should have been. The result of fighting in full armor, no doubt. "Thrawn?" he asked, turning around.

"Here," Thrawn said, emerging from cover and walking over to them, Padmé's ELG-3A blaster in his hand. "Do you still wish to destroy this place?"

Anakin looked over at the row of cortosis-laced clone armor. Dooku's ultimate plan for victory. "Absolutely," he said.

"Then do so," Thrawn said. "Ambassador Padmé and I will check on the freighter."

Anakin looked questioningly at Padmé. "Go ahead," she said. "Dooku can have his battle droids now, for all the good they'll do him. But this . . ."

"Got it," Anakin said. "Be careful. I'll be right out."

The armor might be impervious to his lightsaber. But the pillars holding up the ceiling and the floor above weren't.

He started on the one farthest to the east, to seal off that entrance as quickly as possible in case Solha tried to move the B2 out of the doorway. The pillar was stronger and better-designed than he'd expected, and it took six cuts to finally bring it down.

But when it fell, it fell spectacularly. Apparently the builders had never dreamed the pillar would collapse, and so had anchored it firmly to the ceiling as well as the floor. The result was that as the upper part of the pillar came down it dragged a huge section of ceiling and roof down with it. Even with Jedi speed Anakin was barely able to get out of the way in time.

The debris was still bouncing, the dust thick in the air, when he started on the second pillar.

By the time he reached the end of the chamber, he'd figured out the structural characteristics accurately enough to drop the last pillar squarely across the racks of clone trooper armor.

He spent a moment peering through the clouds of dust at what was left of the chamber, surveying his handiwork and making sure there was no chance that anyone could ever retrieve enough of it to be of any use. Then, picking his way through the debris, he made his way back across the chamber to the easternmost door.

Padmé and Thrawn were outside, crouched behind a section of broken permacrete that seemed to have come from the east wing's roof and top floor. "Is it done?" Padmé asked as Anakin dropped into a crouch beside them. "It was certainly loud enough."

"Buried, crushed, and shattered," Anakin confirmed. He tapped the pile of broken masonry in front of them. "What happened here?"

"Did you forget my ship's diversionary attack?" Thrawn asked.

"I guess so," Anakin said. Across the courtyard, four more B2s were standing guard at the foot of their freighter's ramp. "Let me guess. The other Serennians and the rest of the droids are inside?"

"Most likely," Thrawn said.

"Solha said they were going to disable it," Padmé said. "They've probably had enough time to do that by now."

"Probably," Anakin agreed. "So what now?"

"We prepare to leave this world," Thrawn said. "Ambassador Padmé and I will go there." He pointed to another pile of debris about halfway down the east wing's wall. "You, General, will go to the spot where the shield generator used to be and engage the battle droids. Don't advance, but remain on that spot and merely defend yourself. We shall do the rest."

Anakin frowned. Only the one hatch on the freighter was open, and there was no way anyone would be able to sneak in past the B2s, no matter how engaged they were. Even if Thrawn and Padmé got in, there was no easy way to unsabotage a ship in a timely manner without knowing exactly where and how it had been sabotaged in the first place. "May I ask how you're going to accomplish that?"

"There's no time," Thrawn said, peering up at the stars. "Go. Now."

Anakin took a deep breath. "Okay. Just remember what I said earlier about never letting you hear the end of it." Bracing himself, he ignited his lightsaber and charged into the courtyard.

The B2s swiveled as they saw him, bringing their wrist blasters to bear.

Double vision: bolts at chest, at chest, at head, at chest, at head—

He settled into his defense, letting the Force guide his hands. The battle intensified; he intensified his defense . . .

"Anakin!"

The voice seemed to come from the bottom of a well. He half turned, handing his defense fully over to the Force.

And to his amazement found that, while he'd been focused on the freighter and the B2s, another, smaller freighter had landed in the courtyard behind him. The ramp was open, and two men were lying dead or stunned on the ground beside it where they'd apparently fallen off. Padmé was waving to him from the top of the ramp; she caught his eye, nodded, and disappeared inside. Thrawn was standing beside the ramp, using it for protection as he fired Padmé's S-5 at the droids. "Inside, General," he called.

Once again, the Chiss had somehow pulled off some magic. Turning back to the droids, Anakin backed toward their new transport, continuing to block their attacks as he walked. He reached the ramp, waited for Thrawn to slip around behind him and into the ship, started to back up himself—

"Hold it!" a voice called.

Anakin risked a glance to the side. Padmé's friend LebJau was staggering toward him, R2-D2 clutched in his arms. "He got tangled in some broken plastoid," he called.

Anakin winced. "Take him inside," he said. "Sorry, Artoo."

He waited until LebJau and the little droid were safely through the hatchway, then backed up the ramp himself and stepped inside. He slapped the hatch control—"Go!" he shouted.

And grabbed for a handhold as Padmé rocketed the ship up and out, driving away at full power, twisting and jinking to avoid the B2s' fire. He waited until she'd straightened out, then headed forward.

Thrawn was already seated in the copilot seat when he arrived. "I give up," Anakin said as he got a grip on the back of Padmé's chair. "What hat did you pull *this* one out of?"

"Don't you recognize it?" Thrawn asked. "It was one of the other ships at the Black Spire landing area."

Anakin frowned. "So . . . ? Ah. The Separatists we left on Batuu helped themselves?"

"Exactly," Thrawn said. "You may recall my comment that as long as they were a few hours behind us all would be well."

"So you expected them to come."

"Of course," Thrawn said, his tone the kind Obi-Wan used when he thought Anakin wasn't catching on fast enough. "They're soldiers. They wouldn't simply abandon their duty."

"Of course not," Anakin said sourly. "And you knew they would land right where you and Padmé could shoot up at them from beneath the ramp because . . . ?"

"It was the nearest spot in the courtyard where they would be able to attack you from behind without risking a crossfire from their own droids."

"Speaking of droids, was that LebJau who just came in with Artoo?" Padmé asked.

Anakin nodded. "Artoo was in trouble, and LebJau got him out. There—up ahead—is that the cortosis mining area?"

"I don't know," Padmé said. "Seems to be in the right place, though."

"It is," Thrawn confirmed.

"Take us over there, Padmé," Anakin ordered. "We've got one more job to do."

"I'd urge you to reconsider," Thrawn said. "The presence of outsiders has already damaged this world enough."

"Hey, *we* weren't the ones who did this to them," Anakin countered. "We didn't start it. But we need to finish it."

"What are you talking about?" Padmé asked, sounding puzzled.

"General Skywalker plans to destroy the mine," Thrawn said quietly. "Again, I urge you—"

"There," Anakin interrupted, pointing past Padmé's shoulder at a tall, angled structure in the middle of the darkness, its lights off, apparently deserted. "That must be the main shaft."

"Anakin, are you sure this is a good idea?" Padmé asked carefully.

Anakin looked down at the top of her head, a flash of anger rippling through him. "You taking *his* side now?" he demanded.

"I'm not taking anyone's side," she protested. "I'm just trying to figure out if it's the smart thing to do. We've got the droids reprogrammed, remember? Why not let them waste the cortosis?"

"And what if they figure it out?" Anakin shot back. "Just because Thrawn said cortosis is rare doesn't mean they won't find another stash of it somewhere. Besides, we can't risk them making more clone armor."

"There'll be miners down below," LebJau murmured from the hatchway behind them.

Anakin turned. LebJau's face was set in hard lines, his throat working. "We'll get them out first," he promised. "Thrawn and I can do that. Or maybe you and Thrawn—I need to find and set some explosives."

For a long moment, LebJau gazed in silence at the building coming up on them. He looked down at the lightsaber on Anakin's belt, and sighed. "Sure," he said. "Not like we have a choice. Like we ever have any choice, really."

"Good," Anakin said, turning back around. "Looks like the main door's there on the south. Put us down beside it."

"I hope you know what you're doing," Padmé murmured.

"I do." Reaching over the chair back, Anakin touched her shoulder. "Trust me."

CHAPTER 20

"Lord Vader?" Thrawn's voice came through the blackness. "Come back, my lord."

Vader opened his eyes. To his mild surprise he was still seated at the *Chimaera*'s helm. "I have not left, Admiral," he said, putting some warning into his voice. "There is no need to return."

"My apologies, my lord," Thrawn said, inclining his head.

Vader looked around. Thrawn had been wise enough to clear this section of the bridge, leaving no one to gawk at him, either in the crew pit or on the command walkway above them.

Fortunately for Thrawn. Even more fortunately for whoever that unlucky person might have been.

"They are preparing the *Chimaera* for attack," Thrawn said, answering the unasked question.

"I see," Vader said, turning back to the helm readouts.

They had arrived.

"Yes," Thrawn said. "The system has no name among the Chiss, nor has it any inhabited worlds. In the distance ahead lie two ships in parking drift, most likely part of the moon-transport group. They are largely dormant, presumably awaiting the return of the ships from Mokivj."

"Is there a base?"

"There is nothing except the ships."

"Perhaps the Grysks are nomads, after all. We are undetected?"

"As yet, it appears so." Thrawn hesitated. "I have a plan, my lord. It will require your participation, if you are willing."

Vader eyed him. At least this time the Chiss was asking instead of ordering or assuming. "Tell me your plan," he said.

"I wish you and your First Legion to go aboard the *Darkhawk*. You will intercept the Grysk ship, go aboard—"

"No," Vader said.

Thrawn seemed taken aback. "Excuse me, my lord?"

"I will not go aboard the ship," Vader said. "Commander Kimmund and the First Legion are more than capable of handling a breach and rescue mission on their own."

Thrawn's lips compressed, just a bit, just briefly. "Yet of all of us, my lord, you are the only one who can utilize the Force."

"Does that bother you, Admiral?" Vader asked. "The creature you described on Atollon. It nearly defeated you because you could not understand it."

"In the end it was vanquished."

"Was it?" Vader countered.

Thrawn's lips compressed again. "This is hardly the time to discuss such matters."

"It is the perfect time." Vader waved a hand toward the viewport and the two Grysk ships in the distance. "You propose to take the *Chimaera* against a people whom the Emperor has not yet declared as an enemy. You propose to do so without orders, and in an action that benefits your people and not the Empire."

"We have already discussed this," Thrawn said. "I maintain that it serves both."

"Does it?" Vader countered. "We are on a mission for the Empire, Admiral. The mission is all that matters. Victory is all that matters."

"The future of my people also matters."

"No," Vader said flatly. "Victory is the goal."

"And not revenge?"

"Not revenge," Vader said. "Not even rescue."

For a moment Thrawn was silent. "I understand," he said. "But I believe we can do both."

Vader stretched out with the Force. Again, Thrawn seemed so certain, so confident that he was in the right.

Vader could stop him. Perhaps he *should* stop him.

But he'd seen this confidence before, long ago, in The Jedi. He, too, had had perfect assurance that what he was doing was both right and necessary.

And once again, Vader found himself curious to see whether Thrawn could truly deliver everything he'd promised.

"Very well," he said. "But understand this. All the strength of the creature you faced on Atollon pales in comparison with the power of the Emperor. Are you truly willing to risk his anger?"

"There is no risk," Thrawn said evenly. "This mission will indeed meet with the Emperor's ultimate approval."

"Perhaps," Vader said. It might not, of course. But again, the Chiss's quiet certainty was unmistakable. Whether Thrawn was ultimately proven right as to the Emperor's approval, there was no doubt that he himself believed such approval would be forthcoming. "Very well, I will permit this attack.

"But *this* is how it will be carried out . . ."

"Bridge reports ready, Admiral," Faro said. *Her voice holds tension, her body stance trepidation. She is not convinced the battle can or will be won.* "All weapons systems standing by, ready to activate at your command."

"Thank you, Commodore," Thrawn said. "And the *Darkhawk*?"

"In position, sir." *Her voice holds a fresh layer of uncertainty.*

"You do not believe we can achieve victory, Commodore."

She hesitates, her expression holding reluctance. "I've seen the scanner reports, sir," she said. "I've counted the number of weapons emplacements. Each ship is nearly as big as we are . . . and there are two of them."

"Indeed," Thrawn said. "But we have an advantage."

"Which is, sir?"

"The Grysks have been studying the Empire," Thrawn said. "They must therefore know Imperial ships and weapons. We shall use that knowledge against them."

"And, hopefully, their own cultural blind spots?" Faro suggested.

"Incoming!" Sensor Officer Hammerly called suddenly. "Just out of lightspeed ahead of us. Configuration . . . it's the ship we chased out of the Mokivj system, Admiral."

"Very good," Thrawn said. *Faro's expression holds a degree less uncertainty now.* "Proceed, Commodore. Let us see how we may turn their numerical advantage against them."

"Yes, sir," Faro said. *Her stance still holds tension, but her voice holds only confidence and resolve.* "Signal Lord Vader and the *Darkhawk*," she called toward the comm station. "Tell them their target is on the way."

"*Chimaera,* acknowledged," Kimmund called toward the bridge comm, gazing at the *Darkhawk*'s tactical display. The Grysk ship was headed toward the two drifting ships far ahead, riding a vector that would take them within range of the Imperials lying silent and dark directly in front of them. "Lord Vader, we have target confirmation."

"Very well, Commander," Vader's voice came from the speaker. "Stand ready."

"Standing ready," Kimmund repeated. The Grysk ship was getting closer . . . overshot the mark . . .

And without warning the blaze of a TIE Defender's engines flashed into view directly behind the Grysk. The fighter leapt ahead, its laser cannon blasting away at the Grysk's own thrusters.

The Grysk was caught completely flat-footed. Vader got a double volley into the thrusters before the pilot belatedly jinked in an effort to throw off his attacker's aim.

Too little, too late. Even as the Grysk tried to leap forward, its acceleration faltered and faded away, leaving it running on a locked vector. "Tephan?" Kimmund said.

"Ready," the pilot confirmed. She keyed the *Darkhawk*'s thrusters, kicking them to full acceleration. The Grysk shot past; the *Darkhawk* matched its speed, then started to catch up. The distance between them shrank; Tephan again adjusted her acceleration—

And with a violent *thud* the *Darkhawk* slammed against the Grysk, bouncing once against its hatch before the grapples caught and locked the two ships together.

"Go!" Kimmund shouted. He unstrapped and bounded out of the cockpit, racing toward the hatch. He reached it just as the sizzlers went off, burning through the Grysks' hatch and sending the warped and blackened metal spinning into the enemy ship.

It had been one of the fastest breaches Kimmund had ever launched. Even so, the Grysks were in position, pressed against walls and in recessed doorways. They opened fire, blasting at Drav and Jid as they crouched inside the partial protection of the *Darkhawk*'s own hatchway.

And as the blaze of blasterfire and Grysk lightning guns lit up the corridor, Kimmund spotted the slight bubble of distortion as a cloaked figure slipped from the *Darkhawk* and traveled, unnoticed and unhindered, down the corridor. The aliens' defense formation began to unravel from the rear as Rukh began working his way up the lines, taking out the Grysks one by one. Nearly half of the enemy was down before those in front even noticed.

By then it was too late. Between Rukh at the rear and Drav and Jid in the front, the whole defense disintegrated.

"Rukh?" Kimmund called as he led the rest of the stormtroopers past the Grysk bodies. "Come on, Noghri—give me a direction."

There was a flicker, and the diminutive creature reappeared. "This way," he rumbled, gesturing with his electrostaff. "I smell Chiss this way."

Kimmund nodded briskly. "Viq, Dorstren, take point. Rukh, hang behind them and call out directions. And keep that cloak on—if we need to throw you at them, I don't want them to even know you're there."

"Understood," Rukh said. He did something to his chest, and again vanished.

Mentally, Kimmund shook his head. *Damn,* but he wanted one of those. "Okay, stormtroopers, move it out," he ordered. "Let's show the grand admiral what the First Legion can do."

The Grysk ship had been hit, disabled, and boarded. So far, Grand Admiral Thrawn's plan had gone exactly as predicted.

Now, Faro knew, came the real test.

"Increased power emanations from Bogeys One and Two, Admiral," Hammerly called briskly. "They've spotted the fight and are coming up to speed."

"Very good," Thrawn said. "TIE Commander: Launch fighters in designated sequence."

"Yes, sir."

Faro looked at the tactical. Three squadrons of TIE fighters were streaming from the *Chimaera*'s hangar bay now, expanding to full broadside formation and settling into three well-spaced waves. The two large Grysk ships were still coming to full combat readiness, but already they were reacting to the incoming ships, with Bogey One pulling back a bit while Bogey Two moved toward the TIEs.

A maneuver that was clearly not lost on Thrawn. "TIE Commander, all ships on Bogey Two," he ordered. "Wave Two, open fire as soon as you're in range."

Faro frowned. "Wave One will be in range sooner, sir," she pointed out quietly.

"Indeed," Thrawn acknowledged. "I have a theory, Commodore, which I wish to test."

The TIEs were still out of range when a pair of hatches opened on Bogey Two and two ships the size of light cruisers appeared. They formed into a staggered pair and headed for the TIEs.

"Interesting," Thrawn murmured. "Notice, Commodore, how Bogeys Three and Four take up the same fore–back formation as the main ships themselves. Bogey Three presents itself as the main target, while Bogey Four remains slightly behind in reserve."

"Yes, sir," Faro said, frowning. It was an obvious formation to take, one she'd seen dozens of times. Hardly worth commenting on.

"TIEs: Target Bogey Three," Thrawn said. "Repeat, target Bogey Three only. Second wave only, fire when ready."

The TIEs and cruisers continued closing on each other. "What about the Defenders, sir?" Faro prompted.

"TIE Fighter Squadrons Four and Five, stand ready," Thrawn called in answer. "Defenders, stand ready. Lord Vader?"

"I am here, Admiral," Vader's voice came. "I do not believe three waves of TIEs will be a match for the firepower of two light cruisers."

"Nor do I, my lord," Thrawn said. "TIEs: Hold your course."

Faro took a deep breath. Thrawn was known for his efficiency, spending his troops with the care of a miser spending credits. But he was also known for his ruthlessness and his willingness to do whatever was necessary to achieve his objectives. Right now, Faro couldn't tell which category this operation fell under. They were nearly at firing range . . .

The Grysks were ready. A split second before the TIEs reached range the lead cruiser opened fire, raking the front Imperial line with laserfire.

Three of the TIEs disintegrated in that opening salvo, another two staggering out of formation as each suffered the loss of a solar panel. An instant later the second line of TIEs opened up with their own laser cannons, blazing across Bogey Three as ordered, specifically targeting the cruiser's weapons clusters. The cruiser responded with another salvo, taking out two more of the first-wave TIEs—

"Break off!" Thrawn snapped. "All TIEs: Break off and take evasive maneuvers back toward the *Chimaera*."

He turned to Faro, a small but satisfied smile touching his lips. "Did you see it, Commodore?"

Faro gazed at the tactical, her stomach tightening. What was Thrawn going for? That the cruisers had superior firepower? That the

TIEs had caused only minimal damage to the lead cruiser's fighting capability? "I'm sorry, sir," she admitted. "Apparently not."

"All TIEs: Launch," Thrawn ordered. "Three waves, Defenders in Wave Three. Form up with initial waves and await targeting orders."

He got acknowledgments and turned back to Faro. "Two things, Commodore," he said, lowering his voice. "First: The cruiser opened fire just before the TIEs reached their own range. What does that suggest?"

Faro looked again at the tactical, watching the TIEs and Defenders stream out into the battlefield. Thrawn had suggested earlier that the Grysks had been observing the Empire . . . "They're familiar with TIE firing range," she said slowly. "They therefore let the TIEs get close enough so their own weapons would have maximum impact, but made sure they got the first volley."

"Which means?"

"Which means that they know a great deal about Imperial weaponry," Faro said. As he'd already suggested.

"Indeed," Thrawn said. "And the second fact?"

The two groups of standard TIEs and Defenders had come together and were sorting themselves out as per Thrawn's orders. "I'm sorry, sir," Faro confessed. "I didn't see it."

"You saw it, Commodore," Thrawn assured her. "Which TIEs did the cruiser target?"

Faro frowned again.

And then suddenly she had it. "The Grysks targeted the first line," she said. "But it was the *second* line that was firing at them."

"Exactly," Thrawn said, and there was no mistaking the satisfaction in his voice. "I had suspected that from our earlier encounters, but I needed confirmation. The Grysks' cultural blind spot is that they consider the nearest enemy to be the most dangerous, and will adjust their combat strategy to accommodate that bias."

"And we just fed into that bias by attacking only the nearest of the two cruisers," Faro said, feeling a smile of her own touch her lips.

"Exactly," Thrawn said again. "And so we now have two weapons to use against them."

"*Two* weapons, sir?"

Thrawn looked out the forward viewport. "They think they know Imperial weaponry, Commodore," he said with quiet satisfaction. "But they have never encountered a TIE Defender."

According to the specs Sampa had shown him, Rukh's vaunted personal invisibility cloak was supposed to last for three full minutes. In actuality—Kimmund made a point of timing it—the thing popped him back out after two minutes and twenty seconds.

And now the legion's secret weapon was gone.

Kimmund scowled to himself as their formation continued down the maze of corridors. This ship was a lot bigger than the simple freighter they'd attacked before, with a lot more deck space and a lot more capacity for crew or passengers.

And yet to this point they hadn't run into much opposition. Either the Grysks had been caught by surprise and were still trying to organize a proper defense, or else they were simply biding their time and luring the stormtroopers into a trap.

Kimmund was pretty sure it would turn out to be the second.

"Very near," Rukh muttered. As Kimmund had picked up the legion's pace, the Noghri had responded by dropping into a sort of primate-run, loping along on all fours with his electrostaff strapped across his back. It made him look even more bestial than he already did.

Ahead, a Grysk popped out from the edge of a side compartment and blasted off a shot with his lightning gun, the bolt catching Jid on his right upper chest and staggering him back. Morrtic swung her E-11 around and returned fire, but the Grysk had already ducked back out of sight. Morrtic hurried forward, only to have the hatch close in front of her. Cursing under her breath, she dug into her utility pouch.

"Belay that," Kimmund called to her, dropping to one knee beside Jid. As satisfying as it would be to blast the door and then fry the Grysk, they didn't have the time to spare. "Just seal it and leave him there. Jid?"

"I'm okay, Commander," Jid said, his voice coming out from between clenched teeth as Morrtic gave the hatch control two point-blank blaster bolts. "*Damn*, but that stings."

"Can you walk?" Kimmund asked. Their earlier tangles with Grysk lightning guns had shown that a close-in shot could scramble a stormtrooper's muscles and nervous system, leaving him temporarily unable to function.

"Not yet," Jid growled. "Leave me here—I'll watch your backtrail."

Kimmund snarled a silent curse. The ten stormtroopers he'd left the *Chimaera* with were already down by four: two left to guard the *Darkhawk*, and two more lost to enemy fire. If he now also had to leave Jid behind, they would be down to five stormtroopers and one Noghri. Half his force, and the Grysks had yet to spring their main trap.

Elebe was obviously thinking along the same lines. "Sir, depending on what we find up ahead, we might end up taking a different route back to the *Darkhawk*," he pointed out quietly. "If we leave him here, we may not be able to retrieve him when we're done."

"Don't worry about it," Jid said. "Go on—I'll catch up."

"Sure," Kimmund said. Or else some Grysk would stroll up to him while he was unable to aim and take him out with a single leisurely shot.

But there wasn't anything Kimmund could do about it. He couldn't afford to leave another man behind to guard Jid while he recovered.

"I could carry him," Elebe offered.

"Carry me *and* shoot, too?" Jid scoffed. "You're bad enough when it's just you and the firing range. Go—I'll be all right."

"Right," Kimmund said reluctantly. Leaving another man behind . . . but the mission had to come first. "Elebe, you and Morrtic are on point. Rukh?"

"That corridor, to the right," the Noghri said, pointing ahead.

"Let's go," Kimmund said. Letting Elebe and Morrtic get a three-pace lead, he motioned Rukh ahead and fell in behind him.

"How the *hell* can he possibly know that?" Drav growled from behind Kimmund as they headed out.

"The air currents change," Rukh said over his shoulder as he again dropped to all fours. "The scent rides the currents."

"Just make sure you don't mix up your directions," Kimmund warned. "We can't wander around the ship all day."

"One corridor," Rukh promised.

Morrtic reached the corner and swung around it to the right, her E-11 ready. She paused a split second, then did a 180 to face the other way down the corridor. "Clear," she murmured.

She stayed in position as Elebe rounded the corner beside her, bringing the long muzzle of his DLT-19 heavy blaster rifle around and leveling it to the right, the direction Rukh had indicated. "One hatch twenty meters directly ahead," he reported. "Sealed; no side access."

"There," Rukh said. "In that compartment."

Kimmund muttered a curse. Twenty meters of bare corridor, with no cover and nowhere to run. Traps couldn't get any more obvious.

But he had his orders. Thrawn wanted the Chiss children out, and Vader hadn't disagreed, so that was what the First Legion was going to do.

"Morrtic, Drav: rear guard," he ordered. Bad enough to be walking into a trap. No sense giving the enemy a chance to close in behind them, too. "Stay sharp."

He rounded the corner as Drav took up position with Morrtic, the two stormtroopers standing back-to-back and watching the other approaches. Elebe slipped into formation on Kimmund's right and slightly behind him, while Sampa settled on Kimmund's left. Rukh was somewhere, but Kimmund's full attention was on the hatch and he didn't have time to check on where the Noghri might have gone.

Morrtic had been right. Bare corridor, no cover, no exit. Kimmund glanced around, looking for signs of hidden gunports, but the walls, ceiling, and deck seemed solid. It was just the hatch, then, which would presumably open at the Grysks' chosen time and unleash their carefully prepared firestorm.

The First Legion made a point of keeping their armor in perfect condition, and as a result it was usually able to block almost anything except a point-blank shot from a seriously and probably illegally enhanced blaster. Unfortunately, they'd already seen that Grysk lightning bolts didn't have to penetrate the armor to take a stormtrooper out of the fight.

In fact, Kimmund decided, being left alive but unable to help as he watched his force gunned down in front of him would be worse than being killed outright.

And that was most likely the exact scenario that was about to unfold. Whether all the missing Grysks were waiting behind that hatch, or whether they were planning to waylay the stormtroopers on the way back to the *Darkhawk,* in the end it would all add up the same.

All for a couple of children. And not even Imperial children.

Kimmund was prepared to give his life for his stormtroopers, his commander, and his Empire. He wasn't thrilled about giving it up for alien children.

Curse Thrawn, anyway.

They were three paces from the hatch, and Kimmund had a door-popper blasting cap ready in his hand, when the hatch suddenly slid open to reveal a triple line of Grysks: two lying prone, two kneeling, two standing. All six had their weapons leveled; and even as Kimmund squeezed his E-11's trigger the aliens opened fire at the stormtroopers.

Or rather, they tried to.

Even before the hatch was all the way open the two prone gunners' weapons inexplicably jerked to either side, one left, one right, their blasts arcing harmlessly into the corridor walls instead of their targets. A split second later the two kneeling Grysks' heads simultaneously snapped backward, the backs of their helmets slamming into the torsos of the soldiers standing behind them, all four blasts also going wildly off target as their lightning guns were knocked out of line.

And suddenly Kimmund got it.

"Head shots!" he snapped at his men, shifting his aim to the leftmost standing Grysk. The alien, who had been starting to recover from the earlier impact against his torso, collapsed in a heap on the deck as two blaster bolts shattered his faceplate and sizzled through his skull. The two prone Grysks likewise went limp as Elebe and Sampa fired simultaneous blaster bolts into their helmets. A blaster bolt sizzled past Kimmund's helmet as Drav opened fire from the corridor intersection, dropping the remaining standing Grysk. The leftmost kneeling alien jerked to the side, his weapon twisting toward the ceiling; Kimmund shifted his aim to the other kneeler and sent him flopping backward with his fellows. Before he could turn his E-11 toward the last Grysk the alien's back twisted around and he fell to the deck.

And then, to Kimmund's complete lack of surprise, Rukh popped back into sight, his electrostaff still pressed against the last Grysk's throat.

Kimmund did a quick scan of the room behind the crumpled remains of the Grysk defense. It was a control area of some sort, its walls lined with consoles marked with curved arcs and circles of subdued light. In the center, half hidden behind a large console, a pair of blue-skinned Chiss girls were peeking anxiously toward him. There were no other hatches he could see in the compartment, and no more Grysk. "I thought your gadget was out of juice," he said as he stepped over the alien bodies and strode toward the children.

"That was what I wanted you to think," Rukh said, falling into step beside him. Kimmund sniffed, a whiff of burning skin making its way through his air system. Apparently, despite his attempt to keep the Noghri clear of the shooting by ordering head shots from his soldiers, Rukh had caught the edge of one of the blaster bolts. "As I likewise wanted any Grysks monitoring our progress to assume."

"Nicely done," Kimmund said, glancing at him. Now that he was looking, he could see a slight limp in the Noghri's right leg that hadn't been there before. "You okay?"

"I can travel," Rukh said.

"Traveling without getting gunned down would be nice, too," Kimmund pointed out. The two children had stood up, but were still half hidden behind the console, as if that offered any real protection. "It's all right," he called to them. "We're friends. Grand Admiral Thrawn sent us to rescue you."

Not even a flicker of a response. Clearly, this pair didn't under-stand Basic, either. "Come with us," Kimmund tried again anyway, beckoning them toward him. "Come on, we don't have all—"

Abruptly, both girls' glowing red eyes widened. One of them half turned and jabbed a finger toward a section of wall between two con-soles. Kimmund shifted his gaze, frowning as he followed her finger—

A hidden gunport suddenly opened and the muzzle of a lightning gun poked through.

Cursing, Kimmund swung his E-11 toward the gunport. But Sampa was already on it. Even as the lightning gun tracked toward the three stormtroopers he sent two blaster shots into the opening. The lightning gun jerked, pointed briefly at the ceiling, then slid out of sight.

Kimmund turned back to the Chiss, to see the other girl point suddenly at the wall behind her. This time, Kimmund made sure his blaster was lined up with the gunport when it began to open, firing through it before the Grysk could even get his own weapon into posi-tion.

"They see the future," Rukh grated.

"So they do," Kimmund said, his lips curling back from his teeth in a macabre grin. "So they do." He beckoned again. "Come on, kids. We're getting out of here."

He pointed at the two gunports. "And *you* are going to point out every attack before it happens. Got it?"

He held out his hand. Hesitantly, the two girls came out from be-hind the console. One of them looked at the outstretched hand . . .

"Show them you're human," Elebe suggested.

Holstering his E-11, Kimmund pulled off his helmet and tucked it under his left arm. "See?" he said, giving the girls his best smile. "Not a Grysk. Not even a droid. Human." Once again, he held out his hand.

This time, the girl reached out and took it. "Move out," Kimmund ordered quietly, offering the second girl his other hand. "Drav and Morrtic at point; Chiss girls behind them, Elebe and Sampa behind them, Rukh and me at the rear. Vanguard and rear guard's job is to block any attack on the girls; Elebe and Sampa's job is to have blasters lined up wherever the girls point. Let's go."

And as they maneuvered their way down the corridors, and the increasingly panicky Grysk attacks were steadily fought off or blocked practically before they could even be launched, a stray thought whispered through Kimmund's mind.

He could really, *really* get used to this kind of combat.

"Commander Kimmund, Admiral," Kimmund's voice came in Vader's helmet. "The Chiss prisoners have been recovered; Imperial forces have returned to the *Darkhawk*."

"Thank you, Commander," Thrawn's voice came in response. A cool voice, Vader noted, a voice that was neither surprised nor impressed by the First Legion's success.

Because that was, after all, simply what Thrawn had ordered and expected them to do. "And now the Grysks have lost the ability to navigate across unfamiliar regions."

"Do you want us to destroy the ship before we leave it, sir?" Kimmund asked.

"Unnecessary," Thrawn said. "It is sufficiently disabled to keep it from further combat, and I have need of the *Darkhawk*'s resources elsewhere."

"Yes, sir," Kimmund said. "Casting off now."

"Well done, Commander," Thrawn continued. "And now, Lord Vader, you may prepare for your attack. The enemy believe themselves superior to Imperial forces. Let us prove them wrong."

"We shall," Vader promised. "Defender Squadron: Form up on me."

And so the children were safe. Force-sensitive Chiss children, alive and well.

Mentally, Vader shook his head. All those private meetings. All those secret conversations. All his personal misgivings about what Thrawn and the Emperor were doing.

But he realized now that he had nothing to fear. Thrawn's loyalties would always be split between the Empire and his own people, a fact the Emperor undoubtedly knew. No matter how high Thrawn rose in the ranks of the military, he would never have the necessary standing to challenge Vader's position at the Emperor's side.

"Lord Vader, you will lead the Defender squadron as Wave Three," Thrawn continued. "You will match speed and firepower with the TIEs, and you will not use missiles or shields until cleared to do so."

"Acknowledged," Vader said. Captain Skerris had argued long and hard against that part of the plan. Long enough, and hard enough, that Vader would have sent him to his knees had the man been under *his* command.

Thrawn had been more patient and forgiving. Briefly, Vader wondered if the pilot's attitude would someday come back against him.

"All TIEs: Attack," Thrawn ordered. "Take out the cruisers and engage Bogey Two."

"Acknowledge," the TIE commander said. "All right, Imperials. Grand Admiral Thrawn wants to see carnage. Let's make some."

The TIEs leapt forward, sweeping toward the Grysk ships at full power. Vader let the first two waves pass, then drew his Defender squadron in behind them.

The first attack had been a test, a free shot Thrawn had offered the Grysks in order to confirm his analysis of their tactics. This time the enemy was going to have to work a lot harder for prizes. Even as the cruisers opened fire, the TIEs veered off their vectors, swerving to the sides and re-forming in pairs to swarm the cruisers.

And every attack the cruisers launched was at the leading fighter of each pair.

Vader nodded to himself. So Thrawn had been right about the Grysks' tactical pattern. Now, with the cruisers fully engaged, it was time to see whether or not they could change that pattern.

"Defenders; TIE Four: Follow me," he ordered. Sweeping up and over the cruisers, he drove his Defender out of the battle and turned toward Bogey Two, the lead Grysk ship. Around him, the other Defenders arranged themselves into a broadside as the fourth TIE squadron swept through their formation and formed up in front of them.

"Admiral?" Vader called.

"I place the Defenders under your command, my lord," Thrawn said. "You may act on your own discretion."

Once, Vader reflected, he might have considered that an off-handed comment, a veiled hint that this part of the mission wasn't important enough for the grand admiral to bother with personally.

But having watched Thrawn's interactions with Commodore Faro, and having heard him give her an almost identical order, he knew now that wasn't the case. What Thrawn was telling Vader was that he trusted him to command that part of the operation.

Whether a Chiss's trust for a Sith Lord was a subtle insult wasn't really the point. And Vader didn't think any insult was intended, anyway. The Jedi had seen enough of Thrawn's style and way of speaking to understand that that was simply how he was.

"Very well, Admiral," he said. "TIE Four: Prepare to veer off. Defenders, prepare to raise shields and go to full speed."

Bogey Two was looming ahead. This time the larger ship didn't wait until the TIEs were nearly to their own range before opening fire. Their lasers lashed out—

"Veer off!" Vader snapped. "Evasive and attack. Defenders, mark gunports."

Bogey Two fired again, and again, and again. The TIEs swept over and past, dodging the lasers and returning fire as best and as accurately as they could. Two more were hit, disintegrating into flaming debris. Vader gave the Grysks one more volley—

And as that final blaze of laserfire lanced out from the big ship, he finally had all the data he needed. "TIEs: Pull back," he ordered. "Defenders: shields and full power. *Go!*" He keyed the shields and pulled the throttle all the way back.

A Dark Lord of the Sith never gasped in surprise. But if Vader had been anything else, he would have. Certainly The Jedi would have reacted as he was jammed back into his seat. Only in Vader's proto-type TIE Advanced x1 had he ever felt such power in a fighter before, or the incredible balance between speed and nimbleness. A laser burst blazed straight at him—

It sizzled into nothingness, its only effect being a brief wave of luminosity flickering around the edge of the Defender's shield.

And with that, Vader knew they had won.

"All Defenders: Attack," he ordered. "Clear out the gun emplacements. TIE Four, form up again and move into the spots we've cleared. *Darkhawk*, come in behind TIE Four. Concentrate on anything that looks like a cruiser or fighter hatch. If there are other enemy ships, I want them to remain inside."

He took a deep breath, listening to the chorus of acknowledgments. The feel of a fighter; the thrill and burden and satisfaction of command . . .

But those were The Jedi's memories. Not his.

Another laser bolt splashed off his shields. Arming a missile, he sent it into the center of the emplacement. A flare of fire and debris blew into space. He armed a second missile, chose his target, and fired.

And then, right at the edge of the Defender's sensors, back behind the main Grysk warships, Vader spotted another ship: small, courier-sized, unlike any of the configurations he'd yet seen.

Doing its best to sneak away.

He looked back at the battle. Among the *Chimaera*, *Darkhawk*, Defenders, and standard TIEs, the Grysks were minutes from defeat, their defenses crumbling in front of him. From this point on, Vader and his fighter would neither add to nor detract from that inevitability.

Turning his Defender onto an intercept course, he set off in pursuit.

Someone from the *Chimaera* called his name, once, then a second, more urgent time. He ignored both hails. The mystery ship had spotted him now, but instead of turning to engage it increased its speed, heading toward deep space. The Defender slowly but steadily closed the gap . . .

But the timing was too short, the other ship's lead too big. Long before Vader reached firing distance the ship escaped into hyperspace.

For a long moment, Vader gazed at the spot where it had disappeared, the possibilities and implications churning together through his mind. Then, turning the Defender around, he headed back toward the battle.

The Imperials would win the day . . . and then he and Thrawn would have a talk. A very long, very serious talk.

"Bogey Two fully engaged," Faro reported. *Her voice holds new confidence, and her stance holds eagerness.* "Bogey One is pulling back."

"Acknowledged, Commodore," Thrawn said. "Move the *Chimaera* to attack Bogey One. Maintain distance from Bogey Two."

"Because as long as the TIEs are attacking Bogey Two, they're its main threat," Faro murmured. *Her voice holds understanding.*

"Indeed," Thrawn said. "You wondered earlier how we would defeat two ships nearly as large as ours. You now have an answer?"

"Yes, sir," Faro said. *Her voice holds grim anticipation.* "We persuade them to let us take them on one at a time."

"Very good," Thrawn said. "Move the *Chimaera* into position, and commence attack."

"Defender Four, there is an emplacement to starboard of the weapon Defender Six destroyed," Vader's voice came over the speaker. *The voice is different, but it holds the same intensity and focus. The word patterns are different, but the cadence and intonation are the same. The brashness has abated, but the firm sense of loyalty is the same.*

"Sir?" Faro asked tentatively.

"Yes, Commodore?"

"Sorry, sir." *Faro's voice holds apology and concern.* "The way you were looking out at Bogey One . . . are you all right, sir?"

"I am," Thrawn said. "I was pondering the problem of mixed loyalties, and the decisions one must sometimes make. Lieutenant Lomar, hail the Grysks."

"Yes, sir." *The comm officer's voice holds no confusion or concern. But he is not as astute as Commodore Faro.* "Ready, Admiral."

"Grysk war vessel, this is Admiral Mitth'raw'nuruodo," Thrawn said in Meese Caulf. "You are hereby delivered notice to return to your homeworlds and abandon your ambitions to extend your rule beyond your borders. If you continue in these endeavors, be assured that you will be defeated and destroyed."

There is no response. But the Grysk silence holds anger and malice.

"End transmission," he said in Basic.

"Sir?" *Faro's voice holds caution.* "May I ask . . . ?"

"I gave my name, and warned them to cease operations against us," Thrawn said.

"Ah." *Faro's expression holds confusion.* "I assume you're not expecting them to listen?"

"The survivors of this battle may take the warning to heart," Thrawn said. "Their masters, unfortunately, will not."

"I see." *Faro looks out the viewport. Her stance and expression hold determination.* "Well, then, when they come for us we'll beat them, too."

Vader's Defender continues to sweep around Bogey Two, alternating between missile and laser cannon fire. He spins the fighter in a tight curve and heads back toward another target, doing a complete roll as he does so. It is a familiar maneuver, carried out with a familiar precision.

It is he.

Without warning, he veers off, heading from the battle zone toward an escaping ship. TIE control calls to him once, then twice, but is ignored. The configuration of the ship Vader is pursuing . . .

"I admire your confidence, Commodore," Thrawn said. "Let us hope that confidence is not unwarranted."

"Yes, sir," Faro said. "But I'm not concerned. We have you, and we have Lord Vader. Whatever the Grysks throw at us, we can take it." *She straightens up, her determination increasing.* "Starting with this group right here. Turbolasers: You saw where the Bogey Two gunports were. Start by targeting the same positions on Bogey One."

THEN

The cortosis miners who shuffled back to the surface at LebJau's order were, for the most part, fearful or angry or just hesitant. But they *did* come out, all of them. They filed past LebJau, Thrawn, and Padmé, throwing glances at Anakin as he moved back and forth between the equipment sheds collecting the tools and explosives necessary for destroying the mine. A few of the miners tried to ask LebJau what was going on, or to accuse him of collaborating with their oppressors.

But for the most part, their anger or fear quickly faded into a weary resignation.

"I don't think General Skywalker has thought this through," Thrawn murmured to Padmé as the final group of miners walked past and headed toward the battered vehicles in the parking area. His expression was uneasy, and Padmé could hear the disapproval beneath the tone. "It would be better to allow the Separatists to waste their resources than to force them to look elsewhere."

"I agree," Padmé said, feeling a twinge of guilt with each dejected-looking miner who passed. "But I've seen Anakin in this mood." She looked sideways at him. "I'm guessing you have, too."

"Indeed," Thrawn said. "But he has feelings for you. Can you not persuade him to rethink this action?"

"What do you mean?" Padmé asked, the all-too-familiar mix of innocence and disclaimer springing reflexively to her lips.

"I understand your reticence," Thrawn said. "But the time for that has passed. I've observed you both, and I know what you're hiding. General Skywalker's plan could create a serious threat to this world. You must stop him."

Padmé shook her head, her thoughts flashing back to that terrible day, that terrible frozen moment when Anakin had confessed his slaughter of the Sand People. "He won't listen to me," she said, blinking back tears. "Once he's decided something, he won't listen to anyone."

Thrawn was silent a moment. "Then there's indeed nothing we can do."

Padmé looked at him. There'd been something new in his voice. "Is there a problem?" she asked. "I mean, another problem?"

"There is no problem," Thrawn said. "But my task here is complete. If you'll again loan me your communicator, I'll take leave of you and your"—he glanced at Anakin—"your associate."

"Of course," Padmé said, slipping off her backpack. She dug out her comm and handed it to him.

"Thank you," he said, keying it on and tapping out a short code. "This has been an interesting experience, Ambassador Padmé. I trust that both our peoples have gained from our brief alliance."

"Any chance I can persuade you to return to Coruscant with us to speak with Supreme Chancellor Palpatine?" she asked as she took the comm back and put it away. "Our peoples should get to know each other. There's a great deal we could accomplish together."

"I'm afraid I have other duties I must attend to," Thrawn said. "In addition, I'm not in a position to take part in official communications." His eyes flicked over her shoulder. "General Skywalker, I must take my leave."

"I understand," Anakin said. Padmé turned, wincing at the bundle of wrapped explosives he'd put together. "But you really should reconsider Padmé's offer. The Republic's going to win this war, and Chancellor Palpatine is the one who'll lead us to that victory. The Chiss Ascendancy would do well to establish good relations with him."

"Perhaps someday," Thrawn said. "But for now, I must depart." He looked up.

Padmé followed his gaze. Above them, a dark shape was dropping toward the ground.

"I'll wait in orbit until you depart to guard against further attacks," Thrawn continued as a sleek ship settled to the ground nearby. "Safe travels to you both."

"I hope we'll meet again," Padmé said. "Thank you for your help."

"And for yours," Thrawn said, inclining his head to her.

The ship's ramp lowered as he walked toward it, the hatch behind it sliding open. He walked to the ramp.

And paused. "One final thought," he said, turning to face them. "I'm concerned by your suggestion that the Separatists plan to infiltrate your government offices disguised in enhanced clone armor. Successful attacks of that sort generally require numbers that the Separatists will have difficulty placing into position."

"There are a lot of clones wandering around the Senate and Chancellery," Padmé said.

"But a single massive infiltration draws attention, while gradual infiltration holds the risk of premature discovery," Thrawn pointed out. "I cannot help but wonder if the armor is intended for some other purpose."

"*Was* intended," Anakin said, leaning on the word. "*Was*. Whatever Solha and Dooku were planning, it's no longer relevant."

"Perhaps," Thrawn said. "Still, it would be wise to think on it, General."

Turning again, he walked up the ramp and disappeared inside. The hatch and ramp sealed, and the ship rose again into the sky.

"You think he could be right?" Padmé asked, suppressing a shiver. There was something in Thrawn's earnestness that had sent a darkness through her.

"I don't know," Anakin said. "And right now, I don't care. Get back to the ship and make sure it's ready. I'll set this thing and we'll get out of here."

"Anakin—"

But he was already gone. With one last lingering look up at the stars, Padmé headed back to their borrowed ship.

LebJau met her at the ramp. "I was hoping I could hitch a ride somewhere," he said.

"You aren't going back to your people?" Padmé asked, frowning.

"You mean the people who'll probably hang me if I stay?" he countered bitterly.

"It's not that bad," Padmé said, trying to sound positive. "Most of the workers at the factory will be able to go back. They'll still need you to work on the super battle droid assembly line."

"*If* the duke lets us," LebJau said. "Fair chance he won't. Especially—" He broke off, waving a hand at the mine buildings. "Even if he does, the miners aren't going to get *their* jobs back."

This is war—the old, clichéd phrase came automatically to Padmé's mind.

But this wasn't Mokivj's war. Or it hadn't been until they'd been dragged into it. The fact that it was the Separatists who'd done the dragging and not the Republic was small consolation.

It wouldn't be any consolation at all to LebJau's people.

"I know," she said quietly. "I'm sorry." She sighed. "Yes, of course you can come with us. Would Batuu work? We have to go there anyway to get my ship."

"Sure," LebJau said, his eyes still on the mine. "I know some guys who went there once. Sounded okay."

"If you know people who go there, it might be wise to change your name."

"Yeah, no big deal." He waved at the ship. "I don't suppose I can have that ship when you're done with it? I know it's stolen, but it doesn't sound like people on Batuu would care. I could probably sell it for a stake."

"Of course you can have it," Padmé said. "It's the least we can do."

She craned her neck as Anakin reappeared at the mine entrance. "Here he comes."

"Okay," Anakin said, hurrying up to them. "Into the ship. LebJau, you need to get clear—"

"We're taking him to Batuu," Padmé interrupted.

Anakin flashed her a frown, shifted the frown to LebJau. "Okay. Sure. In that case, *both* of you into the ship."

Three minutes later they were half a kilometer in the air, hovering a kilometer away from the mine building cluster. "Ten seconds," Anakin warned. "Though there shouldn't be much to see."

"What's supposed to happen?" Padmé asked.

"I'm just collapsing the tunnels," Anakin said. "There should be some ground fracturing, maybe some dust—"

An instant later the area exploded into a blazing geyser of fire and smoke.

Padmé gasped as Anakin twisted the control yoke hard over, trying to get them away from the geyser. Something slapped into the ship's underside, throwing a slight wobble into his maneuver, and a few blazing embers landed on the hull near the cockpit viewport. "What the frost is *that*?" LebJau yelped.

"I don't know," Anakin snapped back, fighting the controls as more globs slammed into both the upper and lower edges of the ship.

"Don't give me *I don't know*," LebJau snarled. "That's my world down there! What the frost did you *do*?"

"I just collapsed the tunnels," Anakin said. The ship was leveling off now, outside the edge of the roiling fountain still pouring from the mine. "It shouldn't—look, I've taken down mines before. I know how to do it."

"But this isn't just a mine," Padmé said, staring at the biggest of the glowing globs on the ship's hull as she suddenly understood. "It's a *cortosis* mine."

"What does that—?" Anakin broke off. "No—that's crazy. It's only supposed to redirect *blaster* energy."

"I guess it can redirect the heat of explosives, too," Padmé bit out, her stomach tightening into a painful knot. "That's *lava* out there,

Anakin. However the cortosis did it, it sent your explosion straight down through the crust into the magma."

For a long moment, none of them said anything. There was nothing to say.

"Doesn't look like it's coming too close to your town," Padmé said at last. Even to herself, the attempt at solace sounded pitiful. "It's blowing away from the factory, too."

"No, it's just pouring lava onto our best cropland," LebJau said bitterly. "And that ash and smoke . . . it's going to be in the air and cropland and water for years. Maybe forever."

Padmé looked at Anakin. His jaw was set, his eyes focused straight ahead. *Collateral damage*—the other cliché came to her mind.

Collateral damage. A planet full of people, just trying to live their lives. The kind of ordinary civilians she and Anakin had once dedicated themselves to protecting.

Collateral damage. And it hadn't started here, either. She'd been doing it ever since she arrived on Mokivj. She'd cajoled and bribed and all but insisted that LebJau and his friends work for her; that they risk everything for this stranger who'd dropped into their midst.

Collateral damage. Had she become so numbed and war-weary that she no longer even saw what she was doing to everyone else around her?

"But I guess there's nothing we can do about it now," LebJau continued. The bitterness was gone, leaving only tiredness behind.

"I'll talk to the Senate," Padmé promised. "*We'll* talk to the Senate," she amended, looking at Anakin. "Maybe they can send some help."

Anakin didn't reply.

But then, he knew as well as she did that the words were meaningless. The Senate had far too many demands on its limited resources to even notice Mokivj, let alone help its people.

Collateral damage.

"Yeah," LebJau said. He wasn't fooled, either. "Can we get out of here now?"

"Sure," Anakin said. "Batuu?"

"It's as good a place as any to start a new life," LebJau said. His eyes, Padmé noted, were still on the magma geyser.

"You can always try the Black Spire cantina," Anakin said. "I'm guessing they go through a lot of bartenders at that place."

"Sure," LebJau said. "I'll think about it."

EPILOGUE

NOW

The Chiss warship drifted away from the *Chimaera* and turned back onto its original vector. A moment's pause; then with a flicker of pseudomotion it was gone.

For a moment Vader gazed out the main viewport after it. The ship wasn't nearly as big as a Star Destroyer, but from what he'd seen of its flankside weapons it would be a formidable opponent.

He sensed Thrawn's presence behind him before he heard the soft footsteps on the command walkway. "All is well?" he asked the Chiss.

"All is well," Thrawn said. "Admiral Ar'alani will return the children to their families, and has promised to bolster the defenses of the colony world from which they were taken."

"Yes," Vader said. "The time has come, Admiral."

"The time?"

"You promised proof that the Grysks are a threat to the Empire." Vader turned to face Thrawn. "If such proof does indeed exist."

"It awaits us in my office," Thrawn assured him. "At your convenience."

Vader strode past him down the walkway, his cloak swirling. Thrawn's office was off the rear of the aft bridge; stretching out with the Force to wave the door open, he walked inside.

Lying in the middle of the desk, taking up half the available space, was a section of half-disassembled machinery. "This is the proof?" he demanded as Thrawn closed the door and crossed to the other side of the desk.

"It is, my lord," Thrawn confirmed. "It is the inner power coupling mechanism from one of the Grysk gravity projectors. Note the meshwork wrapping the three poles and linking to the shield shell?"

Vader frowned. The material looked familiar . . .

He stiffened. *"Cortosis?"*

"Indeed," Thrawn said. "This is what the Grysks use the material for: power couplings and energy management. It cannot dissipate the sharp power gradient of their arc-cannon weaponry, as you saw, and so is of no use to them as armor."

"How does that prove Grysk interference with the Empire?"

"I propose two questions," Thrawn said. "First: How did the Grysks know that cortosis would be an effective defense against blasters and lightsabers?"

Vader stared at the cortosis weave, more of The Jedi's memories seeping back into his consciousness. "You suggest they were studying us as far back as the Clone Wars?"

"I do, my lord." A small smile touched the Chiss's face. "After all, the Chiss were watching you. Why not the Grysks? My second question: Once the Grysks knew the value of cortosis against blasters and lightsabers, how did the Separatists gain that knowledge?"

Vader reached out and touched the edge of the cortosis with a gloved finger. So many dark, dark memories . . . "You suggest the Grysks contacted Dooku. That they offered him invulnerable battle droids as a way to ensure Separatist victory."

"Indeed," Thrawn said. "I believe their plan was to offer him a taste of such a victory, then withhold it until they had obtained his servitude. But he surprised them."

"In what way?"

"We have now seen the Grysk pattern of dominance, my lord," Thrawn said. "On Batuu they forced the Darshi into obedience by holding their ceremonial daggers hostage. With the Chiss, they are attempting to do the same by taking our children. Stealing one species' treasured and honored past; stealing another species' treasured and vital future.

"But Dooku surprised them. Instead of simply armoring battle droids, he armored both droids *and* clone armor. I believe that it was that surprise, and the further reconsideration it forced upon them, that delayed the Grysks' movement into the Empire until now."

"Yes," Vader murmured.

Only it wasn't Dooku who'd created that plan. What Vader knew now—what The Jedi had never known—was that the factory was being secretly overseen by Chancellor Palpatine, who saw in the cortosis an extra guarantee of success for his upcoming Order 66. "You said before that they were sealing themselves away," Vader said.

"I was wrong," Thrawn said. "Or rather, my conclusion was incomplete. I believe now they are ready to make their move, and that the purpose of sealing off the region around Batuu is to discourage Imperial travel there while they take their final steps toward learning how to manipulate humans the way they have the Darshi and the Chiss."

"Why can it not be both?" Vader asked. "They seek to isolate Batuu for study *and* also close all convenient avenues the Empire might use to move against them. Their observations of Clone War battles and subsequent Imperial operations will have taught them that our preferred strategy is to bring large numbers of ships and overwhelming force to bear."

"Indeed," Thrawn said thoughtfully. "Yes. Their own combat pattern, according to legend, is to use many small groups of warships, each group composed of only a few vessels. It is a strategy designed for infiltration over a large area instead of immediate, massive conquest."

"Especially when such infiltration is accompanied by reluctant allies among their target's populace."

"Indeed." Thrawn's eyes took on a new intensity. "You may recall my suggestion that using the cortosis clone armor for infiltration would not be an effective tactic for the Separatists to use against the Republic. In retrospect, that could indicate the hand of the Grysks in molding that particular Separatist strategy."

Vader stared at him.

He knew.

"You made no such suggestion to me," he said. A hollow gesture, but one he had to make.

"Ah," Thrawn said, and Vader sensed a subtle shift in his thoughts. Doubt? Confirmation? "My error. I was thinking of an incident from my past. My point remains: The Grysks stand ready to begin their infiltration of the Empire. The only solution is to eliminate the threat before they are fully prepared."

And there it was. The reason, perhaps merely the justification, for dealing with the grand admiral right here and now. Treason, overt or subtle, was grounds for execution. "So you propose spending Imperial resources against the Grysks," he said. "Thereby protecting your own Chiss Ascendancy at the expense of the Empire."

"You question my loyalty," Thrawn said. It was a statement, not a question.

"I do," Vader said, eyeing the grand admiral's throat. A quick twist, a snapping of the neck . . .

"You misunderstand, my lord," Thrawn said quietly. "Have you listened to the transmission I sent the Grysk ship, the message I knew would be passed on by the survivors of the battle?"

"Would that make a difference?"

Thrawn reached to his computer and pressed a few keys. *"Grysk war vessel, this is Admiral Mitth'raw'nuruodo."* The Meese Caulf words came from the computer's speaker. *"You are hereby delivered notice to return to your homeworlds and abandon your ambitions to extend your rule beyond your borders. If you continue in these endeavors, be assured that you will be defeated and destroyed."*

Thrawn touched another key, and the recording ended. He looked at Vader, waiting.

Vader ran the words over again in his mind . . . and then he saw it. "You identified yourself as Mitth'raw'nuruodo," he said quietly. "A Chiss name.

"And the Grysks always attack the closer enemy first."

"Yes," Thrawn said, and Vader sensed a fresh layer of emotion in his voice. "The invasion is coming, Lord Vader. But I have now bought the Empire time to prepare."

"Perhaps," Vader said. "But that is not all of it."

Thrawn's eyes narrowed slightly. "What do you mean?"

"You know exactly what I mean." Vader gestured toward the bulkhead and the galaxy beyond it. "I saw the ship, Admiral. The ship that escaped from the battle." He paused, but Thrawn didn't respond. "I presume from your silence that you saw it, as well. It was a courier ship.

"A *Chiss* courier ship."

"Perhaps you were mistaken," Thrawn said.

"No," Vader said flatly. "There is more. The personal cloaking device worn by the Grysks. Identical in function to that used by your assassin Rukh. I submit they are all of Chiss design."

For another moment Thrawn remained silent. Then he took a slow, measured breath. "Yes," he said. "Though ironically such devices are of no use to our own people. Yes, it was a Chiss shuttle you saw, my lord. But my message to the Grysks, and its importance to the Empire, still remain."

"Do they?" Vader countered. "Was your message to warn the Grysks away from the Empire? Or was it a warning to whatever group of Chiss are working with them that you are aware of their presence?"

Thrawn smiled faintly. But Vader could sense the pain behind the smile. "Why can it not be both?"

"*Was* it both?"

Thrawn turned away. "There were stirrings of political conflict when I left my people for the Empire those many years ago," he said. "I assumed the Aristocras would settle their differences, as they have so many times before. This time, perhaps they could not. Or perhaps the Grysks have made deeper inroads into our culture than I'd hoped."

Vader gazed at the Chiss, feeling the dark irony deep within him. "So you who have never hidden your contempt for the Republic's handling of the Clone Wars now stand on the edge of your own civil war?"

"Or have already taken our first steps into it," Thrawn said. "If one side is already under the control of the Grysks . . ." He shook his head. "Your earlier thought was perhaps closer to the mark than you knew. Perhaps the true purpose of closing the border is to prevent *me* from bringing the Empire against them."

It was, Vader thought, an intensely arrogant suggestion. Still, having seen Thrawn's abilities, he could well believe that someone would want to keep him away from their plans. "What do you intend to do about it?"

"Meaning?"

"Time is likely critical for your people," Vader said. "Will you turn your back on the Emperor and take the *Chimaera* to your worlds to assist in their survival?"

"I hardly think that would be possible," Thrawn said, turning back to face him. "You, certainly, would oppose such a decision."

"Do you expect me to believe that a tactician of your skill has not yet thought of a way to kill me?"

Another faint smile. "I have, in fact, thought of *three* ways." The smile faded. "I pledged myself to serve the Emperor, Lord Vader, just as I once pledged to assist Anakin Skywalker. Someday, I will indeed return to my people. But not until the threats to the Empire have been dealt with."

For a long moment, they stood together in silence. Vader thought about his secret . . . about Thrawn's loyalty . . . about the Emperor's continued need for him. Perhaps the entire Empire's need for him . . . "Anakin Skywalker is dead," he said.

Thrawn lowered his head. "I know."

Vader nodded slowly. *I know.* Not *So I have heard.* Not *So I was informed.* But *I know.* "We will not speak of him again," he said. "*You* will not speak of him again."

"I understand, my lord," Thrawn said. "But I will always honor his legacy."

For another moment Vader was silent. "I am told you believe the navy should focus on small fighter craft."

A flicker of something crossed Thrawn's face. "I do, my lord."

"The Defender is an excellent ship," Vader said. "I will speak to the Emperor on behalf of the project." He raised a finger. "But it needs to be faster, and more heavily armed." He considered. "The controls, too, should also be made simpler. Not all Imperial pilots are as capable as Captain Skerris."

"Or as you yourself," Thrawn said, inclining his head. "Excellent suggestions. I will transmit those instructions to the Lothal facility upon our return to Coruscant."

"Good," Vader said. "Are we done here?"

Thrawn lowered his head in a respectful bow. "Yes, Lord Vader," he said. "We are done."

ABOUT THE AUTHOR

Timothy Zahn is the author of fifty-six novels, over a hundred short stories and novelettes, and five short-fiction collections. In 1984, he won the Hugo Award for best novella. Zahn is best known for his *Star Wars* novels (*Thrawn, Heir to the Empire, Dark Force Rising, The Last Command, Specter of the Past, Vision of the Future, Survivor's Quest, Outbound Flight, Allegiance, Choices of One,* and *Scoundrels*) with more than eight million copies of his books in print. Other books include *StarCraft: Evolution,* the Cobra series, the Quadrail series, and the young adult Dragonback series. Zahn has a BS in physics from Michigan State University and an MS from the University of Illinois. He lives with his family on the Oregon coast.

Facebook.com/TimothyZahn

ABOUT THE TYPE

This book was set in Minion, a 1990 Adobe Originals typeface by Robert Slimbach (b. 1956). Minion is inspired by classical, old-style typefaces of the late Renaissance, a period of elegant, beautiful, and highly readable type designs. Created primarily for text setting, Minion combines the aesthetic and functional qualities that make text type highly readable with the versatility of digital technology.

THE EMPIRE'S GREATEST ADMIRAL RISES THROUGH THE RANKS
IN THIS GRAPHIC NOVEL BASED ON TIMOTHY ZAHN'S NEW YORK TIMES BEST-SELLING BOOK!
STAR WARS
THRAWN
"STAR WARS fans from all over the galaxy should come see what the THRAWN comic has to offer."
– MULTIVERSITY COMICS
STAR WARS: THRAWN TPB
ISBN: 978-1302911560
ON SALE SEPTEMBER 2018
WHEREVER BOOKS ARE SOLD
DISNEY
LUCASFILM
MARVEL
© & TM 2018 Lucasfilm Ltd.
© 2018 MARVEL
TO FIND A COMIC SHOP NEAR YOU, VISIT COMICSHOPLOCATOR.COM